The
Dark Divide

Book 2 of the Rift Runners Trilogy

JJ FALLON

snapping turtle
snappingturtlebooks.com

First published in Australia in 2012
by HarperCollins Publishers

This edition published in 2013
by Snapping Turtle Books

Jennifer Fallon Media Ltd.
PO Box 638, Rangiora, Canterbury, 7440
New Zealand

Cover design by David Tonkin, Snapping Turtle Books
Cover Images: shutterstock.com

ISBN: 0473254050
ISBN-13: 978-0473254056

PROLOGUE

The first thing the Faerie prince, Marcroy Tarth, did when Hayley Boyle arrived in his magical kingdom of *Tír Na nÓg* was to take her clothes away and burn them, replacing them with a gossamer-thin shift that offered only minimal protection for her dignity and absolutely none from the elements. It was something to do with her clothes being tainted by technology, Marcroy said, although she wasn't really listening to the explanation.

Hayley was too enchanted by *Tír Na nÓg* to notice much of anything. She was still trying to get her head around the events of the past few hours. *Was it only hours?*

This morning she had woken up in St Christopher's Visual Rehabilitation Centre in Dublin, facing another day of "life lessons". Another day of learning to cope with her blindness. Another

3

day of dealing with the aftermath of being hit by a car outside Kiva Kavanaugh's house in the chaos caused by a frenzied paparazzi pack. Another day of wondering if Ren was dead or alive.

Another day of being reminded that, until that moment, she had been a perfectly ordinary seventeen-year-old girl whose best friend just happened to be the son of a movie star. And now she was here. In another reality. With the Faerie.

And she could see.

Although she still wasn't sure if Ren was dead or alive.

I might go mad if I think about this too much.

Her skin had tingled as she and Marcroy passed through the magical veil that separated the Faerie kingdom from the realm of man. Although it was still night out in the real world, it was only twilight in the Faerie kingdom. Magic glimmered from every surface. Even the insects seemed benign and drunk on the magical nectar they consumed. The forest pulsed with life, as if every plant were a sentient being, but even they paled in comparison to the majestic trees where the *Daoine sídhe* made their homes.Hayley gasped with awe when they reached the centre of *Tír Na nÓg*. She stared at one wonder only to discover another so marvellous she was almost unable to comprehend their existence - let alone their size and magnificence.

Intoxicated by the magical forest air, Hayley followed Marcroy all the way up the exquisitely curved stairs in wide-eyed wonder. The *sídhe* had coaxed the sacred trees into growing the stairs, Marcroy explained. The sacred trees of *Tír Na nÓg* were full of hollowed-out caves and broad boughs wide enough to act as platforms. His voice was hypnotic and seductive. It felt like warm liquid chocolate, if it were possible for a voice to manifest such a tactile effect. She was enchanted - with Marcroy, with *Tír Na nÓg* and the beautiful people who lived here. Their strange cat-slit eyes stared curiously at Hayley as she climbed ever upward behind Marcroy, no doubt wondering about this human interloper.

When they realized she was Marcroy's invited guest, the Faerie bowed and smiled and sometimes sang a small refrain in a musical language Hayley couldn't understand. Although she was unfamiliar with the melodies, the songs were so harmonious it was like listening to a treasured music box that constantly refreshed its repertoire, each song trying to outdo the last in purity and joy.

Marcroy led Hayley by the hand, high into the branches to meet his sister, an ethereal creature of exquisite beauty who seemed puzzled by her visitor. Elimyer had long, white-blonde hair, eyes that seemed carved from emeralds, and pronounced points on her ears. She was naked and flawless, as she emerged from the dark entrance of her quarters in the sacred tree and embraced Hayley like a long lost child, which Hayley found rather disconcerting.

She stepped back to examine Hayley at arm's length after Marcroy had introduced them. "Aren't you a sweet little thing? You remind me of my daughter."

"You have a daughter?" Hayley asked, a little surprised. Elimyer looked barely old enough to have a boyfriend, let alone a child anywhere near Hayley's age. She kept her eyes firmly fixed on the Faerie girl's face, uncomfortable with the casual nudity of Elimyer and her kind. At least Marcroy was dressed.

She wasn't sure what she would do if he decided to go native.

The *leanan sídhe* reached forward to gently lift a lock of her dark hair and sniff it. "You are like her in many ways. But you smell different."

"Um... I suppose," Hayley asked, glancing at Marcroy. She wasn't sure about the hair sniffing, but for all she knew, this was how the Faerie greeted one another. "What's your daughter's name?"

"Her name is Trása," Elimyer said, stroking Hayley's head with a vague smile. "You have such pretty hair. So dark and glossy."

"Trása?" Hayley asked, an edge to her voice she couldn't hide. She snatched the lock of hair from Elimyer's hand. "That blonde cow Ren was hanging out with the day of my accident?"

The one who likes to chat up other people's boyfriends, she added silently.

Not that Ren Kavanaugh actually was her boyfriend. Her plans for that eventuality had been cruelly shattered by recent events. First, she was hit by Murray Symes's car, which put her in a coma and blinded her. Second, she was sent to live in that damned rehabilitation facility to learn how to deal with her "disability". And then to top it all off, Ren had whisked her away to this magical alternate reality with the cops hot on their tail just so she could witness the horrific, but effective, removal of the bullet from Marcroy Tarth's chest, which still made her stomach churn when she thought about it.

Now Ren is missing, my sight has been magically restored and I'm a guest of a real live Faerie prince in a magical kingdom that in my reality only exists in, well... faerie tales.

Hayley felt as if she'd been living doggy years, lately. It didn't seem possible all that could possibly have happened to one person in only a few weeks.

Elimyer smiled at her. "Who is Ren, dear?"

"She means Rónán," Marcroy explained, smiling at her. "Hayley is from the realm where Rónán of the Undivided has been hiding all this time."

"All this time? It seems like just yesterday you brought us the news that the Undivided were divided, brother." She let out a vague little sigh. "I really should go beyond the veil more often. It's so easy to lose track of what's happening."

Hayley thought calling Ren's life in her realm "hiding" a little odd, given Ren was barely three when her father, Patrick Boyle, had found him in that lake on the movie set where he was working as a stuntman; the same set where Kiva Kavanaugh got her big break, and, as it turned out, her adopted son. Hayley didn't think Ren had been *hiding* in her reality. Ren - or rather Rónán, as they insisted on calling him here - must have crossed a dimensional rift from this realm to splash down in the lake. There was a good chance someone had hidden him, rather than Ren hiding himself.

She didn't want to question Marcroy too closely, though. In the last few hours, Hayley had gone from trying to face her blindness and despair to standing here, in another reality, cured, swapping pleasantries with a naked faerie. She stifled the urge to giggle nervously. *I must have tripped over and banged my head again*, she decided. *I'm back in the coma. I bet the brain damage I got when the car hit me is worse than they thought, and I've had a relapse.*

It must be. This is fairyland and I'm talking to fairies. This can't be real.

But it was real. Hayley knew it instinctively, even if she couldn't explain exactly why she was so sure it wasn't the result of some exotic fever dream brought on by a head injury and opiate painkillers.

Even more intriguing, this strange turn her life had taken had little to do with her. It was all about Ren and his mysterious origins.

How had Ren taken it when he discovered this world that was his true home? she wondered, wishing he were here now. Hoping that wherever he was, he was safe. She wasn't too sure about that. There had been bullets flying about when he pushed her through the rift.

When he was missing for all those weeks, had he been here? In *Tír Na nÓg*? Had he been as enchanted with the place as she was? How had he coped when he woke up here in this strange world full of impossible beauty and unbelievable creatures?

Marcroy had explained much to Hayley on her journey here, but she still found it hard to grasp.

Had Ren been so fortunate with the explanation he'd been given? Or did he just know this place and all the magic that came with it, because of who he was?

Hayley desperately wished Ren were here now. Marcroy was prettier than any creature had a right to be, but he wasn't Ren, and she could do with something familiar. Trouble was, Hayley had no idea where Ren was. Marcroy said the rift had closed before he came through. Was he back home, trying to explain her disappearance? Had the cops arrested him? Was his mother's stiff-backed lawyer, Eunice Ravenel, trying to get Ren released on bail, as Hayley stood here, trying to grapple with having crossed realities to a world where Ren was a prince and not simply a troubled teen with self-harm issues?

"I have business with Jamaspa on behalf of the queen, Ellie," Marcroy informed his sister, placing his hands on Hayley's shoulders from behind, his breath tickling her ear and sending shivers down her spine. His touch was electric. "So Hayley will be staying with you for a time."

Elimyer's eye lit up. She seemed unduly pleased by the prospect of a houseguest. "That's wonderful! Do you paint, dear? Draw? Write poetry? Play an instrument, perhaps?"

Hayley shook her head. "Not really."

"Pity," Elimyer sighed. She turned to Marcroy, filled with disappointment. "You didn't bring her here for me to inspire her, then?"

"No," Marcroy said. "She is a guest, Elimyer. Not your lunch. Be nice to her."

"A guest like Sorcha?" she asked, with a raised brow and a slight edge to her voice. Hayley got the feeling there was something important being said here - something she should probably know about. She was too enchanted by her surroundings, and far too polite, to question either Marcroy or his sister about it.

Marcroy glanced at Hayley for a moment and then shook her head. "No. Not like Sorcha, Ellie. This one is my friend, not my lover."

"Then she'll be here a little longer than Sorcha, I suppose?"

"Perhaps," Marcroy said with a shrug. "We'll see."

Elimyer took Hayley by the hand, smiling. "You'll be wanting something to eat, I'm guessing," she said, drawing her away from Marcroy. "Trása eats all the time when she's here. Something about being half-human. Are you half-human, dear?"

"I'm all human, as far as I know," Hayley said. She didn't think her father's annual eggnog-fuelled insistence they were descended from a long line of Celtic seers counted with this Faerie creature as evidence she might be anything other than entirely human. "But yes, I *am* hungry."

In fact, Hayley couldn't remember the last time she'd eaten. It was some time last night, but even that seemed hard to pin down. After dinner at St Christopher's. She'd eaten some of her stepmother's delicious, buttery shortbread. Was it only last night? For some reason, time felt different here - as if it flowed at a different pace.

Not that anything about Hayley's life was ordinary, at the moment.

Life *had* been ordinary until just before Ren appeared out of nowhere at St Christopher's - after everyone had just about written him off as dead - to whisk her away to this alternate reality and abandon her here on her own.

Where are you Ren? she wondered silently, as Elimyer beckoned her inside. *When are you going to come and get me?*

Although you were right about one thing. You said you knew some people who could cure my blindness.

But it's done now.

When can I go home?

PART ONE

CHAPTER 1

"*Onushirano shoguno namaewo mouse?*"

"Why do they keep asking who our lord is?" Trása asked. She glared at Ren, breathing hard, as he was, after running behind their samurai captors' horses for the better part of an hour. Climbing to her feet as the samurai dismounted, she brushed the sand from her jeans, and glanced around, peering through the darkness for some hint as to where they might be.

Looking around, and trying to determine the same thing, Ren rubbed his wrists. They were chafed and raw from the hemp rope the soldiers had tied him with, before dragging their prisoners at a stiff trot from the stone circle where they'd jumped into this reality to this torch-lit compound set on the edge of a vast forest. Although Ren couldn't be sure in the darkness, the forest was mostly huge, yellow-flowering *kozo* trees. Ren recognized them because Jack had been cultivating a struggling specimen at home in a large clay pot in his beloved greenhouse - and lecturing any unsuspecting visitors he got on the origins of every single plant in the whole building every chance he got. Jack's hobby lectures enabled Ren to identify the species, but he had never imagined *kozo* trees so tall, or so numerous.

The buildings to their left, and there were quite a few, appeared to be a residence and a number of smaller dormitories and barracks. Beyond them, the fires of a working forge glowed red in the darkness, accompanied by the rhythmic, metallic clanging of a smithy plying his trade. On the other side of the compound, in a much better-lit area that must be running a night shift, given the number of people working, there were a series of open shelters with long tables and several large vats at one end. The air reeked of lye, although Ren had no idea why.

But the odd smell of this place was a puzzle for another time. He turned to Trása, hoping her experience as a rift runner might shed some light on their current predicament. And perhaps some clue to where they were. "Do you understand what they're saying now?"

She shrugged. "Sort of. They're speaking some kind of Japanese dialect, aren't they? With a bit of Gaelish thrown in for good measure?"

"Near enough," Ren agreed, as the man in charge shouted an order to his men to keep the prisoners there until he returned. The mounted warriors were staring at them with suspicion and mistrust. The easiest way for him and Trása to get themselves killed at this point, Ren guessed, was to try to make a break for it. "You ever been to Japan?"

She shook her head. "Not in your realm. But all rift runners are imprinted with languages they might encounter in another realm. I never needed this one until now. Are we still in Eire, do you think?" she added, turning a slow circle to study the mounted warriors with their suspicious stares and their drawn bows aimed squarely at them.

"We're surrounded by a platoon of pissed-off samurai," Ren said. "I'm guessing not."

Trása shook her head. "That doesn't mean much. I've been in realms where the whole world was populated by Chinese who worship the Pristine Ones. There're thousands of them ruled by the *Djinn*, thousands more ruled by Maharajas. There's even a reality I've heard of where the Neanderthal still rule Europe. This could just be a realm where the Japanese are in ascendancy." She moved a little closer to him, until they were back-to-back, and added with a whisper over her shoulder. "If their magic is anything to go by, the *Youkai* here are very powerful. Can you feel it?"

Ren nodded, as another thought occurred to him. "You could turn into a bird and be outta here in a couple of minutes, couldn't you?"

"I'm not prepared to risk it," she said, and then lowered her voice even more to add, "Suppose the magic here triggers Marcroy's curse and I can't turn back?"

"I can break the curse for you, can't I?"

"Sure. Do you know how?" When Ren didn't answer her - because he really didn't know exactly what he was supposed to do to break the curse, she added, "Besides, these samurai look like they don't miss very often. Owls don't take off that fast."

She had a point, Ren supposed, but still, he thought she at least might want to try. They were prisoners here and things were only likely to get worse. Now, while they were still in the open, she might have some chance of escape.

Rule Four of the *What To Do If You're Kidnapped* rules drummed into him by his mother's bodyguards leaped to mind.

Run if you get the chance.

Never run in a straight line.

Make a ruckus.

Get somewhere public as fast as you can.

Granted, they hadn't been kidnapped exactly - they'd voluntarily jumped through a dimensional rift to trespass in this reality - but the situation seemed close enough. Regardless, they had to get away, either by talking their way out of it or escaping, although where they might *escape to* was almost as big a problem as staying put. They couldn't waste time here as prisoners of who-knew-what. Somewhere out there in the maelstrom of infinite realities, his brother, Darragh, and his friend, Hayley, were trapped.

If they weren't in this realm, they were in another - maybe back in Ren's magic-less realm, maybe in the one Darragh and Trása came from or maybe another random reality like this one. Hayley had stepped through the rift into Darragh's realm a moment before Ren and Trása did, so Ren assumed she, at least, was safe and well. Ren had jumped through after Hayley, and he was here with Trása, so he figured Darragh was most likely still caught back in his world with only Sorcha for company and aid.

But who knew for sure where Hayley had finished up?

Was she stuck in Darragh's reality now? Blind and helpless... although even blind, knowing Hayley, she wouldn't be helpless for long. Was she trapped in that incomprehensible world of Druids and Faerie? A world that made very little sense to Ren, even though apparently he belonged there.

How would it seem to someone like Hayley who had no idea what she was stepping into?

And who would explain it to her? His friend Brógán? The great, but scarily taciturn warrior, Ciarán?

Ren wished he'd had time to study Darragh's memories - time to get a handle on this magic thing. He could feel it. The very air in this place trembled with magical power waiting to be tapped. Even more frustratingly, buried in his head, was the knowledge to do something with it. Hidden in his mind was all the magical expertise he needed to be gone from here. He simply hadn't had time to think.

Trása elbowed him and pointed to the main house with its upturned eaves and intricately carved lintels. "He's back."

Ren turned to discover the warrior who had ordered the others to watch them, had appeared on the veranda of the main house. A moment later, a woman stepped out of the house and stopped next to him, and beside her was the largest dog Ren had ever seen. The woman was a walking Japanese cliché - dressed in a red silk kimono embroidered in exquisite golden dragons. Ren had to stifle the urge to laugh, an urge that vanished almost immediately when she stepped forward with small steps and a hollow tapping sound, her wooden *geta* echoing on the veranda's decking. The dog compelled much more respect. Powerfully muscled, with a sleek tan coat, it looked like a well-trained mastiff, the way it walked by her side. It also looked as if it could eat either of them in one or two bites. The woman stepped down into the raked sand of the courtyard and shuffled forward.

She stopped and studied Ren and Trása with dark, cold eyes. The dog sat beside her, his eyes also fixed on them.

"Lord Hayato says you claim to be lost travellers," the woman said in the same, almost-the-Japanese-he-knew the warriors spoke. Even wearing the wooden sandals, she was only shoulder-high to the Lord Hayato, but somehow she seemed much taller. Her hand rested on the dog's head, which was higher than her waist.

"*Warewareniha shogunha imasen,*" he said, repeating what he'd told his captors when they'd first discovered them several hours ago, just after they had come through the rift from Ren's reality. "*Warewareha mayoteiru tabino monodesu.*" We have no lord, we are lost travellers.

The woman stared at him for a moment and then produced a small square of paper from the pocket of her kimono. With brisk, rapid movement, she folded the paper back and forth until it took the vague shape of a heart. Once it was done, she tossed it into the air, closed her eyes, and a moment later the little origami heart vanished in a puff of tiny white flakes.

"His heart is true," she announced. "He speaks the truth."

Her declaration seemed to have little effect on their escort. Or the fixed stare of the huge dog.

There were no lowered bows or sighs of relief. The men continued to glare at them from under their highly polished *kabuto* with suspicion and mistrust. One of them even spat on the ground muttering *"Ronin."*

"He knows your name," Trása whispered with alarm.

Ren shook his head. "He means mercenary, I think," he told her. "It's the almost the same word in Japanese." At least he hoped that was the case. It was too scary to contemplate the alternative.

Ren took a step forward, feigning a confidence he didn't feel, and bowed as low as he could to the woman. He ignored the dog, figuring unless she commanded it to attack, the mastiff would not bother him if he did not bother it. Clearly, this woman was in charge and she'd just magicked up a bit of origami to determine if they were telling the truth. The warriors were probably her minions. Even the stern Lord Hayato seemed to defer to her. Ren grabbed Trása's hand and tugged her down into a bow as well, addressing the woman as he bent over.

"We are honored to be in your presence, *kakka*," he said, hoping that calling her *Your Excellency* was a compliment and not an insult, if her rank was higher than that. Ren wasn't sure about this reality, but he'd seen his mother almost run out of Tokyo a couple of years ago, for mispronouncing an honorific when she met some local dignitaries during a banquet held in her honor after she won her Oscar. He didn't want to make the same mistake.

"And from where have you travelled, *muhousha?*" she asked coldly.

Ren frowned. He'd granted her a title of great respect and she had responded by suggesting he was some sort of criminal. He wondered if the truth-telling spell was still in effect, because suddenly, he wasn't sure if it was a good idea to confess they'd stepped through a rift from another reality.

"From a very distant place, *kakka*," he said as he straightened to look her in the eye. She was a woman in her late thirties, he guessed, and well-used to being in command. "One where the customs are much different to yours. I trust we have done nothing to offend you."

"What is your name?"

"Ren Kavanaugh."

"That is a *yabangin* name," she said, studying them even more closely. Her gaze shifted to Trása and her frown deepened as she studied the girl. Abruptly she turned to Hayato and spoke so rapidly, Ren was only able to catch every third word or so, and they weren't promising as far as he could tell. As soon as she finished speaking, Hayato signalled to several of his men. Four of them immediately dismounted and converged on Trása, one of them unsheathing his *katana* as he went.

Trása screamed as the men grabbed her and forced her to her knees. The mastiff began growling. One of them pulled her long blonde braid aside and pointed excitedly at her delicate, almost pointed ears.

"Hey!" Ren cried in English, rushing forward. "What the hell?"

"She is *Youkai!*" the samurai cried out. "Look!"

Another man raised his *katana*. Trása screamed as her hair was pulled and her head jerked back to expose her throat. Ren was shoved roughly to his knees beside her by the man holding Trása's hair.

"Rónán!" Trása cried in panic. "Do something! They're going to kill me!"

"For God's sake! Call them off!" Ren demanded of the woman who was obviously in charge, still on his hands and knees. "She didn't do anything to you!"

The dog growled low in this throat, forcing Ren to lean back. The woman stood impassively, ignoring his pleas, doing nothing to stop Trása's impending execution.

He scrambled to his feet and tried to lunge toward Trása, but one of the warriors grabbed him from behind. Not that he could have done much against four armoured men with swords, and a dog probably trained to kill, but he couldn't stand by and let them murder Trása just for being Faerie. At least, he assumed that's what they were panicking about, given the way the man had spat the word *Youkai*.

He couldn't understand that, either. This world fairly dripped with magic. The woman commanding them to slay Trása wielded it with impunity. Why the fuss over one half-*beansídhe* interloper, even if she was annoying at times?

Faerie were magical creatures, and without them, humans had no magic. In Ren's limited experience - and certainly his brother's memories offered nothing to contradict the impression - one tended to appease the *Tuatha* if one wanted to use their magic, not kill them on sight.

And yet, in this reality, being identified as even half-Faerie, seemed enough to get you slaughtered on the spot.

"Trása!" he called to her, as he struggled to shake off the men holding him back. "Change!"

"*What*?" She screamed as they forced her to her knees.

"Change into a bird and fly away!" he cried in English, as she thrashed about in the grip of the man trying to keep her still long enough to line up the blade so he could cut her throat. Fortunately, the men trying to hold Trása didn't understand what he was saying. There was still a chance at least one of them could get away. "Fly away! Now!"

"But what if I can't change back?" she sobbed between cries as she fought them with every once of strength she owned.

"I'll find a way to change you back," he promised urgently. "But even if I can't, better a live owl than a dead Faerie!"

Even through her desperate struggles, Trása must have seen the logic in his words. Without warning, she went limp in the arms of her captors. Her sudden capitulation took them by surprise. The warriors stepped back from her for a moment looking puzzled and more than a little concerned.

It was enough. Before they could grab her again, the half-human, half-*beansídhe* girl morphed into the white owl shape she favoured, flapped her wings once, and launched into the air with a screech of protest.

The dog lunged forward, snapping at her tail feathers while the woman in the kimono screamed in anger, as Trása flew away into the darkness to freedom.

CHAPTER 2

Everywhere Marcroy looked through the shimmering event horizon of the rift, there were rotting corpses.

The smell wafting back through the open rift was beyond awful. Marcroy's eyes watered with the stench of it, and he hadn't even stepped through the rift to other side.

Nor would he. For Marcroy Tarth, stepping through this rift would be just as fatal as it had been for the thousands of dead Faerie who lay rotting around this abandoned stone circle in the other reality.

The earth around the stone circle on the other side of the rift was piled three-deep in bodies, most of them obviously fleeing something in their own realm. What had driven so many to throw themselves through a rift into a world without magic? What had driven them to face this certain death? These *sidhe* must have known what they were doing. They must have felt the dearth of magic with the first breath they took of this new reality's depleted air. Still, they stepped through rather than stay behind and face - what?

Marcroy looked at the *djinni*, Jamaspa, who had opened the rift to show him this carnage. "How many more?" he asked, utterly shaken by the sight of yet another decimated world. There were no obvious signs of civilisation around the stone circle on the other side - that might mean the circle was in an out-of-the-way place, or it could mean this entire world was dead, all other mortal forms of life gone - along with the magic. It would not be the first realm to suffer such a fate.

And while the Undivided lived, it wouldn't be the last, either.

"We have lost count," Jamaspa told him, his ephemeral blue form shimmering with emotion.

Marcroy stared at the carnage for a long, silent moment, and then turned to the *djinni*. "I don't need convincing, Jamaspa. I understand the Undivided must be stopped. I have done nothing but work towards that end for years now."

"Granted," the *djinni* agreed. He waved a wisp of blue smoke that might have been his arm in the direction of the rift and it shimmered close. The dreadful piles of bodies disappeared, replaced by the welcome ordinariness of their own sunset-reddened stone circle, just outside the entrance to *Tír Na nÓg* in the realm Marcroy called home. Inside *Tír Na nÓg*, the *sidhe* remained blissfully unaware of the fate that had befallen so many of their race from other realms. "Unfortunately, you took it upon yourself to fix things without

23

consulting the Brethren." Jamaspa sighed heavily, making his whole ephemeral blue body bob up and down. "Do you remember asking me not so long ago, cousin, if my rift runners were mistaken about the future that awaits us if we do nothing?"

Marcroy nodded, picturing himself and the *djinni* looking down over *Sí an Bhrú*, remembering their conversation very well. "You said the Undivided twins, RónánDarragh will destroy us – *Tuatha, Djinn* and all the others of our kind. I believe you made some sweeping claim that you had seen the destruction in other realities where they were allowed to rule united." Marcroy stared at the *djinni*. "This is what you meant, I suppose."

Jamaspa nodded, making his whole body bob up and down. "And now you know I was not exaggerating."

"If I recall it correctly, your exact words were "for the sake of all the *sídhe* races of this realm, we must destroy the Undivided." But they are missing and powerless. How can they have caused this?"

The *djinni* frowned. He seemed uncomfortable. "The Brethren were... remiss, perhaps... in not specifying the destruction of RónánDarragh would be most beneficial if it happened *before* they were old enough to breed."

Marcroy was growing impatient with the *djinni*. He couldn't see the problem. As far as he was able, he'd done everything the Brethren had asked of him. He devoted much of these past nineteen years to the task. Everything had gone according to plan. They were days away from success. "RónánDarragh in this realm have no offspring. When the transfer happens at *Lughnasadh*, the far less-powerful and problematic Broc and Cairbre will become the

Undivided. Unless..." His voice trailed off, as he wondered what had become of Brydie Ni'Seanan, the attractive and undoubtedly fertile young woman the queen of the Celts had so blatantly thrown at Darragh a few weeks ago, before he disappeared into another realm.

"If you speak of the young woman Álmhath threw into Darragh's bed, she is taken care of," Jamaspa assured Marcroy. "She will not be giving birth to any child of the Undivided."

"Then we have nothing to fear," Marcroy said, glancing up at the last traces of the sunset. It was going to rain tonight, he guessed, looking at the formation of the clouds. He turned back to Jamaspa, "It is done, and you may inform the Brethren accordingly. Wherever they are, Darragh and his missing brother, Rónán, will perish on *Lughnasadh*, their line will end with them and the threat of Partition will be gone."

Jamaspa didn't appear impressed by Marcroy's assurances. "And if they *don't* perish?"

He looked at the *djinni* in surprise. "How can they not?"

The *djinni* morphed into a more human shape without warning, and sat himself down on the edge of the nearest standing stone. The sun was almost completely set now, darkness stalking the land. In the distance, the faint sounds of the night creatures coming awake to hunt and play could be heard, if one listened closely. Marcroy ignored the sounds to concentrate on his blue companion's alarming suggestion.

"What are you not telling me, Jamaspa?" he asked, suddenly ill at the thought that he had skirted so close to breaking the treaty of *Tír Na nÓg* just to discover it may have all been for naught.

"There are rumours," Jamaspa said. "Unfounded, unreliable and untraceable. But they have been heard in several realms now. Rumours that in some realities, the Undivided have not achieved Partition, despite spawning the twins who can easily achieve it. Rumours that hint at a foe capable of defeating them before they had a chance to mature."

"If they are only rumours, what difference do these rumours make to us?" Marcroy asked.

"Perhaps a great deal," Jamaspa said, watching Marcroy closely. "In every realm where the Undivided have achieved Partition, they have turned on the *sídhe* and set out to destroy them. You have seen the result for yourself, now, Marcroy. Once Partition is achieved, the Undivided are effectively immortal, as far as we know. Certainly we've not heard of any *sídhe* having success in killing them."

It occurred to Marcroy that perhaps the animosity of the Undivided toward the *Tuatha Dé Danann* was justified. In some of the realms where the magically gifted humans had managed to free themselves of any need for cooperation with the *sídhe* races, their animosity might have had something to do with the Brethren's determination to be rid of them. Sending assassins, as a rule, was not the best way to open a dialogue with an enemy.

"You think there is someone or some*thing* who can kill them?" Marcroy asked, a little impatiently. "Even if they are capable of achieving Partition?"

Jamaspa nodded. "One of the rumours we've heard claims that twins capable of severing their magical ties with our people were destroyed by their predecessors. Those twins were the rare Undivided who *didn't* perish during the transfer of power from one generation of Undivided to the next."

Marcroy thought about that for a moment. He didn't see how it was possible. "Humans cannot channel *sídhe* magic on their own. That's why we protect them with the triskalion tattoo. Without it, the magic would kill them."

"*If* they're human," Jamaspa agreed.

"How can they not be human?" Marcroy scoffed.

"To wield *sídhe* magic," Jamaspa pointed out, logically enough, "one has to be mostly *sídhe*."

Marcroy rolled his eyes at the very suggestion. "You don't think we wouldn't have noticed the Undivided were *sídhe* before now?"

"That would depend on how much trouble the *Matrarchaí* have taken to conceal it from us."

"I would suggest they've not much *sídhe* blood in them," Marcroy said, "because every single one of them has died during the transfer to his or her successors."

"Granted," the djinni conceded. "But if RónánDarragh, were to survive..."

Marcroy didn't hear the rest. He was remembering the investiture of RónánDarragh when they were babies. *The tall stones of Beltany casting their shadows over the stone platform where the infant heirs lay. The long, complicated ceremony full of absurd ritual. The sacrifices to the gods and goddesses.* He remembered stifling a yawn as Orlagh stepped forward to take each of the year-old twins by the hand - Rónán by the left and Darragh by the right - to brand them magically with the symbol that would act as a conduit between the *Tuatha* and the Druids.

Marcroy remembered waiting, expecting the children to howl with pain. It was more than a surface tattoo the *Tuatha Dé Danann* queen was bestowing on them. She was branding them to the bone, searing the magical symbol into the boys so deeply that even losing that limb would not interrupt the flow of power.

But the boys hadn't cried...

These boys - these magically gifted psychic twins born of a human woman - obviated the need for the treaty. There was no need for spells or magical tattoos, Jamaspa had told him, a few days later, when he came to warn Marcroy about them. These children could take from the *sídhe* that which had, until now, been given under very specific conditions.

"You knew," he accused the *djinni*. "Back when you first came to me, you knew then that they were part-*sídhe*."

Jamaspa shook his head. "I didn't *know*. I still don't. In fact, we won't know at all, for certain, until the power transfer at *Lughnasadh*. If Darragh survives it, then we have our answer. And maybe our weapon. So the other twin you devoted so much time to hiding will also need to be brought home."

The ramifications were mindboggling. Marcroy didn't know what to think. He was certain, however, that nothing good could come of any Undivided having the temerity to survive what was, effectively, his own execution. "I don't see how Darragh or his brother can help us fight off the *Matrarchaí*, even if they are almost all *sídhe*, which I seriously doubt." Even as he said it, he could hear the lack of conviction in his own voice.

"That's because you are not thinking this through, cousin," Jamaspa said. "Consider for a moment. What is the one thing we Faerie cannot do? What we cannot even contemplate doing?"

"Breaking *sídhe* law," Marcroy answered without hesitation.

"Then imagine," the Djinn suggested. "If RónánDarragh are mostly *sídhe*, without even knowing it, they are bound by *sídhe* law, *too*. They must defend us. They have no choice."

Marcroy paused as he slowly realized what Jamaspa was saying. "And you think the rumours in other realms that some Undivided seeking Partition were destroyed because the *eiléféin* of our RónánDarragh must have turned on their heirs when their heirs have tried to annihilate the Faerie? As *sídhe* themselves, they could do nothing else."

Jamaspa smiled. "See! I told the Brethren you weren't as foolish as you seem."

Marcroy was stunned. "But this means, if Darragh and his brother survive *Lughnasadh* we can win. We are saved. This is excellent news!"

"If it's true."

"I suppose we won't know until *Lughnasadh*," Marcroy said, rubbing his chin, wondering how he was going to manage this. He needed to bring the Undivided home. Both of them. He needed to know whether they were going to survive the transfer of power, and if they did, he needed to be the one to reveal the truth to them. He would become their mentor... their guardian... the father figure both boys had always lacked.

He would be the reason they chose to save their true people.

The idea that he might be the saviour of the *sídhe* races in this realm was very enticing to a *sídhe* as ambitious as Marcroy. Such a deed would come with great reward, great prestige - perhaps even admittance to the ranks of the Brethren, who hadn't opened their ranks to a new member in several thousand years...

Marcroy could already taste the delicious ambrosia of success. The heady taste of being hailed as a hero, not just by his own people, but every *sídhe* in this realm. He was already scheming, already trying to plan how to make it happen.

The first step was obvious - bring Darragh and his brother back to this realm. If they survived the transfer, to have any hope of success, he had to keep RónánDarragh close.

In theory, it was all too easy...

Pity, then, Marcroy had no idea what had become of the Undivided.

CHAPTER 3

The media circus that had taken up residence in the car park of Dublin's Castle Golf Club with alarming speed and seemed undaunted by the early-morning rain or the fact they were not permitted any closer to the action. Now it was daylight and the full extent of the carnage wrought on the club's pristine fairways and greens was apparent.

There was plenty to keep the cameras rolling and the reporters talking into their microphones and cameras, as they breathlessly reported on what little they knew about the last night's events, which was - Pete Doherty was quite certain - barely anything at all.

After all, Pete had been in the thick of things for most of the night, and he knew next to nothing about what had happened down there on the ninth hole, so he was pretty certain the media was no better informed.

The Gardaí had cordoned off the car park and another area around a metallic-silver Audi parked at an odd angle with its doors open. His own unmarked patrol car would soon be subject to a similar level of forensic scrutiny. It was down on the fairway, wrapped around the trunk of a large oak tree.

Uniformed officers were on duty to keep the paparazzi pack at bay. Over by the elegant, two-storey clubhouse, another crowd of curious onlookers had gathered, despite the rain, to watch all the excitement. There was an ambulance parked on the edge of the green, its back doors open, the paramedics wearing high-visibility fluorescent vests sitting on the back step of the ambulance sipping coffee from polystyrene mugs. They were waiting for someone to treat. Other than Pete, nobody was injured, but there had been shots fired and people were still missing. Pete made a mental note of the Audi's licence plate and turned to glance over his shoulder, more than a little annoyed that Inspector Duggan was sending him home. She wasn't concerned about his supposed concussion - she thought he'd screwed up by letting the Kavanaugh kid escape last night. He watched through the rain-streaked window of the patrol car as it slowly headed across the carpark for the gates. The line of uniforms scouring the rough around the fairways weren't just looking for evidence, he knew. They were looking for bodies.

"Jesus wept!" the officer driving the car exclaimed, slamming on the brakes. "There's two of you!"

Pete jerked against his seat belt with a grunt and squinted through the beating wipers, looking at the figure that stepped in front of the patrol car taking him home on Inspector Duggan's orders. The reporter brazenly blocked their way as the car headed away from the chaos that smart-arsed Kavanaugh kid had managed to wreak while kidnapping his cousin from St Christopher's Visual Rehabilitation Centre last night.

"It's okay," Pete assured the driver, as he jerked open the door. He was angry enough at being sent home and excluded from the action. He certainly didn't need the added complication of an over-enthusiastic reporter who figured Pete owed him a favour or two just because they were related. "I'll take care of this."

He climbed out of the car, pulled up the collar of his coat against the drizzling rain and approached the reporter, who eyed him up and down with a frown.

"That's an impressive shiner you've got brewing there, my friend," the reporter said, his frown changing to a mischievous grin as he examined Pete's face more closely. "You gonna get a medal for it? Mum'll be thrilled."

"What are you doing here, Logan?" Pete asked, glad his brother hadn't asked for details on how he had acquired the two rapidly blackening eyes he sported. He would never hear the end of it if his twin learned a girl had knocked him out cold.

"Same as you. My job." Logan thrust the mike he was holding toward his battered and bruised brother and assumed his very best on-camera voice. "Care to give me an exclusive, Detective-Sergeant Doherty?"

"Fuck off," he said pleasantly, knowing his use of an expletive would render the tape unusable for the evening news. He pushed away the lens Logan's cameraman shoved in his face, "Get that thing away from me, George, or I swear I'll shove it sideways up your-"

"Keep filming Duggan if you can spot her," Logan ordered George hastily, before turning back to Pete. George obliged and moved the focus off Pete and onto the action across the course - or what little they could see of it. Logan took Pete by the arm and drew him aside, out of George's hearing. "Off the record then. Brother to brother. What's really going on down there, Pete? Did you catch the Kavanaugh kid?"

"No comment, *brother*," Pete told him, amused Logan had even bothered to try such a tactic. "I know your idea of *off the record*."

"Is it true Ren Kavanaugh kidnapped some girl from a hospital in the city last night?" Logan asked, undeterred, "and made his getaway in a stolen patrol car? *Your* patrol car, perchance?"

"Why are you even asking me, Logan?" Pete sighed, wondering where Logan had heard about *that*. He probably had a police scanner in his car. Or the TV station had one. Nothing was really a secret anymore. "You know I'm not going to tell you anything."

"Ah, but you're wrong. Your silence is very revealing."

Logan glanced past Pete at the chaos across the fairways, where a cluster of patrol cars and a whole platoon of Gardaí were scouring the course, looking for any sign of the fugitive, Ren Kavanaugh, and his missing cousin, Hayley Boyle. Pete doubted they'd find anything. Kavanaugh was proving to be a right little Houdini, and if he was still hiding on the golf course somewhere, surely they would have found him - or the girl he'd kidnapped - by now.

His brother frowned at the police for a moment and then turned to Pete with a cheerful smile. "So... if you won't tell me anything useful, any chance you can do your favourite brother a favour and line me up an interview with old Iron-Britches Duggan before you go?"

"Don't be ridiculous."

"She likes me."

Pete shook his head at his brother's eternal optimism wondering, if they were so much alike to look at, how they could be so different in so many ways. "She smiled at you at last year's Christmas party, idiot. That doesn't mean she likes you. It just means she was hitting the eggnog a bit too hard."

"Hey... if the eggnog gets me an exclusive..."

"You have absolutely no morals or integrity, Logan."

"Takes one to know one, Pete." His brother grinned at him, punching his arm playfully. "*Identical* twins, remember?"

Pete stared at Logan for a moment, and then shook his head, as the hazy memory of what had happened to him last night began to coalesce into some semblance of a useful recollection.

Jesus wept! There's two of you! His driver had just said that, when Logan - Pete's twin brother - stepped in front of the patrol car. Pete remembered saying exactly the same thing driving away from St Christopher's last night, just before some dark-eyed apparition appeared in the front seat and cold-cocked him into unconsciousness.

Jesus wept. That's it! There's two of them.

Impulsively, he hugged his brother, suddenly grinning. "Thanks, bro."

"For what?" Logan asked, immediately suspicious of Pete's smile.

"Can't explain. I'll see you later." He turned for the car, anxious to be gone. He had some checking to do. He'd find something to prove it to Inspector Duggan. Something to prove it to himself. "You gonna be at Mamó's birthday on the weekend?"

"Of course," Logan said. "Aren't you?"

"Should be," Pete said, climbing back into the car. "I'll see you Saturday night."

He slammed the car door before Logan had a chance to ask him anything further, and told the constable to drive off. Logan stared at him suspiciously for a moment through the windscreen and then stepped back to let the patrol car pass, moving George out of the way, as the cameraman concentrated on filming as much as he could of the investigation across the fairways.

Pete leaned back against the headrest and closed his eyes. He already had a headache, but couldn't imagine going home yet. Even if he wanted to, he knew he'd never sleep. Not now.

Logan had nailed it.

Jesus wept! There's two of you!

Chelan Aquarius Kavanaugh - adopted son of the famous actress, Kiva Kavanaugh, spoiled brat and escaped fugitive on the run from a charge of murder and now kidnapping - had an identical twin brother, and Pete Doherty, one way or another, was going to find him and prove he wasn't seeing double.

CHAPTER 4

Trása's escape from the samurai compound had come at a cost. She'd lost some tail feathers to that beast of a dog and one of the arrows loosed in her direction had grazed her wing. Unsteady and shaken, she flew on in agony, grateful, nonetheless, that the injuries had not damaged her flight feathers. If that had happened, she might as well have stayed with Rónán, let them slit her throat and feed her remains to the mastiff.

It would have been a quicker and much less painful way to die.

She flew far from the torch-lit compound, deep into the *kozo* forest, before she felt safe enough to land, despite the injury to her wing. At least her avian eyesight gave her an advantage. Trása needed to find somewhere to transform, something she couldn't do if she simply landed high in the branches of a tree and tried to change there.

Turning back into a human might break the branch she'd landed on and send her plummeting to the ground.

Not much point in escaping one death - so it had been drilled into her at in *Tír Na nÓg* - simply to find another by being careless.

Of course, that was assuming she *could* resume her true form. Trása might be trapped as a bird here, just as easily as she was in her own realm. The magic in this reality was strong. It wouldn't surprise her at all if Marcroy's curse held power here too.

Trása wouldn't know, however, until she tried to change. If she could change without a problem, then it would be safe to change back into a bird again, and see if she could help Rónán.

Exhausted and in agony from her wounded wing, she spied a clearing in the vast forest that seemed far enough away from any signs of human habitation to make it safe to land on the ground. There was no telling what animal dangers lurked beneath the forest canopy. Her owlish eyesight was excellent, but she couldn't see through the leaves to know if a fox or a vole lurked beneath, waiting for an owl foolish enough to land on the forest floor. Trása would need to transform as soon as she landed. Before anything big enough to view her as edible came along and decided it was time for breakfast.

The clearing was small and shadowed as Trása swooped towards it, the rising sun yet to find the forest floor. She circled it a few times to ensure it was clear of predators, before coming into land on the leaf-strewn ground. As soon as her claws touched the moist carpet of rotting vegetation, Trása imagined herself as human again.

A moment later, she was standing in the clearing, naked, shivering, bleeding from a flesh wound on the fleshy underside of her upper arm, but filled with a relief so intense she wanted to cry. Gasping, she checked herself over, thrilled to discover the only injury was the arrow-nick. Unharmed, but cold and filled with an insatiable hunger - common for shifters changing from a form that needed much less food than another.

Trása healed the arrow wound with a thought. It had been intensely painful when she was trying to fly with a wounded wing, but it was barely noticeable now she was human again. She was freezing. It was just on dawn and she had nothing to wear until she could steal some clothes.

That meant finding a human settlement of some kind.

That in itself, was a straightforward exercise. She merely had to fly around until she spotted a village or a farmhouse from the air. There would be a washing line somewhere, with clothes she could appropriate without being seen. Of course, the problem she would have then, was carrying those clothes back to where they were holding Rónán prisoner, so she didn't have to rescue him while stark naked.

What she needed was a *Leipreachán*. A lesser *sídhe* who could vanish and reappear at will. Then she could make him carry her clothes wherever she needed them.

The thought made her hesitate, as it occurred to Trása she was standing in the middle of a vast forest in a realm seeped in magic, and yet there was no sign of a single *sídhe* - lesser or otherwise. In Trása's realm, if a magical creature had landed in a forest and transformed from animal into human form, there'd be curious lesser *sídhe* come to investigate. They couldn't help themselves. Faerie were curious beyond reason, and instinctively drawn to others of their kind.

Were they too terrified to approach? Was she so strange to these foreign *sídhe* that she frightened them? Had the rift implosion that brought Trása and Rónán here blown them across the world, as well as across realities? Had they landed in this realm's version of Japan? Were they in a place where her long blonde hair and pale skin marked her, not as Faerie, but as an alien creature they didn't know or recognize?

Shivering, Trása cocked her head, straining to hear the tell-tale signs of *sídhe* in the undergrowth - but there was nothing. The first rays of the sun were kissing the leaves in the upper reaches of the forest canopy. How could that be? This world was drenched with magic. Trása breathed it in with every breath. It oozed out of her every pore. How could it not be swarming with every kind of *sídhe*?

Her forehead creased with concern. That heartless bitch in the gorgeous kimono, who so casually ordered her samurai to slit Trása's throat, had called Trása *Youkai* in a voice fairly dripping with contempt. The *Youkai* were the Faerie of Japan and the Korean peninsula in Trása's realm. She'd met a few of them back in her own reality, when they had come to *Sí an Bhrú* to pay their respects to what was left of the Undivided. They had seemed proud and exotic creatures, not unlike her own kind, and somewhat were disdainful of humans.

Their contempt had seemed odd at the time, but now - with this apparent lack of any other *sídhe* - it was positively frightening. Where were the *Youkai*? They had to be here somewhere, Trása reasoned, because there was too much magic for them to be extinct. She had visited worlds where the *sídhe* had been annihilated... the reality Rónán had been sent to by her father was one. Here, though, she could taste magic on the very air. There ought to be *Youkai* giggling behind every bush, hiding in every tree and lurking under every blade of grass.

"It's okay," she called out, turning a slow circle to see if she could coax someone out of the forest. Things would be easier for her and Rónán too, if she could enlist the help of her own kind to set about rescuing him. "I won't hurt you! Look! I'm *Youkai*, too."

She repeated her call in the rusty Japanese she'd been imprinted with months ago but never had reason to use until now. It was greeted with the same eerie silence as the call in her native tongue. Trása waited for some time, knowing that shyness sometimes overrode the curiosity of the lesser *sídhe*, but there was no answer. The forest was silent. In the distance she could hear the birds who made their homes amog the *kozo* trees, chattering among themselves, but it was the chatter of real birds greeting the rising sun, not magical creatures hiding in bird form.

Trása was at a loss about what to do next. She had never visited a magical world where there was no Faerie. Even in Ren's reality, where the magic was almost non-existent, she'd had a *Leipreachán* to help her, although until now, she'd never really considered Plunkett O'Bannon's annoying presence to be actually helpful. She was a little shocked to think she was missing him now.

Where could the *Youkai* be? Had the humans imprisoned them? The woman in the red kimono hadn't used magic the way Trása was accustomed to, but had folded a piece of paper into a shape first, and the magic seemed to have been released when it disintegrated into dust at her command. That made less sense to Trása than the missing *Youkai*.

Trása's stomach rumbled. She felt hollow inside, but she wasn't convinced it was just because she was hungry. Filled with uncertainty, she shivered again. Despite the rising sun, it was chilly in the clearing and she still had nothing to wear. She needed to get out of here. Now she was sure she could change shape at will, she had one less thing to worry about, and she would be warmer in bird form with feathers to protect her and much less body mass to heat, than she would as a human. With her arm now healed, she should be able to fly safely enough, but with daylight approaching, and the samurai on the lookout for a large white owl, she decided it wasn't a good idea to change back into the bird form she favoured.

She closed her eyes for a moment, wondering if she could recognize the call of any of the other birds in the forest. She would be much less conspicuous in daylight if she could blend with the local bird population. Trása wasn't even sure if she was still in Eire, although some aerial surveillance would tell her, soon enough. Sailing around the skies in the middle of the day disguised as a common barn owl might draw unwanted attention, if they weren't indigenous to the area.

At the sound of a raucous call Trása would have recognized anywhere, she smiled. It was a seagull. They must be close to the sea here. Gulls were easy to emulate, they could fly long distances, sociable, unafraid of humans and likely to go unremarked when hanging around a human settlement. The samurai would think her nothing but a precocious scavenger if she assumed the form of a gull and flew back to the compound where they were holding Rónán.

And maybe... if she were lucky, someone would toss her some food.

Trása closed her eyes again, and formed the image of a seagull in her mind. A moment later, plump, white and grey, she launched herself upward toward the rising sun to search out Rónán, her delicately grey-tinted wings flexing in the faint breeze.

It was time to see what she could do to save the only man in this reality capable of saving her.

CHAPTER 5

Riding around in the trunk of a car, even one as roomy as a Bentley, Darragh was starting to feel as if the world was closing in on him, a feeling in no way helped by the fact that Sorcha - who should have been protecting Rónán, wherever he was - lay curled up beside him like a spooning lover, muttering to herself in her native tongue about the indignity of it all.

Darragh had no way of knowing how long they'd been trapped in the back of Rónán's mother's car. He didn't know if it was day or night. He had no way of knowing how similar her chauffeur, Patrick Boyle, was to his alternate reality version - Amergin. Would Patrick betray them in the same way Amergin had so heinously in their own realm? The police here wanted his twin brother, Rónán, and for all Darragh knew, Patrick was helping them. He and Sorcha might well be on their way to the nearest Gardaí station.

When Patrick opened the trunk to let them out, Darragh and Sorcha might be safe. Or they might be arrested.

"This was a foolish idea," Sorcha growled, as they hit another bump that forced an involuntary grunt from both of them. She shifted a little, trying to get comfortable. "This man you have placed your trust in is Amergin's *eileféin*. He will betray you as surely as Amergin did."

Darragh shook his head in the darkness, refusing to believe it. The trunk smelt of carpet and petrol fumes. "Patrick is like a father to Rónán," he whispered, not sure if their voices would carry to the passengers in the car, who had no idea - Darragh hoped - there were stowaways aboard.

"Amergin was like a father to you, too," Sorcha pointed out in a sour whisper. "That didn't stop him betraying you in our realm. I'm quite certain it won't stop him betraying us in this one, either."

Darragh had no answer to that, other than his faith in his brother's memories that the *Comhroinn* - the magical mind sharing of the Druids in his reality - had given him. He had to believe Rónán's high opinion of Patrick was deserved because, really, Sorcha had a point. Right until Amergin confessed his betrayal on his deathbed, Darragh would have sworn the Druid was the most trusted man in the entire universe.

Was fate so cruel? Are we so naïve and unlucky, that we could be betrayed twice by the same man in two different realities?

He cried out suddenly, as a sharp pain slashed across his face.

"Be quiet!" Sorcha hissed.

"I'm sorry," he whispered back, reaching up to touch his cheek gingerly. His fingers came away sticky with blood. "Something cut me. On the face."

"How...?" Sorcha began, and then Darragh felt her shrug in the darkness. "Rónán is alive then."

"So it would seem," Darragh agreed. He wasn't sure if Rónán was safe, however. For him to manifest a wound inflicted on his brother in another reality, the wound had to have been caused by a weapon forged of *airgead sídhe*. Faerie silver.

It did not bode well that Rónán had been gone only a few hours and was already wounded with a magical weapon. Where was he? Had he slipped while handling his own weapon or was he under attack? Darragh had no way of knowing, and only one small consolation. The psychic link between them only worked on magical injuries. At least, wherever he was, Rónán was not suffering the indignity of a sprained ankle in a realm devoid of magic.

They rocked forward as the car came to a stop. His heart in his throat, Darragh realized they were about to find out what Patrick Boyle planned to do with them. He heard faint voices, then footsteps. The car started again. A few moments later they stopped and the engine died. More footsteps, the trunk lid lifted and daylight flooded in, temporarily blinding both of them.

"You okay in there?"

Darragh squinted in the painful light, noting - with a great deal of relief - that Patrick seemed to be alone.

"We're fine," he said, a little warily. "Are we somewhere safe?"

"Temporarily," the man who reminded him so uncomfortably of Amergin said, glancing around. "I just dropped Kiva off at the RTE studios in Donnybrook. Your mam has a TV interview scheduled this morning. No thanks to you. She's calling it damage control." The man glanced around again and then stepped back and beckoned them out.

"Where are we?" Sorcha asked, frowning at the unfamiliar surroundings.

"St Vinnie's Hospital car park. Should be safe enough for the moment."

Cautiously, Sorcha and Darragh climbed stiffly out of the car and looked around. It was well past daybreak now. They were in a multi-level car park between rows and rows of abandoned vehicles, although none seemed as large or stately as the Bentley. The air smelled of petrol fumes and stale urine but there were no people around that Darragh could see. His ankle was throbbing, and he wasn't sure if he'd be able to put much weight on it, but he wasn't going to confess that to Patrick. The chauffeur hadn't betrayed him yet, but that didn't mean he wouldn't.

"Have you got any cash on you?" Patrick asked.

Darragh shook his head. He hadn't planned to spend more than a few hours in this reality. What need for coin of the realm?

"You'd be a fool to use a credit card they can trace."

He nodded in agreement, not sure what Patrick meant about cards being traced. He was quite certain, if he found the the time to trawl through his twin brother's memories – acquired in the

Comhroinn - that Patrick's warning would make sense.

"Here then," Patrick said, pulling out his wallet. He thrust a number of paper notes at Darragh. "That should be enough to get you home. If you catch the DART at Elm Park you'll be home in a few minutes."

The DART? He means the train. By Danú, he expects us to travel by public transport?

"You'd better not let anybody see you," the chauffeur added, frowning. "You know where old Jack keeps his spare key in the glasshouse, don't you?"

Still coming to grips with the notion of navigating his way through the mass-transit system of this realm, Darragh thought about it for a moment and realized one of Rónán's clear memories included the location of the next-door neighbour's spare key.

"Take a cab from Blackrock Station," Patrick ordered. "Have it drop you at Jack's place. Let yourselves inside and then lie low until I get there."

"What if Jack is home?" Sorcha asked.

"It's Friday, so he should be at his gardening club meeting until after lunch," Darragh said. He realized he knew a lot about the old man who lived next door to Rónán. Darragh was relieved Patrick was sending them to Jack.

Jack had already helped them solve the problem of what to do with the man they'd kidnapped yesterday. It was fair to assume he might help them again.

"Don't worry, Patrick. We'll be fine," Darragh said.

The chauffeur studied Sorcha for a long moment, making no attempt to hide his suspicion about who she might be and what she was doing with the boy he thought was Ren. "You planning on introducing your friend anytime?"

"This is Sorcha," Darragh said, not sure how he was going to explain her presence without telling Patrick much more than he had time for now.

"What have you done with my Hayley?" Patrick asked her.

Sorcha apparently couldn't think of any better response than the bald truth. "Nothing. I don't know where she is."

Patrick stared long and hard at both of them and then turned to Darragh. "You've got some explaining to do when I get home, Rennie, me lad. Make no mistake."

"He's not-" Sorcha began, but Darragh grabbed her arm to silence her.

"Thank you, Patrick. We are indebted to you. And I promise," he added truthfully, "Hayley is safe and I will explain everything when we have more time. Although I'm not sure you'll believe me."

"We'll see about that," Patrick replied, not looking at all happy with either of them. "Now move it. I have to be back to pick Kiva up in twenty minutes. I'll see you later, and by then you'd better have a good explanation for what's been going on these past few weeks, and what's happened to my Hayley, Ren Kavanaugh, or I'll be ringing the Gardaí and handing you over to them myself."

"I'll tell you everything," Darragh promised.

"Then go," Patrick urged, as the sound of another car approaching reached them. "Keep that hood pulled up and don't let anyone see your face."

Sorcha wanted to add something, but Darragh never gave her the chance. Patrick was letting them go, and they needed to take the opportunity. Besides, he'd mentioned Jack's place, where - if Ren's memories were reliable - he would be safe. Jack O'Righin had helped them once, after all. Darragh assumed he wouldn't mind helping them again.

At least Jack knew the truth about them, which would make things a little easier. The ability to cross through the rifts was lost to this realm and explaining it was not only tedious, it would make him sound like a lunatic. Better to stick with those who knew the truth and save himself the trouble of telling the story over and over to people who wouldn't believe a word he was telling them.

Leaning on Sorcha for support, and gritting his teeth against the pain, Darragh limped toward the exit sign and the ramp that lead down to the street. He kept hold of Sorcha until they were out of sight of the Bentley. When he let her go, he pulled up the hood of his sweatshirt. By the time they reached the car park entrance he'd figured out that if he stayed on the ball of his foot and avoided putting any weight on his ankle, he could walk without help. He would pay for it in a couple of hours, he suspected, not looking forward to the pain. He could already feel the skin pulling as the swelling tightened about his joint. He would need to do something about his ankle when they reached Jack's place. Rónán's memories included a medicine called codeine - Jack had some, he thought which might help the pain, something Darragh - who was magically able to heal most minor but painful and debilitating injuries like this in his own reality - was not looking forward to the next few hours.

In the reality where he belonged, a simple thought would have cured Darragh's injury, but here, where there was no magic, ice and a hefty dose of codeine - according to Ren's memories - was the next best thing for a sprain.

Darragh and Sorcha crossed over the network of narrow streets of the hospital campus onto a road filled with bumper-to-bumper traffic. As he watched Darragh realized, with a sinking heart, how little he really knew about this reality. He understood what he was looking at, knew where he was and how to get home from here on his own, but his brother's most recent memory of this place had only put him here late at night. In the rain.

After Hayley was hit by the car that caused her blindness.

The memories of that night - disconcertingly - included Trása kissing Rónán, which Darragh wasn't expecting. He had to push away a sudden surge of jealousy along with the unwanted - and unhelpful - memory.

"What's the matter?" Sorcha asked.

"Nothing. Are you all right?" Sorcha had stopped by his side and was bent over, gasping heavily, as if she were having trouble breathing. He had never seen her like that before.

The warrior grimaced and straightened with a visible effort. "It's the air in this realm, I think. It's making me nauseous. Aren't you finding it hard to breathe with all these fumes?"

"It'll be better once we get to Jack's place," Darragh told her, trying to convince himself as much as Sorcha. He had no way of knowing if that was the case, but he couldn't afford to despair. And she was right. The air - especially near the roads - stank like a tar pit.

"I hope it does," Sorcha grumbled. "I don't like this place, Darragh, and I don't want to stay here. You have to find us a way home."

"I don't like it here either," Darragh agreed. "So let's find the train station and be gone from here."

"What's a train station?" Sorcha asked.

Darragh studied her for a moment and then sighed. With Sorcha for company, it was going to be an interesting ride. Wherever Rónán was, Darragh had to believe his brother would get him home again. Whatever it took.

If not, they were both lost. Forever.

CHAPTER 6

A couple of the samurai had loosed arrows at Trása as she escaped, but she'd had the presence of mind, even in owl form, to swoop and dive erratically toward the trees. A few moments after she took off she was lost in the darkness of the forest, leaving the samurai making hand signs to ward off evil. Ren could hear her calling out to him, even after she vanished from sight, perhaps to let him know she was there.

Maybe she was trying to comfort him... and assure him rescue was at hand?

Or was she so completely avian when she changed shape, that she forgot who Trása was and who she was supposed to be? Ren figured there must be some residual understanding was when someone changed into an animal. How else would a shapeshifter remember to return to their normal form?

"*Bakamono!*"

A deathly silence fell over the compound at the woman's angry shout. Even the mastiff returned to heel, looking disappointed he'd not been able to catch the owl. Ren gave up wondering about shapeshifters and decided to concentrate on his more immediate problem - keeping his own head attached at the neck. He had to get out of here alive and then find a way back to his own reality to rescue Darragh and Sorcha. He needed to find Hayley. He needed to save her and set things to rights in his reality - and in all the other realities he'd managed to screw up lately with his blind optimism and ignorance.

"Idiots! You let the *Youkai* get away!" The woman turned and pointed at Ren. "And look! There the other one stands, free as a bird, mocking you!"

By the time Ren registered that he was "the other one" the rest of the samurai were on him. Ren's face was pushed into the chilly, damp sandy ground, his arms wrenched behind his back and held there. He forced his head up a little to look at the woman, wondering if she was about to order his death, too.

"Where are the rest of your filthy kind?" she demanded, shuffling over to him in tiny steps forced on her by the tightness of her kimono.

"What... kind?" he asked, spitting out grit and sand so he could speak. "What are you talking about?"

"She means the rest of the stinking *Youkai*," someone above him explained with a helpful kick to his solar plexus.

"I'm not *Youkai*," he grunted, his eyes watering with pain. He hoped his Japanese was close enough to theirs to make him understood. "I'm like you. I'm human. *Ningen.*"

"You are *Youkai,*" the woman insisted, looking down at him with contempt. "I can smell your stench from here."

"Chishihero-*sama*! His hand! Look at his hand!"

Behind his back, someone had spotted Ren's tattooed hand. His left arm was unceremoniously wrenched around so Chishihero could study the triskalion branded into her prisoner's palm. She was silent for a moment and then ordered the men to make him kneel before her.

They dragged Ren to his knees and forced him to lower his eyes, which placed his face about the height of the woman's elaborate sash.

"The mark on your hand," Chishihero said, in a Japanese dialect close enough to the language he spoke for him to understand it. The additional memories he'd acquired from his brother filled in more gaps, to the point where he was likely to be fluent himself, after hearing these people speak for a little longer.

"The symbol is magical. What does it mean?"

"*Wakarimasen,*" Ren said. *I don't know.*

"You are lying."

Ren couldn't tell if Chishihero knew that because of the truth spell - or if she was guessing. Either way, he was in trouble.

"I don't know what it means," he insisted. "It's been there all my life." That much, at least, was true. The truth spell *was* still in effect because his last statement made her hesitate.

"You are dangerous, I think," she said eventually.

There was no safe answer to that. Ren shrugged. "I mean you no harm, Chishihero-*sama,*" he said, figuring if her men addressed her as that, it might be safe for him to do so. "I only wish to find my way home."

"And where is your home?"

"*Eburana.*" Ren said, guessing the alternate-reality Japanese name for the Dublin his brother was familiar with was near enough for this realm. He'd decided one thing already - this was a reality steeped in magic. There would be no advanced technology here, and certainly no history that might have given rise to the Republic of Ireland, as he knew it. Dublin was an ancient city, so it was possible, even in this realm, that they had heard of it. Besides, the answer would tell him if the exploding rift that had separated him from Hayley had jumped him and Trása into a reality in roughly the same geographical location as the one they'd stepped through on the Castle Golf Club course, or if they'd been thrown across the world and landed in this reality's equivalent of Japan.

The woman struck him, backhanding Ren across his face. Her large silver ring sliced his cheek. "You mock me at your peril, *Youkai.*"

Ren fell backwards with the force of the blow. His cheek was stinging and he could feel warm blood welling along the cut. The warriors stepped back and did nothing to aid him.

"Shall I arrange to send him to Tsubasa-sensei, Chishihero-sama?" Hayato asked with great deference, avoiding Ren's eye, acting as if nothing had happened. Ren didn't know who this woman was in the grand scheme of things in this reality, but she commanded the loyalty of these samurai. He struggled to his feet, determined not to be struck again by Chishihero or anybody else.

Chishihero watched him, studying Ren thoughtfully for a few moments and then she shook her head. The mastiff eyed him like he was dinner. "No, Hayato... I cannot risk it. Letting the *Youkai* escape was bad enough. A *yabangin Youkai* with a magical brand and no master is far too dangerous."

"If we confined it..." Hayato began, rather tentatively.

The woman let out a short, sceptical laugh. "Confine it, Hayato? You and your incompetent minions have already proven once this evening that you can't contain a magical beast. I don't have the time to be responsible for its imprisonment and ensure it doesn't escape like the other one. If I leave the plantation now, we'll never meet this season's *washi* quota and I will risk nothing that will incur the wrath of the Empresses." She cast her gaze over Ren again and shrugged, turning on her heel, saying, "I'll send the *Sensei* its hand for study and a report on the incident after you've killed it. Come, Kiba." The mastiff dutifully turned, following her back to the house.

"Whoa!" Ren cried, when he realized the "it" she was planning to murder and dismember was *him*. "Kill me? Send bits of me for study? Are you serious?" He looked around at the samurai. Perhaps they were smiling because this was their boss's idea of a sick joke, but he knew it wasn't. The woman would have slit Trása's throat without blinking. He shouldn't be surprised she was ready to dish out the same fate to him.

"Don't let it speak," Chishihero warned Hayato. "It has magic. Give it a voice and it will enchant you and your men and before you know it, you'll be letting this one escape, too."

JJ FALLON

"Fuck you, lady," Ren said in English.

Chishihero glared at Ren, but didn't respond. Instead, she turned on her heel with Kiba at her side and began to walk back toward the main house with the small mincing steps her kimono and wooden sandals forced her to take, leaving odd tracks in the raked sand of the yard.

Hayato gave his men a hand signal, which must have meant something along the lines of "kill the prisoner now" because as soon as he made it, the samurai closed in on Ren with bared *katanas*.

Ren's heart began to gallop as a realized he had only seconds to live.

He refused to accept his life could end like this. Ren had just discovered he had a twin brother. He'd just found out he was a Druid prince capable of wielding unthinkable magic. He'd just pushed his best friend through a dimensional rift to an alternate reality to cure her blindness. He'd just discovered his true home.

He'd just seen Trása morph into a bird and fly away...

It wasn't going to end like this.

Not here. Not now.

The samurai were closing in, their blades reflecting the torchfire in the courtyard. They were seconds away from slitting his throat.

Ren's head filled with the sound of blood rushing through his ears. His eyesight began to blur as the overwhelming desire to be somewhere else overtook him. As the first touch of cold steel kissed the flesh of his throat, the world disappeared and the pain in Ren's head exploded into a darkness so intense, he was sure he must be dead.

CHAPTER 7

Brydie's imprisonment in the amethyst jewel where she had been trapped by the *djinni*, Jamaspa, had robbed her of all sense of time. There was no day, no night, no mealtimes, no desire to sleep. She dozed off at times, but that was more from boredom than from a need to rest.

She knew her captor now, although his intentions remained vague. The *djinni* who had trapped her in this jewel claimed he meant her no harm, but neither was he inclined to release her, even when she couldn't offer him a satisfactory answer to his questions.

Jamaspa asked many questions - some didn't make sense but others were specific. She answered all of them honestly, because she couldn't see any reason not to. The *djinni* wanted to know where Darragh went at night. More importantly, he wanted to know how Darragh had managed to sneak out of his chamber undetected. Brydie knew the answer to neither question, but her repeated denials made no impact on the *djinni*. Jamaspa was convinced she simply couldn't recall and that keeping her trapped inside the jewelled brooch Marcroy Tarth had given her on the way to *Sí an Bhrú* , would somehow jog her memory.

Brydie had no idea how long she'd been trapped. Time was meaningless here. She could pace restlessly when she grew bored with waiting, even when she tried to count her steps in order to calculate how small she now was, or how large her prison might be, there seemed to be a different number of steps each time.

Was anybody on the outside missing her? Queen Álmhath had left for Temair days, perhaps weeks, ago. She might be wondering why she hadn't heard from her court maiden. More likely, the queen believed Brydie was so besotted with Darragh of the Undivided, that she'd had neither the time nor the inclination to send a message to her mistress to let her know if her mission to conceive Darragh's child had been successful.

And here in *Sí an Bhrú*? Would anybody miss her?

Probably not.

She was a stranger in the Druid stronghold and she had spent little time in the common areas of the fortress before she'd moved into Darragh's chamber. Brydie's foolish decision to play along with Darragh's deception by covering for him when he sneaked out to search for his lost rift runner was costing her dearly, and not just because it made Jamaspa believe she knew more than she did. It was likely that most people here barely remembered her brief visit to *Sí an Bhrú* .

How would they know she was missing, if they didn't remember she'd been here at all?

Brydie thought it odd that she wasn't more lonely or frightened. She figured the spell Jamaspa had used to trap her in Marcroy's amethyst brooch had suspended all her bodily functions, as well. Brydie felt as if she was were breathing, but surely there was no air inside this tiny space. She doubted she was *actually* breathing, just going through the motions, protected by the enchantment that had trapped her here. She was never hungry, never thirsty and not once had she felt the urge to evacuate her bladder or bowels - something of a relief given the tiny space she occupied.

She could tell when he was coming, too. Jamaspa, from what she had seen of the *djinni*, could move about like a wisp of smoke. He seemed to have the ability to travel in and out of the jewel at will. When he was back, she could feel him, and see him, too, in a . Although he often refused to appear in a form on which she could focus, she knew when he was here, even if she couldn't look him in the eye. The amethyst would darken to a purple so deep it made the night seem bright. When Jamaspa spoke, his voice was so resonant and commanding, it sent shivers down her spine.

Brydie could feel him coming now, her skin prickling with gooseflesh.

What does he want this time? she wondered. *Will he ask the same questions, over and over? Or has he thought of something new to ask me?*

"Are you well, little human?" his voice boomed, reverberating through her bones. She found him both fearsome and yet oddly compassionate. He didn't seem to care that he had trapped Brydie in this jewel to extract information from her, but he did seem concerned that she might not be enjoying herself. The *djinni* loomed over her like a nightmare and then worried he might have frightened her with his looming.

"Can I even *get* sick in here?" she asked, looking around the polished faceted walls of her gemstone prison. It was time she asked a few questions of her own, Brydie decided. She wasn't going to get out of here by answering "I don't know" to everything.

"What do you mean?" the *djinni* boomed, his voice rich and loud. Brydie had to stop herself covering her ears.

"I mean... am I dead? Shrunk down to the size of a flea? Is my spirit trapped in here with you, while my body lies rotting on the floor out there? Or am I stuck in here, whole and entire, and when you get sick of asking me the same questions and getting the same answers, over and over, you'll finally set me free and I'll be back to normal?"

The *djinni* was silent for a time, before remarking with a frown in his voice, "In Persia, a human captive would never dare question one of the *Djinn* in such an impertinent fashion."

"Oh?" she said, trying to find a place to look, so she knew she was addressing the *djinni* and not the wall. "How do you know that? You make a habit of trapping innocent women with your family jewels, do you?"

There was a moment of heavy silence, before Jamaspa said, "No human captive would dare make fun of the *Djinn*, either."

"Well, they ought to come see me then," Brydie retorted cheerfully, rather pleased she'd been able to rattle the *djinni* a little. "I could give them a few pointers."

"Tell me how Darragh of the Undivided leaves this chamber undetected," the *djinni* asked apparently deciding not to engage in any further idle chatter with his prisoner.

"I don't know," Brydie sighed. She leaned against the cool, smooth interior of the gem and sank slowly to the floor. She might as well get comfortable. Experience had taught her these questions could go on for quite a while.

Brydie woke a few hours later. Or it might have been minutes. Perhaps days. Jamaspa's questions had gone on for hours, it seemed, leaving her wrung out and Jamaspa no closer to the truth he sought. She sat up as a shadow passed over the jewel, wondering if the *djinni* was back, but there was no sign of him. This shadow was outside the gem.

Someone was moving about in Darragh's chamber.

Brydie scrambled to her feet and began to bang on the walls of her tiny jewelled prison, even though she knew it was useless. She could hear what was happening outside the jewel, but people outside couldn't hear her. She was certain it was impossible to see that there was someone trapped inside the brooch. When she'd owned the brooch, she studied its faceted surface, admiring the color and the precision of its cut. She hadn't seen anybody moving about inside it, and if she had, she would have assumed it a trick of the light.

Who could even imagine there might be somebody trapped in here?

And even if they did discover her there, how were they supposed to get her out?

If Brydie could catch the attention of someone... if a Druid came into the room looking for something... if he or she sensed the spell... maybe they could help?

Perhaps it was Darragh, come home at last. If the Undivided couldn't undo a spell wrought by an evil *djinni*, who else could?

But that sparked off another set of unsettling questions. Would Darragh notice she was gone? And if he did, would he care? Wouldn't he simply assume she'd left *Sí an Bhrú* and gone back to Temair without saying goodbye? Why would he think something evil might have befallen her? They'd known each other for only a few days.

Surely, he would sense the magic worked in his own bedchamber, she thought, more from wishful thinking than any real knowledge of the subject. And if he did sense it, wouldn't he want to know the source? Was he powerful enough to sense the enchanted jewel lying amid Brydie's discarded clothes?

The shadow moved again and darkness enveloped her as a hand scooped the brooch off the cloak. Whoever had picked up the brooch, peered at it closely for a moment, turning it this way and that - knocking Brydie off her feet in the process - to study it.

"Hey!" she shouted uselessly. "In here! Look closely, you fool! Can't you see me?"

Her shouts meant nothing, of course, but she continued to do whatever she could to attract the attention of whoever had picked up the brooch. Was it a maid? A thief? That was unlikely here in the very heart of *Sí an Bhrú* .

Brydie tried to make out the person, drawing back with a yelp when a giant eye loomed toward her, as the curious person holding the jewel examined it more closely.

"Colmán!" she shouted, when she recognized the shiny trinkets woven into his pointed, forked beard. It made sense. Who else but the Vate would be snooping around Darragh's chamber if he wasn't there?

"Colmán! In here! Can't you see me?"

He couldn't hear her cries for help. He just studied the brooch a few moments longer before clasping his hand around it and slipping the brooch - and Brydie along with it - into his pocket, knocking her off her feet again and plunging her into darkness, and removing all hope she may have had of being rescued.

It was some time again before Brydie saw the light of day. Buried in the depths of Colmán's pocket, jostled along by his uneven gait, she had no way of knowing what her future held. She called out for Jamaspa, but he did not come. The *djinni* had other places to be.

Other trapped innocents to tend to, perhaps?

Maybe Brydie had nothing to worry about. Even now, she might be on her way to being rescued. The queen may have discovered her fate and sent Colmán to fetch the jewel so her trapped court maiden could be released. Even now, Colmán might be taking her to someone who could reverse the *djinni's* spell and release her from her amethyst prison.

Brydie's heart began to race. Suppose the opposite were true? Suppose the Vate had taken the jewel in which she was trapped and nobody knew about it? Suppose he'd coveted the valuable stone and had decided to sell it now Brydie was gone and there was nobody about to claim it?

Suppose Jamaspa couldn't find her again?

What would happen to her then?

She began to panic a little. *Am I stuck here forever?*

A glimmer of light and a rough jolt threw Brydie off her feet as Colmán lifted her out of his pocket and placed the jewel on a table. A moment later a large eye loomed over her and then receded a little and Brydie realized she was looking at Torcán's betrothed.

"Is there no sign of her at all?" Anwen asked, in a voice that seemed filtered through treacle.

"None, my lady," Colmán informed her. Brydie turned to look at him through the faceted walls. He looked like a giant - as did Álmhath's future daughter-in-law - and he was tugging on his forked beard as if he were trying to pull it out by the roots. "There is no sign of the court maiden or of Darragh. She left her cloak and this brooch behind."

"So where is Darragh?" the young woman asked, her suspicion obvious even to Brydie.

"He has gone into seclusion to await the power transfer, my lady," Colmán informed her, which was an outright lie, Brydie figured, because he didn't even try to make the sentence rhyme. In one of their many late night talks, as they lay in the dark pretending - and sometimes not pretending - to make love, Darragh had told her that was the easiest way to tell if the old man was lying. When he was telling the truth, Colmán was painfully conscious of his role as the chief bard charged with memorising the history of the Undivided, and being a traditionalist, he went to great pains to speak in rhyme. When he was lying, Darragh had told her with a laugh, the Vate was so busy concentrating on the lie, he forgot all about rhyme.

Anwen, however, seemed to think the reason for Darragh's absence was quite plausible. "Do you suppose he took Brydie with him?"

"It's possible, my lady," Colmán conceded. "He was much taken with her."

Anwen nodded. "Very well, then. On behalf of Queen Álmhath I thank you for returning Brydie's cloak and the brooch. I will see to it the items are kept safe until her return."

"They seemed too valuable to leave lying about," Colmán agreed. His head bobbed out of sight for a moment - perhaps he was bowing to someone - and then he turned and walked out of Brydie's line of sight.

A few moments later, she was thrown off her feet as the brooch was picked up again. Another huge eye stared into her crystal prison and then pulled back far enough for her to realize it was the queen's son, Torcán. "Since when did Brydie own something as valuable as this?" she heard him ask his betrothed.

"Your mother says Marcroy Tarth gave it to her on a whim on the journey to *Sí an Bhrú* ," she heard Anwen reply, although the court maiden was no longer in view with Torcán holding the brooch.

"Do you really think she's gone into seclusion with Darragh?"

"She could be dead, for all I know," Anwen replied, "and the Druids wouldn't tell your mother about it. Particularly if Darragh killed her."

Torcán sounded sceptical. "From what I saw of the two of them together, Darragh seemed rather more inclined to bed her than kill her."

"Maybe he did both," Anwen snapped back. She sounded angry. And rather less concerned about her fellow court maiden than Brydie would have liked. "Either way, if something has happened to her, we have to be certain the queen is not connected to it."

"Mother took her to *Sí an Bhrú*, Anwen. And the whole world saw her all but throwing Brydie at Darragh."

"But she never returned with us, Torcán," Anwen reminded him. "As far as the world - and more importantly, Brydie's family - is concerned, Brydie is still here at *Sí an Bhrú* and the last anybody saw of her, my sister court maiden was in the bed of Darragh of the Undivided. The responsibility for her fate, therefore, rests with him."

"What do we do with the rest of her things?"

"Burn the cloak," Anwen ordered without hesitation. "As for the brooch... if Marcroy sees it, he'll recognize it at once as the jewel he gifted to Brydie." She was silent for a moment and then appeared next to Torcán. "Melt down the gold and have the jewel reset into something for me. But not a brooch. Something else."

Brydie's eyes brimmed with angry tears.

Torcán nodded in understanding, smiling. "Some things are better hidden in the open, yes?"

"And some things are better if they never see the light of day," his future bride replied, somewhat ominously.

But that wasn't what upset Brydie.

She was coming to terms with her enchanted prison. She was even a little intrigued by the possibility of listening in on the goings on in Álmhath's court - something she would never have been able to do as a mere court maiden.

What upset Brydie more than words could say, was the idea that her amethyst prison - the jewel in which the *djinni* Jamaspa had magically entrapped her - was going to be set into a gift for that self-serving bitch, Anwen.

CHAPTER 8

Ren landed heavily against a tree, as if he'd been shot into it by some giant, invisible catapult. He grunted with the pain, gasping to drag air into his lungs as the rough landing winded him. After a few moments, the spearing pain in his chest began to subside and he had time to take note of his surroundings. He could hear voices in the distance, but he seemed - for the moment - to be safe among the *kozo* trees.

How he got here was a different question entirely.

The voices were growing louder, more panicked. Ren pushed himself to his hands and knees and crawled through the undergrowth towards the sound. Dropping flat onto the damp, leafy ground, he realized he was still perilously near the samurai compound. In fact, he was barely fifty feet from where he'd been standing a few seconds ago, about to have his throat slit. Ren reached up, feeling his neck gingerly with his fingertips. His hand came away smeared with blood, but it was a small flesh wound. In the compound, he could hear the chaos as the samurai searched for their quarry.

Somehow, Ren realized, he'd teleported himself out of the compound to safety.

Ren closed his eyes, wondering how he'd accomplished this remarkable feat. The memories he shared with his brother weren't sorted in any easily accessible manner. There was no instruction manual on how to use his magical powers. Darragh had learned his skills over a lifetime of instruction, controlled training and experimentation. Important things Ren needed to know were so second nature to his brother and Darragh's memories of learning them had faded into nothingness. Others, like struggling to master some obscure Siberian folk dance to honor a visiting Russian diplomat, were fresh in his brother's mind.

There must be something about teleporting, but it was unlikely Darragh had the same name for this unexpected skill as the one Ren had assigned it. Until he worked out what Darragh's name for it was, Ren wouldn't be able to examine his brother's memories and work out how to do it again.

In the meantime, he was safe enough, although not for long. Ren could hear Hayato ordering his men to start searching the forest, yelling at them to hurry, while Chishihero screamed at him, ranting about the empresses, and her *washi* quota, and the general incompetence of Hayato and his samurai.

Ren glanced around, wondering where he was. The forest seemed unremarkable in every direction, just row after row of plantation trees. The orderly lines were a sure sign this was no uncultivated wilderness. It also meant there wasn't a lot of undergrowth. Other than a bit of brush near the edge of the forest, it was disturbingly well-kept. That meant little or no cover when they came looking for him, which was going to be any minute now.

He closed his eyes, trying to recapture the feeling he'd had when he zapped himself clear of his executioners, but Ren had no idea of how he'd magically teleported himself out of the compound. Only that he'd done it.

Frustrating as that was, it also meant getting away the old fashioned way, on foot.

Unfortunately, the stone circle where they'd landed in this reality - and arguably their best chance of getting home - lay on the other side of the compound. That was assuming he ever found Trása again. Or if she found him. Actually that was much more likely, because she could fly while he was stuck on the ground.

Over in the compound, men were mounting up, milling about as they shouted to one another. Ren wondered if he could risk doubling back around the compound to the other side, and following the road back to the stone circle. They might not come into the forest to search for him - if they assumed that any prisoner who could blink himself away at will would go further than the trees nearby.

Ren glanced up at the sky. The moon was long set. It was the darkest part of the night. He was tired, cold, still damp from the rain in his own reality, and fed up with magic and the trouble that came with it.

He took a deep breath and with a final glance over his shoulder at the compound through the trees, crouching low to the ground, took off at a run between the trees, staying parallel to the compound. If he followed the fence line, it would eventually lead him back to the road, and from there he could track beside it to reach the stone circle. Once he was there...

Well, who knew what would happen. Maybe Trása would find him. Maybe, if he had the power to teleport himself around at will, somewhere, buried in his mind, was the secret to opening a dimensional rift.

One way or another, Ren figured, he was going to find a way home.

Ren fell asleep just before dawn. By then he was profoundly lost, with no idea where he was, where the compound was, or where he might find the stone circle that could send him home. He remembered stopping to rest a while ago, exhausted beyond hope, determined to close his eyes for no more than five minutes.

When he woke, it was bright daylight, and there was a little girl standing over him, poking him with a sword.

"Okinasai! Okinasai!"

"Whoa! I am awake!" Ren cried, pushing the sword point away.

The girl standing over him was about twelve or thirteen. She had long, wavy dark brown hair, black eyes and was dressed in a faded woolen shirt, that crossed over the front and tied up at the sides, and a pair of patched woolen trousers that had known better days. She didn't seem to be entirely Japanese, although that was the language she spoke. Ren climbed cautiously to his feet, keeping a wary eye on the *katana* the girl carried. "Be careful with that thing, will you? Somebody might get hurt."

"Are you the *Youkai* they're searching for?" she asked, studying him with a frown.

"You gonna run me through with that thing if I say yes?" he asked in English. When she responded with little more than a blank look, he repeated the question in Japanese.

To his surprise, she shook her head and hefted the sword until the flat of the blade rested on her shoulder and then smiled at him. "Of course not. I'm to take you back to the Ikushima compound."

"Thanks," Ren said, looking around to see if the child had companions nearby who might be a little more keen to spill his blood than she was. "But I just left the compound, mostly because they were trying to slit my throat. Not too keen on going back to that, I have to confess."

"Not the Tanabe compound," she said, a little impatiently. "The Tanabe are *kusobaka*." Ren smiled. He thought the people who tried to kill him and Trása were stupid shits, too. He was warming rapidly to this young lady.

"I'm going to take you back to *Shin Bungo*." She turned and pointed to her right. "Over there."

"You're not friends with the Tanabe... people, then?"

She spat on the ground in disgust. "I would fall on my sword before I called any Tanabe dog a friend."

"Fair enough. What's your name?"

"Kazusa."

"Tell me, Kazusa," Ren asked, climbing to his feet. "Are you familiar with the theory of *my enemy's enemy is my friend*, by any chance?"

Kazusa pursed her lips for a moment and then shook her head. "I am not. But it seems a reasonable assumption. Will you come with me of your own free will, or must I make you?"

Ren bit back a smile. Now he was on his feet, he was pretty sure he could take down a twelve-year-old girl, even one armed with a *katana*, but she seemed fairly certain of herself. Maybe she was some sort of kiddie ninja and could slice him into sushi in the blink of an eye. It wasn't likely, but Ren was quickly learning that what seemed likely was no longer a safe way to anticipate danger.

"I'll come voluntarily. For now." This girl was offering him somewhere else to go that wasn't the compound of Chishihero and her henchmen. That had to count for something.

"Empty your pockets."

"Excuse me?"

"I must check that you are not carrying any *washi*," she explained. "Namito was very firm on that. 'If you find the *Youkai*, be certain he cannot bewitch us with *ori mahou*', he said. He was quite adamant about it."

Ren shook his head, a little confused, but did as she asked, turning his pockets out to prove he had no paper in them. *Ori* and *maho*, in the Japanese Ren spoke, roughly translated as folding and magic. Chishihero's truth spell with the little *origami* heart almost made sense, if that's what Kazusa was worried about. He decided not to tell her he had no idea how to make anything out of folding magic, or that he didn't need it. He needed to discover what was going on here first. He needed to find out if Kazusa was offering him help or just a different type of trouble.

"Good enough?" he asked, as she inspected his pockets closely, disinterested in the other contents. Apparently, all she cared about was paper.

"Good enough," she agreed. "Walk ahead of me."

Suspicious little thing, aren't you? he said to himself, as he returned his pockets to their previous state. "Where are we going?"

"I will show you the way."

"Is it far?"

"Not especially."

"Is there food there?"

She poked him in the back to get him moving. "There is," Kazusa informed him, as she shouldered the *katana* again. "It remains to be seen, however, *Youkai*, whether or not my brother wishes to waste it on you."

CHAPTER 9

It was raining again by the time Darragh and Sorcha reached Jack's place, which was fortunate because it kept the paparazzi next door in their cars. Darragh's ankle was swollen and throbbing by the time Sorcha retrieved the key from its hiding place in the glasshouse and they let themselves into the kitchen. Rónán had a memory of Jack owning an impressive first aid kit, which Sorcha located in a cupboard under the kitchen sink. By the time Jack got home from his gardening club meeting, Darragh's ankle was bandaged, he was almost dry and feeling very little pain due to the helpful contents of a small white bottle in the kit labelled "codeine".

"What the feck are you two doing here?" Jack demanded. He entered the kitchen through the back door, shaking the rain from his coat as he spied

Darragh sitting at the table. He didn't need to have it explained to him that this was Darragh and not Rónán. Jack had seen them together and could tell the boys apart at a glance.

"There was trouble at the rift," Sorcha explained, coming up behind the old man. She had a kitchen knife in her right hand and a scowl on her face that did not bode well for Jack's future if he refused to help.

Jack ignored Sorcha and stared at Darragh. "Trouble at the rift, you say? Is that how you cut your face?"

Darragh fingered the bruised slice across his cheek. It was still there which meant Rónán hadn't yet realized he was able to heal the injury magically. It seemed odd to Darragh that Ciarán or Brógán wouldn't have explained to Rónán by now that he could heal himself.

"No. This is an injury Rónán received in another reality."

Jack looked around then, as if expecting to see Darragh's brother. "Where's Ren?"

"Safely through to the realm where he belongs," Darragh assured the old man, although he had no real way of knowing. He was certain Jack would toss them out if they intimated that something ill had befallen his twin.

"Not so safe, if somebody's already smacked him in the face. What are you and Attila the Hen, here, still doing in this realm?" he asked, full of suspicion and doubt.

"Something happened to the rift," Darragh explained. "I sprained my ankle and couldn't get to it before it closed."

Jack stared at both of them with a doubtful expression, shaking his head. "So you came here? To my house? Next door to Kiva's place? Are you mad? This is the first place they'll look for you! Christ, half the fecking Dublin press corps is parked outside your mother's place!"

"That woman is not Darragh's mother!" Sorcha sounded offended. "His mother, and Rónán's too, was the Druidess Sybille-"

"Whose stupid idea was it you come here?" Jack cut in, ignoring Sorcha's interruption.

"Patrick's," Darragh said as Jack slumped into the chair opposite at the table. "He said he'd come for us later."

"Jaysus, you didn't tell him I helped you find Hayley at that rehab centre, did you?"

Darragh shook his head. "Hayley made it safely through the rift. Patrick doesn't realize I'm not Rónán, and he hopes I'll tell him what happened to her."

"There's a conversation not to be missed," Jack muttered sourly. "Jaysus-fecking-Christ, what am I supposed to do with you two now?"

"Shelter us until we can find a way home," Sorcha said.

"How long is that going to be?"

"Until I can contact Rónán, that's all," Darragh said, making it sound straightforward and everyday. "Once I arrange for him to open the rift on the other side, we can leave, and you'll never see us again."

Jack frowned, as if he believed the promise a little too glib to be genuine.

A fair assessment, Darragh conceded. He had no way of knowing if he could contact his brother, no

79

way of knowing if he would ever find his way back to the reality where he belonged. The mechanics of their return were something he didn't feel the need to burden Jack with. Better the old man keep thinking that contacting another reality was no more complicated than dialling up... what had Rónán called it... the puddle phone?

Jack remained unconvinced. "You can't trust Patrick Boyle," he warned. "You've nicked his daughter, lad. He isn't trying to help *you*. He's trying to find Hayley."

"We can explain what happened to her," Sorcha said.

The old man snorted at her. "To be sure you can. And when Darragh delivers your lunatic explanation about how he sent her off to an alternate reality to be healed by Faeries, his next call will be to the good Doctor Symes who's gonna have Ren-Mark-Two here declared criminally insane, You won't see the light of day again, lad, not until you're my age. *If* you're lucky."

Darragh held up his right hand, displaying the triskalion. "But it's obvious I am not my brother. His tattoo is on his left hand."

Jack shook his head. "It won't matter. They'll convince themselves that's where it's always been, because that'll make more sense than what you'll be telling them."

"Then we must silence Patrick Boyle," Sorcha declared. "If he cannot speak, he cannot betray us." She hefted the carving knife pointedly and added to Jack, "I am with you, old man, in your belief that his betrayal is not only likely, but inevitable."

"Patrick is not Amergin," Darragh reminded her, weary of her insistence the similarities between the men made Patrick in any way predictable. Or certain to betray them.

"He is near enough to be dangerous," Sorcha replied.

"Who the feck is Amergin?" Jack asked.

"Patrick Boyle's *eileféin*," Darragh replied with a sigh. He didn't want to have this discussion with Jack. He wanted to have it even less with Sorcha.

"His *what*?" Jack asked, climbing stiffly to his feet. He walked over to the counter and took the electric kettle from the bench to fill it at the sink, asking, "Anybody else want a cup of tea?"

"No, thank you," Darragh said, seeing a welcome opportunity to change the subject. "I hope you don't mind, but we helped ourselves to breakfast before you-"

"An *eileféin* is the alternate reality version of a person from our reality," Sorcha explained, undeterred. "It turns out Patrick Boyle is the *eileféin* of the most heinous traitor ever spawned by man in our reality, the Vate of All Eire, Amergin."

Jack turned the kettle on and then pulled out a battered enamelled mug from the sink. "Seriously?" he asked, as he rinsed it under the tap. "Kiva's house boy? Pussy-whipped Patrick? The Vate of *All* Eire? Can't see it, myself. But that's why it's an *alternate* reality, I suppose."

"They're not *exactly* the same person," Darragh pointed out. "Obviously your history has diverged significantly from ours. But his bloodline runs true enough for him to be considered *eileféin*."

"Which means what, exactly?" Jack asked, dropping a teabag into his chipped mug before shovelling an alarming amount of sugar into it.

"It means he's likely to betray us," Sorcha announced at almost exactly the same time, as Darragh replied, "Nothing."

Jack's gaze swung back and forth between them for a moment. Then he smiled. "I'm sensing a differing of opinions here."

"Sorcha mistrusts everyone," Darragh explained.

"Then she's obviously the brains of the outfit," the old man said.

The kettle bubbled to a boil and switched off. Darragh was secretly fascinated by the self-heating kettle, but he couldn't afford to let himself be distracted by the gadgets and gimmickries of this realm.

"Patrick will do nothing until he's spoken to us about Hayley," Darragh assured him. "I know him better than both of you, and that is what I believe."

"You've been here a couple of days, lad," Jack reminded him. "You don't know squat. Fetch the milk for me, would you, love?" he added to Sorcha who was standing closest to the fridge. She scowled at being addressed as "love" but did as Jack asked.

"I have Rónán's memories," Darragh told the old man with complete confidence. "Rónán trusted Patrick with his life."

Sorcha handed the carton to Jack and slammed the fridge door, turning on Darragh impatiently. "Do I have to keep reminding you and your credulous brother exactly what happens when the Undivided trust Amergin? Or any other manifestation of him in any other realm?"

"Why do you assume Amergin would betray us?" Darragh asked. "Perhaps the defining event in our reality was the interference of Marcroy Tarth.

With no Faerie lord here to corrupt him, Patrick could prove to be our greatest ally."

"You'd not be wanting to bet twenty-to-life on that, lad," Jack said, bringing his tea back to the table. "He certainly hasn't shown any guilt about tossing me into the shite-hole with you."

"What do you mean?"

"I mean that if the Gardaí find you sitting here, shooting the breeze in my kitchen, I'll be in a shiteload of trouble, lad, along with you."

"Do you want us to leave?"

Jack hesitated, and then he shrugged. "You can stay. For now. At least until you talk with Patrick. You're going to have to convince him Hayley is safe and well, though, or he'll be calling the Gardaí from here."

"And then what?" Sorcha asked.

The old man shrugged. "And then you'd best figure how to get home, lass, because you're not going to last long in this reality waiting for faeries to come rescue you."

"The Faerie are the cause of our problem, not the solution to it," Sorcha complained.

Jack looked at Sorcha in wonder, shaking his head. "It's fascinating the way you can say that with a perfectly straight face."

"Is there any way to tell if the authorities know we're still in this realm?" Darragh asked, mostly to distract Sorcha who was looking a little offended.

Turning back to Darragh, Jack shrugged. "The TV, maybe. They were all over this on the morning bulletins."

"Do you have a TV?" Sorcha asked.

Jack smiled. "You really are from another world, aren't you?"

CHAPTER 10

It turned out to be a long walk to Kazusa's compound. Or rather, her family's compound. For the better part of an hour, as the sun climbed steadily higher in a bright, cloudless sky, Ren allowed Kazusa to poke and prod him, guiding him this way and that through the trees, pointing him the direction of her home. After about an hour, they broke out of the *kozo* trees onto a low ridge that looked down over an emerald valley, surrounded by more carefully planted stands of trees. The distant hills were terraced in what seemed to be rice paddies. Nearer the ridge, fat black-faced sheep grazed on the edge of a settlement clustered around a large walled complex of brick buildings with red tiled roofs, quite unlike the wooden buildings of the Tanabe compound. There were armed samurai patrolling the top of the wide, mud-brick walls surrounding the buildings. It might have been a village or a concentration camp. It was hard to tell from this distance. It wasn't a fort, he figured. Much of the village was outside the thick walls, and despite the armed men patrolling the top of the walls, they didn't seem high enough to deter an invasion. It was almost as if they'd been built to contain, rather than repel.

"That's home?"

"*Hai*. That is *Shin Bungo*, home of the great and glorious Ikushima clan."

"Impressive."

Kazusa smiled. "One day, we will be the most powerful clan in *Airurundo*."

"Says who?" Ren asked, wondering at this girl's self-assurance. She had answered an important question for him, though. She'd called this place *Airurundo*, not *Nippon* or *Nihon*. They were still in Ireland. The exploding rift had sent them to some wacked-out reality where the Japanese ruled Ireland. Ren couldn't imagine how far back in history his reality had diverged from this one for that to happen.

"My brother, Namito, says so," Kazusa informed him proudly. "He says that when the Empresses are-" She stopped abruptly, her eyes narrowing, as she hefted the *katana* off her shoulder and pointed it at Ren's belly.

Kazusa had been lugging the heavy sword for a while, and the weight of it was telling on her. Her arm was trembling with the strain of holding it level. Ren could have disarmed her in an instant, if he'd wanted, but she was taking him somewhere they might not want to kill him on sight - somewhere he might get food, and water and some idea of how he was going to get home. Ren was content to let Kazusa believe she had the better of him. For now.

"Are you loyal to the Empresses?" she demanded. Her eyes narrowed as she studied him, waiting for his answer. "Given what you are, I'd be surprised if you said yes. But you might be loyal to them. That might explain what you're doing here."

"If I say I'm not, are you going to kill me?"

"I'm more likely to kill you if you say yes," she replied with an alarming amount of vehemence.

"In that case, may the evil bitches rot in hell," Ren said pleasantly. "How many empresses are we hating, exactly?"

"What sort of question is that?" Kazusa asked, rolling her eyes. "It's that way."

"Excuse me?"

"The path down to the village. It's over there." She pointed to the left with her trembling sword.

Puzzled by her odd behaviour, Ren spied the faint game trail they'd been following and set off toward the edge of the ridge, where the ground sloped less sharply, heading down towards *Shin Bungo* and hopefully some answers. He glanced up at the sky for the thousandth time, hoping to spot Trása, but if there were any owls about this morning, he couldn't see them.

Trása, wherever she was at the moment, and in whatever form she had assumed, was on her own.

Shin Bungo turned out to be the last thing Ren was expecting. It wasn't a concentration camp, or a fort - despite its outward appearance - it was a fireworks factory.

That explained the thick walls. They weren't trying to fight off their neighbours. These walls were built to contain an explosion.

Kazusa's family had been in the fireworks business for generations, she explained, as they reached the valley floor and headed for the compound entrance. She was much chattier now they were within shouting distance of home. The Ikushima factory, Kazusa informed him as they walked along the rutted road beside the wall, had been here long before the *kozo* plantations surrounding them had spread out so far, planted by the greedy newcomers sent by their noble families in the middle kingdom, the *Chucho*, to seek their fortune here in the colonies.

Ren filed that away for future reference - even in this reality, Ireland was occupied. Not by the British, this time, but by the Japanese.

It was not a recent event, Ren figured. There had been more than one wave of immigrants to Ireland from *Chucho*. Kazusa spoke of more than eight generations of fireworks masters in her family, and although she clearly had some Asian heritage, she was not the pure Japanese of Chishihero or Hayato. Hardly surprising, Ren thought. Eight generations in a new country... at that point, you were no longer immigrants. You were locals and you were probably marrying the natives and having kids with them, too.

Kazusa didn't have much good to say about this latest wave of immigrants who, Ren gleaned, were responsible for a great deal of trouble in her part of the world. He gathered there were moves afoot by the neighbours to move the Ikushima family's factory to a remote area because of the risk to the surrounding forests. Kazusa scoffed at the very idea, claiming her family had been here much longer than those wretched *kozo* trees, and if they wanted magic so badly, then they shouldn't have killed all the *Youkai*.

Ren hadn't been paying much attention to Kazusa's chatter until then, but that dragged his attention back with a savage jerk. "Whoa! Hang on, did you say they killed all the Faerie?"

Kazusa shrugged. "Well, maybe not all of them - you're proof enough of that - but they're pretty thin on the ground these days."

Ren stopped walking. He needed to get this cleared up now. The last time someone decided he was *Youkai*, they tried to slit his throat. "I'm not Faerie, Kazusa. I'm human."

Kazusa never got the opportunity to argue the point. Someone spotted them from the walls. A shout went up and a few moments later the gates swung open, and a dozen or so mounted samurai galloped out to surround them.

Here we go again. Ren raised his hands in a gesture of surrender. The lead horseman skidded to a halt, swung his leg over his horse's neck, and jumped to the ground. He was heavily armoured, and when he removed his *kabuto*, his long dark hair was gathered up into a thick ponytail on the very top of his head. Kazusa dropped her sword and threw herself at him. The warrior hugged her briefly and then pushed her away, holding her at arm's length.

"I told you not to leave the compound."

"And I told you there was no chance of finding the *yabangin Youkai* by thundering around horseback," she shot back, looking very smug. "I found him. Sleeping in the Tanabe forest."

"You went into their forest?" The warrior muttered something under his breath, and shook his head, as he let her go. "You are forbidden to enter the forest, Kazusa. If the Tanabe found you..."

"They wouldn't hurt me, Namito. Even Chishihero wouldn't dare."

"No, but she would hold you for ransom," he warned. "And if you go onto their lands again and they catch you, I won't pay it."

Kazusa was grinning broadly, and even Ren could tell the young man didn't mean a word of his threat. He finally turned his attention to Ren and bowed politely before addressing him. "Thank you, *wagakimi*," Namito said. "For bringing my sister home safely."

"He didn't escort me home!" Kazusa objected. "He was my prisoner!"

Namito ignored her. He tucked his helmet under his arm, revealing a young man not much older than Ren. He had distinctly Asian features and startling blue eyes that were out of place in such a handsome, oriental face. He bowed once more, smiling. Namito must have appreciated the fact that Ren had humoured Kazusa by allowing her to capture him and bring him here. "I am Namito, *Daimyo* of the Ikushima. The *Youkai* are welcome here."

"Except I'm not *Youkai*," Ren replied, bowing to his host. He needed to clear that up at the outset. Being *Youkai* in this reality was a health hazard. "My name is Ren. Ren Kavanaugh."

Namito nodded sympathetically. "Of course, it would be foolish to announce such a thing. The Ikushima will honor your wish to remain anonymous, *wagakimi*." He glanced at his men who nodded agreement. Then he turned to his sister. "Do you understand, Kazusa? You are not to tell anybody about Renkavana. No bragging to your friends that you captured a *Youkai*."

Kazusa scowled at her brother, but nodded. "He's not much of a *Youkai* anyway," she said. "He can't even heal himself."

Everybody turned to stare at him. Ren realized Kazusa was talking about the cut on his face. The cut Chishihero inflicted on him when she'd struck him. Not used to having the power to heal his own wounds magically, it had not even occurred to Ren to fix it. As soon as he thought of it, though, he realized the knowledge was there in his mind, among all the other unsorted and confusing information he'd acquired from his twin brother's mind during the *Comhroinn*. All he had to do was will the healing to happen.

But if he did heal it - now Kazusa had drawn attention to his injury - there would be no denying he was *Youkai*. The Undivided, the Druids and the complicated hierarchy of magicians from Darragh's reality were unknown here. In this reality, as far as Ren could tell, there were the *Youkai* - who were mostly dead - and the human sorcerers who wielded magic with origami.

There seemed to be no room in the middle for a human who could wield magic because he happened to be branded with a magical tattoo.

Namito didn't see a problem with Ren's injury, though. He smiled down at his sister, explaining, "Of course he wouldn't heal it, Kazusa. That would reveal what he is." Namito looked to Ren. "I apologise for my sister, Renkavana. She has never met one of the *Youkai* before. Will you be bringing your mate to join us?"

"My *what*?"

"The female *Youkai*," he explained. "The Tanabe captured you and your mate together at the *rifuto* stones, but she escaped in the form of a bird before Chishihero could have her killed."

Namito had an impressive spy network, Ren realized, if he knew about Trása already. And that they had come through the rift at the stone circle in the forest. Although it did explain what Kazusa had been doing, scouring the Tanabe plantation for escaped *Youkai*. She must have heard her brother talking about it and decided to help. Ren couldn't imagine any circumstance where Namito would send this little girl out to search for rogue *Youkai* on her own.

"I don't know where Trása is," Ren told him, thinking the truth was the safest course for the time being. "What do you know of the rift stones?"

"Not much," Namito said. "And here is not the place to discuss it. Will you accept the hospitality of the Ikushima, *wagakimi*?"

He says that like I have a choice, Ren said to himself, but he smiled and bowed, wondering if the Ikushima were planning to kill him too, but were just being polite about it.

"I would be honored," he replied. *Manners cost nothing*, as Kerry Boyle was fond of saying. And if there was any chance he could find his way home, he needed allies. Until he found Trása and figured out how he was going to get back through the rift to the reality where he belonged, Kazusa and her brother would have to do.

91

CHAPTER 11

It was dark before Patrick knocked on Jack's back door. By then, Darragh and Sorcha had spent an informative day watching the television, learning about the chaos at the golf club and the unsuccessful attempts of the Gardaí to locate the fugitive, Ren Kavanaugh, and his missing cousin, Hayley Boyle, whom Rónán was now accused of kidnapping, in addition to the other charges laid against him several weeks ago, when Trása had burned down a warehouse and with the help of the *Leipreachán* Plunkett O'Bannon, framed him for murder.

Or rather, Darragh had been watching TV. Sorcha had complained the shiny box gave her a headache just after lunch, and had gone to lay down in one of Jack's many empty guest rooms, which was an extraordinary thing for her to do. Normally, Sorcha behaved like a caged cat, prowling around looking for trouble, always alert to any danger.

Darragh could never remember Sorcha opting for a lie-down over patrolling the grounds. He wondered if this realm was making her sick. He'd gained a lot of information in the *Comhroinn* with his brother, including Rónán's knowledge of biology, germs and the nature of disease. It was possible, he realized with the benefit of his brother's high school education, that Sorcha had contracted something in this reality for which her immune system was unprepared. Although rift runners jumped safely between realities regularly in Darragh's world, they were always either part-Faerie, or human magicians with the ability to heal themselves as soon as they reached a magical realm. Maybe the mere act of channelling Faerie magic gave Druids some immunity. Darragh was certainly feeling no ill effects from this realm.

But Sorcha was neither Faerie nor Druid.

Perhaps this realm wasn't just making her ill. It could be killing her.

Sorcha's health, however, was the least of his problems. Darragh had to convince Patrick Boyle his daughter was safe first, so Patrick wouldn't turn him over to the authorities. They had no reason at all to believe he wasn't his brother, and would be happy to lock him up and throw away the key for murder, arson, and now, kidnapping.

Darragh was waiting in the dining room. In the background, he could hear the television in the other room. Yet another report about the Castle Golf Club and the search for the fugitive, Ren Kavanaugh. The reporter was explaining the same thing reporters had been explaining all day long - nobody knew a damned thing.

"... *says Inspector Duggan, who is leading the investigation. She is refusing to say if there were any injuries following the shoot-out last night, or if indeed, this investigation is in any way related to the investigation surrounding the escape from legal custody of the son of the Oscar-winning actress, Kiva Kavanaugh, despite her appearance at the scene this morning. This is Logan Doherty. Back to you, Liam...*"

Jack led Patrick into the dining room, saying nothing. He disappeared for a moment and the TV went silent before he reappeared and went to the sideboard, took out two glasses and a bottle of Powers Irish whiskey, pouring his visitor a glass without asking if he wanted one. He thrust the half-full glass at Patrick. "Have a seat."

Patrick looked down at the glass in his hand, staring at it as if he didn't know how it got there, and then took a long swig, before he uttered a word.

"What have you done with my Hayley?" he asked finally.

"As far as I know, she's safe and well," Darragh said.

"Don't fuck me about, Ren," Patrick warned. "You tell me where she is, or I swear, the Gardaí'll be knocking down Jack's door in the next ten minutes."

"I'm happy to tell you everything you want to know, Patrick, but you're not going to believe me," Darragh warned.

"Aye," Jack agreed with a sour laugh. "He's got that much right." The old man pulled a chair out from the table and offered it to Patrick. "Seriously,

Paddy. Take a seat so the lad can explain what's going on."

"Do the IRA have her?" he asked, glaring at Jack.

"What the feck would the IRA want with your wee lass?" Jack asked, offended by the question. "Now take a seat and listen to the lad. And keep an open mind. Trust me, fella, you're going to need it."

With some reluctance, Patrick Boyle did as Jack asked, and took the seat opposite Ren at the polished dining table.

Darragh took a deep breath. He had spent much of the day running though various scenarios in his head about how this conversation would go, and they all ended in Patrick not believing a word of what he told him. For Amergin's *eileféin* to even begin to accept what Darragh was about to reveal, he needed to be convinced Darragh wasn't lying.

There was one very simple and effective way of doing that.

"How well do you know Ren Kavanaugh, Patrick?" Darragh asked.

Patrick scowled at the question. "You know the answer to that."

"Would it be reasonable to assume that you have been a father to him? That it is unlikely any man in this world knows him better?"

"That would be a fair call," Patrick agreed warily.

"Is he in the habit of lying to you?"

"I would have said no, right up until you started dealing drugs, burning down buildings, killing people and kidnapping my daughter," Patrick replied. "That's not the Ren I know."

"Ren has a tattoo on the palm of his hand, doesn't he?" Darragh asked, ignoring Patrick's snide remark. It made little difference in the scheme of things. Either Patrick was going to believe the evidence of his own eyes, or he wasn't. Whether he got snippy about it or not was irrelevant. "It's been there since you dragged him out of that lake up in County Donegal where you were employed as Kiva Kavanaugh's stunt double?"

"Of course," Patrick said impatiently. "But if you think that's going to excuse-"

"On which hand is the tattoo?" he cut in, placing both palms on the table in front of Patrick.

"What?"

"Which hand?" Darragh asked. "You know Ren better than any man alive. You just said it. So which hand is the tattoo on, Patrick?"

"The left," Patrick snapped.

"Are you certain of that?"

"Of course, I'm fucking certain of it!" he said, rising to his feet as Darragh turned his palms over for Patrick to see them. "What's the point of this, Ren? Just tell me what you've done with Hay-"

"Absolutely certain?" Darragh asked softly.

Patrick froze, staring at Darragh's right hand with a look of utter disbelief. He slowly resumed his seat, staring at Darragh with dawning comprehension. "Oh, my God. You're not Ren."

Amergin would have come to the same conclusion just as quickly. Darragh nodded. "Rónán is my brother."

Patrick studied him closely for a few moments, and then shook his head in wonder. "Jesus, you're exactly like him."

"We're identical twins," Darragh agreed, stating the blindingly obvious, mostly because he considered it necessary to drive that point home before he tackled the rest of his story. If Patrick didn't accept that inescapable fact, Darragh would lose him completely the moment he uttered the unfortunate words "alternate reality".

"So was it you who took Hayley? Or Ren?"

"I'll get to that," Darragh promised. "First I have to know you believe me, Patrick. I need to know you understand I am not the young man you know as Ren. I know much of what he knows, for reasons you would not comprehend, but I am not him, and I do not have your daughter."

Patrick took a large gulp of whiskey and turned to look at Jack seated at the far end of the table, watching them. "Do you believe him, Jack?"

The old man nodded. "Aye. But then I've seen them standing side by side, so it's a little easier for me to grasp."

"Okay," Patrick conceded, turning back to Darragh. It was impossible to tell what he was thinking. It couldn't be utter disbelief because he wasn't reaching for his cell phone to call the police, so that was something to be grateful for. "Let's assume for a moment I accept you are Ren's twin brother. Where is he then? Was it you who was burnt down that warehouse? And where is my daughter?"

"Before I can explain anything, I need to tell you how Rónán came to be in that lake up in County Donegal when you rescued him. Once you understand that, the location of my brother and your daughter will be easier to comprehend."

Patrick leaned back is his chair and crossed his arms. "Okay, then. Lay it on me."

"Excuse me?"

"He's willing to listen to you," Jack explained.

Darragh nodded and took another deep breath. "Rónán - that's his real name - tells me you're familiar with the concept of alternate realities in this-"

"Alternate realities?" Patrick spat, jumping to his feet. "Alternate fucking *realities*? Are you kidding me? *That's* your explanation?"

"Do you have a better one for this?" Darragh asked, holding up his tattooed palm.

"I could think of a dozen better explanations off the top of my head!" Patrick shot back. "You could be Ren and that tattoo you're sporting on the wrong hand could be make-up, and don't tell me it's not possible. Ren grew up on movie sets. He probably has the cell phone numbers of half the make-up artists in the country, if not the world, stored in his phone. Kiva would certainly know them, although the idea Ren comes from an alternate reality is a step up from her first suggestion that he was left behind by aliens."

Darragh offered Patrick his right hand. "Do you want to check it's real? I am not Ren, Patrick. I am his brother, and my name is Darragh."

"I know," Patrick said, in a less belligerent tone. "And do you know how I know you're not Ren?"

Darragh didn't respond, certain it was a rhetorical question.

"He would never try to spin me such a ridiculous fucking yarn to get himself out of trouble." He drained the last of his whiskey and then raised his empty glass to Jack in mocking salute. "Explains the generous proportions of the drink, though. Suppose you thought I'd swallow this blarney easier if I was pissed?"

"The alcohol helps," Jack conceded.

Patrick let out a derisive snort as he slammed the glass onto the table. "I'm not going to sit here and listen to this nonsense. You may be Ren's brother, lad, but you've taken my Hayley. There's going to be an accounting for that, let me tell you."

"She is being held as a hostage until Ren has been exonerated," Sorcha announced from the door.

Darragh looked up in surprise. He didn't even know she'd come downstairs.

Patrick swung around to stare at the newcomer. Sorcha was still dressed in the jeans and t-shirt they'd borrowed from the accountant's house. Her long dark hair was dishevelled and she looked pale, but still commanded attention when she spoke, even without her weapons.

"Who the hell are you?"

"I am the one negotiating Ren's surrender," Sorcha announced, looking at neither Darragh nor Jack. "Something I will not permit until the crimes committed by the half-breed mongrel, Trása Ni'Amergin, are attributed to the right perpetrator."

"What the fuck is she talking about?" Patrick asked in confusion.

Darragh was wondering the same thing.

"I am talking about clearing Ren Kavanaugh's name," Sorcha said, stepping into the room. She was a head shorter than any man present, but acted as if she towered over them. "Once we know it is safe for him to return, your daughter will be returned to you unharmed."

"That's extortion."

"It is also the only way you are ever going to see your daughter alive again," Sorcha informed him with chilling certainty. "So you may go, and you may contact whomever you see fit, to ensure the threat to him is removed. Once that is done, Hayley will be returned to you."

Sorcha was making this up on the spot, Darragh realized with despair. They couldn't do anything of the kind.

"And if I don't? If I walk out of here, call the cops and have the whole frigging lot of you arrested, what then?"

"I can get a message to the people holding your daughter much faster than you can get the police here," Sorcha told him. "One hint that you have betrayed us, Patrick Boyle, and you will never see your daughter again."

CHAPTER 12

The reception Ren got from Kazusa's brother was in stark contrast to his treatment at the Tanabe compound.

Chishihero of the Tanabe had tried to kill him.

Namito and his sisters put on a banquet for him.

After being offered an opportunity to bathe and change into clean clothes - albeit a *yukata* much the same as those on offer in Japanese hotels in his own reality, Ren was led to the main house across a raked courtyard, where dinner and the rest of the clan were waiting for him. Despite feeling he was wearing a borrowed dressing-gown, the informal, unlined kimono tied with a narrow obi around the waist was a welcome change from the damp filthy jeans and borrowed t-shirt that he'd been wearing when he jumped into this reality.

The house was a little smaller than the main residence of the Tanabe, but it was much older, and seemed to belong in the landscape. The people of the Ikushima - especially the servants - looked mostly Caucasian. Kazusa's claim to her family's lengthy residence was reasonable. They'd been here so long, it was hard to tell where the colonial Japanese ended and the indigenous Celts took over. Namito's striking blue eyes and distinctly Japanese features were not uncommon in the Ikushima compound. He guessed Chishihero and her Tanabe clan were more recent immigrants.

Dinner was already laid out when he arrived. It was a traditional Japanese table setting with a steaming bowl of rice on the left of each place, a bowl of *miso* soup on the right and several other delicious-smelling dishes served in delicate porcelain bowls. Finely carved ivory chopsticks lay in front of the rice bowls.

Ren bowed as he entered. He remembered that much about his lessons in Japanese etiquette. The studio had sent Kiva's entire entourage to protocol lessons after his mother almost had them run out of Japan for inadvertently insulting someone. Ren had found the classes the most interesting part of the trip - not counting their visits to Space World and Tokyo Disneyland. He was so intrigued by the customs that when his school had added Japanese to the curriculum last year, he'd signed up for it right away.

He wondered now if it really wasn't the just the remarkable coincidence it seemed to be at first glance. Darragh had the ability to see glimpses of the future. Arguably, Ren should share the same talent. But while Darragh grew up knowing what he was seeing and learning to focus his Sight, Ren was oblivious to it. Was his interest in learning

Japanese a manifestation of a gift he knew nothing about?

Did my subconscious know that I would need this one day?

It was an interesting idea, and one he could only discuss with Darragh. But first he had to find Darragh, and that meant finding a way home. There was no sign of Trása, but he wasn't too worried about her. This place oozed magic. Kazusa claimed the *Youkai* were all dead, but it seemed unlikely, given the magic in this realm. It may have suited them to let the humans think they were no longer around. Trása was half-*beansídhe*. She'd probably found the local *Youkai* and was being coddled and comforted in their version of *Tír Na nÓg*, while bemoaning the terrible accident that brought her here, not for a moment caring what might be happening to Ren.

She may even believe he was already dead. After all, they had been trying to slit his throat just after she left, and she hadn't hung about to find out if the Tanabe had carried out their intentions.

Dinner was an informal affair, Ren gathered. Everyone was dressed in much the same fashion as Ren, in cotton *yukata*. He entered the room after kicking off his wooden *geta*, stepping on to the straw *tatami* mats in bare feet and discovered his hosts had seated him with his back to the the *tokonoma*. Ren couldn't read the hanging scroll in the *tokonoma* alcove, but he knew the place in front of the *kakejiku* scroll was always reserved for special guests. That made him very suspicious. Kazusa had escorted him here at the point of the sword, and now he was the guest of honor?

There were four other places set at the low table beside Ren's. As *Daimyo* of the Ikushima, Namito sat at the head. On his left sat Masuyo, Namito's grandmother. She was a tall, gaunt woman who seemed to be suffering from some ailment. Her wrinkled skin was papery and pale, and as far as Ren could tell, she was a Celt, despite her Japanese name. She bowed stiffly, as if it caused her great pain, but watched him with pale eyes that missed very little. Next to her, and nearest the entrance, sat Daichi, an older man who was introduced as the commander of the Ikushima samurai. He was short and stocky and seemed almost as suspicious of Ren as Ren was of him. Opposite Daichi was Kazusa, looking very pleased with herself. Ren gathered she was not often present at meals with the adults. She occupied that frustrating limbo between childhood and adulthood where she was too old for one and not old enough for the other. Her role in bringing Renkavana to *Shin Bungo* could not be denied, however. Tonight she was a grown-up.

Sitting between Kazusa and Namito was a young woman who bowed low to Ren as he took his place. Namito introduced her as his sister Aoi. She raised her head and smiled shyly at him, almost taking Ren's breath away. He guessed this was what Masuyo might have looked like when she was young - slender, elegant, with porcelain skin, thick straight black hair and wide-set, sapphire eyes. She was a beauty, and her brother acted as if he knew her value. Kazusa rolled her eyes as Ren stared at her sister. She was used to - and unimpressed by - the reaction of men when they met Aoi.

"Why don't we be seated?" Masuyo suggested, smiling as she watched Ren watching Aoi.

They sank onto the cushions, the men sitting cross-legged, the women with their legs folded to one side. He could all but see the magic crackling the air in this reality, otherwise he could almost have convinced himself he was in his own world, in some high-priced Japanese restaurant.

"*Itadaki-masu*," Namito said. *I gratefully receive.* The others around the table repeated the mealtime salutation before reaching for the food.

"Who would have thought," Masuyo announced, reaching for her soup, "that I would sit down to dine with *Youkai* in my lifetime."

"You must forgive my *Obaasan* her manners," Namito said to Ren. "She is old and quite overwhelmed to meet one of your kind."

"I'm delighted to meet her too," Ren said, smiling at the old woman, who was watching him like he'd sprouted horns and a tail. "But, truly Namito, I am not *Youkai*. How could I be? Kazusa tells me they are all dead, here."

Namito nodded, picking up his chopsticks. "You came through the *rifuto* stones, *wagakimi*. *Youkai*, even from another realm, are still *Youkai*. That's why the Tanabe were so anxious to be rid of you before anybody discovered your arrival."

"It's why they wanted to kill you," Kazusa informed him cheerfully.

"Manners, little sister," Aoi chided softly.

Ren turned to Namito for an explanation. He shrugged. "My sister speaks true. The *Konketsu* and all who support them will go to great lengths to prevent you opening a rift back to your own reality."

"Why?" Ren asked. He was hoping, given the trouble his presence seemed to be causing, that they would be glad to be rid of him.

"The *Konketsu* fear that *Youkai* from other realms will see what the Empresses have done here... and seek vengeance."

Ren was silent for a moment, slurping his noodles to give him time to think. It was obvious they knew how to open rifts. All he needed to do was find out how they did it and he was home, preferably before anyone in the reality he'd just left realized Darragh was still there and tried to make his brother pay for Ren's alleged crimes.

There was that not-so-minor problem of the looming autumn equinox. If he didn't find a way out of here, return to his own reality, collect Darragh and then make it back to the Druid reality before *Lughnasadh*, it wouldn't matter anyway.

Perhaps he should stop denying he was Faerie to these people. Did it matter if they thought he was? While it would get him killed among the Tanabe, apparently, here among the Ikushima, it seemed to be worth a great deal.

"Do you travel often to other realms?" Ren asked, as casually as he could manage. *What are the chances somebody here in this room can open a rift? Maybe Granny Masuyo is a great wizard? Or the shy and delightful Aoi?*

"Not any longer," Namito explained. "Not since the Empresses forbade it."

"Kazusa mentioned the Empresses earlier," Ren said carefully. "You're not that fond of them, I take it?"

"It would be treason not to be loyal to Empresses," Namito said stiffly. "Kazusa was speaking out of turn if she implied otherwise."

Touched a nerve, there, didn't I? He glanced at Kazusa who was slurping her noodles with great determination and avoiding her brother's eye as well as the gaze of everyone else at the table.

"Well, to be honest, I don't know the first thing about your Empresses and whether or not I ought to be loyal to them. As you say, I came through the *rifuto*. First chance I get, I'd like someone to open it for me so I can go back through." He hoped he hadn't broken any taboos by being so blunt over the dinner table, but as Trása reminded him when they arrived, it was only a couple of weeks until *Lughnasadh*. If he hadn't found a way back to the Druid realm by then, he - and Darragh along with him - would die when the Faerie queen transferred the Undivided power to the new heirs. He didn't really have time for social niceties. "Whatever it is the *Konketsu* have done here," he said, hoping to reassure them, "well, I think we'll just have to invoke the Vegas clause." In response to their blank looks, he added, "You know... what happens in this reality, stays in this reality..."

Aoi looked at him in confusion. "Surely, if you are *Youkai* you can open a rift yourself, Renkavana? That is what Chishihero will assume."

"He can't even heal a little cut on his own face," Kazusa reminded her sister. "How do you expect him to know enough *ori mahou* to open a doorway to another world?"

"Is that how they open rifts here?" Ren asked. "Using folding magic?"

"Isn't that what they do in your realm?" the old lady asked suspiciously.

"No... it's more... hell, I have no idea what it is. It's certainly not origami."

"*Ori mahou,*" Kazusa corrected. She turned to her sister, "See? He's hopeless."

"Not so hopeless as you think," Masuyo said, studying Ren closely. "Just because his magic is not the same as ours, doesn't make him any less useful for... other things."

The old woman may not be the head of the household, but Ren got the feeling she was the power behind the throne. And he didn't like the sound of the *other things* she spoke of. They sounded ominous.

"I'm not sure my magic is of any use here," he said, conveniently overlooking his miraculous escape from the Tanabe. "I don't know the first thing about your *ori mahou.*"

"Told you," Kazusa muttered, loud enough for everyone at the table to hear.

"Really, I just want to find my way home."

"What of your mate?" Masuyo asked. "The one who turned into a bird and flew away? Don't you want to find her?"

"She's not my mate," Ren told them. "And I'm sure she'll find me if she wants to. For the record, she's the *Youkai,* if you're looking for one."

"Do you not have a life mate, Renkavana?" Aoi asked with a coy smile.

"No way! I'm only seventeen," he said, realising as he said the words, he was wrong. He was older than that, almost nineteen, in fact. The mystery of his actual date of birth was now solved with the acquisition of his brother's memories. The realisation stopped Ren in his tracks for a moment. He hadn't expected that little snippet to burble its way to the forefront of his consciousness without warning. "Or thereabouts," he added, with a frown.

"And in your realm," Masuyo asked, "one does not have to be *Youkai* to wield magic?"

"No," he said. "They need one of these." He held up his tattooed left palm for them to examine. "You have the tatt, you have the magic."

"So anybody can be branded and then taught to use magic where you come from?" Kazusa asked. With the prospect of magic being available to the masses, she was suddenly a little less dismissive of Ren's brand of sorcery.

"No... the ink is magical, I think. It doesn't take on everyone."

"Perhaps it only takes on those with *Youkai* blood running in their veins," Masuyo suggested, reaching for the fish. "Magic is magic, after all. Just as the sun rises and sets in all the different realms in the same fashion, I imagine things as fundamental as who can and cannot wield magic are also the same."

Ren shook his head. "In my realm, mixing Faerie and human blood in those who can wield magic is frowned upon." *God, did I just say that? I sound like Darragh*, he thought, as he realized it was his brother's knowledge he was quoting. He was calling Darragh's reality "my realm" now. Did that mean Darragh's memories were starting to blend with his? When would he no longer be able to tell the difference?

And was the same thing happening to Darragh back in Ren's world?

"Whereas here in this realm the opposite is true," the old lady was saying. Ren dragged his attention back to the conversation. "Here, without *Youkai* blood in them, one cannot so much as light a candle with magic. Rather inconvenient, after one has eradicated all the *Youkai* from their realm."

Ren stared at her in surprise. Kazusa had said the same thing, but coming from a child, it seemed an exaggerated claim. "They're *all* gone?"

"You're the first I've met in my lifetime," Masuyo said. "And I'm older than I have any right to be."

"Then where is all the magic coming from?" Ren asked, without thinking.

Namito smiled. "So you *can* sense it?"

"Sense it?" Ren asked with a shrug, realising he'd well and truly blown any chance he had of denying his magical ability now. "This place reeks of it. Every breath you take is dripping with it."

Masuyo smiled and looked to her grandson. "See, Namito. I told you it was worth the risk."

"It won't be if the Tanabe learn he's here," Namito said to his grandmother with a frown, and then he turned his attention back to Ren. "The magic comes from the *kozo* trees. They are the trees from which the *washi* is made - the paper used by those who wield *ori mahou*."

"Like Chishihero?"

"Like her," Namito agreed with a frown. "She is of the *Konketsu* – those who are part *Youkai* and part human. Only they can perform *ori mahou*."

"So... if I want to find my way home, I need to find someone like her who knows folding magic to open the rift?" Ren asked cautiously, aware of how such a suggestion might sound to the enemies of such a person.

Masuyo shook her head with a thin smile. "Chishihero cannot help you, Renkavana. Even if she did not kill you on sight, she is a minor member of *Konketsu*. Otherwise, she would not be stuck out here in the colonies with us in the wilds of *Airurundo*. She would be at the Imperial court, serving the Empresses themselves."

So much for Plan A, Ren thought as the conversation moved on to Masuyo's childhood memories of her visit to the Imperial court. Kazusa and Aoi couldn't get enough of these stories. Ren only half-listened to her speaking, because something else the old woman said bothered him.

Magic is magic, after all. Just as the sun rises and sets in all the different realms in the same fashion, I imagine things as fundamental as who can and cannot wield magic are also the same.

Suppose she was right about that? Ren wondered. *What does that make my brother and me?*

And if she was right, why hadn't anybody mentioned before now that Ren and Darragh - and probably all the Undivided to come before them - might be Faerie?

CHAPTER 13

Pete Doherty hated family gatherings and he'd been dreading this one for days. Normally, he'd keep himself distracted by working, but his suspected concussion and Inspector Duggan's fear that Pete was seeing double after he was laid out during the Kavanaugh kid's escape, meant he was stuck at home, discovering just exactly how much crap there was on television on a Saturday afternoon.

Even so, with nothing else to do all day, he still managed to be late for his grandmother's birthday gathering. Bracing himself, he opened the front door of her house to a wave of music and laughter coming from the living room.

Pete didn't hate his family - quite the opposite. He just hated being the less blatantly successful one. Not that he considered himself a failure, nor did he resent his brother's high profile. It was just irritating that it was so public. Pete's career in the Gardaí had been stellar. He'd studied at Cambridge. He had a masters degree in criminology. But if he ever took a bullet in the line of duty, the one everybody would see on national television going on and on about it, would be his twin brother, Logan.

A door opened down the empty hall. The music and the chattering grew louder for a moment as his mother emerged from the room carrying a tray of empty glasses. She was dressed, as always, in an elegant suit, probably from some fabulous designer in Paris. Logan would know which one. All Pete really knew was that his mother ran a very successful modelling agency and dressed that way because it was one of the perks of her job. He had never, now he tried to recall, seen her dressed in jeans and a t-shirt.

His mother glanced up when she saw him and smiled. She was a beautiful woman, one of those ageless women who seemed to reach their mid-thirties and never get any older. He'd run into one of his colleagues when he was having lunch with her once, and later, back at the office, the man had asked if Pete was dating her. To this day, he still thought Pete was lying about her identity, because he simply couldn't believe this woman was his mother.

"Peter, *ma cherie*! We were starting to worry you weren't going to make it!"

"Didn't think anybody would notice if I was here or not," he said, shouldering the door closed.

She smiled sympathetically. "I would have noticed, *cherie*. This is probably the only chance I'll get to see you before I leave."

He walked the length of the narrow hall to kiss his mother's cheek. As usual, the faint aroma of Chanel No 5 clung to her perfectly styled hair, the perfume she'd worn as long as he could remember.

"What exotic destination are you off to this time?"

Pete's mother was always travelling. She had done most of his life, leaving him and his brother and sister to be cared for, more often than not, by their grandmother, whose birthday it was today. His mother never spoke much about her job, insisting it would bore them to tears, but she always brought them back a gift, no matter how small, to remind them that even though she was away, she was thinking of her children.

"Nowhere exciting," she said. "Just a quick trip across the Atlantic. I'll be back by next Thursday. Are those for your grandmother?"

Pete held up the large bunch of roses he was carrying. "Think Mamó will forgive my tardiness when she sees these?"

His mother chuckled, a warm throaty sound that Pete always associated with warmth, happiness and home. "I think she'll tell you how well they'll go with the roses Logan brought her. You two really should phone each other beforehand, you know, when you're coming to these sorts of events. You're always getting people the same present."

"Logan's here already then?" Not that he'd needed to ask. Logan's red Porsche was parked out in the street.

His mother nodded and jerked her head towards the living room. "He's inside. Brought a lovely girl with him. She's been in a few commercials your Mamó's seen, so he's her favourite, for the moment."

She focussed her eyes on Pete and added pointedly, "Your twin brother, at least, seems to be trying to give me grandchildren." She glanced past Pete with a questioning look. "Did you bring someone with you, perhaps?"

He glanced over his shoulder at the empty hall. "Obviously not."

She seemed rather disappointed, but undeterred. "Are you seeing anyone at the moment, maybe?"

"Maybe." It was the safest answer he could give. Experience had taught him long ago that to answer in the affirmative meant the third degree about whom he was dating. A negative response would trigger a lecture about how he was wasting time, because all the good girls in the world would be married to other men soon, if he didn't start taking his duty to get married and give her grandchildren seriously. Like his brother.

"Are you... close... with this *Mademoiselle... maybe*?"

"It is possible to ever have a conversation with you that doesn't end up asking me if I'm getting laid?"

"You should let me introduce you to some of my girls, *cherie*," she laughed. "Come down to the office sometime, and I'll let you browse my portfolios."

"You sound like a madam running a very expensive line of hookers, when you say that, mother," he warned, smiling. "And if you don't mind, I'm quite capable of finding my own... portfolios."

She laughed again, placing the tray on the small telephone table near the door. She opened her arms to her son. "Then get a move on, *cherie*. Your *Mamó* wants more great-grandchildren. *I* want grandchildren."

"*Mamó* has plenty of great-grandchildren already," he reminded her, lowering the roses, as she hugged him. "My female cousins seem to be single-handedly trying to over-populate the planet. Why does she need more?"

"She is greedy, *cherie*," she told him, squeezing him tight. "And it's time for you and your brother to do your part. You and Logan are special. You owe it to the human gene pool to continue your line."

"No pressure then."

She squeezed him affectionately and stepped back from the embrace, holding Pete at arm's length, for a moment, which allowed his mother a clear view of his face. Her eyes widened with concern when she saw his bruises. "*Mon Dieu*! What happened to you?"

"Perp got outta hand. I'm okay."

She frowned, eyeing him with a worried expression. "Are you sure?"

"Positive. I'll be fine. I might even be the family hero for a day or so."

"I'd not count on that, *cherie*," she warned. "While you are being beaten up by out-of-hand-perps, Logan's been investigating that business with the actress's boy. You know? The one they want for burning down that warehouse and murdering that homeless man. I believe he has some amazing exposé lined up that is going to make him famous." His mother smiled, used to her son's flair for the dramatic. "He's in there telling everyone about it."

"Knowing Logan, all he's found out is where Kiva Kavanaugh gets her nails done," Pete said, rolling his eyes. *Jesus, I was the one who interrogated*

Ren Kavanaugh! If I wanted to big-note myself, I could blow Logan out of the water.

Stupid bastard didn't even get past the barricades at the golf club, he was tempted to tell his mother.

He doesn't know the first thing about the Kavanaugh case.

But he said nothing. That was the difference, he supposed, between being a cop and a TV reporter.

"Need a hand with that tray?" Helping his mother with the drinks seemed like a much better idea, right at this moment, than watching everyone go all doe-eyed about Logan rubbing shoulders with celebrities.

"It's okay, Pete," she chuckled and she picked the tray up. "Go in there and give your *Mamó* her flowers. She's been asking where you are."

"Better get it done, then," he said. "Sure you don't need a hand?"

"Go!" his mother ordered, fully aware of why Pete was stalling. "Get it over with."

Pete opened the kitchen door at the end of the hall for his mother, before he turned, squared his shoulders and opened the door to the living room. He was met by a wall of laughter and warm air. *Mamó* liked to keep the heating on, even when it wasn't cold, and there was an Elvis song playing in the background. Today was his grandmother's eighty-seventh birthday, and like everyone else in the family, Pete was of the opinion that if she wanted to heat the place up until it felt like downtown Cairo, she ought to be allowed to do it.

The room was crowded to overflowing. Logan was standing near Mamó's chair with a drop-dead-gorgeous redhead on his arm. Pete thought she looked vaguely familiar, but he didn't watch enough TV to be certain. Logan was holding court about his latest exploits. The young woman seemed content to smile and nod and not add anything substantive to the conversation. Clustered around them were Pete's aunt, Maureen, her husband, Sean, his twin uncles, Liam and Gerald, his grandmother's younger sister Aileen, and a few distant cousins visiting from Belfast, whose names he couldn't immediately recall. And that was just the adults. There was another cluster of nieces, nephews and younger cousins crowded around the coffee table, doing their best to devour every chip and dip platter as fast as was humanly possible.

On the table under the window, behind his grandmother's throne-like floral armchair, was a crystal vase filled with three-dozen spectacular red roses that must have cost what Pete earned in a week. His own supermarket-bought dozen roses seemed paltry by comparison.

"Peter!" his grandmother cried happily when she spied him. "You came!"

He smiled and made his way to her chair, stepping over children and a rather put-upon tabby trying to flee the smothering attentions of his cousin Kelly's four-year-old daughter, Siobhan. When he finally made it to her chair, he leaned over, kissed Mamó's wrinkled cheek, and presented her with the flowers. "As if I wouldn't be here for your special day, *Mamó*," he said loudly. She was going deaf and the ambient noise in the room meant she'd barely be able to hear a word he said. "Happy birthday."

"Thank you, darling," she said, smelling the roses as if she had never seen anything more wonderful. *Mamó* was good like that. She never treated any gift - no matter how valuable or insignificant - any differently from another. "They're lovely. What happened to your face?"

"Got hit by a girl," Pete said. He'd learned long ago that telling the truth in this family was sometimes a better way to lie, than making something up. "Laid me out cold, she did."

Mamó laughed. "All right then," she said, patting his cheek. "I understand. It's a police thing. You're not allowed to tell me what really happened, are you? Why don't you get a safer job, darling? Like Logan?"

Wow... that only took about a minute. That's a new record.

"I like having a *real* job," Pete said loudly, glancing up at his twin with a grin. "Hey, Logan. Didn't notice you standing there."

"Sure you didn't," Logan laughed. "This is Tiffany. She's a model-slash-actress."

"Really? Fancy you dating a model." He smiled, shaking the young woman's proffered hand. "Hi Tiffany, I'm Pete."

Tiffany smiled at him, her eyes wide. "Hi Pete. God, you look so much like Logan."

"I get that a lot," Pete said, glancing at her brother.

"Tiffany is signed with Mum's agency. You got a minute?"

"Sure," Pete said, glad he wasn't required to comment on Tiffany's modelling career.

"*Mamó?*" Logan said loudly. "Pete and I are going to help Mum with the drinks. Will you look after Tiffany?"

The old lady looked up at him. "Eh?"

"We're going for drinks." He turned to Tiffany. "Do you mind? I need to talk to Pete about something."

Tiffany shrugged. "Sure."

Before Pete had a chance to object, Logan had him by the arm and was dragging him out of the living room. Pete waved to his heavily pregnant cousin as they passed her, but Logan never gave him the chance to stop and say hello or enquire how long it would be before he had another cousin whose name he'd have to remember at family gatherings. A moment later, they were in the hall, holding the door open for their mother as she returned with the drinks tray.

"Can you bring your grandmother's tea in with you?" she asked her sons, as she passed them. "It's on the counter."

"Be there in a minute," Logan promised her, before hustling Pete into the kitchen. Logan finally closed the door on the noise from the hall and turned to look at his brother. "You look like shit."

"Love you too, brother."

"Does it hurt?"

Pete flexed his fist for a moment and eyed Logan's face thoughtfully. "Wanna find out?"

Logan grinned. "No, I'm good. Are you still working the Kavanaugh case?"

"Is that what you wanted to see me about?" Pete asked, shaking his head. "Jesus, Logan, you know I can't tell you anything."

"That's not why I'm asking," Logan said. "I might have something for you."

"Like what?" Pete asked suspiciously, knowing Logan would want something in return.

"We've been going through some of the CCTV footage they have of the Kavanaugh kid, since he popped up on the radar again the other day."

"Shouldn't the Gardaí be doing that?"

"Well, you are," Logan agreed, pushing aside the steaming cup and saucer on the small table that reeked of Earl Grey with a healthy dash of Irish whiskey awaiting delivery to their grandmother. "But some of the good citizens of Dublin like to get paid for their efforts..."

"You mean you paid someone for *evidence*?"

"You call it evidence, I call it spectacular investigative journalism," Logan said with a shrug.

"Chequebook journalism," Pete corrected.

"Whatever you call it, it works. The Gardaí don't have all the tapes."

Pete sighed. "What did you find?"

Logan reached inside his jacket pocket and produced a folded envelope. He opened it and pulled out a grainy ten by eight black and white photo and laid it on the table, using their grandmother's cut glass salt and pepper shakers to hold down the edges. The photo was of Ren Kavanaugh, the shot taken inside what appeared to be a cluttered antique shop. "Seems your boy has an interest in art-deco crystal."

"When was this taken?" Pete asked. They knew almost nothing about where the Kavanaugh kid had been in the past few weeks. "And where?"

"It was taken in a suburban antique shop a few hours before Ren Kavanaugh appeared at the St Christopher's Visual Rehabilitation Centre to kidnap Hayley Boyle."

"What's he doing in an antique shop?"

"Buying a salad bowl, according to the store owner."

"A *what*?"

"A salad bowl. He insisted on crystal. The girl claiming to be Jack O'Righin's granddaughter was with him."

"Jesus," Pete muttered. "Does Duggan know about this yet?"

"Not yet, but that's not what I wanted to show you."

Logan pulled out another photo of Ren Kavanaugh and placed it on the table. This one had been taken on the red carpet in London a few weeks ago. Ren was wearing a tux and looking rather glum.

"What's this?"

"The London premiere of *Rain over Tuscany*."

"Is that you in the background?"

"I was there. With Tiffany. Don't you ever watch the news?"

"Not the sort of news show that thinks you walking down a red carpet in London with some model-slash-actress Mum fixed you up with because you can't get a real date is actually news... no... not as a rule."

"You think you're so funny, don't you?"

"Hilarious. What's this photo got to do with the other photo?"

"Look at his hands."

Pete took the second photo and placed it beside the one of Ren in the antique shop. In the shop, Ren's right hand was extended, palm up to collect his change. In the second photo, Ren's left hand was raised to shield his eyes from the lightning storm of flashbulbs.

Both hands were tattooed with the strange and inexplicable triskalion the boy had been found with when he was barely more than a toddler.

"What about them?"

"Christ, Pete! Aren't you supposed to be a detective? Take another look!"

Pete examined the tattooed hands again and then shook his head. "They're on opposite hands. I see that. But that's probably just a flipped negative."

"There's no flipped neg, Pete," Logan assured him. "These are both digital images. Besides, if you look at the exit sign over the door in the shop and the advertising banners at the film premiere, they're both the right way around."

"What are you suggesting?"

"That there're two of them." Logan waited for a moment, as if expecting his revelation to have a fanfare attached. When Pete didn't visibly react, he said, "And yet you don't seem surprised."

"It's because I *know* there's two of them. I've seen them," Pete said, staring at the photographs. "Side by side."

Logan looked more than a little disappointed. "Duggan never said anything about Ren Kavanaugh having a twin at the press conference."

"That's because she doesn't believe it. I tried to tell her, but she thinks I'm concussed and seeing double."

Suddenly his brother beamed at him and pointed at the photos. "For an exclusive, I'll give you proof."

Pete shook his head. "I can't make that sort of deal with you."

"I figured as much," Logan conceded. "Who else suspects the Kavanaugh kid has a twin besides you?"

"Nobody," Pete said. "At least nobody I've spoken to. Why?"

"What about the owner of the Audi?"

"How do you know about that?"

"Call it a wild guess. Reporter's intuition, if you like. Or maybe it's just screamingly bloody obvious, Pete."

Pete stared at him in confusion.

"God, you really are concussed, aren't you? They weren't fingerprinting that Audi in the car park of the Castle Golf Club to check if it had been cleaned well enough. There were cops crawling all over it."

Pete shrugged. "The car belongs to some financial analyst who lives nearby. Claims he was too pissed to drive Wednesday night, so he left his car at the club and walked home across the course. When he went back to get it on Thursday the car was gone. His wife reported it stolen a couple of hours before Kavanaugh turned up at St Christopher's."

"Do you think Kiva knows her boy has an evil twin?"

"Evil twin?"

"The other twin is always evil," he chuckled. "I mean... look at you and me."

Pete studied his brother for a moment, recognising the look in Logan's eye. He was bursting to tell him something, at the same time feeling insufferably smug that he knew something Pete didn't.

"What are you going on about?"

Logan pulled another photograph out of the envelope and slammed it dramatically on the table in front of Pete. "I lifted *this* frame from the footage we shot at the golf course yesterday morning."

Pete stared at the photo, not sure what he was supposed to be seeing. It was a blow-up of Kiva Kavanaugh's Bentley, parked under a tree near the rough opposite where the action had taken place last night - just before someone fired shots at Ren Kavanaugh and he had vanished into thin air.

The trunk of the car was open. Kiva's chauffeur was standing at the back, looking over toward the car park where the press had gathered *en masse*.

Pete leaned in closer. "Is that...?"

"Looks like," Logan said, grinning.

"Jesus."

"*Now* do I get my exclusive?"

"I have to show these to Inspector Duggan," Pete said, gathering up the photos. "Now."

Logan nodded. "I'll get my coat."

"I didn't say you could come."

"No chance those photos are going anywhere without me," Logan told him, as he snatched them out of his brother's hand. "Do you want to tell *Mamó* we're leaving, or shall I?"

"You tell her," Pete said, figuring he was better off with Logan on his side than working against him. "You're her favourite. What about the redhead?"

"Who? Tiffany? I'll give her a cab fare home."

Pete raised a curious brow, smiling. "So she's not the future Mrs Logan Doherty, then?"

"Hardly," Logan laughed. "When I finally get married, she's going to have a brain that's not pickled in champagne and nail polish remover. The lovely Tiffany has only three topics of conversation, I'm afraid - me, me and me."

"So why did you bring her home to meet the family?"

"To impress *Mamó*. And keep Mum off my back about grandchildren."

Pete wished he'd thought to do the same. "You sleeping with her?"

"No, Pete. We share a mutual love of needlepoint."

He grinned. "Ask a stupid question..."

"It's okay," Logan assured him. "You can't help it. You're the stupid twin."

"How do you figure that?"

"Which one of us got the why-haven't-you-met-a-nice-girl-and-given-me-grandchildren lecture tonight?"

Pete bowed to his brother conceding defeat. "Point taken. You are the smart one."

"The good-looking one, too," he added, sliding the photos back into the envelope. Then he picked up the steaming cup of whiskey-laced tea. "I'll meet you out front. We'll take the Porsche. It'll be faster."

"You only want to do that because with me in the car, if you get pulled over for speeding, you think I'll get you out of a ticket," Pete accused.

"Better make sure we don't get booked, then," Logan said, fishing his keys out of his pocket with his free hand and tossing them to Pete. "You're driving."

CHAPTER 14

The following evening, after Ren spent an interesting - if entirely wasted - day, being shown around the Ikushima fireworks factory, he was invited to dine with the family. This time, however, Aoi insisted on escorting Ren back to his room after dinner. Namito didn't seem to mind, saying he and Daichi had business. Masuyo claimed she was tired and intended to seek her bed, and ordered her younger granddaughter to do the same.

That left Ren with only Aoi for company and the distinct feeling that this was some sort of set-up.

They crossed the raked sand of the courtyard, following the white path made of different sand to the rest of the yard. Ren didn't know what it was, but it felt grainy underfoot and seemed to reflect the firelight from the torches spaced at regular intervals along the path.

Somebody, Ren decided, had spent a lot of time lighting torches and raking this yard, to keep it looking so pristine.

He shivered a little as they stepped down from the wooden veranda of the main house. With the setting sun all the warmth of the day had gone. It was the onset of autumn and hadn't been a warm day to start with. Aoi saw him shiver and looked at him with concern. "Are you cold, *wagakimi*?"

"You don't have to keep calling me 'my lord', you know," Ren told her. "Ren will do fine."

"It would be disrespectful, *wagakimi*," she replied.

"But much less annoying," Ren replied in English, certain she would have no clue what he was saying.

"I beg your pardon?"

"It would please me if you called me Ren."

"Not Renkavana?"

"No. Just Ren."

"Very well. If you insist... Ren."

"*Arigatou gozaimasu.*"

"You are welcome," Aoi said, smiling up at him. "We of the Ikushima would do anything to please one of the *Youkai*."

"Why is that?" He was curious, having given up trying to convince anybody in this reality he was an ordinary human. "Your neighbours thought I was *Youkai*. They called me feral and tired to slit my throat."

"That is because of the Empresses," Aoi explained. "They have decreed all *Youkai* be killed on sight."

"Yeah," he said, wondering what the Faerie in this realm must have done to piss off the Empresses so badly. "Your *Obaasan*, Masuyo said that last night. And she has a point. If the only people who can use magic need *Youkai* blood, it's a bit silly to run around the countryside eradicating them all from your realm."

"The *Konketsu* are very protective of their bloodlines," Aoi shrugged, as if it were nothing to be surprised about. "They fear *yabangin* blood polluting their pedigrees."

It sounded more as if they were breeding dogs than magicians, with all this talk of bloodlines and pedigrees and being polluted by feral Faerie. "But *Konketsu* would have to be part *Youkai* anyway, wouldn't they?" he asked. "If they're using magic and Masuyo is right that you can't wield it any other way?"

Aoi nodded. "Of course."

That brought up a tricky question - despite the fact he'd been here more than a day, and his hosts were treating him like royalty. "So how come you're feeding me, instead of feeding me to the hounds?"

Aoi glanced around, as if making certain they could not be overheard, before answering him in a low voice. "There are some among us who believe the *Konketsu* are corrupt."

"Some like the Ikushima?"

She frowned. "Please, do not say that - even in jest."

Hey, you brought it up, he was tempted to point out, *and you haven't killed me. Yet.* But he kept the thought to himself. Aoi was being remarkably forthcoming, and he didn't want to do anything to jeopardise his chance to discover how he might find one of these *Konketsu*, because he was going to need one of them to open a rift for him if he ever wanted to get home.

"I'm sorry. What do you mean by corrupt, exactly?" Ren had a mental picture of dark-robed magicians lurking in alleys, taking kickbacks for working black-market spells - which would have been fine if it meant all Ren had to do was bribe the right wizard.

He was certain the truth was going to prove far more troublesome.

"They are supposed to share the magic, but they don't," Aoi explained, her anger apparent in her tight whisper. "They hoard it for themselves. If one is not of the Great Families, it's almost impossible to find a *mahou tsukaino sensei* prepared to do anything for the rest of us. Unless you're willing to pay dearly for it."

"Is that why you don't have a magician here?" Ren asked. He wasn't sure that was it, but he needed to know if they were holding out on him. For all Ren knew, the solution to his problem might be sitting in one of the many outbuildings scattered around the compound, meditating on the price of rice in the paddy fields, or whatever magicians did for fun.

Aoi shook her head, her expression so forlorn he didn't doubt she was telling him the truth. "Not since Ichirou died, and that was before Kazusa was born. I barely remember him."

"And you're not one of the Great Families, so there's no *Konketsu*?"

She nodded. "*Obaasan* says it's a trade tactic as old as time. She claims it's why the Empresses ordered all the *Youkai* killed. The rarer a thing is the more valuable it becomes."

The old girl might have a point, Ren thought. If magicians were thin on the ground, you could charge quite a bit for magic, something that would prove difficult if there were Faerie about, doling out their wizardry for free. But the information left Ren with a dilemma. Aoi and her family had sheltered him, fed him, and kept him safe from the Tanabe, and while he was grateful, he realized they lacked the one thing he needed to escape this reality.

There was no polite way of telling Aoi that. And even if he did, what good would it do? The people who had what he needed to get home - the Tanabe - were determined to murder him on sight.

The most frustrating part of it all was that Ren *knew* how to open a rift. He could draw the knowledge from his brother's memories. But he couldn't do it without the right tools. In Darragh's world, they used carved jewels - rubies - to open the rifts, and the stone circles to focus their power. What he lacked was a ruby, any way of finding a suitable one, or the faintest idea about how to carve the magical symbol for his reality into its depths.

That was a skill owned by the *Sídhe* and one they had never shared with the Druids. It was, he supposed, their way of maintaining some control over who could go rift running.

He was about to ask Aoi if she knew of any other way to open a rift - besides dealing with some hideously expensive magician on the take belonging to a clan who wanted to kill him on sight - when a yell went up from the main gate. There followed a shouted exchange too fast for Ren to follow between the guards along the top of the wall. A moment later, Namito and Daichi burst out of the main house, unsheathing their *katanas* as they ran.

"What's going on?" Ren asked, as other doors opened around them and other men ran toward the walls, arming themselves as they ran.

Aoi summed the situation with a glance and then grabbed Ren's hand. "Come with me."

"Why? What's happening?"

"We are under attack. Quickly, you must hide before they see you!"

"Is it the Tanabe?" he asked, wondering if they were attacking because of him, how they'd known he was here. Did they have spies in the Ikushima compound, just as the Ikushima had spies in theirs?

"Of course it's the Tanabe," Aoi told him impatiently, taking him by the arm. She was trying to pull him away from the gate. "They-"

Her words were cut off by a massive concussion that shook the ground, and knocked two of the Ikushima samurai off the wall.

"What the fuck was that?" Ren asked, as he staggered against the force of it. It felt like an earthquake and sounded like a bomb had gone off.

"Chishihero," Aoi said.

"That was magic?"

"Of course. Now please, Renkavana, you must hide."

"No way," he said, shaking free of her grasp. "I want to see this." A whistling noise sounded somewhere behind them as he turned and ran toward the wall, scrabbling up the nearest wooden ladder until he was standing on top, amid a cluster of samurai in various states of undress. As he reached the top, and looked down over the huts clustered outside the walls, the whistling noise turned to a loud bang and the night was banished by a blinding flare that exploded in sky overhead, exposing everything for a good hundred yards around the compound. The occupants of the huts were nowhere to be seen. They'd either managed to get inside the walls or were hiding in their houses.

Beneath the wall in front of the village, the Tanabe forces were arrayed.

There were forty or fifty of them, all mounted, all carrying bows that at this distance, could have hit every man standing on the walls. That the bows remained slung over the warrior's shoulders was probably a good sign. They were attacking, but they weren't going for a bloodbath.

At least, not yet. Not until Chishihero had done her thing.

Ren spied her at the head of the troop with Hayato at her side. She was busy folding something. Probably another magical concussion grenade. The mastiff, Kiba, sat calmly at the side of her horse, waiting for the command to attack.

A moment later, Chishihero looked up, finished with her folding. The flare was fading fast, so Ren couldn't make out what she'd fabricated, but he felt it. A split second before the next blast of magical energy slammed into the gate, the *origami* shape disintegrated into a shower of confetti. Ren felt the magic surging.

He was almost knocked off the wall by the force of the explosion.

The Ikushima men picked themselves up and remained standing like a row of proud sitting ducks, waiting for the next blast and for Chishihero to blow them off the wall.

Ren scrambled to his feet, pushing his way along the wall, until he reached Namito. The young warrior frowned when he saw Ren, pushing him behind Daichi, so he could not be easily spotted from the ground. "You must hide, Renkavana," Namito warned. "It is you they have come for."

"Screw that," Ren replied in English, as another flare exploded overhead. Then he asked, in his almost fluent Japanese, "Why are the Tanabe warriors just sitting there? And why aren't you fighting back?"

"It is high treason to interfere with one of the *Konketsu* when they are working," Namito explained with a shrug. "Once Chishihero has finished her-"

"You're going to sit here and wait for her to finish bombing you? Dude, she's trying to blow your walls down!"

The young man shrugged. "There's nothing we can do, *wagakimi*. Chishihero may work whatever magic she pleases. The battle proper cannot commence until she is finished."

"Are you shitting me?"

Namito seemed unnaturally accepting of the situation. "Only another *mahou tsukai no sensei* may challenge the *Konketsu*," the young lord told him. "We have none."

Enough of this bullshit. He was one of the Undivided. That must count for *something*, even in this reality where they'd never heard of Druids. "You do now," Ren announced, sounding full of bravado, even to himself.

Before he could question exactly how he was going to save the day, Ren turned to face Chishihero, stepping through the cluster of waiting samurai, until he was standing on the edge of the wall - another bit of foolish posturing, he realized a little too late.

Another one of her concussion blasts and he'd be off the wall, on the wrong side, at Chishihero's mercy.

A third flare exploded overhead. Ren stepped forward, trying to look menacing as he feverishly trawled through the jumble of his brother's memories for something magical that might save these people. Unfortunately, as Darragh had warned him several times, the *Comhroinn* had shared their memories, not given him the experience needed to bring any sort of finesse to his magical ability. At his appearance, the Tanabe suddenly stiffened, sitting taller in their saddles.

Hayato unsheathed his *katana*.

Chishihero stopped folding her next bomb and looked up at him. Although the light was fading fast, she looked... frightened.

"Leave now," Ren announced loudly, in what he hoped was a commanding tone, "and I will spare you!"

"You dare challenge us, *Youkai*?" Hayato called back. "Surrender yourself now! As the law commands!"

"Your law," Ren shouted back, opening his palm and extending his left hand. "Not mine."

Ren closed his eyes for a moment, calling on the easiest trick he thought he could manage. Fire.

Almost as soon as he thought of it, flames danced across his palm painlessly, as if the triskalion branded into his hand was alight. Everyone around him gasped. He didn't think it was an impressive trick, but he'd done it without folding anything, which is probably why they were so awestruck. Ren was fascinated by it too, and had to remind himself to keep focussed on the problem at hand.

Chishihero wasn't impressed. She looked up at his paltry flame and laughed scornfully, her fear fading at the realisation that she was facing an inferior foe. "Is that all you can do, *Youkai*? Make a little fire?"

"It's all I need to do, lady," he called back.

"I can blow these walls to dust," she shouted up at him.

"I can burn your forest down."

His words brought a gasp, even from the Ikushima.

Another flare shot up into the sky, showering the night with sparks, lighting the worried faces of the Tanabe. Ren glanced up at the white flare thinking their precious *kozo* forest was in far more danger from a random spark from one of their fireworks than his untested powers.

"You would not dare burn the Empresses' forest," Chishihero called up to him, after a long pause.

"Try me," he called back.

Hayato and Chishihero consulted for a few moments and then the *Konketsu* held up her half-folded magical bomb and symbolically crushed the paper with one hand.

"It is done, *Youkai*," she called up to him through gritted teeth. "But this is not the end of it. The Empresses will hear of your threat to destroy their forest - and the treason of the Ikushima." She turned her attention to Namito, adding, "Enjoy your brief victory, *Daimyo*. It will not last long. You will be killed, your sisters sold into slavery, your grandmother turned out into the winter to roam the roads as an outcast, your warriors disgraced and *Shin Bungo* destroyed. Trust me when I tell you... no power that this*yabangin Youkai* you're harbouring owns can save you from the wrath of the Empresses now."

With that, she gathered up her reigns as Hayato gave the order to withdraw and the Tanabe turned for home, leaving Ren surrounded by the accusing stares of the people he'd just saved and the sickening realisation that his foolish attempt at heroism may well have sentenced everybody in *Shin Bungo* to death.

CHAPTER 15

It took Trása two exhausting and worrying days, but finally she found the entrance to this reality's *Tír Na nÓg*. She'd spent so long searching for some remnant of the *Youkai* in this realm, she was half-expecting it not to exist at all.

She was considering abandoning her search for *Tír Na nÓg* to find Rónán when she stumbled over it. Trása was so excited to discover an entrance into the Otherworld, when she finally spied it, she almost flew straight into it without stopping to wonder why it lay open and untended by even the smallest of the *sídhe* creatures normally posted to guard such things.

Trása could travel in and out of *Tír Na nÓg* in her own reality with impunity. She was known there, and had never been challenged or prevented from entering or leaving. Had a *sídhe* from another reality arrived at the veil seeking entrance, however, they would have attracted all sorts of attention.

Trása stepped through the veil to a world full of magic and little else. Although the trees grew abundantly, and the air hummed with magic, just like the world outside this *Tír Na nÓg*, it seemed empty of all her kind.

Trása wept.

She was tired and hungry and hadn't been able to find Rónán. For all she knew he was dead - and Darragh with him in a matter of days, wherever he was - murdered by the same people who'd tried to murder her.

They were probably the same people who had murdered all the other *sídhe*.

Exhausted by her searching and two days on the wing with nothing but crabs and small fish to eat, Trása finally cried herself to sleep, curled into an abandoned bower that had once been home to someone like her - lost, alone and lonely.

Trása woke sometime later, feeling a tickle on her nose. Sitting up abruptly, she caught sight of something out of the corner of her eye. It vanished into thin air at the very top of the branch where she'd been sleeping. She jumped to her feet and ran to the edge of the wide branch. The leaves shimmered as she moved, but it was the only movement she could see now she was fully awake.

"Wait!" she called out. "Come back! I won't hurt you!"

Silence greeted her plea. Whatever lesser *sídhe* was out there, it was too frightened to show itself. Or it might have waned away to somewhere safe, miles from here and she was calling out to no-one.

It didn't matter. The important thing was that she had spied a lesser *sídhe*, and where there was one, there would be more. How many more, she didn't dare hope.

Trása sat down, dangling her legs over the edge of the branch, as she tried to puzzle it out. She was sure she was still in Eire, but the landscape was different - the topography of her homeland was the same, and she'd identified enough landmarks that not even a completely different human history could erase, and she had found *Tír Na nÓg*.

This was Eire, and it had been colonised by the Japanese.

For some reason, they had killed all the *Tuatha Dé Danann*, and yet maintained the magic. Or perhaps they had not killed all of them - there were still a few lesser *sídhe* around, but they were so frightened they were not even willing to answer the summons of a *Daoine sídhe*.

The only way to talk to one of the wee folk, she decided, was to trap one.

It was easy to bait a trap for a lesser *sídhe*. Human children in every reality she had ever visited did it all the time. They would set up a basket or a box, bait the trap with something shiny, and wait. More often than not, helpful parents would trip the trap while the child slept, leaving behind a treat, which entertained everyone except the *sídhe*, who considered the practice barbaric, demeaning and misleading.

There was only one way to truly catch a *Leipreachán* - summon him by his real name to a trap baited with bacon.

That presented Trása with another problem. Finding bacon would be easy enough. Seagulls were scavengers. Nobody would remark on one scratching through a midden heap in search of a scrap of meat. The problem came from knowing the *Leipreachán's* name.

Trása knew the true name of only one *Leipreachán* - told to her by her uncle, Marcroy Tarth, before she stepped into the reality where Rónán had been thrown, in her search for the missing Undivided twin. Marcroy had given her Plunkett O'Bannon's true name, because without it, he wouldn't have done a thing she wanted while they were away.

That meant the only *Leipreachán* in this reality who could fall into her trap was Plunkett's *eileféin*.

Assuming he had one.

The idea of having only that annoying *Leipreachán* for company in this abandoned place depressed Trása even more than the thought of being alone. It would be just like being in Rónán's reality again, only without the benefit of television.

But she couldn't see any other way. She couldn't open a rift. There was magic aplenty to allow a rift to be opened, and a stone circle to focus the magic, but she had no jewel. Without the help of a *Leipreachán,* it might take her years to find one.

She had to find a way to open a rift. She needed to know if Rónán and Darragh lived. She wanted to be released from the curse that in her own reality kept her trapped as a barn owl. But first, Trása had to find a way to get home.

And she was running out of time, because if Rónán still lived, then so did Darragh. In only twelve days, back in the reality where they all belonged, the Druids would transfer the Undivided power to the new heirs and that would kill them both.

In twelve days, Trása knew, if she ever hoped to return to her own reality in human form, she had to stop the power transfer happening. In twelve days, RónánDarragh must return to their own realm united in order to remain the Undivided and keep their powers.

Only then could they free her from Marcroy's curse.

By the following evening, Trása's *Leipreachán* trap was almost complete. She'd seen a human settlement not far from the entrance to *Tír Na nÓg,* further along the coast. She had fought off a local flock of gulls to secure, from the local butcher's midden heap, three scraps of bacon than hadn't quite turned. She'd carefully flown them back here to *Tír Na nÓg,* all the way fighting off the urge to swallow them. She'd spent the rest of the morning weaving a loose basket from twigs and long stalks of grass.

When she was done, she examined her handiwork with a frown. The basket was too flimsy, the bacon too meagre. Would it be enough? Would Plunkett's *eileféin* even have the same true name in this reality?

"Only one way to find out," she said aloud, her voice sounding hollow and strange in this magical place which should have been filled with music and laughter. She looked around at the silent majestic trees, wondering if they felt the loss of their magical occupants as much as she did.

Trása's next task was to fashion a sling for the trap so she could carry it to the one place she was certain there were *Leipreachán* lurking in this realm.

If they were there, she would find them. Once that was done, she changed back into bird form. This time, however, she changed into a speckled hawk. Stretching her wings to check she had the dimensions right, Trása picked the sling up with her beak and took to the air, off to catch herself a *Leipreachán.*

Trása burst through the veil carrying her baited trap, and turned for *CuanMó,* surprised to discover it was already dark. In *Tír Na nÓg,* time never moved at quite the same pace. She thought she'd been gone a few hours but a whole day had passed. That posed a real problem for Trása. *Tír Na nÓg* was the safest place in this realm to hide, but in her own realm, being half-*Beansídhe* meant she was immune the Faerie kingdom's time effects.

In this realm, where she didn't really belong, she *was* affected. She would have to be careful about how much time she spent in that *Tír Na nÓg.* Days, even months or years, might slip by unnoticed if she wasn't careful.

The realisation only increased the urgency of her mission. She needed to find a way home. Soon. If things weren't quite the same in this realm, who knew what other differences there were and how they might affect her? Or her magical abilities?

Trása was pondering that, beating her powerful wings occasionally to stay aloft with her burden, when the sky suddenly exploded with light. The shock forced a cry of pain from her, as the light seared her retinas, causing her to drop her bundle.

Screeching with frustration, white spots dancing before her eyes, she swooped down to search for it, as another explosion rent the darkness. She scanned the forest beneath her, realising she had little chance of finding her precious *Leipreachán* trap in the dark.

Another explosion. Now she changed direction and realized it was fireworks to the south.

That meant humans, she realized. Not the poor fisher-folk she'd found in their rude little village further to the north in her quest for bacon for her *Leipreachán* trap. Fireworks meant civilisation. People. Perhaps magicians with knowledge of how to escape this realm. Perhaps people who knew what had happened to Rónán.

Perhaps people like the woman in the kimono and her samurai, who'd tried to kill her.

She'd have to risk it, Trása decided, but it was hard to concentrate while in bird form. Another bright white shower of sparks illuminated the night. It was too far south to be the same compound where she had so narrowly escaped having her throat slit, but not far from it.

Trása was torn with indecision. If she flew south to investigate, she might never find the bundle she'd dropped to build her *Leipreachán* trap. The chance of spotting something as small as a bundle of twigs on the ground as she flew back over the forest, even with an eagle's eye, were infinitesimal. On the other hand, it was dark and she couldn't see now, anyway, despite having a rough idea of where the sling and its contents might have landed.

More fireworks lit the clear night. Somewhere out there, someone was celebrating something.

That decided her. Celebrations meant food. Real human food. Dancing. Crowds. It meant alcohol, too. Drunks meant loose tongues and a chance to find out what was happening in this realm - maybe even a chance to discover if Rónán still lived. And as she knew well from her time in Rónán's realm, drunks were the best targets for *Tuatha* hoping to steal the other essentials of life.

Hungry and craving human companionship more than she had thought possible, Trása abandoned her search for the fallen sling and with a flap of her powerful, speckled wings, turned south to join the party.

CHAPTER 16

Inspector Duggan was a tough, all-business sort of woman. Until he and Logan pulled up outside her house in his brother's red Porsche 993, Pete had never really thought about Brendá Duggan's life outside of the Gardaí. She had a husband - he knew that from the Christmas party last year - and a couple of kids. There were photos in her office of two teenage kids and a yellow Labrador he assumed were hers, but as a rule, Pete spent as little time in Inspector Duggan's office as he could manage. One rarely got hauled in to face the Inspector, just to be told what a wonderful job they were doing.

He certainly didn't socialise with Brendá Duggan, ask about her weekends, or have any idea what his boss's reaction would be when he and his TV reporter brother turned up on her doorstep at ten o'clock at night, claiming to have proof she was hunting not one Chelan Aquarius Kavanaugh, but two.

As he pulled on the handbrake and shut down the burbling purr of the 993's engine, he glanced at the neat semi-detached house where the inspector lived. All the reasons they should just turn around and go home seemed plausible now, than the notion of getting out of the car, walking up the path and ringing the doorbell.

"Maybe we should leave this until Monday," Pete said, studying the house. There were lights on downstairs, so someone was still awake, but it might be the Inspector's husband, one of her kids...

"Since when did cops keep office hours?" Logan asked.

"Since I decided your ludicrous theory about Ren Kavanaugh having an evil twin could get me busted back to traffic duty."

"*My* ludicrous theory?" Logan said. "Hey, I'm not the one insisting he saw those boys standing side by side." He held up the manila envelope to remind Pete why they were here. "I'm just the one with the photographic evidence of it."

Logan had a point. There were photographs to prove Ren had a twin and that Pete wasn't crazy. More importantly, there was evidence Patrick Boyle, father of the alleged kidnap victim, knew more about had happened in the past few days than he was saying. "Okay, then. Let's do it. Just do me a favour."

"Sure."

"Let me do the talking. Duggan might have acted as if she liked you at the Christmas party, but she already thinks every time there's a leak from our office, it came from me telling you more than I should. Don't make it worse."

"I'll behave," Logan promised. "I'll turn on the charm. You watch, I'll have her eating out of my-"

"Just don't embarrass me, okay?"

Although Pete had been secretly thrilled to be driving Logan's precious 993, he climbed out the car with some difficulty. The Porsche was insanely low to the ground. Logan managed it with ease, because he had more practice getting in and out of the vehicle. They walked up the path side by side. At the front door, Logan rang the bell before Pete could chicken out and suggest they leave again.

A few moments later the door opened. A solidly-built man going grey at the temples, wearing a plaid dressing gown and holding a steaming mug of tea greeted them with a scowl. Before Pete or Logan could utter a word, he called over his shoulder, "Bren! It's for you."

"Sorry for disturbing you so late, Mr Duggan," Pete said.

The man shrugged. "Happens all the time." He studied Logan for a moment and then frowned as he recognized him. "You're that TV reporter, aren't you?"

Logan smiled. He was used to being recognized. He positively wallowed in it. "Yes sir, we met at your wife's office Christmas party last year. Logan Doherty." He offered his hand to Mr Duggan, who studied it with disdain.

"Thought that bit you did on film censorship the other night was a load of shite," he said, taking a sip of his tea. "Why don't you report on some real news for a change?"

Logan was too smart to take offence at the comment. He smiled and lowered his hand. "To be honest, Mr Duggan, I couldn't agree more. I thought this weekend's Conference of European Classifiers was about the most boring thing I've ever had to cover."

"Leave him be, Ethan," Inspector Duggan said, coming up behind her husband.

He stood back to let his wife pass. "I'm going up to bed. Try not to wake me when you finally come up." With that, Ethan Duggan took his mug of tea and headed for the stairs, without so much as a goodbye.

Brendá Duggan was also in her dressing gown - a well-worn pink fluffy creation with a badly embroidered pocket that said "Happy Mother's Day" in red. It had probably been a gift from one of her kids when they were smaller. The fact that it she was still wearing it made Pete rethink his opinion of her. He'd long ago concluded Duggan had iced water running through her veins and a heart carved out of granite. He would never have picked her for the sentimental sort.

She eyed the brothers standing on her doorstep and shook her head. "You boys into metal music at all?"

Pete shook his head, wondering at the question. "My daughter is. Your unexpected appearance on my doorstep at this hour, reminds me of a song she's rather fond of playing over and over and over."

"Ma'am?" Logan asked, looking even more confused than Pete.

"No good can come of this," Duggan said.

The brothers continued to look at her oddly. She shook her head. "That's the name of the song. I think the band is called Catatonic, or something like that. You'd better come in, I suppose."

Logan smiled and offered Duggan his hand. "Nice to see you again, Brendá."

"That remains to be seen," she said, standing back to let them enter. They followed her down the hall and into what was obviously a newly-renovated kitchen. Pete thought he remembered her talking about it being upgraded some months ago, but as there were few things in this world he cared about less than his boss's renovation plans, he'd paid no attention at all. "You boys want a coffee? Kettle's hot."

"I'm fine, thanks," Logan said. "But please, don't let us stop you."

She waved them to a seat at one of the high stools at the breakfast bar, and picked up her half-drunk coffee. "Okay. What's this about?"

"Do you remember me telling you there were two Ren Kavanaughs?" Pete said.

"Do you remember me telling you to take the medication they gave you at the hospital and to stay home and rest until your concussion was better?"

"It's not concussion if there's photographic proof," Logan said, before Pete could respond. He turned to his brother. "Show her, Pete."

Duggan sighed. "Show me what?"

Pete opened the envelope his brother produced and did exactly what Logan had done to him - placed the photo from the antique shop and the one from the film premiere on the counter in front of Inspector Duggan, side by side.

She put her coffee down and studied the two photographs for some time before she said anything. Finally, she looked at Pete. "Where did you get these?"

"The first one is all over the net. It's from the London premiere of *Rain over Tuscany*, when the Kavanaugh kid made himself an instant celebrity by dropping the F-bomb on national television," Pete explained.

"And this one?" she asked, pointing to the second grainy photo.

"It's the CCTV footage from a small antique shop about six blocks away from the Castle Golf Club taken Thursday afternoon," Logan told her.

"I've heard nothing of this."

"The owner saw the news on Friday evening while he was eating his dinner and says he recognized Ren from his mugshot. There's a girl with long blonde hair with him on the rest of the tape, although she's not in this shot. He didn't get names - they paid cash - but I'm assuming it's the girl claiming to be O'Righin's granddaughter."

"Paid cash for what?"

"An art deco crystal salad bowl," Pete told her.

Duggan pursed her lips, frowning, and then looked up, her eyes boring into Logan with a gaze that had withered many a hardened criminal. "How did you get this tape?"

"Business has been slow in antiques lately, I gather. The shop owner contacted my producers to see if he could sell it to us."

Duggan was not pleased by the news. "And your producers, being the law-abiding citizens that they are, bought the damned thing instead of contacting us and letting the Gardaí establish the chain of evidence. Thanks for that." She studied the photos for a moment longer, scowling. "The tattoos are on different hands."

"See," Logan said, nudging Pete. "She spotted it."

"It might be a ruse to confuse us," Duggan remarked, still studying the photos thoughtfully. "The tattoo could be fake. This kid grew up on movie sets. He probably has knows half the make-up artists in the country. The hair on this one is longer, but I suppose that could be accounted for by the time between when the photos were taken."

"You don't seriously think he'd go to the trouble of replicating the tattoo on a different hand, do you?" Logan asked. "If he wanted to hide the tattoo, all he had to do was wear a glove."

She lowered the photo saying, "It's a damn sight more plausible than the idea Ren Kavanaugh has a hidden identical twin who's suddenly appeared out of nowhere." She looked at the twin brothers and smiled. "However attractive that notion seems to the two of you."

"You think he's that clever? He's a kid. He'd have to know he was on camera, hope the cops found the tapes..." Logan shook his head. "Occam's Razor, Brendá."

Duggan stabbed at the photo with her finger. "This isn't proof of anything, Logan. Thanks to the way you acquired this tape, it's reasonable doubt, that's all. Besides, think of the logistics of what you're suggesting. This kid has been photographed by the paparazzi every other day of his life since he was three years old. You don't think if there was an identical twin brother out there somewhere, with a tattoo on his opposite hand, somebody wouldn't have noticed by now?"

She had a point, Pete realized. It made perfectly good sense and he had nothing with which to counter her logic, except for this grainy CCTV photo and the fact that he had seen them together. He knew - however unlikely it might be - Ren had a twin and he was here, helping his brother kidnap Hayley Boyle and escape the law.

"There's another photo," Logan said, turning to Pete. "Show her the one from the footage we shot at the golf club."

Pete did as Logan suggested. Duggan took the photo and examined it closely for a long, long time.

"We'd need to get this blown up and enhanced."

"We did that," Logan said. "And I can show you the tape we lifted that frame from. It's exactly what it looks like. Someone is dropping out of that tree and into the trunk of Kiva Kavanaugh's Bentley."

"I'll need to see *all* your footage," Duggan said. "No holding out on me, Logan. Every frame you took at the golf club yesterday morning, and every other bit of coverage I can get, from whoever else was there filming. Someone may have got a better angle than you and doesn't realize what they have." It was hard to tell if Duggan was excited by this break or unimpressed. She was very hard to read.

"We haven't got time for that," Pete said, a little frustrated by her determination to plod through one rule at a time. "If Ren Kavanaugh is at his mother's house, she'll have him out of the country by morning, if he's not already."

The inspector shook her head. "That may be, Pete, but I can't get a warrant to search the house of someone as high profile as Kiva Kavanaugh based on one frame of film that could well turn out to be a trick of the light. Bring me something I can take to a judge, and we'll storm the place with the ERU. But until I have proof, lads, what you have is nothing more than a fanciful theory."

"What do you want us to do then?" Pete asked, before Logan started arguing with her. And he was going to. Pete could tell just by the way he was leaning forward with that intense, I'm-not-letting-this-go look he often wore when he was onto something. It was what made him a good reporter, Pete knew. And the same trait that made Pete one of the youngest detectives in the NBCI.

"Go home," Inspector Duggan ordered. "Get some sleep."

"But-"

"But nothing," she cut in. "This is wild speculation and conjecture. It's tabloid fodder, nothing else. So unless you can bring me some solid evidence or some trace of Hayley Boyle soon, I have to face a distraught father tomorrow and admit that after an extensive and fruitless search, in all likelihood, we may have to confront the possibility that she's dead."

"The footage we shot at the golf club may prove she home, tucked up safe in bed," Logan argued, pointing at the photo of the Bentley with its trunk open.

Duggan shrugged. "Then prove it, lads. Because I have no intention of following up the news that his daughter is probably lost forever with the accusation that Patrick Boyle is guilty of helping his daughter's killer escape - unless I'm absolutely sure he did."

CHAPTER 17

*I*t shouldn't be so easy to take a life.

The assassin pondered that thought as he approached the cradle rocking gently in the centre of the warm, candle-lit chamber. Ana would have set the cradle rocking to soothe the twins before she left the room, trusting their visitor so profoundly that it would never occur to her the children might be in danger.

He reached the cradle and stopped to study it for a moment. The oak cradle was carved with elaborate Celtic knot work, inlaid with softly glowing mother-of-pearl brought up from the very depths of the ocean by the magical Walrus People, the mara-warra. It had been a gift from Queen Orlagh, centuries ago and had rocked generations of twins to sleep since then.

Generations that would end now. Tonight. By his hand.

He glanced down at the blade he carried. The **airgead sídhe** *caught the candlelight in odd places, illuminating* the engraving on the blade. He hefted the razor-sharp weapon in his hand. Faerie silver was useless in battle, but for this task, would suffice.

Warmed by the fire crackling in the fire-pit in the centre of the large round chamber, the twins slept peacefully, curled together like soft, precious petals, the one on the left sucking her thumb, the other making soft suckling motions with her mouth, unconsciously mirroring her sister. The girls were sated and content, blissfully ignorant of their approaching death. Even if they had been awake, it was unlikely they would recognize the danger that hovered over them. The man wielding the blade above their cradle - the man come to take their lives - was a friend, a dependable presence they trusted to keep them safe.

"You can't seriously mean to do this."

He glanced over his shoulder. A figure stood in the shadows by the door, a presence that was both alien and familiar. A presence so like him it may have been nothing more than a corporeal manifestation of his own conscience.

"It has to be done. You know that."

The figure by the door shook his head and took a step further into the room. He found himself staring at a mirror image of himself, except his reflection's face was filled with doubt and anguish, while his was calm and resigned to what must be done.

"They are innocent," the anguished manifestation of his guilt announced.

"They are our death."

"If preventing our death requires the death of innocent children, then perhaps we deserve to die."

He didn't answer, turning back to stare down at the twin girls he had come to murder. It wasn't who they were, but what, that made their deaths so necessary.

Why am I the only one who sees that clearly?

His conscience took another step closer. "I won't let you do it."

"How will you stop me?" *he asked as he raised the blade. One of girls was stirring - they were too alike to tell which was which. She opened her eyes to smile up at him, her face framed by soft dark curls. Her sister remained asleep, still peacefully sucking her thumb. Which will be harder? he wondered idly. Killing the one who is asleep and ignorant of her fate, or the one staring up at me with that sleepy, contended smile?*

"I'll kill you if I have to, to stop this."

The assassin smiled down at the twins, dismissing the empty threat. "Even if you could get across this room before the deed was done, you can't kill me without killing yourself, which would achieve precisely what I am here to prevent."

He moved the blade a little, repositioning his grip. The candlelight danced across its engraved surface, mesmerising the baby. He was happy to entertain her with the pretty lights for a few moments. His mission was to kill her and her sister, after all, not to make them suffer.

There was a drawn out silence, as he played the light across the blade. Behind him, the presence that was both his conscience and his other half remained motionless. There was no point in him trying to attack. They were two sides of the same coin. Neither man could so much as form the intent to attack without the other knowing about it.

The girls would be dead before anybody could reach the cradle to stop him.

"There must be another way." *There was note of defeat in the statement; a glimmer of acceptance.*

"I wouldn't be here if there was," the assassin replied, still staring down at the baby he was destined to kill. *"You know that,"* he added, glancing over his shoulder. *"You're just not willing to accept the truth of it yet."*

The man held out his hand, as if he expected the blade to be handed over; and for this night to be forgotten, somehow. Put behind them like a foolish disagreement they'd been wise enough to settle like men. *"They're just babies..."*

"They are our death and the death of much more besides."

"But they're innocents..."

The assassin shook his head. *"Only because they lack the capacity yet to act on the evil they were bred to manifest. Once they are grown..."*

"Dammit... they're your own flesh and blood!"

The assassin gripped the blade tighter and turned back to the cradle, steeling his resolve with a conscious act of will. It didn't matter who they were. It's what they were. That was the important thing.

It was the reason they had to die.

"They are abominations, bred to cause chaos and strife."

"You don't know that."

"Of course I know it," he said, growing impatient with an argument he considered long resolved. He turned to glare at his opponent. *"I see the future. So do you. And I dare you to deny the future you see isn't just as filled with chaos and strife because of the women these girls will become..."*

Darragh jerked awake, appalled by the clarity of the dream. He'd experienced the same dream often, for most of his life, but never had it been so sharp, so real, before. He sat up and rubbed his eyes, looking around Jack's guest room. The beds in this reality were too soft. He had taken to sleeping on the floor since being stranded here, dragging the mattress from the sprung bed base to the corner and sleeping on the floor where it was darker, firmer and he didn't feel as if he were being swallowed by a fluffy white cloud whenever he lay down.

"Are you awake?"

The muffled question came from outside the door. Darragh looked up and eyed the glowing numbers on the digital clock across the room. They read 3:45. In the morning.

"Yes, Sorcha. I'm awake."

He felt rather than saw the warrior slip into the room, heard the door snick shut and her padding barefoot across the floor to where he lay. Even wearing flannelette pyjamas that belonged to their host, she stepped as if she expected to be attacked at any moment. She stopped and loomed over him, as if silently rebuking him for his temerity. What was he thinking, trying to sleep at three in the morning?

"The old man is finally gone."

"You woke me to tell me that?" he asked, pushing himself up on his elbows. Jack was on an early morning flight to America for his book tour. He'd made them promise before he left, that if they were caught in his house, they would swear he knew nothing about it. Other than that, the old man had not had much to say about their continued presence in his home.

Worryingly, Darragh had heard nothing more from Patrick since he left on Friday, clearly unhappy about Darragh's inability to explain the whereabouts of both his daughter and Rónán.

Sorcha glared at Darragh. "It's time to call home," she told him. "I have everything ready."

Darragh sighed. It wasn't going to be easy to do what Sorcha wanted, but it was proving impossible to convince her of that. He yawned, and sat up, rubbing his eyes. "You'll need rainwater."

"I remember what the mongrel *Beansídhe* said," Sorcha told him, looking rather miffed that he thought she needed reminding. "Rainwater, a crystal bowl, no synthetic fibres and a magical talisman." She pointed to his tattooed right palm as she mentioned the talisman.

Darragh glanced at the tattoo and shook his head. "The last time we tried this, Rónán was here. Even with both of us, we barely got through."

"That doesn't mean you can't contact home, just that it will be difficult," she said, undeterred. Sorcha was extremely uncomfortable trapped here in Rónán's world. She wanted to go home. Badly.

So did Darragh, but he was a little more pragmatic about the logistics of escaping this reality. Somehow, in this realm with no magic, he had to arrange for someone to open a rift from the other side. And he had to do it soon. Not only were the authorities in this realm searching for his brother - and by default, him - in the reality where the Undivided twins belonged, the transfer would happen any day now. When they took the power from The Undivided and gave it to the twins they'd found to replace him and his brother, he and Rónán would die.

And yet... if Rónán had made it safely back to their reality, why hadn't he come back for his brother already?

Why hadn't he healed the cut on his face?

"Rónán will come for me."

"I'm not prepared to assume that," Sorcha said, taking a seat on the edge of the bed frame.

"Fair enough."

"And because it seems we're stuck here for the time being, we need to discuss what we're going to do about Warren."

Darragh turned until he was sitting cross-legged on the mattress facing Sorcha. His ankle gave him less trouble that way. "Jack took care of him."

She shook her head in the darkness. "Jack distracted him for a time. At any moment, that man will report us to the authorities. He identified Jack. He can tell them where we are. We gave Jack our word that in return for sheltering us, we would ensure he remained untainted by our presence here. We cannot hold to that promise while Warren lives and is in a position to betray us."

Darragh nodded, unable to argue with her logic. "Granted. But how will the authorities even know who he is?"

"I've been watching television. It seems they can track people down from the objects they own in this realm. Sometimes by the records they keep. Sometimes the traces of the sweat they leave behind."

"How is that possible?" Darragh asked, wondering if the answer to his question was buried somewhere in the memories he had acquired from his brother during the *Comhroinn.* For a reality that had no true magic, they seemed to be able to achieve some rather magical feats that neither Sorcha nor Darragh could explain.

"I don't know," she said. "We just have to deal with the fact that they can." And then Sorcha added with a frown, "Warren has to die, Darragh."

"I know."

"You knew it days ago, and yet you let your brother talk you out of doing what needed to be done, at a time when it could easily have been taken care of. Instead, you let Jack propose his preposterous massage parlour plan and you let the man who could betray us, walk away."

"Rónán wasn't ready to make that sort of decision." He remembered the look on his brother's face when Sorcha suggested killing the owner of the car they'd stolen and whose house they'd used as a hideout on their first night in this realm.

"All the more reason for you - who understands these things - to make it for him," she said.

Darragh nodded in reluctant agreement. The rules of their realm were much less shaded in grey when it came to making decisions about those who were a threat to them. "When should we do it?"

"I'll take care of it," Sorcha promised. "You must stay here and try to contact Ciarán. You are too well-known in this realm to be roaming about. Thanks to your brother's fame and the mongrel's treachery, your face has been shown far and wide. We cannot risk you being mistaken for him."

As usual, Sorcha had a point. "How will you find Warren?" he asked, accepting that he could not help her with this task.

"I have his address," she told him. "And Jack left us money in case we need it. I can get there on public transport. Jack tells me it is less traceable than a cab."

Darragh frowned. He knew Sorcha was a capable woman - she was over eighty years old, after all, even if she didn't look a day over twenty five - but still... this wasn't her world.

She could see his doubt and was impatient with it. "Warren's house backs onto the golf course," she reminded him. "Once I reach the course, I'll be able to make my way there unseen."

"Assuming the Gardaí have left the course."

"You need to trust me, Darragh," Sorcha said, rising to her feet with a faint grunt. "I know what I'm doing. You follow your destined path and I will follow mine."

Darragh studied her in the darkness, frowning. The grunt she let slip when she stood seemed very unlike her. Sorcha was a lithe and healthy woman. "Are you all right?"

"Of course I'm all right. Why?"

"I don't know... you seem..." he shrugged, finding it difficult to pinpoint his concern. "... less spry than usual."

"It's the beds in this realm," she said. "They're too soft."

"Do what I've done. Take the mattress off the bed and put it on the floor."

"Perhaps I will," she agreed, and then she was gone, slipping out of the room as silently as she had entered it.

Darragh lay back down and folded his arms behind his head. Sorcha would be gone the better part of the day, he guessed, taking care of the Warren problem. Jack had left the country. For a short time, he had this huge house to himself. He needed to head downstairs and see if he could make contact with someone in his own realm. Once he'd let them know where to find him, it was only a matter of time before someone came for him.

In the meantime, he was hiding in the house next to the home where his brother Rónán had been raised - the place Rónán had lived his life in ignorance of who he was.

Darragh smiled in the darkness. He would attempt to make contact with his own realm and then, when he was done, he would sneak through the garden wall to the estate next door.

After all, this was, perhaps, the only time in his life he would have a chance to see how his other half had lived.

CHAPTER 18

Trása liked cats. She liked their independence. She liked their arrogance. She just wasn't very good at being a cat.

Trása could turn into anything she chose but the avian form came easiest to her. Her uncle, Marcroy Tarth, favoured wolves, but he was just as adept at being a field mouse, if it suited his purposes.

She sat down in the shadows and studied the compound, a little bemused. There were people running about shouting, armed men, hysterical children and no sign of a party. This wasn't a community celebrating. They were preparing for war.

The people here were like the people in the fishing village where she'd found the bacon to bait her *Leipreachán* trap. They were a very attractive people - a mixture of Celts and Asians, blended in that odd way that seemed to bring out the best of both races. The Japanese, Trása realized, had been in Eire for a very long time, indeed.

She watched the chaos for a time, wishing her grasp of the language were better. Much of what they were saying, as they ran hither and fro, had to do with preparing for another attack. Apparently, as far as Trása could make out with her feline awareness, there had already been one attack this evening. The panic seemed to be about the prospect of more attacks to come.

No wonder they were excited.

This compound was quite different from the one she and Rónán had been taken to, when they first arrived in this reality. This one seemed older than the other place, more sprawling, and yet more solid than the postcard-pretty timber buildings with their upturned eaves. There were more children here, more women and they were dressed less formally - many in what looked like dressing gowns - although that could have something to do with the time of day, rather than the local fashion.

The reason for the fireworks, she deduced, wasn't to celebrate, but to illuminate the battle. There were no causalities she could see, but everyone was acting as though the world was coming to an end.

Foolish humans, she said to herself, the thought colored by her feline disdain for all things non-feline. Trása rose to her feet, rubbing the side of her jaw along the corner of the wall, and padded silently through the mÂ☐lée to the largest building she could see through the forest of legs running back and forth. The main house was the centre of the action. Her long, beautiful black tail swished back and forth elegantly and she made her way forward, trusting the humans in her path to get out of her way, rather than the other way around.

She was a cat, after all. She shouldn't have to get out of the way of any other creature on Earth.

When she finally reached the main house, she leaped the short distance to the veranda, unbothered that it was completely dark now. She stopped, stretched her spine out luxuriously, and decided the first thing to do was find the kitchen, and after that, a comfortable place to sleep for the night. Somewhere warm, soft and not likely to be disturbed by dogs.

Trása didn't get more than a few steps before she was forced to abandon her plan for a meal and a snooze. A familiar voice reminded her of why she had come.

"I'm so sorry, Aoi," she heard Rónán saying as she rounded the corner. He was talking to a young woman with the most startling blue eyes dressed like a geisha without the white makeup. Had she not been weeping, Trása thought, with feline disdain, the geisha girl might have been quite pretty. "I didn't realize it was a crime to wield magic without permission of the *Konketsu.*"

"It's not just that," Aoi sniffed. "You have confirmed for the Tanabe that we are harbouring *Youkai.* The wrath of the Empresses will be terrible."

What's he done now? Trása wondered, as she sat down to watch. The young woman seemed very upset. *Why do they think Rónán is one of the Tuatha Dé Danann?*

"Look, I said I was sorry," Ronan repeated. "If I'd known waving a bit of magical fire around was going to cause this much trouble, I'd have let them storm the gates."

"We can fix the gates, Renkavana," Aoi sobbed. "We cannot fix this."

With that rather melodramatic declaration, Aoi turned on her square wooden heel and fled inside, something that lacked a certain amount of grace and dignity accompanied, as it was, by the clacking noise of her *geta* against the wooden decking of the veranda, and that she stopped to remove her shoes before she ran inside.

"Jesus Christ!" Rónán muttered in English, as he watched her leave.

If Trása had been capable of it, she would have smiled. Rónán was learning, she gathered, that not everyone appreciated magical intervention. She was mildly impressed to discover he'd found something magical with which to intervene. Perhaps his brother's memories were beginning to make sense to him, although by the sound of it, he hadn't done much more than make a bit of fire. She did wonder how he managed to escape the woman in the red kimono, and whether he'd used magic for that, too. It seemed unlikely. Perhaps Aoi had helped him? If she had, she was regretting it now.

Rónán watched Aoi leave and then turned and stepped off the veranda, following the raked path until he reach a small hut some distance from the main house. As he entered the hut, which seemed little more than a bedroom and a small washroom, Trása slipped in behind him on to the woven matting, waiting until he had closed the sliding door, before rubbing up against his leg to tell him she was there. She hadn't meant to announce her presence quite so affectionately - her feline instincts had taken over before she had time to consider the implications.

Smiling, Rónán bent down and scratched her under her jaw, sending a delicious thrill down her spine. She started purring, rubbing harder against his hands, astonished at how good it felt to be petted like that.

"Hey, puss," Rónán said, squatting down beside her. "You're a friendly little thing, aren't you?"

"*Mmmmm*," she said to herself, forgetting her words were nothing more than a rumbling purr.

"Like that, do you?" he asked, still scratching her under the chin. She turned her head sideways, to enable easier access to that annoying spot just behind her ear that she could never quite reach. "Glad somebody around here appreciates my efforts."

His words jerked Trása out of her feline bliss and back to annoying reality. Enough of this nonsense. She hissed at Rónán and moved away from him, resuming her human form as she went.

"What the fuck!" Rónán jumped back in fright as Trása morphed from a house cat into a full-grown person.

She rose to her feet, naked and annoyed. "Yell a little louder," she suggested. "I don't think they heard you in Antarctica."

Rónán seemed a little taken aback by her sarcasm. And her words. "You were listening in," he accused. "When I was talking to Hayley back at St Christopher's. That's exactly what I said to her."

"I was standing guard," she corrected. "Your voice carries. So does Hayley's, by the way. Pass me the blanket."

"What?"

"The blanket, moron. It's cold in here. I'm freezing."

"I thought Faeries didn't feel the cold."

"Whatever gave you that idea?" as asked, looking at him oddly.

"I remember when we were back in the warehouse in Dublin. It was icy in there and you were hardly wearing anything. You claimed you didn't feel the cold."

"I was trying to distract you with my feminine wiles," she said with a shrug.

"That's bullshit."

"It was Plunkett's idea. Can I have the blanket or are you not finished staring?"

Rónán did as she asked, passing her the soft woven blanket from the futon against the far wall, although not as hastily as he once might have. Trása wondered if that was the influence of Darragh's memories too. The boy she had been able to divert with her enticing bare midriff back in the other reality would have blushed himself crimson at the sight of her naked body. The young man standing before her now seemed much less naïve. Given it was little more than a month since the incident in the warehouse, the change in his demeanour was unlikely to be the result of anything else.

Once she was covered, she glanced around the hut, pursing her lips thoughtfully. "So... you've found yourself a cozy little niche here, haven't you? How did you get away from Madame Butterfly and her henchmen?"

"How do you know who Madame Butterfly is?"

"Well... I don't, really. I just heard the name on TV in your reality. How did you get away?"

"Long story," he said with a shrug. "Where have you been?"

"*Tír Na nÓg.*"

"So there are Faerie here?"

"Not so's you'd notice," she said, pulling the blanket a little tighter against the chill. "I think there are some lesser *sídhe* around, but I haven't been able to find any to talk to yet. I was on my way to trap myself a *Leipreachán* when I saw the fireworks over this place and decided to see what all the fuss was about. What did you do, Rónán?"

"I didn't do anything."

"Your girlfriend was crying and wailing like you've destroyed their whole world."

"Aoi's not my girlfriend," he said impatiently. "I've been here two days. Her brother is the *Daimyo*. And all I did was scare off Chishihero when she came here looking for you and me. The trouble seems to arise from the fact that I used magic to do it. Apparently that's a capital offence around here."

Trása could resist smiling. "You mean you committed a capital crime *without* my help? And all this time you've been acting like you'd never do anything the slightest bit naughty unless I set you up first."

Rónán didn't seem to appreciate the irony. "Yeah... well, the only thing I'm sure about, Trása, is that we have to get out of here. We need to find a way to open that rift again. Time is running out."

Trása's smirk faded at the reminder. Not only would Rónán and Darragh die in a few days if they didn't stop the Druids transferring the power of the Undivided to the new heirs on *Lughnasadh*, if the boys died, Trása would never be able to return home unless she fancied a short and unwelcome life as a barn owl.

"Do you know how we can open it?" she asked.

"They don't use jewels here," he told her. "They use something called *ori mahau*. It means 'folding magic'. Apparently the magic comes from the *kozo* trees they make all the paper from."

Trása nodded. It made sense. There could not be this much magic in a world unless there was something constantly replenishing the supply. Magic trees would do it. "So we just need to learn how to fold whatever it is that they fold to open rifts here, get enough magic paper to work the spell and we're home free."

Rónán shook his head. "You make it sound simple."

"In theory, it is," she agreed. "Bet it isn't, though."

"Would the lesser *sídhe* know how to do it?"

Trása shrugged. "Maybe."

"Then you should probably find one and ask him."

She rolled her eyes. "Now who's making things sound too simple?"

CHAPTER 19

Kiva Kavanaugh's house was huge. It wasn't as big as *Sí an Bhrú*, of course, but scores of people occupied Darragh's home. *Sí an Bhrú* was a community. Amazingly, this house was built to accommodate only two people - Rónán and his adoptive mother, Kiva.

Darragh had watched the housekeeper, Kerry Boyle, had driven away earlier, clutching a purse and a list scrawled on the back on an envelope. Perhaps she was going shopping. Whatever the reason, she might be gone for some time. He didn't know where Kira might be. Of Patrick Boyle, Darragh's rescuer and the *eileféin* of Amergin, the Druid who had betrayed the twins so heinously in their own realm, there was no sign.

Darragh limped across the lawn from Jack's place and let himself in the back door. It was a keypad lock, but thanks to the *Comhroinn* he had his brother's memories and knew both the code and how the lock operated. He stepped into the kitchen and glanced around. It was a large room, not dissimilar in layout to Jack's kitchen next door, with its white cupboards, black granite counter tops and shiny stainless-steel appliances. This kitchen was much cleaner than Jack's, however. Kerry Boyle was a better housekeeper than Jack O'Righin and his once-a-fortnight cleaning lady, Carmel.

The house was silent but for the inevitable hum of electrical appliances on standby. Darragh found it odd that the people of this realm didn't notice the sound. It was quietly driving him mad, and among the many reasons he couldn't wait to get home.

Not that he was going to be able to get back to the reality where he belonged any time soon. He'd had no luck connecting with his own realm. Darragh had suspected, even before Sorcha went to such pains to set up the paraphernalia required to contact their own realm, that it wouldn't be enough. Even with the combined magic of both Darragh and his brother Rónán, in the park, they had barely made contact the last time.

On his own he had no chance.

Sorcha would find it hard to accept that when she returned. She was determined to get home and did not want to entertain - even for a moment - the possibility that they were stranded here until someone came to get them.

She would have to accept it now, Darragh thought, as he gingerly limped through the kitchen into the hall. It was deserted and silent. The whole building evoked a wash of confused emotions. He stepped onto the floral carpet runner to muffle his footsteps and slowly headed towards the stairs.

Although he knew the layout of the house and was familiar with every room, the room he really wanted to see was Rónán's.

The stairs were wide, the banister made of polished oak. Darragh marvelled at the cleanliness of it. *Sí an Bhrú's* floors were made of stone and compacted earth Even when it was clean and tidy, spiders nested in the shadows, worms burrowed under the floors and all manner of insect and rodent creatures who shared the world with men, occupied the nooks and crannies of his home.

This place was sterile. Heartless, even. There was something missing. Something only the presence of other creatures could provide. It was as if the house, magnificent as it was, lacked a soul.

Darragh stepped onto the landing and looked around, sweating a little from the pain of climbing the stairs. To the left were the marvellous double doors to the master suite where Kiva slept. Inside - so his brother's memories informed him - was her large four-poster bed, her endless wardrobe, her closet devoted to shoes, her ridiculously decadent black marble bathroom, and her Japanese meditation room. Even Rónán's memories couldn't provide a reason for the latter, but it was there, and Darragh didn't feel the need to visit it. He turned right, down the silent, echoing hall toward Rónán's room.

He hesitated before he opened the door. His ankle was throbbing, but he was more afraid of what emotions might overcome him, standing in this place that featured so prominently in his brother's life.

And then he scoffed at his own foolishness and opened it. Every step Rónán took in Darragh's realm would be the same for his brother. If Rónán could cope with the experience, so could he.

The room was exactly as Rónán's memories recalled it. The wide bed, with its soft goose-down quilt, in the black and white geometric pattern Rónán favoured after finally convincing Kiva's decorator he had outgrown the dinosaur theme she was so fond of. Darragh realized he could name most of the books on the shelves, all of the computer games and if he'd been brave enough to turn on the computer and try his hand at the internet, he knew Rónán's hotmail password.

Leaving the bedroom door open, Darragh limped further into the room. He slid open the wardrobe doors to find Rónán's school uniforms hanging neatly at one end, still in the dry-cleaner's plastic covering. Beside them was a large selection of more casual clothes.

Darragh studied the clothes for a moment and then smiled and began to peel off the dirty hoodie he wore. It belonged to Warren's teenage son. Like his stolen jeans, they had never fitted properly. Here was a whole wardrobe full of clothes designed to fit him perfectly. He pulled out a pair of Levis, a red and black checked shirt, and a comfortable-looking leather jacket that his borrowed memories told him was one of Rónán's favourites. Once he'd dressed in the clean clothes, he turned his attention to Rónán's shoe collection, settling on a pair of thick woollen socks and well-worn, calf-high, tooled-leather Western boots.

He smiled as he studied himself in the full-length mirror of Rónán's bathroom, amazed at how well the boots fitted, despite his swollen ankle.

Darragh found many clothes of this realm a little silly, but to see himself dressed like this...

On impulse, he opened the drawer under the basin. There were scissors in there, he knew. Pulling them out of the drawer, he faced the mirror. But for his longer hair, he and his brother were identical. On a whim, he began cutting his long brown locks, snipping them to the length of Rónán's more closely cropped style. When he was done, he gathered up the strands of hair from the floor and flushed them down the toilet.

"By *Danú*," he said aloud, as he stared at his reflection in the mirror. The haircut was a little ragged, but it was near enough to Rónán's style. He couldn't help but grin at the young man staring back at him. "I'm Ren Kavanaugh. It's uncanny."

He held up his right hand. The tattooed palm, in his reflection, was now his left. It truly was as if he was standing here, looking Rónán in the eye.

"Wait until we meet next time, brother," he told his reflection, thinking of Rónán's reaction the first time they'd met in Breaga. "*What the fuck*, indeed."

"Kerry! Is that you!" a voice called out behind him. "Why is the door to Ren's room open? I told you, nobody is to touch his room until... Oh, my *God*!"

Darragh froze as Kiva appeared in the mirror behind him, standing in the door of the bathroom.

There followed a moment of stunned silence as Kiva stared at Darragh in disbelief. And then, before Darragh could say anything, or offer any sort of explanation, Kiva threw herself at him and hugged him so hard he could barely breathe.

"Oh my God, Ren, you're back!"

She squeezed him tightly for a moment longer, while Darragh tried to figure out something to say, and then she stood back and held him at arms length, studying him through tear-filled eyes.

"Oh, my God, Ren! I thought you were dead," she said, sniffing back her tears. "The police thought that O'Hara character had arranged to have you killed. Oh, my God! And then they said you were back, and that you'd been to see Hayley... and now she's missing..."

"I'm sorry... Mum," Darragh said, feeling awkward and at a complete loss as to how he should deal with Kiva. He hadn't expected to encounter Rónán's mother from this realm, and his brother's memories of her were of surprisingly little help, full as they were of conflicted and ambivalent emotion.

"I know you are, sweetheart," she said, smiling through her tears. She reached up to touch his wounded face. "I know you never meant any of this to happen. Oh, my God... But don't worry, darling, I'll call Eunice. We can sort this out. If she can arrange for you to surrender to the-"

"No!" Darragh said, pulling away from her, desperately trying to claw through his brother's memories for clues about the best way to deal with Rónán's mother from this reality. "No police. Call them and... I'll leave... and... you'll never see me again."

"Okay... okay... I won't call anyone. I swear." She tried to hug him again. "Just promise me you won't run away again."

"Very well," he agreed hesitantly, letting her embrace him, figuring that was slightly less off-putting than her constant repetition of the phrase "Oh, my God".

"Are you hungry, sweetheart?" Kiva asked, letting him go, searching his face for something Darragh couldn't fathom. "Let's go down to the kitchen. Kerry's out shopping, Neil's at school and Patrick has taken the car to get new tyres. We're all alone, I promise."

Darragh nodded, unable to think of anything else to do. Until he could escape from Kiva's well-meaning, but smothering, ministrations, he had no choice but to play along with the notion that he was Ren. She clearly hadn't spotted the difference between him and his brother. Patrick had spotted it almost immediately. That said much, Darragh thought, about the relationships Rónán had with both his mother and the man who had saved him from drowning when he was first tossed into this realm.

Kiva took Darragh by the hand and led him downstairs, almost as if she was afraid he would disappear if she let go. She was alarmed by his limp, but he assured her there was nothing to worry about. Darragh let her rattle on nervously as they walked, not sure of half the things she was speaking about. She talked of school friends he could barely recall, friends of hers he didn't give a fig about, news that meant nothing to him. Perhaps she was afraid to be quiet for fear of the awkward silence that was bound to fill the space between them.

"Did you want something to drink?" Kiva asked, as she pulled out one of the stools at the kitchen counter for him. "Something to eat, maybe? There's some left-overs in the fridge, I think."

"Thanks... Mum," he replied uncomfortably, taking the seat she offered, "but really, I'm fine."

Kiva looked disappointed. Darragh realized she wasn't asking because she was concerned he was dehydrating or starving, she just needed something to keep her occupied.

Poor woman, he thought. *She has no idea how to cope to with any of this. And I can't tell her the truth. She's not equipped in any way to deal with the concept of alternate realities, magic, or her adopted son having an identical twin.*

Kiva sat opposite him, smiling nervously. She was dressed in a silk dressing gown, her hair unbrushed and dishevelled. She must have been sleeping when he sneaked into the house. Darragh cursed his own foolish curiosity, knowing Ciarán would be furious at him for being so careless. And extracting himself from this awkwardness was going to be... difficult.

"So..." Kiva began with a forced smile. "Where have you been, all this time?"

Darragh shrugged. "Here and there."

She nodded. "Murray said not to press you for details, but-"

"Murray? You mean Doctor Symes?" Darragh asked, the name provoking an overwhelming feeling of dislike - a feeling he had acquired from his brother, he realized.

"He said you'd come back. Even when everyone thought you were dead and only I refused to believe it, he was on my side. He said you'd come back, and that when you did, the most important thing to do was *listen* to you." She smiled so sympathetically, Darragh was quite sure she was acting. "So here I am, sweetheart. Ready to listen."

It was only a few paces to the door, Darragh calculated, but if he ran now - assuming his ankle would bear the strain - Kiva would be straight on the phone to the authorities and he'd be lucky if he made it back to Jack's place before all the Gardaí in Dublin descended upon him.

On the other hand, Kiva clearly wanted to help her son - or at least the young man she believed to be her son. It might be safer here than at Jack's, if she was prepared to shelter him and Sorcha until they could find a way home to their own reality.

"What did you want to know?" he asked, stalling for time while he tried to figure a way out of this messy situation.

"I just want you to talk to me, Ren," she said, leaning across the counter to take him by the hands. "Tell me what happened. I can help you, darling. We'll get you the best lawyers in Europe. Murray will testify you have problems. Even if we can't get you acquitted outright, he says we could have you treated in a private mental hospital and you'd be out in a matter of months."

She was squeezing his hands as she spoke. Any minute now, Darragh knew, she would glance down and spy the tattoo on his right palm that should have been on the left, and there wouldn't be any answer he could offer that would satisfy her.

"A couple of months?" he repeated, trying to sound interested in the prospect.

"Of course," Kiva added carefully, "you'd have to tell us where you took Hayley, so we can bring her home."

"You wouldn't believe me," Darragh told her honestly.

"She's safe then?" Ren's mother asked. It was clear she was worried for her chauffeur's daughter. She was family, after all. Hayley's stepmother was Kiva's cousin. Darragh was beginning to understand Rónán's conflicted feelings for this woman. Somehow she could be both magnanimous and self-centred at the same time.

"Of course, she's safe. Ro..." He caught himself just in time, as he reminded himself Kiva had no idea the young man sitting in her kitchen wasn't her son, Ren. If Darragh started referring to his brother in the third person - and by a different name - he'd seem even crazier than she already feared he was. "*I* would never hurt her. She's... my best friend." Rónán's memories were quite clear in that point. But vague assurances of Hayley's wellbeing weren't going to satisfy Kiva for long. His safety, Darragh suspected, and Kiva's willingness to protect him from the forces arrayed against his brother, were dependent on her believing he was going to divulge Hayley's whereabouts any minute now. Or at the very least, ensure her safe return.

He smiled at Kiva, Rónán's memories supplying the words he needed to keep Kiva onside. "You know I love you, Mum," he said, mindful of her desperate need to have that sentiment reinforced at every opportunity. Rónán had rebelled at offering her such assurances, out of little more than pig-headed resentment, as far as Darragh could tell. But he had no need to rebel against Kiva. Quite the opposite. He needed her. She was vulnerable so he suspected it would take remarkably little to secure her aid. "Truly. I didn't mean to hurt anyone, Mum. Especially you."

"I know that, sweetie," she said, her eyes brimming with fresh tears. "But we need to know what you've done with Hayley..."

"She's safe, Mum, I promise," he repeated.

"Why did you come back for her?"

That was an easy question to answer. He could answer that as if he was Rónán without even stopping to think about it. "When I heard she was blinded in the accident, I figured it was my fault."

"So you kidnapped her?"

"I didn't kidnap her. I helped her get to some people who could help her get better, that's all. Just like you did."

Kiva wiped her eyes, looking at Darragh in confusion. "Like *I* did?"

He nodded, recalling how Rónán had found Hayley at St Christopher's when they arrived in this reality. Trása had found a story about Kiva and her chauffeur's daughter in a magazine at Warren's house. "I read what you did. In the *OK Magazine* story with the image of you and Hayley taken at the hospital. They wrote you were covering the cost of all her treatment and her rehabilitation, and I thought, well... if my mother is willing to do so much to help Hayley, then so should I."

"Then you weren't trying to silence her?" Kiva said, as if Darragh's story - despite sounding vaguely ludicrous to him - reinforced what she wanted to believe. Interesting that she used the word "silence". The authorities here must believe Rónán had kidnapped his friend because she knew something about the drug deal and murder he was accused of being involved in. The one Trása and that damned *Leipreachán*, Plunkett O'Bannon, had so effectively staged to frame his brother, in the hope that a sentence of life imprisonment would prevent his return to the reality where he belonged.

"Of course not!" he said, looking wounded on his brother's behalf. "How could you think such a thing, Mum? I love Hayley like she's my own sister."

"But where have you been, Ren?" Kiva asked, shaking her head. Darragh figured she desperately wanted to believe her son, but he'd vanished for the better part of a month. She wanted something plausible to explain his absence. If she had that, then she might believe the rest of his tale. "You've been gone for weeks."

"O'Hara's men kidnapped me," he said, telling her what she probably believed, rather than the truth. "It took me this long to escape."

Kiva's hand flew to her mouth as she gasped in horror.

"I had nothing to do with the deal he had in the warehouse that burned down," Darragh added hastily, making sure he established Rónán's innocence from the outset. "But his men were just like the cops. They couldn't believe it was just a coincidence I happened to be there that day. They wanted to find out what I knew."

"Oh my God, Ren... did they hurt you?"

"I... I'd rather not talk about it," Darragh said, looking away. He was at a loss, not sure how much longer he could keep this charade up. Kiva seemed like a nice person. He didn't want to mislead her, but he could see no way of telling her the truth.

Before he could say another word, however, she had jumped to her feet and hurried to his side to embrace him. "It's okay now, baby," she said, holding him tight. "Try not to think about it. We'll get you through this, honey, I promise. We'll get the best help. Murray will be there for you. We'll get you all the assistance and care and the treatment you need. Don't think about what they did to you, darling. Be brave."

Darragh wasn't sure what she was imagining had been done to him, but he did nothing to correct her assumptions. He wasn't sure there was anything he could do, to change her mind. She was an actress, after all. She thrived on drama. So he simply hugged her back and let her gush about how she would make everything better - Hayley apparently forgotten - wondering how he would get out of this mess.

CHAPTER 20

For the second night in a row, Ren spent the night with Trása curled into the crook of his arm. He hadn't realized she'd spent the night there until he woke the next morning to find a warm black ball of fur snuggled up next to him. He smiled at the sight of her, amused that in human form she professed disdain and irritation for him and yet in feline form - where disdain and irritation seemed much more likely sentiments - she apparently found him more than acceptable company.

He stroked her gently, fascinated by her feline eagerness to be petted, until her human awareness kicked in and she realized what she was doing. At that point, the cat jumped off the bed and turned to glare at him, transforming into the half Faerie-half human girl she was meant to be.

"Just you watch where you're putting those hands, boyo," she sniffed, snatching up the blanket from the bed to cover her nakedness. Ren was sure she was neither self-conscious nor shy about her nudity. She just didn't want him getting an eyeful. Had he been Darragh, Ren suspected - with the benefit of his brother's memories - Trása wouldn't have minded a bit.

"I'm sorry," he said, pulling his knees up to his chin, grinning. "You looked like you were enjoying it."

"It's the height of bad manners to take advantage of someone when they're in animal form."

"Is it?" he asked. "Gee, I must have missed that lesson. In my reality, they concentrate more on boring stuff, like... you know, maths and science... that sort of thing. Can't image what they were thinking at that expensive private school my mother sent me to, leaving transmogrification off the curriculum."

"It's rude to poke fun at people, too," she said glaring at him.

Ren smiled. Trása looked genuinely annoyed. She couldn't see the absurdity of what she was saying which made this whole bizarre world even more ridiculous.

"I'm sorry."

"So you should be."

He glanced up at the high, narrow window above the door. The very first rays of dawn had already lightened the sky. It wouldn't be long before the whole compound was awake. Trása needed to be gone by then. One suspected *Youkai* was enough for the Ikushima to handle. He wasn't sure what they would do if they discovered they had a real Faerie to contend with.

"Will you go back to *Tír Na nÓg*?" he asked.

Trása shook her head. "I need to catch me a *Leipreachán* first," she said. "Now I know where to find you, I'll head to Breaga. There's always *Leipreachán* around there. At least there is in my realm." Then she frowned, and added. "Shit."

"*Excuse* me?"

"I lost the trap I built. And the bait."

"What do you bait a *Leipreachán* trap with?" he asked. Although Ren knew he wasn't dreaming, when discussing things like *Leipreachán* traps - it was hard not to wonder if the entire conversation was really the result of taking something mind-altering. He was half-expecting to wake, any moment, on the couch in the psychiatrist's office, Murray Symes leaning over him, notebook in hand, hoping to learn something useful from his disturbed patient's chemically-induced hallucinations.

"Bacon, of course," Trása told him, exasperated that she had to explain something so obvious. "Can you get me some from the kitchens?"

He shrugged. "I suppose. What about the trap?"

"That's actually the easy part," she said, looking thoughtful. "I'll have to build another one when I get to Breaga, though." She stopped for a moment and then threw her hands up in frustration. "I just don't understand why I need to. I mean... why aren't there any *Daoine sídhe* around here?"

"According to the people here, the Empresses had them all killed."

"I know," she said, frowning. "You told me that yesterday. But I don't see how they could kill them all. Or imagine a reason why they'd want to. I mean... they obviously use magic in this realm. Why destroy the people who know most about it?"

"Maybe they wanted to destroy the competition?" Ren asked with a shrug, wondering what he was supposed to have learned since their discussion yesterday that warranted asking the question again. "I don't know."

Trása pursed her lips and studied Ren for a moment. "I think you need to find out. It may affect our ability to get home."

"Why don't you ask your pet *Leipreachán* when you catch him?" Ren suggested. "I'm not exactly the flavour of the month around here after the other night. They probably won't tell me anything. I'm half expecting them to send me back to the Tanabe in chains with a written apology for all the trouble I've caused, pinned to my *yukata*."

"I doubt that," she said. "You and Madam Oopsy-Daisy seemed pretty friendly to me."

"Her name is pronounced Ow-ee," Ren said. "And I'm pretty sure she was just being polite."

"Whatever," Trása said, as if she was tired of discussing it. She glanced over her shoulder at the window and the rapidly brightening day. "I need to get going. I've wasted enough time here. There's something decidedly off about this world. I intend to find a way home and be gone from here as soon as possible. You coming, or staying?"

"I don't think they'll let me just walk out of the compound," Ren told her. "I can't change into a bird and fly away like you can, you know."

"Then how did you get away from the Tanabe?"

Ren had avoided answering the question so far, whenever Trása asked. He wasn't sure if she would let the subject drop quite so easily this morning. He shifted on the futon, crossing his legs as he said with a shrug, "They were slack. I saw an opportunity, and I took it."

Trása eyed him curiously. "You're lying."

"Why would I lie?" he asked, looking at her with what he hoped was wide-eyed innocence.

"Because you don't want me to know the answer, that's why," she said, sounding puzzled, rather than offended. "And you know what? I don't care. Just get me some bacon and I'll be on my way. Maybe, when I found out how to get out of this crazy place, I'll come back and let you know. Or maybe I won't."

"Yeah," Ren said, with utter certainty. "You'll come back."

Trása didn't get a chance to answer. Someone knocked politely on the door. Before Ren could react, Trása was back in feline form, disinterestedly washing her face with her white-tipped paw, where only a moment before she'd been standing there, arguing with him.

"Come in."

The door slid open to reveal Aoi standing on the veranda, dressed less formally than she had been the night of the Tanabe attack. Now she wore a simple white *yukata* which Ren still thought of as little more than a glorified dressing gown.

"Good morning, Renkavana," she said with a low bow. She glanced at Trása and frowned. "I didn't realize you came with a pet."

"I didn't," Ren said, giving Trása a gentle push with his foot to hurry her out the door. "It's a stray. Wandered in here the other night like it owned the place. I didn't have the heart to kick it out."

Aoi seemed to accept his explanation and paid Trása no more attention. Trása took the opportunity to slip past Aoi and escape the hut. Hopefully, the next time Ren saw her, she would have some news about getting out of this crazy realm.

"My brother asked me to escort you to him," she told Ren. "He wishes to discuss your future plans."

That'd be nice if I had any future plans, Ren thought, *other than getting the hell outta here.* "Okay. Lead me to him."

"He is waiting for you in the drying yard," Aoi explained, taking a step to one side to allow Ren to exit ahead of her.

Ren wasn't sure if the drying yard was meant to have any special significance, and figured it would be impolite to ask. He'd been all but ignored by his hosts since his ill-advised rescue the other night. His meals had been delivered to the hut, and nobody had spoken to him. He wasn't sure if he was a guest or a prisoner. The request to discuss his future plans made him hope his status was that of a guest.

He followed Aoi through the compound toward the high brick wall that separated the fireworks factory from the residential areas. The daylight increased with every step. The wall was a wise precaution, given the explosive nature of the work that went on in the factory, but it was too close to the houses of *Shin Bungo* for safety, Ren thought. He looked around for Trása but couldn't see any sign of her, or a black and white cat. Perhaps she'd left for Breaga already, to take up her search for a *Leipreachán.* He hoped that when she caught one, he'd be able to explain what the hell was going on in this world.

Aoi made no attempt at small talk. Ren couldn't read her well enough to tell if she was angry or had nothing to say. When they reached the brick wall, she waved her hand at one of the guards on duty, who hurried to push the big, brass-studded gate open for them.

The smell hit Ren as soon as he stepped through the gate. It was an odd mixture of cordite and wet paper. This was the part of the factory Ren hadn't toured yet. Before him stretched a vast sea of low tables covered in paper balls. That's what they seemed to be at first glance, but he realized that these were the paper shells used to contain the fireworks for which the Ikushima were so famous. There were thousands of the thick brown paper shells on the tables, ranging from golf ball to basketball size. The reason the fireworks factory was located so close to a forest harvested for paper became apparent. And the reason they must be at war with the Tanabe. The *kozo* trees the Tanabe harvested for their magical origami paper must be the same as the paper the Ikushima used for their fireworks.

Namito had given Ren a tour of the parts of the factory involved in creating the firework powders, explaining how the powders were mixed to produce the different colors. It had was interesting in a Discovery Channel documentary sort of way, but it wasn't until Ren entered the drying yard that the full impact of the economic battle waging between the Tanabe and the Ikushima hit home.

It still didn't explain the absence of the Faerie in this realm, but it was easy to see why the Ikushima, who'd colonised this area of Ireland hundreds of years ago and planted their *kozo* trees to provide themselves with a renewable resource, were so miffed. The more recent Tanabe immigrants wanted the same trees to make paper so they could wield the magic they had stolen from the *Youkai.*

"Renkavana!"

He looked to find Namito walking toward him, also dressed in the ubiquitous *yukata* everyone favoured. The *Daimyo* was not smiing as he approached, which Ren took to be a very bad sign.

"*Ohayou gozaimasu,*" Ren said with a bow, hoping his "good morning" was formal enough. And that he hadn't pronounced it so badly it sounded like something different or - with his luck - something very rude.

Namito wasn't in the mood to be polite. He glared at Ren for a moment and waved his arm to encompass the entire yard. "You see all this?"

"I see it," Ren agreed warily.

"This is what you have endangered with your bravado."

Ren wasn't sure if he could say anything to answer that. *I hope you catch your* Leipreachán, *Trása, he begged silently, wishing telepathy was one of his gifts. And that you find us a way home. Soon. Because I have a feeling this isn't going to end well.*

"Our spies in the Tanabe compound report that Chishihero has sent word back to *Chucho* to inform them the Ikushima are harbouring *Youkai.*"

"And you're not in the least bit interested when I tell you I'm not *Youkai*, are you?" Ren asked, realising that Namito's almost unthinkable lack of civility meant he was in a lot of trouble.

"Your denials are meaningless," Namito said with a shrug. He waved his hand again, motioning a number of armoured samurai forward. "From now on, I can do nothing but protect my family and my people from the wrath of the Empresses."

The wrath of the Empresses sounded dire, Ren thought as he glanced around the vast drying yard, wondering if it was worth making a run for it.

I did it once, Ren told himself, as the guards closed in on him. *Surely I can zap myself away again?* He reached for the magic - tried to recall how Darragh wielded it with such finesse. But he had nothing. It felt like dry sand sliding through his fingers. Whatever ability Ren had tapped into a few nights ago when the Tanabe were trying to kill him was lost to him now. The other night he was in imminent danger of having his throat slit, and that must have made a difference. This time, Namito was only having him arrested.

"To that end," Namito added, motioning his sister forward, "and with the knowledge that the *Youkai* may come and go as they please, regardless of what restraints I might employ, my sister has volunteered to guarantee your safety."

"Thank you," Ren said to Aoi, touched by the gesture, but not sure what it involved. It must be a pretty big deal, Ren figured, or Namito wouldn't be making such a big deal. Aoi stood beside her brother, her head bowed. "Do you understand what this assurance means, Renkavana?"

"That she likes me?" Ren ventured. He felt bad for Aoi, because he had no intention of staying in this realm a moment longer than he had to. He'd done enough damage to the Ikushima for them to be well rid of him, and the clock was ticking on his life in another realm. As soon as Trása learned how to open a rift, Ren would be gone, no matter how many honorable assurances the lovely Aoi made on his behalf.

"It means that if you try to escape, she must commit *jigai*."

Ren looked at Namito blankly for a moment. He had never heard the word before and despite his gift for learning languages, he had no idea what the *Daimyo* was talking about.

"*Jigai*?"

Ren's lack of understanding did little to endear him to Namito. "It is the female version of *Seppuku*," the samurai lord explained. "Surely, the *Youkai* are not so devoid of honor they do not understand what that means."

His heart skipped a beat. Ren knew what *Seppuku* was. "She has to *kill* herself if I escape?" he asked, staring at Aoi in horror. "No freaking way! Why would you promise to do that? You don't know me! You're insane!"

"You came to the defence of the Ikushima against the Tanabe," Aoi said, raising her head to look him in the eye. "I believe, that despite being *Youkai*, your heart is good. I have assured my brother of this and he has taken me at my word. I do not fear *jigai*, Renkavana, because you will not let me down. You will not escape. So I do not have to die."

Namito was watching Ren closely. "Then is it understood," he said. "My sister's life is in your hands, Renkavana. I trust you are worthy of this honor."

Interesting that they considered Aoi's ludicrous oath an honor, when Ren considered it nothing more than inspired lunacy. But he had to concede one thing.

It worked.

He nodded slowly and reluctantly. "I won't try to escape unless you release Aoi from her oath."

Namito bowed to him formally. "You have much honor, Renkavana," he said. "For a *Youkai*."

I had a different word in mind, Ren thought, as he bowed to Namito in return, *but we can go with honor, if you like.*

"*Daimyo* Namito. Aoi," Ren said in English with a smile and in a tone so pleasant and respectful, Namito and Aoi would never guess the true meaning of his words. "I just want you to know that I think you and your whole family are raving fucking lunatics. I am also here to tell you that first chance I get, I'm going to make you choke on this ridiculous oath, dipshit, because I am out of here, soon as Trása finds a *Leipreachán* to show us how to open a rift."

Namito smiled tentatively, leaned across to his sister, and asked, "Do you understand what he's saying?"

"He's sealing his oath with a prayer to the gods in his own tongue, I think," she whispered back.

"Ah," Namito said, turning to Ren. He smiled again and bowed even lower. "Then it is settled."

"Absolutely," Ren agreed, bowing just as low to Namito.

"In that case," Aoi added, holding her arm out in the direction of the gate, "shall we retire to the main house for breakfast, gentlemen? *Obaasan* is waiting and she has prepared a fresh bowl of *natto* for us."

Why don't we, Ren agreed, suddenly not surprised that in a world where a sticky web of fermented soybeans and raw egg was typically served with breakfast, suicide was seen as an honorable way to ensure someone's cooperation.

CHAPTER 21

Brendá Duggan stared at the footage playing on the monitor of Pete's computer, shaking her head. "After all this time? That's all you've got?"

The squad room was all but deserted. It was almost seven, and the rest of the NBCI not involved with the Kavanaugh case had gone home for the day. Those assigned to it were either still in the field interviewing possible witnesses, tracking Ren Kavanaugh's movements prior to kidnapping Hayley Boyle from the St Christopher's Visual Rehabilitation Centre, or down the hall in the conference room, which had been turned into the command post for the investigation, carefully compiling evidence.

The main office was nothing more than a long room of empty desks, fluorescent lights and a depressing and pervasive aroma of stale coffee.

"We called all the major news services," Logan said. He was sitting beside Pete wearing a visitor's pass clipped to the pocket of his chequered shirt. They were both unshaven and bleary-eyed, and had been pouring over these images for two days now. They knew little more now than when they started.

"This is the best we could get," Pete confirmed. "The CNN guy got a slightly better angle than George, but it was still a blur."

"Nobody else caught a shot of Boyle opening the trunk of the car?"

"Every other camera at the golf club was following Kiva Kavanaugh across the fairways," Pete said.

Logan nodded in agreement. "To be honest, were it not for my cameraman having a hangover that morning and being a bit slow on the uptake, we probably wouldn't even have this."

"This" was depressingly brief. As Logan said, the big news item of the day was Kiva's arrival. What her chauffeur was up to didn't rate as news, because at that point, the TV cameras had been following what they assumed was a car chase with the fugitive Ren Kavanaugh. It wasn't until after Kiva and her chauffeur had left the Castle Golf Club that news of Hayley Boyle's abduction from St Christopher's became widely known and the role of her father became newsworthy.

Logan's cameraman had caught less than ten seconds of something - or someone - seeming to drop into the open trunk of the Bentley. The footage they had didn't even show him closing it, or what he did after that, because the camera had turned to follow Kiva. Not until she returned to the car did they have another shot of Patrick Boyle. That footage showed Kiva briefly talking to him followed by a comforting hug, before he opened the door for her and she climbed into the back of the Bentley. As he drove through the pack of press waiting in the car park, his expression was inscrutable, revealing nothing.

Surely, that meant something, Pete thought. The press might know nothing of his daughter's disappearance, but Patrick *had* known and didn't seem all that concerned.

"You have squat," Duggan told them, looking as disappointed as Logan and Pete were. Pete got the feeling that despite her insistence the brothers were pursuing a theory with as much credibility as the Loch Ness monster, she was secretly hoping they were right. It would certainly make the case much easier to solve.

And remove the guilt all cops felt when a child went missing and they were unable to do anything to bring her home safe and sound.

"It still doesn't explain why he would open the trunk at the golf club."

The Inspector threw her hands up. "I don't know, Pete. To check the spare tyre? Change his hat? Reload the CD stacker? God, there'd be a thousand plausible explanations. Sorry lads, I can't get a warrant for *anything* based on this."

"It's enough to question Boyle, isn't it?" Logan asked, seeing his exclusive slip away. "Or maybe I could..."

"Or maybe you could stay out of it," Duggan told him sternly. "I'm only letting you in here, Logan, because I'm not going to be accused of leaving any stone unturned. But this isn't an exclusive and it doesn't give you the right to go off half-cocked and do anything more to impede my investigation than you already have."

"There's a girl's life at stake here," Logan reminded her.

Duggan was unmoved, and unimpressed by the reminder. "According to your theory, Sherlock, she's in no danger at all because she's probably home safe and sound with her father. Or are you suggesting he had nothing to do with her disappearance but is protecting Ren Kavanaugh from us, even knowing full well that the boy may be responsible for her death? You can't have it both ways."

Pete wished he knew what to say that would change her mind. She was right about them lacking proof, but that didn't alter the fact that there were sufficient oddities here for them to add up to something suspicious. And he'd seen them. Both of them.

"Could this be a publicity stunt?" Logan asked thoughtfully, hitting replay on the monitor. "I mean, *Rain Over Tuscany* is nearing the end of its cinema release. And Kiva was due to appear on *Oprah* this week until Ren inconsiderately reappeared. It might be her chauffeur's daughter that's gone missing, but it's her son who's accused of doing the kidnapping. Pick up a newspaper. Turn on a TV. Kiva Kavanaugh is everywhere these days."

The Inspector snorted at the very idea. "That's ridiculous. Nobody would do something like this as a publicity stunt."

"Ever heard of Fairlie Arrow?"

"Who?" Brendá asked.

"It doesn't matter," Pete said, wishing Logan would just shut up about it. It was all right for him to sit there with his temporary visitor badge and tell the inspector how to do her job, but Logan would be gone soon, and Pete still had to work with her.

"Happened about ten years ago," Logan said, anxious to show the Inspector he knew something she didn't. "An Australian singer faked her own abduction - supposedly by an obsessed fan - hoping to use the media attention and public sympathy to revive her career."

Duggan nodded thoughtfully. "I remember something about that. She'd checked into a local motel, hadn't she?"

Logan nodded. "And sat down to watch the fun unfold on national television. The motel cleaner recognized her and called the cops."

"I take your point, Logan," Duggan conceded. "But Kiva Kavanaugh isn't some washed-up lounge singer looking for her fifteen minutes. She can't move without someone taking a photo of her."

"And she's had nothing but trouble and bad press ever since that kid of hers mouthed-off at her film premiere in London a couple of days before all this crap started."

Pete shook his head. He didn't buy the publicity stunt theory for a moment. "It doesn't make sense. If she's set this up to deflect attention from Ren's other charges, where did the twin come from? And why have him mixed up in a kidnapping and make things worse for him?"

"I don't know," Logan said. "But Kiva Kavanaugh hiring a look-alike to confuse the issue and using her chauffeur and his kid to help out, makes a damn sight more sense than Patrick Boyle doing something like this on his own."

"Something like *what*, Logan?" Duggan asked impatiently. "You have no proof he's done anything."

"What about the other photos? The tattoo that seems to have shifted on the Kavanaugh kid's hand?"

"Smoke and mirrors. For all you know, this is all part of the set up."

Pete realized the argument had circled back to where it was the other night, as they sat in Brendá Duggan's kitchen, staring at the conflicting photos of Ren Kavanaugh. Two days of going cross-eyed staring at TV monitors and CCTV footage, bloodshot eyes and a pounding headache, and they hadn't achieved a damn thing.

"Inspector?"

Brendá looked over her shoulder at the uniformed Garda standing at the entrance to the squad room. "Yes, Eileen?"

"Commissioner Byrne is on the phone, ma'am. He says it's urgent."

Duggan turned back to Pete and Logan. "That'll be *my* boss asking for a progress report."

"You gonna tell him about this?" Logan asked, pointing at the monitor and the frustrating, shadowy twenty seconds of footage that posed more questions than it answered.

"Tell him what exactly?" she asked in exasperation. It was a rhetorical question apparently, because the Inspector turned on her heel and headed back toward her office down the hall without waiting for a response.

As soon as she was out of earshot, Pete punched Logan on the arm. "Are you *trying* to get me busted back to traffic?"

Logan grinned. "Don't sweat it, little brother. You can come work for me when she fires you. I could use someone to carry my equipment around."

"Yeah," Pete agreed, ignoring the little brother jibe. Logan had three minutes on him at best, but he was fond of reminding Pete about it whenever he wanted to needle him a little. "And your make-up."

Logan laughed. "Touché. Did you want a coffee? A real coffee, I mean, not that toxic waste you serve in the-" he stopped abruptly, and nudged Pete's arm to get his attention. He was staring at the entrance to the squad room. "You have a visitor."

Pete spun around in his chair to see who the visitor was.

Standing at the entrance to the squad room, cap in hand, looking about uncertainly, was Kiva Kavanaugh's chauffeur, the father of their missing kidnap victim, Patrick Boyle.

CHAPTER 22

Darragh spent the night in his brother's bed. With Kiva convinced he was Ren, there was no way to avoid it, and in truth, Darragh didn't want to avoid anything about his brother's life - with the possible exception of the people trying to arrest him. It was both strange and enlightening to see the world - even for a short time - through his brother's eyes.

For this chance, he had come to this realm. For a chance to walk in his brother's shoes, Darragh had risked everything. It wasn't whimsy that made him seek out his brother's life. He had a head full of Rónán's memories and without any context, those memories were likely to drive him insane. He needed to understand them better. He needed to put a face to the people, the places and the experiences that loomed large in his brother's mind.

He needed to understand why Rónán had been so determined to come back to this realm to save his friend Hayley. That understanding was critical. Armed with the right jewel, Rónán had the capacity - once he realized it - to jump across realms at will. As one of the Undivided, such travel was limited, and there were sound reasons for those limits. Their current predicament was proof enough of that. But Rónán had to *want* to return to his own realm and in order for Darragh to help him realize that, he needed to understand what Rónán was leaving behind.

As one of the most influential figures in his life was his adoptive mother, Darragh needed some insight into their relationship. If Rónán could leave Kiva behind and move on without too many regrets, it would be best for everyone. But if Kiva's absence from his brother's life would harm Rónán, then Darragh was more than happy to have her brought through the rift. Provided, of course, Kiva's *eileféin* in their reality - assuming she had one - was located and eliminated.

Kiva Kavanaugh loved her son Ren. Darragh didn't doubt that for a moment - and neither did Rónán, his twin's borrowed memories told him. But after a day in her company, he doubted Rónán would be irreparably damaged by her absence. Kiva loved him in a way that seemed to have more to do with how her son's behaviour reflected on her, than what he might want or need. As they'd talked - Darragh deliberately telling Kiva what she needed to hear to assuage her suspicions - he began to wonder if it mattered *what* he told her. Kiva's focus was almost exclusively on how they were going to manage this crisis in a way that wouldn't look too awful in the tabloids.

For much of the previous day they had been alone. To keep Kerry away, Kiva had called her cell phone and told her housekeeper to forget the groceries. She claimed a headache and said was planning to spend the rest of the day in bed so Kerry might as well take the day off, too. After all, with all this business about Hayley, it was unreasonable of Kiva to expect her parents to be putting in a full day's work. Kiva then made a similar call to Patrick, telling her chauffeur to keep the Bentley after the new tyres were fitted and return it tomorrow, as she wasn't planning to go out today.

Another call to her publicist and her stylist to cancel their scheduled appointments and the job was done. Kiva and her son were alone and unlikely to be disturbed.

Darragh didn't mention Sorcha to Kiva - he wasn't sure how she would fit into the whole "I was kidnapped by an evil drug lord" scenario he was selling her. Not that it was an immediate problem. The warrior was nowhere to be found since leaving Jack's place in the early hours of yesterday morning. She had gone to kill Warren, and Darragh didn't expect to see or hear from her again until the job was done.

Now she believed he was home again, Kiva wasn't planning to let the boy she thought was Ren out of her sight. Darragh couldn't shift in his chair without her fussing over him and when he tried to use the bathroom, she waited for him outside the door until he was done.

Four or five years ago, Darragh gleaned from his brother's memories, Kiva had starred in a film where she played a psychiatrist engaged in a battle of wits with a serial killer, trying to draw out the location of his last victim before she suffocated in her watery prison. Darragh couldn't help but feel Kiva was playing the role again to deal with him now. Her language seemed at odds with her personality. Whole sentences seemed to have been lifted straight from the script of *Death by the Third Degree*.

Kiva had a huge dilemma and she seemed to swing from one position to another without any noticeable reason Darragh could detect. On one hand, she genuinely seemed to want to bring Hayley home, safe and sound. On the other, she was desperate to protect Ren from the consequences of what she believed were his actions.

She wanted neither outcome quite as much - Darragh concluded after a while - as she wanted to protect her career. Finding Hayley in a blaze of publicity would make her a hero, but one overshadowed somewhat by the kidnapper being her son.

Darragh found Kiva pathetically easy to placate. She desperately wanted to be seen as a good mother, and there was nobody who could give her that assurance more than her own son. So Darragh had spent most of the previous day telling her everything his brother had never told her. It wasn't hard. He had shared Rónán's memories, but he had none of his twin's emotional investment in this woman. It cost him nothing to say the words she so desperately wanted to hear.

Although it was callous to think of her in such terms, Kiva was a means to an end for Darragh. If making her feel better about her parenting skills was all it took for Darragh to be safe until he could return to his own reality, he was happy to oblige.

And perhaps, once he and Rónán were gone from this reality for good, Kiva would be able to console herself with the knowledge that her last few days with her son were happy ones, and that the problems plaguing her troubled child were not her fault.

The only potential problem arose late in the afternoon when Patrick unexpectedly returned with the Bentley to find Kiva and "Ren" sitting at the granite counter sharing a pizza.

Darragh had never tasted anything quite like pizza, and was trying very hard not to act as if it was the first one he'd ever had. Kiva had some restaurant on speed-dial who delivered food to the house. Not long before Patrick arrived they'd delivered a steaming, cheesy platter of bliss, which Darragh was devouring with gusto when Patrick walked in. Caught mid-mouthful, he didn't get a chance to say a word before Kiva jumped to her feet and ran to Patrick, placing herself firmly between him and her son.

"Now Patrick, please, don't do anything rash..."

Patrick stared past Kiva at Darragh, his expression impossible to read. Kiva had no idea Patrick had helped to bring Darragh here. She also knew nothing of their earlier conversation when Darragh had told Patrick who he really was.

He couldn't imagine what the man must be thinking now, seeing Darragh, wearing Ren's clothes and with his hair freshly cut, sitting in Kiva's kitchen eating pizza as though there was nothing amiss. Especially as his daughter was still missing, and he believed she was being held hostage by Darragh and Sorcha until Ren's name was cleared.

"Hello, Ren," Patrick said in a flat, emotionless tone.

"Patrick."

"You're back, then."

Darragh put down his half-eaten slice of pizza and wiped his hands, wondering if he was going to have to fight his way out here. He hoped not. His ankle was still throbbing and he could barely walk. He couldn't maintain the balance required to engage in unarmed combat. Or run.

"So it seems," he agreed, in a cautious tone.

"Patrick..." Kiva began, but he cut her off.

"Has he told you where my Hayley is yet?"

"He says she's safe, but-"

"Have you called the Gardaí then?"

"No!" Kiva said, "And I forbid you to do it either, Patrick. Not until Ren has had a chance to explain-"

"Oh, I think the lad's had plenty of opportunity to explain," Patrick said, his eyes boring into Darragh with an intensity that reminded him of Amergin in his darkest moments. In that instant, knowing what his *eileféin* had been capable of, Darragh was grateful for the lack of magic in this world.

Patrick must be feeling utterly betrayed. He had saved Darragh and Sorcha once in this reality, already. And Darragh had confided in him. He'd told him his fantastic tale about being Ren's twin from another realm. He'd even convinced Patrick, apparently, that Hayley had been sent there to make her well. Sorcha's additional threat to harm Hayley if any harm came to them, must have had some effect, too. Patrick must have believed them, at least in part, because he'd done nothing since then to betray Darragh's presence to the police or anybody else in this realm.

Yet, after making Patrick believe all that, here he was sitting in Kiva Kavanaugh's kitchen, eating pizza and claiming to be Ren.

This is what it feels like, Amergin, another, less noble part of Darragh whispered silently, *to be betrayed.*

"Where's your friend?"

"What friend?"

"The woman. Sorcha."

"I don't know," Darragh said, which was the truth. He really had no idea where Sorcha was at present.

"Who is Sorcha?" Kiva asked Darragh.

"Nobody," Darragh told her. His gaze was still fixed on Patrick, trying to predict what he would do next.

"Are you going to tell me what you did with Hayley?"

"I already did," Darragh said, his eyes locked with Patrick's.

Kiva must have assumed he meant the explanation he'd given her. She opened her mouth to speak, but before she could utter a word, he turned on her. "Fuck you, Kiva, if you'd rather feed this lying little arsehole pizza, while you arrange for him to get away with murder, just so you won't look bad in the papers."

Kiva was shocked by the accusation, but she was a mother protecting her son, and she burred up like a whelping pit bull protecting her pup. "How dare you speak to me like that, Patrick Boyle! Ren is just as much a victim in all this as your daughter! In fact, she probably led him on. Half the trouble he's ever been in, Hayley was there egging my son on. You have no idea what he's been through these past few weeks. No idea what's been done to him! Look at him! He's injured. And he's-"

"And he's feeding you exactly what you want to hear," Patrick told her, his voice filled with contempt. He turned to Darragh again and shook his head. "He's pretty fecking good at that. Well, you know... fuck you both. I'm done with you." He tossed the keys to the Bentley on the counter. "I quit."

Kiva looked panicked by the idea. "You can't just quit, Patrick."

"Yeah," he said. "I can." And with that he turned on his heel and left, slamming the kitchen door behind him.

Rónán's mother stared at the door for a moment and then turned to Darragh, forcing a reassuring smile. "Don't worry about Patrick, darling. You know how he is. He always quits when he's even a little pissed off."

"I don't know," Darragh said, frowning. Patrick appeared more than *a little pissed off*. "He seemed pretty serious."

"I'll talk to Kerry. She'll make him see reason. Tomorrow we'll all be friends again. You'll see."

"What if he goes to the Gardaí?"

Kiva shook her head. "Patrick would never do that," she said confidently. "He is a like a father to you Ren. That at least we can be sure of. Patrick would never betray you. Never."

Despite Kiva's prediction about Patrick's loyalty having an ominous "famous last words" ring to it, by the following morning Darragh was beginning to believe Kiva had the right of it. No Gardaí had arrived in the dead of night to take him away. Tuesday dawned bright and clear. Darragh slept heavily, limping downstairs late mid-morning to find Kiva making him waffles for breakfast - or rather she toasted a pile of frozen waffles from the freezer and topped them with cream from a can and a maple syrup from New Zealand she said Ren liked.

Kiva had noticed the pain Darragh was in from his sprained ankle - a concern that drew a gasp of horror from her when he explained he'd gained the injury jumping out of a moving car. She had given him two of her painkillers to help him sleep. The pills had knocked him out cold. When he woke his mouth was furry, he was bleary-eyed and groggy and felt as if he'd spent the night drying to drink Ciarán under the table at *Sí an Bhrú*.

After their late breakfast, Darragh followed Kiva into the living room. She fussed over him, settling him in front of the TV, making sure his ankle was elevated on the big, padded leather ottoman. She applied a remarkably expert bandage to his wounded ankle, courtesy of the training she'd done for her starring role as war nurse in *Nightingale's War*, the widely-panned World War I epic she'd made when Rónán was six years old. She joked as she tied the bandage off, that at least she'd gotten something out of the film, other than bad reviews. Kiva left Darragh with the remote control and a steaming cup of hot chocolate, while she went into the study to put off another day's appointments. Darragh wondered how much longer she thought she could keep doing that, particularly as Patrick had not been heard from since yesterday afternoon.

Surely, by now, he would have told his wife, Kerry, that Ren was back and Kiva was hiding him?

Surely one of the people in her entourage would become suspicious of her efforts to keep them away?

Darragh knew it was time to leave. He'd learned what he needed to know and he was living here on borrowed time. He needed to get out of this alarmingly comfortable armchair, positioned so perfectly to catch the morning sun, and escape this place while Kiva was occupied with her calls. He needed to get back to Jack's house next door, find Sorcha, and leave this place forever. He had to get back to the Castle Golf Club with Sorcha so that when Ciarán opened the rift from the other side, he'd be there to take advantage of it.

Darragh rubbed his eyes. The warmth of the room, the ankle pain and the lingering lethargy from Kiva's painkillers made it easier to ponder a decision than act upon it. He drifted off, lulled by the sun, the inexplicable excitement of the audience watching a chubby talk-show hostess and her equally chubby guest discuss the most effective strategies they used for sustained weight-loss.

A shout and a shattering of glass woke him abruptly. Somewhere in the house he could hear Kiva screaming. There were other shouts, too. Male. Gruff and threatening.

Darragh scrambled out of the armchair, rubbing his eyes with the heel of his palms, trying to clear the wool from his mind. He cried out involuntarily as he shifted his weight onto his injured ankle. Seconds later the room was full of dark-uniformed men carrying short, ugly weapons that painted a spray of red dots across his chest and face. They were yelling at him to get down. Darragh wasn't standing on anything, so he wasn't sure what they wanted, but then one of them yelled at him to get on his knees. Darragh complied, still confused.

As soon as his knees hit the floor they were on him. He was pushed flat on his face, his arms jerked behind his back and secured with cold metal handcuffs. He cried out again when something was tightened around his bandaged ankle. The shouts kept on from other more distant rooms in the house - men shouting "clear!" against a background of Kiva screaming at them to leave her son alone. They dragged Darragh upright and he discovered he was shackled hand and foot. The short chains around his ankles allowed him only the shortest steps.

He hadn't uttered a word, or had time to defend himself. These warriors of Rónán's realm were exceptionally good at this, he realized. He was amazed that Brogan and Niamh had extracted his brother from their custody. Could they achieve the same feat a second time?

Another man, this one not wearing the dark uniform with ERU emblazoned across the back, walked in. Even if Darragh hadn't known him from Rónán's memories, he would have known him.

This was the detective Sorcha had knocked out in the car. The one who had captured Rónán at St Christopher's.

He looked inordinately pleased with himself when he entered the living room to find Darragh already in chains.

This will be interesting, Darragh thought. *This man knows I'm not Ren Kavanaugh.*

Pete studied Darragh for a moment, and then turned him around. He grabbed his hands and forced Darragh's palms open for a moment and then turned him back around and looked him in the eye.

"You're the other one," he said.

Darragh nodded. If this man was prepared to admit he wasn't Ren Kavanaugh, then surely he must order his release?

Even knowing he hadn't captured the right twin, it seemed he wasn't going to admit it here. He simply eyed Darragh up and down for a moment and said, "Chelan Aquarius Kavanaugh, you're under arrest for-"

"Jesus wept! Look at that!"

Everybody in the crowded living room turned toward the ERU officer who had spoken so out of turn.

The man had lifted his goggles and was staring at the large, flat screen TV hanging on the wall over the ornamental fireplace. Darragh and Pete turned with everyone else, just in time to see a large commercial airliner flying into the side of an impossibly tall building, somewhere on the other side of the world.

PART TWO

CHAPTER 23

"It is a necklace fit for a queen, *Prionsa*."

From her amethyst prison, Brydie snorted at that suggestion, and at Prince Torcán, who was bending over the table with an idiotic smile on his face, looking at the Indian-styled gem-encrusted collar. Staring into the stolen jewel in which the *djinni*, Jamaspa, had magically trapped Brydie.

The collar was intended for Anwen. It was - at Anwen's suggestion - going to be Torcán's wedding gift to his bride. Or so the goldsmith had informed his wife as they chatted in his workroom while he beat the metal into submission, and threaded the scores of polished stones onto fine gold wire.

Typical of Torcán, Brydie thought, *to give his betrothed something fashioned from a stolen gem to cover up the disappearance of one of his mother's court maidens.* And to give her something so pretentious.

Even Álmhath didn't swan about all day in a crown, and she was a queen.

It augured much for the future of their marriage. A gift fashioned from deception.

"You have done well, Master Goldsmith," Torcán said, placing the collar back on the bench. Brydie was knocked off her feet by the careless way he dropped it. She scrambled upright, cursing Torcán. Not that it did any good. He couldn't hear or see her any more than the goldsmith who'd been working on the collar for days could see, or his wife, or even his large black hound who sniffed around the jewel a few times to see if it was edible, scaring the life of out Brydie as his massive pink tongue enveloped the stone.

That had been a close call. It was bad enough being stuck in here, doomed to see and hear everything happening on the outside but unable to take part. How much worse could life become if she was fated to spend the rest of her days stuck in a dog's lower intestine?

Fortunately, the goldsmith had returned to his workshop and shooed the dog away, saving Brydie before she had a chance to find out, but the incident made her weep. She had not seen Jamaspa for days, not since the day Colmán had handed over the brooch to Anwen and Torcán. She concluded that the *djinni* didn't know where she was. He knew where to find her when the jewel was set in Marcroy's brooch, which she had left in Darragh of the Undivided's bedchamber. But now that the stone had been removed, the gold melted down and the jewel set in an entirely different piece - Jamaspa may never find her again.

If he couldn't find her, how could he release her from this purple-tinted prison? She was stranded. The jewel's magic meant she wouldn't age or need sleep or food or anything like it, suspended in her own private bubble of the present, as she was. And that meant she might be here for eternity.

Brydie was plunged back into darkness as the goldsmith and Torcán settled on the price for the necklace. Soon she was lifted up again and placed, much more gently, into a dark, beautifully embroidered bag. It was soft and thick and even through her purple-tinted lens, seemed a rich shade of emerald green. Bracing herself for an uncomfortable trip to the palace - on horseback - Brydie didn't waste a single moment wishing she were Anwen. Torcán's wife would have to put up with Torcán for one thing, but with succession among the Celts often through the distaff line, even the prospect of one day becoming queen was by no means certain.

Trapped in the darkness of the soft green velvet bag, Brydie could only wait until Torcán decided to give his betrothed her gift. That could be days. Anwen and Torcán were not due to be married until *Lughnasadh*. If Torcán was planning to Anwen on their wedding day, Brydie could be stuck in this smothering darkness for weeks.

Brydie had forgotten, however, that Torcán did little his mother didn't either directly order, or approve. He took the necklace straight from the goldsmith's shop to his mother's private chamber in Temair and showed off his prize.

"It's rather... ostentatious, don't you think?" Álmhath remarked when Torcán unveiled the necklace for his mother's approval.

"Do you think so?" Torcán asked. "The goldsmith tells me they're all the rage among brides in the Gupta Empire."

Álmhath frowned at her son. "This is not the Gupta Empire, Torcán. Next you'll be suggesting I pay Anwen's family a ridiculous dowry like the maharajahs do."

"Lucky she doesn't have a family, then," her son pointed out.

Although she was out of Brydie's line of sight, the queen sounded concerned. "Are you sure this is a good idea?

"Anwen said we must disguise the jewel in another setting," Torcán reminded her, a little testily. "The thing is the size of a pigeon egg. The only way it won't stick out like a beacon is if it's buried among enough other gems for it not to draw attention to itself."

The queen snorted at that. "I can hear a greedy jeweller talking there. Master Goldsmith must have seen you coming."

Torcán did not appreciate his mother's derision. He turned to her impatiently, tossing the necklace onto the table, again knocking Brydie off her feet. "If you thought this was such a ridiculous idea, why go along with it? Why not just toss the jewel away, Mother, and be rid of it? That seems to me a far safer thing to do than risk Marcroy recognising the gem from the brooch he gave Brydie and demanding to know what happened to its former owner."

For once, Brydie found herself agreeing with Torcán. He was absolutely right. She climbed to her feet thinking it was stupid of Anwen to insist on keeping the gem if the queen was going to pretend she had no knowledge of Brydie's whereabouts. She'd have been better ordering Torcán to toss it into the sea to be certain it could never be found again.

Brydie was extremely grateful Anwen hadn't doomed her to an eternity trapped inside the jewel, lost and with no hope of rescue. But the queen of the Celts was nobody's fool. Nor was she so strapped for material wealth that one amethyst - no matter how large or well-polished - would make the slightest difference to her one way or another...

Unless Anwen knows I'm here, Brydie thought, sinking to the floor, letting that awful thought fester as Torcán and his mother argued on about the tasteless ostentation of Torcán's wedding gift to his bride.

Does she know? How could she?

Álmhath was not a greedy woman. She obviously didn't covet the gem for herself, and it had been Anwen's suggestion to set the stone into something she could wear. But why not hide it somewhere safe and out of sight?

There were a thousand things Álmhath could have done with the amethyst rather than allow Anwen to flaunt it.

Maybe that's what she's doing, Brydie wondered. *She's not trying to hide the jewel because she's sending Marcroy a message.*

It was all too confusing. There seemed no rhyme or reason to the world these days. Not since Álmhath had tapped her on the shoulder in the sacred grove and told her *Danú* had a task for her.

Her job had been to seduce Darragh of the Undivided. She'd been sent to steal his seed. His bloodline was so precious that Álmhath and the

Matrarchaí were afraid they would lose it when the pwer of the Undivided was stripped from RónánDarragh at *Lughnasadh* and passed on to the new twins Marcroy had found. Both Darragh and his missing brother would die that day and their line would be lost forever.

Brydie glanced down at her belly, wondering if she'd achieved her aim. Was there a child there, waiting to be born? There was no way to tell. While she was trapped in this jewel, nothing would change, nothing would grow, no child - even if one had been conceived - would come of her union with Darragh of the Undivided.

How long until *Lughnasadh*? It was hard to keep track of time, but Brydie thought it might be ten days or so until then. Even if she hadn't found a way out of her jewelled prison by the Autumn equinox, she hoped that when Darragh returned, he would find a way to stop the transfer happening. She'd liked the Druid prince - she liked him much more than she was expecting to like a young man she'd been ordered to sleep with for the express purpose of falling pregnant. He was smart and funny and - once he got over his first impulse to strangle her for being Álmhath's spy - had a healthy lack of respect for his own importance. That had surprised Brydie most of all, because the Undivided were unique and raised to know it. She'd expected him to be much more full of himself.

"Nobody will be paying attention to Anwen anyway," Torcán complained. The argument with his mother about the wedding necklace still raged in the background. "Not with the investiture of the Undivided heirs happening on the same day. I'm quite peeved about that, by the way. It should be our day."

Álmhath rolled her eyes. "You are a fool, Torcán," she snapped.

"Well, maybe we'll get lucky," her son replied. "I hear reports from *Sí an Bhrú* that nobody has seen Darragh for days. Perhaps the ceremony is keeping him away? Perhaps running away is his way of preventing the transfer from taking place? I mean, it's a cowardly course of action, to be sure, but I suppose if he's not prepared to die for his people-"

"It won't matter," Álmhath cut in. "Marcroy assures me the transfer will take place whether Darragh is there or not."

"Can he do that?" Torcán asked in surprise.

"The *Daoine sídhe* can do anything, it seems," the queen informed her son with a scowl. "I have asked that the ceremony be delayed until Darragh is here, so we can witness the transfer ourselves and be satisfied that it happens as planned. But I have been denied."

"Why?" Torcán asked, looking confused. "There are Undivided heirs now. Surely it makes sense to give them time to settle into their new roles before burdening them with all that power. And they're children, aren't they? Small children, at that. Aren't we sick of letting children sit on the Undivided throne?"

Álmhath nodded. "There are many Druids chafing under the ministrations of a divided Undivided. There are others who see a chance to grab power with two more Undivided twins requiring a regency, rather than Darragh who appears to be developing opinions of his own. There are Partitionists aplenty out there, too, who hope the whole system will fall apart if the power transfer fails, and a large number of *Tuatha Dé Danann* hoping for the same thing, I suspect, although allegiance to their oath to protect the Treaty of *Tír Na nÓg* doesn't allow them to admit it."

Torcán perked up as he realized what his mother was saying. "But if the transfer fails, then the Druids would lose their magic, yes?"

"Not while RónánDarragh live," the queen said. "But if anything happened to them before new heirs were found, then yes... that would be the end of the Druids and their magic."

"But that's a good thing, isn't it? I mean... it would devastate them. The Druids would lose their power over us if they didn't control the magic."

"And we will be destroyed along with them," Álmhath reminded him. "Once the *Tuatha* are no longer compelled to share their power with us, we will no longer be their allies. Worse, there will be an imbalance of power that will only be resolved when one of our races is destroyed. Think of that, my son, before you get too excited about losing the unbroken line of the Undivided."

Torcán pulled a face. "Pity there's not a way to have *Tuatha Dé Danann* magic without having to grovel to the *Tuatha Dé Danann*."

"Maybe there is," the queen said cryptically.

Brydie wasn't sure if Torcán appreciated what his mother was telling him, but she did. This power transfer taking place on *Lughnasadh* with one and perhaps both of the Undivided missing might fail, and if it did, then the Treaty of *Tír Na nÓg* would be void and that could mean more than the end of the Druids.

Could there be a way to circumvent the treaty, and the obligations that went with it, yet still retain the magic?

Is that what the *Matrarchaí* was working toward?

Is that why you sent me to Darragh's bed, Álmhath?

It was all very intriguing, Brydie decided, although the irony of having such a bird's-eye view of the inner circle of Álmhath's court only because she had been cursed while carrying out the orders of her queen was not lost on Brydie.

She sat down and crossed her legs. If she was going to witness the schemes and manoeuvrings of Álmhath's court she might as well get comfortable.

There was, after all, nothing else for her to do.

CHAPTER 24

As she lay in wait for Warren to appear in the backyard of his home bordering the Castle Golf Club, Sorcha pondered the matter of whether or not to thank the goddess for her bounty. Had she been hiding in this tree, waiting for a hind or hare to happen along, she would not have questioned the need to thank the goddess. But she wasn't going to kill Warren for food so there was no point in thanking *Danú* for her bounty. She was not going to kill him in battle, so there would be nothing noble or heroic about his death. She would kill him for one reason only - to fulfil her oath to Ciarán to protect Rónán of the Undivided - difficult now that Rónán was no longer even in this realm, but still needed her protection.

Rónán was gone, but Darragh remained. The people of this realm would not understand that Darragh was not his brother and Rónán's crimes would be blamed on him. If he were caught in this realm, he would be punished for them.

Sorcha did not share Darragh's blind faith in his twin. The Rónán she had observed was a conflicted, confused and spoiled young man. Having been in the realm where he was raised for almost a week now, Sorcha was beginning to understand how he got that way, but she wasn't convinced he was as reliable or as honorable as Darragh believed. If he was, they would be gone from here by now. If Rónán was even half the man his brother believed him to be, why hadn't he opened a rift for them immediately after the other rift had closed so unexpectedly? Or ordered Ciarán to do it for him, if he didn't know how?

For that matter, if Ciarán was able to open a rift, why hadn't he done it himself? He didn't need Rónán's permission. He was strong enough, and had the required jewel to open it. There was no reason for him not to do it.

Rónán was alive, obviously. Darragh still lived, which meant somewhere in their own realm, Rónán was still drawing breath. Was he incapacitated in some way? A prisoner, perhaps? Was Ciarán also a prisoner?

Had Rónán taken the opportunity to seize the power of the Undivided for himself?

Eighty-five years had taught Sorcha to believe the worst of men, rather than be disappointed by expecting them to do the right thing. She had no way of knowing if she and Darragh had been stranded here because of fair deeds or foul, so she had to do the only thing she could. Protect Rónán and his brother, Darragh, until she knew for certain - one way or another - that Rónán had betrayed her.

To do that, she needed to act. She needed to eliminate all threats to the young men she had sworn to protect.

Right now, that meant killing the man whose car they had stolen from the Castle Golf Club when they arrived in this realm. The man in whose house they had sheltered. The man who could identify Jack O'Righin as the one who had aided them in their quest to find Hayley Boyle, and through him, lead the authorities to Darragh.

And if it turned out that in their own reality, Rónán had betrayed her and his brother? Well, she would take care of that problem when she got home.

If he *had* betrayed them, Rónán would regret it someday soon. Sorcha would see to that.

Sorcha shifted a little in her perch. The bark of the tree pressed into her face, making it itch a little. It annoyed her that she was itching. There was a time she could have lay along a branch, waiting for her quarry like this for days without being bothered in the slightest, but since coming to this world, she seemed to be losing her battle fitness. Her joints ached. Her muscles felt as if they were wasting. In the chilly darkness, as she watched Warren and his family through the window having dinner in the kitchen of their home, she wondered whether it was the polluted air in this reality or the lack of magic making her feel so... old.

Warren and his family were seated at the counter eating food out of cardboard containers with chopsticks, laughing at something on the wall-mounted television that was out of Sorcha's line of sight. She knew they were watching the television. Their attention was locked on that corner of the room and the reflected flickering light from the screen painted interesting shadows on the windows. His wife was a tall, thin woman, his daughter in the first blush of womanhood and his son - a sullen young man with unnaturally black hair - was more interested in some device he was holding in his hands, than in the rest of the family.

Further along the street, the lights were coming on in the neighbouring houses, where other families were settling down for their evening meal. Behind Sorcha lay the vast dark expanse of the golf course, silent and pristine here at this end of the course away from the carnage Rónán and his companions had wreaked a couple of nights ago. Even the lights from the clubhouse were not visible from here. In the houses either side of Warren's house, there were no lights on upstairs yet, which meant it was likely there was nobody in those rooms overlooking this house, and therefore nobody looking down into Warren's backyard.

Sorcha turned back to study the family. She hoped she wouldn't have to kill them all. Warren was the only one she needed to silence, perhaps the wife if he'd said anything to her. Sorcha was guessing he hadn't. There seemed to be little or no tension between the couple. She would have expected them to behaving in a rather more strained and uneasy manner, if he'd just confessed he'd allowed a naked *Beansídhe* to take his car, sleep in his home, harboured a wanted man and spent an afternoon in a massage parlour with an infamous terrorist.

She needed Warren to come out into the yard, although she was not sure how she was going to coax him out of the house. If he didn't come out soon, she would have to go in after him. Every time the telephone rang, it might somebody asking about his car. Without her even knowing about it, someone might be arriving any moment at the front door, to ask Warren what he knew about the people who had stolen his car. Time was Sorcha's enemy and she knew she had to act soon, or not at all.

If it came to "not at all" then everything would be lost.

But just as she was ready to despair that Warren was never going to leave the house, he climbed to his feet and tossed his cardboard food containers into a drawstring plastic bag that his wife had retrieved from a container in the corner with a lid that cleverly opened when she pressed on a pedal at the base. His wife tied the bag off and handed it to her husband. With a grimace, Warren pushed himself off his seat and headed for the back door.

Finally! Sorcha swung forward and lowered herself silently to the ground. She landed and dropped into a crouch, stunned by how much her knees jarred on impact. She bit back a cry of surprised pain, hoping her stillness and the shadows under the tree would render her invisible. Warren opened the door, closed it and walked to a tall plastic bin on wheels lined up against the back wall of the house.

Sorcha shadowed him, easing the long-bladed kitchen carving knife from the side of her boot. She'd found the weapon in Jack's kitchen drawer, and was impressed by the strength of the metal and the keenness of the blade. One slice would be all it needed to slit Warren's throat.

Warren disposed of the plastic bag then glanced over his shoulder toward the kitchen, checking he was unobserved. Curious, Sorcha waited for a moment as he moved out of the light of the kitchen windows and leaned against the wall. He reached into his pocket and pulled out a pack of cigarettes. He took a cigarette from the pack and a match flared, lighting his face momentarily.

His wife doesn't know he does this, Sorcha realized, smiling to herself. Warren had more than his fair share of guilty secrets.

He drew on the cigarette, until the tip glowed red, and sighed contentedly, leaned back and closed his eyes as he inhaled the smoke.

That was the chance Sorcha was waiting for. Silent as the smoke curling from the tip of his cigarette, she ran the short distance from the shadow of the tree to the shadow of the house where Warren was enjoying his guilty pleasure. She was on him before he opened his eyes, not giving him a chance to cry out before she slashed the blade across his prominent Adam's apple. A spray of warm blood drenched Sorcha as she caught the body and quietly eased it to the ground so he made no noise when he fell. The cigarette hissed, and was extinguished. Warren's eyes were wide with shock and recognition as he realized who it was who had attacked him and a moment later, the life in his eyes was extinguished.

Sorcha glanced over her shoulder toward the kitchen. Nothing was amiss. Warren's wife was moving about, the children out of sight from this angle. Warren probably hadn't been gone long enough for his wife to notice he was missing.

It was time to be gone from here, but Sorcha was soaked in Warren's blood. She could not move about in this realm like that. She quickly peeled off the clothes she was wearing until she was naked, ignoring the bitter chill of the evening. She dropped the clothes beside the body, wondering what the authorities would make of them, given they had been stolen from his son's wardrobe. She fled, at a crouching run, towards the house next door. There was washing on the clothesline and an ornamental fishpond in the yard next door where she could wash off the blood. She had to be quick as someone might come looking for Warren any minute. If she was discovered, there was no explanation she could offer. She could say nothing that wouldn't make things infinitely worse.

The clothes from the house next door were too big for her, but they would have to do. The dress she stole was floral and meant for someone much older, and there'd been a ratty knitted cardigan on the line next to the dress, so she took that against the chill, even though it was already damp with the falling dew. She slipped out of the yard and down the driveway of the next house where she emerged onto the street, just to in time to hear a high-pitched scream of horror as someone - Warren's wife or daughter - discovered the body.

Danú take your soul, Warren, she prayed silently as she walked away from the house as if nothing was amiss. *May your sacrifice be worthy of the cost. May Arawn find you a cozy place in hell.*

Warren was taken care of. Now Sorcha needed to make certain Darragh returned home, so that his death was not wasted.

CHAPTER 25

If it had been up to some of Pete's older colleagues in the NBCI, a half an hour alone in a small room with Ren Kavanaugh's twin would have given them all the information they needed. Pete didn't actually disagree with that. He was quite sure someone like old Frank Murphy, the longest serving member of the squad, would have emerged with the location of Hayley Boyle in no time at all, if nobody was really worried about the condition the boy would be in, once he had it.

Fortunately for the young man in question, there were rules against that sort of thing, and for anybody who'd bothered to look at the stats, they knew it didn't work anyway. There would be no police brutality in Brendá Duggan's squad. Not only had she forbidden Frank Murphy and everyone else - including Pete - to question the boy, she'd brought in a civilian to do it for them. One Dr

Murray Symes, the shrink who'd been treating Ren for most of his teens.

The same guy who ran Hayley Boyle down in the first place.

Frank shook his head and muttered to himself about the foolishness of it all. Pete was in complete agreement - the first time he and Frank had ever agreed on anything. He was livid. It was, to his mind, the stupidest idea he'd ever heard of.

"Symes knows Ren Kavanaugh intimately," Brendá Duggan informed Pete when he charged into her office to object.

"That kid is *not* Ren Kavanaugh," Pete said.

"You can't prove he isn't, Pete."

"The tattoo is on the wrong hand."

"His mother swears that boy is her son. I'm afraid her opinion trumps your concussion."

Pete was fighting a losing battle on that point, so he abandoned it for the moment. "You're not seriously going to let Symes talk to the kid, are you? You're handing them an insanity plea on a platter."

Duggan didn't seem to be in the mood to discuss it. "Hayley Boyle has been missing for five days. You know the stats, Pete. If we don't find her soon we're not going to find her at all. In case you hadn't noticed, the world is going to hell in a hand basket right about now. I'm going to lose half my manpower to anti-terrorist units by the end of the day. I've already had the commissioner on the phone about it. We don't have the time to coax the truth out this kid, and I'm not ready to let Frank Murphy beat it out of him. Symes can tell when the boy is lying. He knows how to push the kid's buttons. He'll get the truth faster than we will and time is of the essence."

"How can he be impartial? Is it even legal? Does Ren's mother know about this? And what about her lawyer? Surely she isn't going to allow it?"

"His mother *suggested* it," Duggan told him. "Can't say I blame her, either. Kiva Kavanaugh is in damage control. If Hayley Boyle turns up dead, we could go her as an accessory after the fact for hiding the boy. She's in the mood to be very cooperative, and I'm not going to look a gift horse in the mouth."

"If you want him to talk to a shrink, why not call Annad in?"

"I tried," Brendá said. "He's got the flu. Symes is the best we can do on short notice."

Pete shook his head in disbelief, but he wasn't giving up. "Can I sit in on the interrogation?"

"Only if you promise to let Symes take the lead," Duggan said. "And that you don't pick a fight with Eunice Ravenel."

Pete sighed, a little bothered Duggan knew him that well. "I'll be good."

"You'd better be," Duggan warned. "Nobody on this Earth gives a rat's arse about what some actress's kid is up to because of what's happening in New York, or else we'd be knee deep in reporters right now. Even your brother has abandoned us. So let's make what little time we have count. I want Hayley Boyle home or... her fate determined."

"Do you think she's already dead?" Pete asked.

Duggan shrugged. "It's up to you and Symes to find out."

The boy everyone but Pete thought was Ren Kavanaugh sat in the interview room with his lawyer, the inimitable Eunice Ravenel. Pete observed them for a time through the one-way mirror in the observation room. The young man sat

235

at the table, his hands clasped together on the desk in front of him. He was still dressed as they'd found him in Kiva Kavanaugh's house, in jeans, a leather jacket and a tooled-leather Western style boot. His other foot was bandaged - apparently he sprained it jumping out of a moving car escaping the henchmen of the drug lord, Dominic O'Hara - if you believed his mother.

Eunice was wearing a severe black suit and heels that were so tall, slender and dangerous-looking, Pete was surprised she was allowed to wear them in an interrogation room. She was pacing the room with a sharp clack-clack of her stilettos.

"Are you Mr Doherty?"

Pete turned to find a tall, distinguished, grey-haired man wearing a dark suit and visitor's badge, standing at the entrance to the observation room. "Dr Symes?"

The man nodded and stepped into the room. He looked into the interrogation room for a moment, studying the boy.

"Has he said anything yet?"

"Not to us," Pete said. "He was lawyered up before he even got here."

"I would prefer to talk to him without her there."

"Yeah... good luck with that."

Symes shrugged. Pete figured that he'd known, even before he asked, that they were already skating around the edges of acceptable police practice. Getting rid of a minor's legal representation while he was being interrogated wasn't going to happen, no matter how special and clever Symes imagined himself to be.

"What did he say when you arrested him?"

"Not much of anything," Pete said. "Nobody did, really. Right about when we stormed the house, that plane hit the World Trade Centre in New York. I don't think anybody was paying much attention to the what the kid was saying for a while there."

Symes's eyes narrowed with interest. "What was Ren's reaction?"

"To the plane hitting the building?" Pete had to stop and think for a moment. Like the rest of the world, he was still trying to come grips with the spectacular scope of the attack himself. "I dunno... gobsmacked I think. Like the rest of us."

The psychiatrist nodded, but Pete didn't think that was because he'd gained any insight into the boy's behaviour. It was just what he did to make it seem that he was pondering deep thoughts. "You must allow me to do the talking," Symes said, turning from the window to look at Pete. "Ren is a troubled young man, but he has an intelligent and clever mind. He has also been in therapy for a number of years and understands the process. He will see a trap coming if you try to ambush him."

Pete threw his hands up. "Boss said to let you ask the questions," he said. "I'm just here to make sure you don't try to beat a confession out of him."

Symes scowled at that, apparently not appreciating Pete's sense of humour. "Shall we begin?"

"Why don't we?" Pete said.

"Hello, Ren," Murray Symes said, as he stepped into the interrogation room.

The boy looked up at the psychiatrist blankly for a moment, as if he didn't know who he was, confirming Pete's belief that this wasn't Ren Kavanaugh, but his identical twin. Ren would have had an immediate reaction to the appearance of his shrink. This boy stared at Symes for a moment or two and then nodded, as if he'd worked out whom it was he was dealing with. "Dr Murray Symes."

"I believe you know Pete Doherty."

The boy looked up at him and nodded.

"I wish to reiterate my objection to this," Eunice announced, before she could be included in the introductions.

"Noted and fallen on deaf ears," Pete told her, in agreement with Ren's lawyer for once. "His mother has given her permission and waived his doctor-patient privilege. You'll probably have awesome grounds for appeal when this goes to court, Counsellor, but right now, there's nothing either of us can do to stop it."

Murray took the seat opposite the boy, leaving Pete to sit opposite Eunice next to the recording equipment. He reached across, pressed record and glanced at his watch. "Interrogation of suspect believed to be Chelan Aquarius Kavanaugh," he said, for the benefit of the recording. "Time is six thirty eight pm, September eleven, two thousand one. Present are Dr Murray Symes, Ms Eunice Ravenel, Detective-Sargeant Peter Doherty and the suspect." He nodded to Symes once he was done. "He's all yours."

Murray had been studying the boy closely while Pete took care of the recording equipment. Eunice glowered at both of them. Ren... or rather the boy everyone *thought* was Ren, seemed unnaturally calm and unbothered by the situation.

"How have you been, Ren?"

Wow... ten years of med school and that's the best he can come up with?

"My name is not Ren," the young man replied. "I am Darragh."

I knew it! "Darragh who?" Pete asked, before he could stop himself.

"I am Darragh of the Undivided," he replied calmly.

"Can I speak to Ren?" Symes asked, throwing Pete a warning look.

Darragh shrugged. "I suppose. If you can locate him. I've not had any luck getting through to him myself, but if you have technology in this realm which will allow it, I would appreciate a chance to speak with him also."

The answer seemed to surprise Symes. "Technology?"

"You have no magic here," Darragh said, as if such a glaringly obvious fact didn't need stating. "How else would you accomplish it?"

"So you think it's going to take magic to allow us to speak to Ren?"

"More than you have, I'm afraid," he agreed.

"When did Darragh arrive?" Symes asked carefully. Pete wanted to scream at him. He could see where this was going. Symes obviously thought the kid had developed a multiple personality disorder, when in fact he was telling the cold hard truth. The bullshit about magic might be the boy trying to mess with their heads, but this was no manifestation of Ren Kavanaugh's troubled psyche. This was a different kid.

"I came through the rift with Rónán last Wednesday."

"The rift?"

"It's how we cross dimensions. I understand that's not a concept you are familiar with in this reality."

Symes laced his fingers together on the table in front of him thoughtfully. "So... you... Darragh... come from another reality? Is that what you're saying?"

"Yes."

"And where is Ren now?"

"He's back in our reality, I suppose. That's where we were headed when your Gardaí attacked us."

"Us being...?" Symes prompted.

"Rónán and me. Sorcha, of course, and his friend Hayley."

"He's sent her away from her family, then," Symes pointed out.

"To restore her sight," Darragh reminded him. "There is a cost for every action, Doctor. I believe that is a law in this realm, as well as mine."

"So... what's this other *realm* like?" Symes asked. "The one where you come from?"

Darragh paused before answering. "I'm not sure I can do it justice by describing it," he said, his eyes flickering up and to the right.

Symes's mouth flashed the briefest smiles, as Darragh stumbled over a description of his imaginary world. Pete was watching him closely. His body language suggested he was remembering, rather than lying. Either this kid was a consummate liar, or he really believed what he was telling them.

"The biggest difference would be the magic, I think."

"I see," Symes said, steepling his fingers. He was easier to read than the kid. The shrink was puzzled now. "So the story you told Patrick about Hayley being a hostage. Was that a lie?"

"Yes."

Still watching him closely, Pete marvelled at how completely the boy believed what he was telling them.

"Why?" Symes asked. "Because you just couldn't bring yourself to tell him you'd sent your cousin through to another reality to be healed?"

"Wasn't there another woman with you?" Pete asked, even knowing he shouldn't. But Symes was wasting time. This kid didn't have a personality disorder. He had a twin brother.

"Do you mean Trása?" Darragh shrugged. "Given the trouble she has caused recently, I would hesitate to call her a friend."

"I mean Sorcha."

"She went through the rift with Ren and Hayley," Darragh said.

"And they left you behind?"

"Could we stop for a moment, Detective?" Symes asked tightly. "I'd like to have a word. In private."

"Interview suspended at six forty-eight," Pete said for the benefit of the tapes. He stood up and pointed at the door. "After you."

"You were instructed not to say anything!" Symes informed Pete as soon as they stepped into the hall and the interrogation room door snicked shut.

"You were instructed to make him to tell us where Hayley Boyle is," Pete reminded him. "Not lay the groundwork for your next published paper on multiple personality disorders."

"Excuse me?" Symes gasped, looking horrified that anybody would dare speak to him in such a manner.

"He's not pretending to be somebody el-"

"No, he *believes* he is somebody else," Symes cut in. "Or at least, I'm here to establish if he truly believes it, if you would stop interrupting long enough to let me get a word in."

"He believes it, because he *is* someone else," Pete insisted. "That tattoo is on the wrong hand."

Symes shook his head. "That doesn't prove anything. The tattoo could easily have been on his right hand all along, and people not remember it correctly. If you'd studied psychology at all, young man, you'd know how unreliable eye-witness testimony is because of the human capacity for self-delusion."

"Don't worry, Doc," he shot back, wondering if it was worth pointing out that he *had* studied psychology. He had a Masters in Criminology from Cambridge, but decided it wasn't worth it. Symes would still think he knew best, no matter what Pete had studied. "You're giving me a grand lesson in the human capacity for self-delusion right now."

Symes glared at Pete. "If you cannot be silent in there, Mr Doherty, I will insist Inspector Duggan has you removed."

"And if you don't get anything useful out of that kid in the next hour," Pete replied, "I'll have you arrested for obstructing justice."

Pete was fairly certain he couldn't do that, but he was determined to get the last word in, so he turned and opened the door before Symes could respond. He took his seat at the table, flicked on the recording equipment and leaned into the mike, "Interview resumed at six fifty-one."

"So... *Darragh*," Symes asked, "how long have you been in this... reality?" He spoke to the boy carefully and with an air of understanding and tolerance that made Pete want to scream. It was clear Symes believed he was pandering to Ren's delusion. Pete didn't buy this nonsense about jumping through a rift from another reality, any more than Symes did, but he was damned sure Symes wasn't talking to Ren Kavanaugh.

"I told you, we came through the rift with Rónán last Wednesday."

"And this... other world you have been in... that's where Ren has been hiding all this time?"

Darragh nodded. "Of course."

"You... or rather Ren, told his mother he'd been kidnapped by men associated with Dominic O'Hara. You told her you were injured escaping him."

"You don't have to answer that, Ren," Eunice advised.

"Rónán's mother did not strike me as someone who could deal with the truth," Darragh replied, ignoring her advice. "I told Kiva Kavanaugh what she wanted to hear. Or what she wanted to believe. I was trying to be nice to her."

"How is that nice?"

"It will make the separation easier for her to bear."

"What separation? Do you mean separation from you?"

"From Rónán," Darragh corrected, shaking his head. "Once I return to my realm, we will not be back."

"Who is Rónán?" Pete asked.

"The young man you know as Ren," Darragh explained patiently. "In the realm where he belongs, he is Rónán."

"You said you were trying to be nice. Is that how you feel about your mother? That you should be nice to her?"

Darragh looked at him for a moment, a little confused. "I barely remember her."

"You spoke to her only an hour or two ago," Eunice reminded him. Even she seemed to be getting a little impatient with his insistence that he wasn't Ren.

He turned to Eunice, shaking his head. "My mother was the Druidess, Sybille of Aquitania."

"A Druidess?" Symes asked in an even voice. If he was surprised by Darragh's answer, he was too experienced to let it show.

"Of course."

"This is your mother from the *other* reality?"

Darragh looked at Symes with great concern. "Obviously. Am I not explaining this clearly enough for you, Doctor?"

Pete bit back a smile at Darragh's question and the shrink's thinning lips, which gave away more than Symes imagined. The good doctor might claim to have intimate knowledge of what made Ren Kavanaugh tick, but this kid was pretty adept at pushing his buttons, too.

"And this *realm*? This is the other reality you took Hayley to?"

Darragh nodded. "Rónán was hopeful magical healing might prevail where your technology had failed her."

Pete was watching Darragh closely for some tiny giveaway tic or movement that might prove useful, but the boy was calm and undaunted by his surroundings. He recalled the last time he'd interviewed Ren. The kid had been a real smart-arse - full of attitude and teenage rebellion. This kid was the opposite. He was calm and collected, even cooperative - except for the bullshit story he was pedalling about coming from an alternate reality.

"My brother was well-intentioned, Doctor. He meant her no harm."

"I knew it!" Pete exclaimed, unable to contain himself. "You're Ren's twin brother, aren't you?"

Darragh nodded calmly and looked Pete straight in the eye. "Why do you sound so surprised, sir? You have seen us together."

"Thank you!" Pete cried in relief, glad people would stop accusing him of seeing double. Now the kid had confirmed his story. He glanced over his shoulder at the one-way mirror, behind which he was fairly certain Brendá Duggan was watching the proceedings. "So you're not Ren Kavanaugh, are you?"

"No, of course not."

"And your brother's tattoo?"

"Is on the opposite hand to mine," Darragh said, as if such a thing were so obvious there was no need to mention it.

"Detective... please..." Symes began, but Pete ignored him. The shrink had been brought in to interrogate Ren Kavanaugh, and this wasn't Ren Kavanaugh.

"Do you know where Hayley Boyle is?"

"I told you, she has been sent to my realm to have her sight healed."

"You planning to stick to that story?"

"It's the truth," Darragh said.

Pete stood up. "Then we're done here," he said. He glanced at his watch. "Interview ended at seven twenty-three pm."

"What are you going to do?" Eunice asked. She seemed even more unsettled about this than Symes.

"Not your problem, anymore, Counsellor," he said. "You heard him. He's not your client."

"That's absurd!" Symes exclaimed, not wanting to give up his multiple personality theory so easily. "Turn the recorder back on. We're not done here yet."

"Yes, we are," Pete said. "We're done. And so is Hayley Boyle, if I'm not mistaken." He turned to the boy, adding, "Isn't that right, Darragh?"

Without so much as a flicker of remorse, the young man looked Pete in the eye and nodded in agreement. "I fear you speak the truth, sir, because unless you know how to open a rift to another reality, nobody in this realm will ever see Rónán, Trása or Hayley Boyle again."

CHAPTER 26

Brydie spent much of the next few days in the dark. Although Anwen had thought up the plan to hide the jewel that once belonged to Marcroy, it was Torcán who had ostensibly commissioned the jewelled collar for his bride as a gift. Brydie supposed Torcán - having been given credit for the idea - was waiting for the right moment to present it to her, so she could wear it at the ceremony. Brydie couldn't see anything while the necklace was in the bag, but she could hear voices sometimes, but muffled, so she couldn't really make out what they were saying. She spent her time trying to decide why the queen had allowed Marcroy's gift to be reset into something her future daughter-in-law would wear.

She was no closer to working it out when she was unceremoniously knocked off her feet, as the necklace was shaken out of its velvet bag and

247

dumped on a table. A large eye loomed over her for a moment, studying the jewel, and then moved back a little to reveal Anwen staring down out her.

In a fit of childish pique, Brydie poked her tongue out. Then she laughed.

Anwen has no idea I'm trapped in here.

That set her pulling all kinds of silly faces at the court maiden. It was childish, but Brydie had nothing better to do with her time, and the idea that Anwen's own bridal gift was making fun of her amused Brydie no end.

A few moments later Brydie was knocked over again as Anwen raised the necklace up and tied it around her neck. Now, instead of having to look at Anwen, Brydie discovered she had an excellent view of the queen.

"Do you like it?" Álmhath asked her future daughter-in-law.

"Very much, *an Bhantiarna.*"

Brydie felt, rather than heard, Anwen reply. Resting on the young woman's upper chest, as she was, the sound reached her through touch as much as her ears, which gave Anwen's voice an interesting, and not unpleasant, timbre.

"Well, try to look surprised when Torcán gives it to you tonight at supper," the queen said. "He'll be disappointed if he knows you've seen it already."

The light vanished as Anwen's fingers covered the jewel, momentarily. "It's a great responsibility to be trusted with something so precious, *an Bhantiarna,*" Anwen said.

Responsibility? Brydie thought. *That's odd. Why would Anwen think the queen entrusting her with the necklace is a responsibility?* It wasn't as if it was a family heirloom. It had been finished only a few days ago. Anwen would know that, wouldn't she?

"Well, if you're right about what it contains, I can't think of anywhere safer to hide it out of Marcroy's reach. At least, not until you've found a way to release her." The queen took a seat at her table, shaking her head. "I should never have let Brydie accept a gift from Marcroy. I knew at the time it must be a trick of some kind."

Oh, by Danú , she knows!

Filled with elation and relief, Brydie stood up and pressed her face against the faceted surface of the jewel. *She knows. Someone knows I'm in here! How long before I'm free?* She began to wave madly at the queen, shouting as loud as she could, but Álmhath was too far away. Brydie wanted to weep with joy. She had so much to tell the queen... about Jamaspa, about Darragh...

Well, maybe not so much about Darragh, she decided.

Of course, the queen couldn't hear her cries, and perhaps it wouldn't have made a difference, even if she was peering into the amethyst with a magnifying glass. Nobody else had been able to see her trapped in here. Why should the queen be any different? She probably didn't realize Brydie could see and hear her.

The relief of simply knowing the queen knew she was trapped in this wretched stone, and was working toward her release was exhilarating. The news banished the slowly escalating despair Brydie was trying to overcome. She had hope. Eventually, the queen would find Jamaspa, or another of the *Djinn* and she would be freed. Maybe any one of the *sídhe* could release her. Maybe Marcroy himself could save her? He should take some responsibility for her predicament, after all. He was the one who had given her the brooch...

Wait... how does Álmhath know I'm in here? Brydie wondered.

No Druid had noticed the magicked jewel or the young woman trapped inside. Anwen hadn't said anything to Colmán when he handed over her belongings.

How does the queen of the Celts know something magical that the Druids don't?

She was still pondering that mystery, when another presented itself, even more unsettling than the idea that the queen of the Celts had some sort of unsuspected magical ability.

"It will be a tragedy," Anwen said, "if that bloodline is lost, after all we've done to nurture it."

Álmhath took a seat opposite her court maiden at the table, bringing Brydie much closer to the monarch, bringing her near enough to see the strain and weariness on her face. She smiled encouragingly. "We will prevail, my lady. All is not lost."

My lady? Why is Álmhath addressing Anwen as an equal?

"That's only because it's not *Lughnasadh* yet," Anwen replied, reaching for the wine decanter. "By *Danú*, how did Marcroy find those boys? We had them so well hidden."

"Not as well hidden as you thought," Álmhath said.

It struck Brydie as very strange that Álmhath was speaking to Anwen as though she was the courtier and Anwen the monarch. It was true Anwen was soon to become her daughter-in-law, but in private the balance of power seemed reversed. Álmhath was trying to reassure Anwen. In public, Anwen tended to behave like a spoiled brat who considered her betrothal to the queen's son licence to do whatever she pleased. Brydie thought she might understand the queen granting Anwen some leeway in private but this went beyond appeasement. If she hadn't known any better, Brydie could have sworn Anwen and not Álmhath was the woman in charge.

But the greater mystery was the boys the queen spoke of. Did she mean Broc and Cairbre, the Undivided heirs Marcroy announced he'd found, only a day after Brydie arrived in *Sí an Bhrú*? Those rare, psychically linked twins who would soon become the channel for *Tuatha* magic?

The Tuatha have found something they weren't meant to find. We are now in somewhat of a bind, because of it. That's what Álmhath said to Brydie in the wagon on the way to *Sí an Bhrú* and sent her to Darragh with instructions to fall pregnant. Is this what she meant by *something they weren't meant to find*? Had Marcroy Tarth located the Undivided heirs Anwen had hidden from him? From the Druids?

Why would she hide the twins?

Why would she confide in Álmhath about it?

And why was the queen of the Celts answering to one of her court maidens, even if that maiden was betrothed to her only son?

"The *Matrarchaí* have overcome worse, *an Bhantiarna*," Anwen said. "We will survive this."

The queen shook her head, unconvinced. "This is not the same as your people coming through the rift to stage an accident to hide the fact that the Undivided are long-lived," Álmhath said, shaking her head. "Or one of our midwives smothering a newborn with pointed ears, or cat-slit eyes."

Anwen rose to her feet, turning to the fire so Brydie could no longer see the queen. "The *Matrarchaí* have been developing this bloodline for two thousand years. There are those who believe we were only one generation short of achieving Partition in this realm."

Brydie couldn't see Álmhath's face, but she sounded concerned. "I know you don't want this to happen now, but I've never understood why. Is there a problem with the new twins? Are they inadequate in some way?"

Anwen shook her head. Brydie could tell by the way she was thrown this way and that by the movement of her neck. "BrocCairbre will be *adequate* as the Undivided, but that's the problem. They are not RónánDarragh." She sighed, her breath making the jewel tremble for a moment. "In this realm, it will set us back... assuming we can recover at all. I am not sure my sisters will be interested in pursuing Partition here, if the transfer goes ahead."

She turned to face Álmhath who had gone quite pale. Even through the tinted filter of the amethyst, Brydie could see it. "You can't mean to abandon us, my lady. Not now. Not after everything we've done for you."

The court maiden shrugged. Once again Brydie could tell simply by the direction she staggered as Anwen raised and lowered her shoulders.

"I'm still not convinced Marcroy - or perhaps one of the other Faerie races of this realm - doesn't suspect what we've been up to. Perhaps they have taken it upon themselves to thwart our plans. It always struck me as too convenient that it was Rónán they tossed through a rift as a child."

"You mean, if they wanted to find a way to subvert the Treaty of *Tír Na nÓg*, why this generation? Why not the one before? Or the one before that?"

By the movement in the stone still tied around Anwen's neck, Brydie guessed she was nodding. She sat back on her heels, astonished by what Anwen was saying. She remembered the conversation she'd had with the queen on their way to *Sí an Bhrú*, when Álmhath had told Brydie what she expected of her.

"*The* Matrarchaí *are the reason the line has never been broken,*" the queen had told her. "*The reason why, after sixty-six generations, humans still occupy* Sí an Bhrú."

Brydie had been stunned by what the queen was telling her, but it was starting to make sense. "*The* Matrarchaí *know the secret of producing the psychic twins needed to preserve the Treaty of* Tír Na nÓg."

Álmhath had nodded, smiling grimly. "*Your father said you were a bright girl.*"

Brydie recalled adding something about her mother's line, and that Álmhath had told her there was more than one bloodline. "*Yours happens to be one of the stronger ones,*" the queen had explained. "*Fortunate indeed that your last bleed was near a fortnight past. We may not have much time, so it's important you conceive as soon as possible.*"

"*Why is time suddenly a problem?*" she'd asked.

"*The* Tuatha *have forced our hand,*" the queen had told her, frowning. "*If we don't act soon, there may not be a line to preserve.*"

"I wish I knew what the *Tuatha* are up to," Anwen sighed again, and for a moment Brydie was plunged into darkness as she placed her fingertips on the stone. "I wish she could tell us what she knows."

Danú , *she really does know I'm in here...*

"Do you think Brydie discovered the truth about what they're up to?"

"She discovered something," Anwen said. "Which is why they trapped her."

"Are you sure?" the queen asked, sounding a little doubtful. "I mean... they could have just killed her. Are you sure she's in there? For all you know, she's run off with Darragh and the two of them are rutting like rabbits somewhere, not caring what the rest of us think."

Brydie smiled at that image, but Anwen didn't seem amused at all. "When Marcroy gave Brydie that stone, it was a purple amethyst so clear it was almost transparent. I remember seeing it when you arrived at *Sí an Bhrú*. Brydie was wearing it on her kirtle. She has disappeared. Now look at it now. The stone is so dark it could be mistaken for a topaz. That is the color of a stone possessed by one of undiluted human blood, *an Bhantiarna*."

"So get me out of here!" Brydie shouted, her pleas wasted. Nobody could hear her. But her voice trailed off as she put the pieces together.

The bloodline of RónánDarragh the *Matrarchaí* were so desperate to preserve. Darragh's ability to disappear in and out of his chamber without using the door. Álmhath speaking of staging accidents to hide the fact that the Undivided were long lived. *Matrarchaí* midwives smothering new born babies with pointed ears and cat-slit eyes...

It all added up to one inevitable conclusion, she decided. *The Undivided are not human. They are Faerie.*

And I was selected to continue the line, which means, Brydie realized, not sure how she felt about the revelation, *I am probably mostly Faerie too.*

What does that make you, Anwen? she wondered. *Are you human? Faerie? Or something else entirely?*

And why, when she spoke of achieving Partition, did Brydie get the feeling Anwen wasn't talking about the few old men who sat around the hearth at Temair drinking mead, as they drunkenly fantasised about a world that didn't rely on the untrustworthy *Tuatha Dé Danann* for their magic?

CHAPTER 27

C*uan Mó*, in every reality Trása had ever visited, was a natural ocean bay dotted with hundreds of sunken drumlins - long, narrow, whale-shaped hills formed of gravel, rock, and clay debris. In the reality where Rónán grew up, they insisted the islands had been formed by the movement of glaciers. Trása been to another reality where drumlins were considered unhatched dragon eggs. There was supposed to be an island in the bay for every day of the year, but anybody who could fly over it knew that was a myth. There were barely more than a hundred drumlins.

Still, the bay was impressive, particularly at low tide. Not far from here was, in her own reality, the small village of Breaga.

It was raining when Trása landed in the trees, dropping the parcel she'd carried in her beak. This time she'd fashioned a sling from the torn strip of the sheeting from Ronan's bed at the Ikushima compound so she could have some clothes to wear, as well as the bacon she needed to bait her trap. It may be necessary to seek out human civilisation in human form, she reasoned, and the temperature was dropping, every day a little cooler than the next. This way she wouldn't have to waste time looking for something to keep warm.

The trap was simple enough to recreate - it was little more than a box, made of twigs and leaves. The trap's effectiveness lay in the enchantment she would cast over it, not its structural integrity. It took Trása less than an hour to fashion an effective trap. It took her a little longer to find a suitable clearing in the forest. Once she found a likely spot, she set the trap, baited it with the bacon and then stood back. She closed her eyes, feeling the powerful magic of this realm swirl around her, she called on the gods Flidais and Tuan MacCarell in the Faerie language of her own realm, to bind the *Leipreachán's* secret name into the trap. Then she leaned forward and whispered the name over the trap, felt it settle on the fragile structure, stepped back and waited.

Nothing happened. Not that she'd expected it to have an immediate result. While Trása hoped it wouldn't take much time or effort to catch a *Leipreachán*, the more pragmatic part of her knew better. So after a few moments of silence, the forest disturbed by nothing more than the local wildlife, Trása sat herself down at the base of a large oak tree to wait.

A few moments of the rain dripping on her made her shiver, so she morphed back into her feline form - better something with a fur coat in this weather -

and then clawed her way nimbly up the trunk to the nearest broad branch where it was reasonably dry. Then she settled down under the shelter of the leafy canopy, amidst leaves just starting to turn gold with the oncoming autumn, waiting for the right the *Leipreachán* to happen by.

Trása had dozed off, her paws tucked under her chest for warmth, when she was woken by the infuriated protestations of a creature caught in her trap. She stared down at it for a moment, her feline curiosity piqued, her human awareness not yet fully engaged. After a moment or two she remembered why she was sitting up in the tree. She rose to her feet, arched her back for a moment, stretching elegantly and luxuriously, and then made her way down the trunk. Not until she reached the trap, and the outrageously dressed creature trapped inside it, did she transform back into human form.

"Ye gods!" the *Leipreachán* cried when he saw her, cowering in the corner of the trap. "I be sorry, mistress. I be so sorry..."

"What have you to be sorry for?" Trása asked, peering through the twig bars of the trap, relieved he'd spoken to her in the language of the *Tuatha Dé Danann*. It didn't seem to matter which reality she was in, the *sídhe* spoke the same language, wherever they were. "And why are you dressed like that?"

She was expecting the *Leipreachán* to look just like Plunkett with his little suit and his jaunty cap, given Plunkett's true name had trapped him here, making him almost certainly Plunkett's *eiléféin*. This *Leipreachán* was bearded, and ginger-haired, but he was dressed like a very short, rather portly ninja.

"Does it offend ye, mistress?" he asked, wringing his hands. "I can change into something less offensive if it offends thee."

"It doesn't offend me," she assured him. "What's your name?"

She knew his secret name, but it would have been the worst breach of protocol imaginable for her to call him by that name where others might overhear.

"I be known as Toyoda Mulrayn," he told her.

"Toyoda? Really? Who gave you that name?"

"'Twas the name I be given by the *Konketsu*." He peered at her through the twigs. "You not be *Konketsu*."

"I'm *Beansídhe*," she said. "Well... half-*Beansídhe*, at any rate. I'm going to let you out now, but remember, Toyoda, I know your true name. Don't make me use it."

The *Leipreachán* nodded meekly as Trása lifted the twig trap off him. He sat there in the rain, looking at her for a moment, his bottom lip quivering. "Are ye truly *Beansídhe*, mistress?"

"Yes, I truly am."

"Not *Konketsu*?"

"No, I'm not *Konketsu*."

"And ye came through the *rifuto* from another realm to help us?"

"If you mean the stone circle through a reality rift, then yes, that's where I came from, and I suppose, if you need my help..."

The *Leipreachán* burst into tears and flew into her arms, blubbering like a broken-hearted child.

"Hey there!" Trása said, not sure how to react. The little *sídhe* sobbed in her arms as if a dam had burst after a spring flood. She didn't know what to do, Trása didn't even realize *Leipreacháns* could cry. She'd never seen anything like it in her own reality.

She patted the little man's back, awkwardly. "There... there... Toyoda, it's all right, I'm here now."

"It's so good to have ye here, mistress," Toyoda sobbed, drenching her shoulder with his tears. She'd not had time to dress since he'd sprung her trap, but his tears were warm on her damp skin compared to the gentle rain falling on them in the clearing. "We've missed ye kind so much, mistress. We hide whenever the *Konketsu* come looking for us, but it's been so hard just waiting and waiting and waiting, all the time."

"We?" Trása asked, as she realized he wasn't talking about missing her, so much as the whole *Daoine sídhe* race. "There are more of you about?"

He nodded and leaned back in her arms, staring up at her with adoring eyes. "A few of us. The numbers get smaller every year. We been waiting, mistress. We knew ye couldn't all be dead. And since the other night when the rift opened, we hoped ye'd come back, and now ye and ye mate be here, and we can take back this realm, and-"

"Whoa there, little man!" Trása cried in alarm. "Let's not get ahead of ourselves. How many of you are there left?"

Toyoda shrugged. "I not be sure of the exact number."

"And there are no *Youkai* left in this reality at all?"

He shook his head, sniffing loudly. "Ye and ye mate are the first to be seen in years."

"My mate? Oh, you mean Rónán?" she asked, gently pushing the little man away so she could get dressed. "He's not *Daoine sídhe*, Toyoda. He's human. And for the record, he's not my mate, either."

The *Leipreachán* cocked his head to one side, looking very puzzled as she pulled on the linen coat-like garment she'd borrowed from the Ikushima compound. "He canna be human," the little man said. "He be able to wane like a *sídhe*."

"No, he can't," she said, looking down at him as she tied off the belt at her waist. "Why would you think that?"

"There be wee wood sprites hiding in the *kozo* forest around the stone circle keeping watch," he explained. "They be chattering about nothing else since ye got here. First, they say, ye changed into an owl to get away when Chishihero tried to be rid of ye, and then ye mate waned himself into the forest when she tried to kill him, too."

"Hang on... let's just get something straight here," Trása said, astonished by the information. "When you say "waning" you mean the same thing it means in my reality, don't you? Translocation? Vanishing from one spot and reappearing somewhere else?"

"Aye," Toyoda agreed, wiping his eyes now his tears seemed to by under control. "What did ye think I be meaning?"

"That's not possible," she said. "Rónán is human."

"He may look human on the outside, mistress, but he be more *sídhe* than ye, if he can wane and ye can't."

Trása sat down on the damp ground, confused and more than a little unsettled by the news that Rónán had escaped the Tanabe compound by performing a feat no creature not almost pure Faerie should be able to perform. It explained why he'd been so vague on how he got away. The implications were quite terrifying.

And right now, she didn't have time to ponder what they meant. She needed to know what had happened to the rest of her people in this realm.

"What happened to the *Tuatha Dé Danann*?"

"They be dead."

"They can't *all* be dead."

"The *Konketsu* hunted them down and killed them," Toyoda told her, as he rearranged his belt with its array of tiny weapons that all appeared to be of Japanese rather than Celtic origin. "The rest of them they herded up like sheep and drove them through the rift into realms with no magic. Most of them be dead before they took more than a dozen steps into the other magic-less realms they be pushed into." He sniffed away the last of his tears and added, "When the *Futagono Kizuna* went through the rift to meet with the envoy from the *Matrarchaí*, they told us to wait for them. They said the Empresses were safe in *Tír Na nÓg*."

He'd said the *Futagono Kizuna*. If her translation was correct, he meant *the bonded twins*. That could only mean this reality's version of the Undivided. "So the *Youkai* shared their magic in this reality with humans, too?" She didn't know why the Undivided had left their realm to meet with the *Matrarchaí*. It seemed an odd thing to do, but no more odd than the reason Darragh and Rónán had left their realm to go rift running.

Toyoda nodded. "I hear that be the same for many realms," he said. "And we be fine here until the Empresses met with Lady Delphine. After that, they not be needing the *Youkai* for their power.

They be strong enough to channel it without any help from our kind."

"Who is Lady Delphine?"

"She be the envoy from the *Matrarchaí*."

Trása studied the little man for a moment, wondering if was telling the truth or spinning a fanciful yarn to make his cowardice seem more acceptable. "And the *Konketsu* are human?"

"Not completely. Turns out ye need some *Youkai* blood in ye, and ye have to produce enough *washi* from the *kozo* trees, but once ye do, then ye can wield all the magic ye want with *ori mahou* and ye don't need the *Youkai* at all."

"So they discovered folding magic in this realm and then just killed all the Faerie? That's monstrous!"

"It didn't happen quickly," he told her, shaking his head. "It be quite insidious-like. And it be too late before the Undivided realized what be happening. By then the Empresses be born - although they weren't the Empresses back then. Once the *Futagono Kizuna* were gone, the Konketsu got a taste for *Youkai* blood, and it be all downhill from there." He sniffed and wiped his runny nose on his sleeve. "Now the *Konketsu* fear *Youkai* from other realms will come through the stone circles and see what they have done here. They destroyed most of the *gampi* bushes needed to fold the *ori mahou* to open the rift, which be why ye and ye mate were supposed to be killed on sight. Chishihero would figure if ye can travel through a rift, ye be a danger to the Empresses."

"Didn't you say the Empresses were supposed to be safe in *Tír Na nÓg*?"

His bottom lip began to quiver again. "The *Futagono Kizuna* were betrayed by the man they trusted like a father. That's how the Empresses escaped. Soon as they were free and they realized the *Futagono Kizuna* weren't here to stop them, they ordered the rest of the *Youkai* killed."

Trása's eye's narrowed. "The Undivided in this realm were betrayed?"

"Aye," the little ninja-*Leipreachán* said. "It be a very bad time for all *Youkai* the day that happened."

The parallels between the worlds were a coincidence, Trása told herself. This was nothing like her reality. Even less like the reality she had just come from. It was not unusual for a magical reality to have Undivided - or in this reality the *Futagono Kizuna* - who aided sharing the magic with humans. And sometimes events seemed to occur in a similar fashion, no matter the realm. Rift runners from Trása's reality were not the only Faerie to jump between realms. She had been to worlds where alternate realities traded with each other on a regular basis. Whole economies were built around the stone circles. She'd known other realities where the Undivided - or their equivalent - were betrayed. But she had never seen a reality where the Undivided had turned on their Faerie allies and set out to eliminate them once they'd found a way to wield magic without their help.

Toyoda sighed dramatically. "The wood sprites keep watch over the stone circles now, and we wait..." He began to choke up again.

Trása reached over and patted his shoulder gently, hoping the comfort was enough to forestall his tears. She wasn't sure she could handle too much more sobbing *Leipreachán.*

"But didn't you say the *Konketsu* are part *Youkai* themselves?"

Toyoda nodded. "They be very precious about the blood lines, to keep the magic going, but they be in trouble. The lines be weakening. If the *Konketsu* had known ye mate was *Youkai*, Chishihero wouldn't have tried to kill him, mistress, she'd have tried to steal his seed from him." He straightened his rather ridiculous black hood and added sorrowfully, "If the Ikushima be showing ye mate a good time while he be a guest in *Shin Bungo*, ye can bet they be after the same thing."

CHAPTER 28

"He's killed Hayley Boyle and probably his brother and our mystery girl, Trása, as well," Pete said. "He all but admitted it."

"Pity you'd turned the tape off by then," Brendá said. The inspector leaned back in her chair and closed her eyes, stifling a yawn. It was past midnight, but nobody was going to sleep this night. The whole world had turned upside down in the past day and people didn't seem to know what to do with themselves, so they stayed at work where every office had a TV set on, with clusters of stunned people standing around them watching as the madness in America unfolded on CNN and left everyone wondering what would happen next.

"God... what a day." She opened her eyes again and stared at Pete for a moment. "At least you're not gloating about being right."

The proof Pete needed was sitting in an open file on Brendá Duggan's desk. It was the report comparing Ren Kavanaugh's fingerprints to those taken from the young man claiming to come from another reality. They were different. Similar in many ways, but different enough that they could not be the same kid. Between Logan's photos, Patrick Boyle's confession, his own eye-witness testimony, Darragh's admission that he was Ren's twin and the fingerprint evidence, Pete no longer appeared insane. Now he just looked like a good detective.

The insanity honor firmly belonged to Ren's twin brother, Darragh, with his insistence that he had come from another reality and that he'd sent Hayley back there, to have her sight healed.

There was no sign of his accomplices - Trása and the woman who had cold-cocked Pete in the car who, Darragh had identified as Sorcha - or his twin brother, Ren. Darragh kept insisting they had returned to the other reality with Hayley. Pete knew he was lying but hadn't been able to figure out a way to make Darragh admit it.

"What do you want me to do with him?"

"I have no idea," the inspector said, shaking her head. "Nothing we can do tonight. But we can't hold him for long unless we charge him with something."

"We can charge him with Hayley's murder," Pete suggested. As far as he was concerned *I've sent her to another reality* was simply a euphemism for *I killed her.*

Unfortunately, euphemisms weren't evidence.

"Not going to be easy to prove that without a body."

"We can get him for stealing a car, can't we? I mean, he pissed off with a patrol car from St Christopher's." Pete smiled thinly and pointed to his two black eyes that had faded somewhat around the edges to an ugly shade of dark yellow. "I'd kind of like to add assaulting an officer to the charge list, while we're at it."

Brendá smiled. "I'm sure you would."

"Have you told Kiva Kavanaugh yet?"

"I didn't have to, thank god," Brendá said, shaking her head. "Eunice Ravenel had already broken the news before I got to speak with her. She's at home, probably composing a press release, as we speak."

"What was her reaction to the news that her son has an identical twin she knew nothing about?"

"Shock," Brendá said. "And vast relief. Although given what Eunice Ravenel's firm charges for her services, that might have been for the legal bill she won't have to pay, rather than the welcome news she's not going to be arrested for harboring a fugitive."

"Even though she was? And so was Patrick Boyle, for that matter. And Jack O'Righin, too, if you want to include everyone who helped them get away from the golf course."

"Technically, they weren't doing anything wrong, as the lovely Ms Ravenel went to great pains to point out. Ren was the one on the run. His brother Darragh was not a fugitive at that point. We didn't even know he existed until a couple of days ago, and he wasn't involved in Ren's earlier troubles, so he did nothing wrong. Much as it pains me to agree with a single word that comes out of that smug little bitch's mouth, I fear Eunice has the right of it."

Pete knew she was probably right too. Still, it didn't seem fair that all of them could just walk away from this, scot-free. "Did Darragh say anything useful to Kiva?"

"I gather not. He was trying to convince her he was Ren. He managed to do it too. She was clueless."

That bothered Pete. Ren had grown up far from his brother. They should know barely anything about each other, and yet Darragh had known enough of Ren's life to keep his mother fooled for nearly forty-eight hours. Kiva Kavanaugh was a self-centred woman, but surely she wasn't so wrapped up in herself that she didn't notice the difference between her son and the brother posing as him, if he was just winging it. "I'd like to talk to Darragh again. There's a few discrepancies in his story I want to clear up."

Brendá smiled wearily. "Which one? The one about him coming from an alternate reality? Yes, by all means, let's iron out that minor inconsistency."

"I mean how he managed to fool Kiva for as long as he did. And this woman, Sorcha," he said. "Boyle says he helped two of them get away from the golf course. He says she was as Jack O'Righin's house. Darragh claims she went through the rift with Ren, Hayley and Trása."

"On balance, I'd be going with Patrick Boyle's statement on the matter," the inspector said. "Unless, of course, you're buying the alternate reality thing?"

Brendá Duggan was joking. At least Pete hoped she was. "Yeah," Pete said with a thin smile. "That would be it."

Brendá closed the file and handed it to Pete. "Talk to him then. If you think you need help, see if Annad Semaj is feeling well enough to have a go at him. Eunice Ravenel isn't representing him any longer, but remember he's still a minor. If you get anything useful out of him, I want to be able to use it in court."

"I have to ask you if you want a lawyer," Pete informed Darragh when they resumed their discussion some time later. Symes was gone and so was Eunice Ravenel. Although the shrink had wanted to stick around, Duggan had politely, but firmly informed him his assistance was no longer required.

Darragh shook his head. "I believe my brother had instructions never to say a word to the police without a lawyer present. I do not share his fear. You strike me as an honorable man."

Pete smiled at that. "Honorable?"

Darragh pointed to the recording equipment. "You are recording this, yes? And you have rules you must follow. Why should I fear you?"

"So for the benefit of the recording - you're formally declining legal representation, yes? Even though you're under eighteen?"

"I am, and I'm not under eighteen. My brother and I will be nineteen on October fifth. Your October fifth. The date is quite different in my realm."

Damn, Pete thought. *Just when he was starting to sound sane.*

"My file lists Ren Kavanaugh's birth date as December tenth, nineteen-eighty-three."

"Then your file is wrong, sir."

"What else am I wrong about?" Pete asked, fascinated by this young man's calm assurance. He wasn't lying, Pete could tell that just by watching him, but his story was insane. He was like those alien abductees who could pass a lie detector test, convinced they'd been kidnapped and anally probed by little green men. Whatever stories this kid was peddling, they might not be the truth, but he believed them. It was going to be next to impossible to get the truth from Darragh unless someone could rattle his cage enough to prove, beyond a shadow of a doubt, that his version of events was bullshit.

Darragh smiled at Pete's question. "What else are you wrong about, sir? By *Danú*, I don't even know where to begin."

"How about you start with where Sorcha is?"

"She returned through the rift."

That's a lie, Pete knew. The first actual lie he'd caught Darragh in.

"According to Patrick Boyle, she was in the trunk of the Bentley with you."

Darragh's eyes clouded for a moment, which intrigued Pete. For the first time, he appeared to have shaken the young man's equanimity. "Patrick Boyle? Is that how you found me? Patrick betrayed us?"

"You said *us*," Pete answered. "So Sorcha was with you?" He wasn't listening. Darragh muttered something under his breath, shaking his head, and then looked at Pete, his eyes filled with regret and self-recrimination. "You would think, given how heinously my brother and I were betrayed in our own realm, I would have listened to Sorcha when she warned me Amergin would betray me in this realm, too."

Pete stared at Darragh for a moment, resisting the temptation to simply respond with *"huh?"* Instead, he thought over what the boy had said, trying to find the truth in it. Darragh wasn't lying, he was living a fantasy, but there would be a kernel of truth in it somewhere that Pete had to find if he was ever going to locate Hayley Boyle's body.

"Who is Amergin?" The only Amergin Pete knew of was the mythical ancient poet that every kid in Ireland had probably heard of. He was disappointed. Darragh's story was going to be far too easy to unravel if that was the best he could come up with.

"The Vate of All Eire in my realm," Darragh told him. "At least he was. He has been replaced now by Colmán." Darragh rolled his eyes, adding, "A less-talented bard it would be hard to find in any reality, I have to say."

"Amergin... in your realm, was also a bard?" Pete said, deciding to play along for the time being.

The lad didn't miss a beat. He nodded in agreement. "It is a popular name among parents who hope their sons will achieve greatness."

"And how did this Amergin betray you?"

"He was the one who threw Rónán into this realm."

Neat, Pete thought. *He's really thought about this.* "And Rónán is Ren's true name, you say?"

He nodded. "I'm not sure where the Ren comes from. Perhaps he recalls what our mother called him. She was Gaulish and called him Renan, I believe, more often than not."

"What did she call you?"

Darragh closed his eyes for a moment and then looked at Pete with a rather forlorn expression. "Do you know, I cannot recall. That is so sad. Every year, a little more of Sybille's memory slips away. Soon, I won't remember her at all."

His regret was so heartfelt and genuine, Pete had to remind himself this kid was talking about a world that existed only in his head, and that he had, more than likely, been responsible for killing two people - one them his own brother. It also occurred to Pete that Darragh had rather skilfully taken charge of the whole discussion. They were talking about his alternate reality as if it really existed.

Time to take back the control. "So how is it you blame Patrick Boyle for Amergin's betrayal?"

"I don't blame Amergin," Darragh said. "Patrick Boyle is Amergin's *eileféin*. He was probably always destined to betray us, no matter the reality he occupies, which I should have accepted, instead of hoping Amergin's betrayal was just an aberration brought about by his connection to the *Tuatha Dé Danaan* through his *Leanan Sídhe* wife and the corrupting influence of Marcroy Tarth."

Pete sat back in his seat, shaking his head. "The *Tuatha Dé Danann*? Are you fucking kidding me? Your alternate reality is populated by fairies?"

Darragh seemed puzzled by his reaction. "I have angered you, Pete. Why? I am trying to explain what happened to Rónán and Hayley. Surely her family wants to know what has happened to her? It would ease their minds greatly, I would think, to know that she is well and undoubtedly able to see again, by now." He stared at Pete with a look of such ingenuous expectation, it was hard to believe this was all in his head - a grand delusion he'd created to save himself from... what? A lifetime of abuse? A guilty conscience he couldn't live with? Pete was inclined to believe the latter.

"Yeah, 'she's safe with the faeries'll do it'," Pete said, rising to his feet as he glanced at his watch. "Interview suspended at twelve-forty-three am."

Darragh looked up at him in surprise? "Are we done?"

"We're done," Pete told him. "At least you are."

"Did you want me to explain to Hayley's family what happened to her in person?"

"I want you locked up, medicated, and under constant psychiatric care," Pete told him, realising that Darragh was so convinced of his fantasy, there was no helping him. And Pete knew he was out of his depth here. He had a degree in criminal psychology, but he wasn't a psychiatrist. This kid needed help. Serious help. It was probably schizophrenia, or something like it that caused him to hallucinate like this, but whatever ailed this boy, there was nothing Pete could do, here and now, to fix him.

"I am not insane, Pete," Darragh said calmly as Pete headed for the door. "You're just not equipped to accept the truth."

Pete stopped with his hand on the doorknob. "Okay then, wise guy, explain this to me... suppose I buy your theory. Suppose I suspend all rational thought for a moment and accept that your brother stepped through a rift into another world with Hayley, and Trása and whomever else you care to name. Suppose I accept that you guys can open rifts between worlds at will... then why are you still here? If your story is true, why are you sitting here, under arrest and facing the next twenty years in gaol, if fairies can open a rift and come to get you, anytime they want?"

Somewhat to Pete's surprise, Darragh didn't even hesitate before replying with a worried expression, "I cannot answer that question, Detective Pete, and I fear it means something terrible has befallen my brother and the people I count as allies, because you are right. If they were in a position to save me from this realm, I would be home by now."

CHAPTER 29

Sorcha took her time making her way back to Jack's place. She could have taken a cab, or some other form of public transport. She had money. She could have been home in a matter of minutes.

But she was feeling out of sorts. It wasn't just the necessary, but unpleasant need to kill Warren that unsettled her. She didn't feel right. There was something wrong with her. She felt slower, felt pain in places she'd never experienced it before.

Sorcha put it down to lack of exercise. She'd barely walked a mile since she'd come to this reality, and she wondered if that was causing the problem. She just needed to walk out the stiffness in her joints and she would be fine.

It took her all night and a good portion of the next day to get back to the tree-lined, suburban street where Jack O'Righin lived. She slept along the way, finding a leafy garden with a secluded nook that offered shelter from the elements. She didn't mind sleeping in the open. She preferred it. By the time Sorcha rose in the morning, just as the sun was dawning over the city, she was rested but still not feeling better. If anything, her night in the open had made her feel even more stiff and uncomfortable.

She put aside her discomfort and headed towards Blackrock, following the DART line when she could. Other times she had to backtrack as it became obvious the roads were meant for cars but not people. It took her almost half a day. Her stomach rumbling in complaint, she arrived back at Jack's place just in time to see the ERU storming Kiva Kavanaugh's estate.

Amergin! she thought, reasoning the dead Vate's *eileféin* had betrayed them, just as she knew he would. *You treacherous bastard.*

Keeping to the shadows of the neighbouring high walls surrounding the estates, Sorcha made her way into to Jack's place unseen. As soon as she was inside she called out for Darragh to warn him of the attack next door.

"Lord Darragh!"

They had to get out of here. Now. When the Gardaí didn't find the boy they thought was Ren Kavanaugh at his mother's house, the next place they would logically look - assuming it was Patrick Boyle who betrayed them - would be this place.

"Curse you, boy! Where are you? We have to leave!"

Sorcha ran through the house, calling Darragh's name, but the silence echoed only her footsteps and her fruitless calls.

Darragh wasn't here.

"*Danú*, save me from foolish children," she muttered, as she stopped in the kitchen to catch her breath.

She guessed immediately where Darragh had gone. Next door. To his brother's house. He would not have been able to resist the temptation to see how Rónán had lived. He had a head full of his brother's memories and no way or sorting them into anything coherent. She understood his need, and cursed him for it at the same time.

"You foolish, foolish, boy!" she shouted at the empty house, knowing he couldn't hear her, but feeling a little better for it. She cursed herself roundly for leaving him alone. She should have anticipated this.

Sorcha had to know what was going on. She was tempted to take a peek herself, by climbing the ivy-covered wall between the estates to watch the attack, but she didn't want to risk detection. She couldn't save Darragh if she was also arrested. There was the problem of all those armed men, too. Sorcha could take three or four of them in a fight, armed with a knife or a sword, but she had no defence against bullets, and the men storming Kiva Kavanaugh's house had all been carrying short, ugly guns against which she had no defence.

Or maybe she did? Perhaps Jack had guns in the house?

Sorcha looked around, not even sure where to begin looking for a weapons cache.

Then it occurred to her that in this world where everything was reported on television, there might be something about the raid happening next door on one of the news channels. There was a clutch of paparazzi camped outside the house next door, day and night. Surely one of them was standing in front of the house, talking earnestly into a microphone, one finger to his ear - she had no idea why reporters seemed to do that - breathlessly chronicling the events at the Kavanaugh house as they unfolded.

Darragh was a bright boy and superbly trained by the best of the best. Ciarán had seen to that. Even injured as he was, it would be hard to take him by surprise. He could well have gone to ground at the first sign of the attack, and would elude capture completely, even if he hadn't been able to get away. He could be concealed somewhere in the garden, either here or the garden next door, simply waiting for a chance to slip away...

There was one sure way to find out. She headed into the living room, sat down on the edge of Jack's clever reclining armchair, picked up the remote and turned on the TV.

What she saw puzzled her at first. She thought perhaps she was watching a movie. On Friday night, after Patrick had been to visit, Jack sat down to watch TV. The movie *Independence Day* had been showing. Sorcha was stunned, not sure what shocked her most - that anybody would go to such pains to pretend they'd won a battle that never happened in the first place, or that this reality devoted so much time and effort perfecting whatever it took to make such absurdities seem real.

Sorcha flicked through the channels on the remote control. Jack had shown her how to use it, and she used the remote now, unable to find any channel not showing the same scenes - planes flying into impossibly tall buildings and after a time, the buildings crashing to the ground in an unimaginable swirl of smoke and dust.

"By *Danú*," she muttered, staring at the screen in shock and disbelief. "I think this is actually happening."

She couldn't imagine how such a monstrous thing could be real. But then, until a few days ago, she couldn't imagine a lot of things she'd witnessed in this world. The barbarity of the destruction defined this realm for her. That such violence could rest in the hearts of the same people who could construct something so tall and elegant and amazing was inconceivable. She didn't understand half the things the voices on the TV were saying as they described the destruction and what might have precipitated it, but she gathered there was a god involved. Or the worship of one. Had such a thing happened in her realm, she might have looked upon this devastation and considered it the work of a jealous god, determined to bring down men who had dared challenge him with their creations.

But this wasn't the work of a jealous god. This was humans deliberately hurting other humans and that made her want to weep for this realm and all who inhabited it.

Sorcha lost track of time as she watched the events at the World Trade Centre unfold. She had trouble grasping the scale of the damage. Nothing could have prepared her for such a thing. She didn't know what to do; didn't know if this was a common occurrence in this realm or something so catastrophic and horrendous, that nobody in this realm knew how to deal with it, either.

For a time, Sorcha even forgot about Darragh.

It wasn't until there was a knock at the front door that she was jerked out of her stunned stupor.

Sorcha had no intention of answering the door. She had no idea who might be seeking entry into Jack's house and no plans to engage with them, whoever they were. But the unwanted visitor must have heard the TV. After a few moment of knocking, a face peered in at the living room window.

It was a woman. An older woman, her grey-streaked haired pulled back into a loose bun. She caught sight of Sorcha and waved.

At least she wasn't Gardaí.

Sorcha wasn't sure she could ignore the knocking without raising suspicion now she'd been seen.

She cursed under her breath and headed for the hall. Hopefully she could divert the visitor and be rid of her without having to answer too many questions.

The woman was waiting patiently on the porch when Sorcha opened the door. She smiled and eyed Sorcha up and down for a moment before asking, "Are you a friend of Jack's?"

"Yes," Sorcha said. "I'm his cousin."

"I'm Carmel. His cleaning lady."

Sorcha knew about Carmel. Jack had warned them as he left that they needed to be gone before she got here next Friday to clean the house.

"What did you say your name was, dear?"

"It's Sorcha," she said, frowning. "You're not due until next Friday."

"I know," the woman said. "But I was just coming out of the Frascati Mall when I heard the news on the radio. I called in to see if Jack had left for New

York already. Wasn't expecting anybody to be home, but then I heard the TV and thought I'd better check."

"Jack left a couple of days ago," Sorcha informed Carmel as the woman pushed past Sorcha to let herself in. "Where are you going?"

"To put the kettle on, dear," the cleaning lady informed her as she headed for the kitchen. "God knows I could do with a cuppa right now. You look like you could do with one too."

Sorcha stared after the woman in shock. *Who in Danu's name does this woman think she is?*

And is she right to be concerned about Jack?

Sorcha knew he was in New York, but the size and location of the city was unknown to her - other than it being far away - as was the likelihood that he might be anywhere in the vicinity of the World Trade Centre.

"How do you take it?" Carmel called out from the kitchen as Sorcha closed the front door, wondering if she couldn't get rid of Carmel, whether she should kill her instead.

"Black!" Sorcha called back, looking around the hall for a weapon.

It was then that she caught sight of herself in the large hall mirror. Suddenly, the reason for her aches and pains, the reason for her feeling so out of sorts became apparent.

Staring back at her was an old woman. Dressed in the ill-fitting floral dress she'd stolen from the clothesline next door to Warren's house, and the ratty, too-big cardigan she wore over it, she looked like a little old lady, ready to keel over in a strong breeze.

Her reflection seemed frail. Gone were her lustrous dark locks - her hair had turned almost white. Crow's feet creased the corners of her eyes. She glanced down at her hands and noticed for the first time that her skin had begun to crinkle like old parchment. Liver spots speckled her forearms. She reached up and touched her face, appalled by the dried-out papery texture of her skin.

She knew what was happening. Sorcha was eighty-five years old, but her youth had been preserved by the time she had spent in the magical lands of *Tír Na nÓg*. Since emerging from the Faerie kingdom, she'd aged, but normally, and only as much as a younger woman might expect to age.

But Sorcha was no longer in a reality with any magic to sustain her. The magic was gone here, and with it her youth.

Sorcha realized then, that she had an even more pressing reason to return to her own realm. It had nothing to do with protecting the Undivided. Nothing to do with the approaching *Lughnasadh*.

Nothing to do with saving anybody other than herself.

Because if Sorcha didn't find a way back through the rift to her own realm soon, she was going to die in this realm of old age.

CHAPTER 30

Fortunately for Brydie, once Torcán had officially gifted his future bride with her wedding gift, Anwen seemed disinclined to take it off. That meant Brydie had a bird's eye view of the goings on in Álmhath's court in a way she had never done before, even when she waited on the queen as one of her court maidens. She wasn't sure if Anwen wore the jewelled collar because she knew Brydie was trapped in it and didn't want to smother her, because she didn't want to let the valuable necklace out of her sight, or if she simply liked wearing something so ostentatious. Whatever the reason, Brydie was no longer bored. She was intrigued, and not just by the goings on in Álmhath's inner circle. For the first time since hearing about them when Álmhath sent her to *Sí an Bhrú* to be impregnated by Darragh of the Undivided, she was starting to appreciate the full power and reach of the *Matrarchaí*.

Álmhath had hinted that Brydie's mother, the legendary beauty, Mogue Ni'Farrell, was a member of the *Matrarchaí* and that her bloodline was precious enough to warrant sending Brydie to *Sí an Bhrú* for Darragh to ensure its continuation. She hadn't realized how pervasive the *Matrarchaí's* influence was. Nor had she realized how closely they were allied with the Druids.

To the casual observer, the queen of the Celts tolerated the Druids, resented their influence over her people and undermined their authority at every opportunity. The truth was quite different. The *Matrarchaí* had taken it upon themselves to preserve the unbroken line of the Undivided, she realized now, keeping the biggest secret of all - that the Undivided were part-*sídhe* - well hidden. More than that, they were actively working with the Druids toward breeding a line that would not need the help or intervention of the *Tuatha* to access the magic their entire realm was so dependent on.

Brydie had heard of the Partitionists. Her father had been accused of being one. She'd always thought their political agenda was the separation of the Celts from the interference of the Druids. That's what he went on and on about with his comrades when they sat around the hearth on long winter nights, drinking too much mead. She had believed the separation they agitated for was a political one, but the separation Álmhath was talking about was much more radical and profound. They were talking about separating the Druids and the Faerie - making it possible to keep the *Tuatha* magic without being held to the Treaty of *Tír Na nÓg*.

Sídhe magic to wield at will, without the *sídhe* to inhibit its use.

Exactly why that was necessary puzzled Brydie. The arrangement they had now was working perfectly fine, as far as she could tell. It had changed little for a couple of thousand years or so. Why the need to dispense with the reliance on the *sídhe*?

One generation away from achieving our goal. That's what Álmhath had claimed. Brydie rubbed her belly, wondering if she'd conceived a child when Darragh made love to her. Was this the generation they spoke of? Had Álmhath sent her to Darragh because nesting in her womb was the chance for humans to wield magic in their own right, with no interference from the likes of Marcroy Tarth?

Fat lot of good it does anybody now, she thought. *I'm trapped in a jewel.* She hadn't eaten in days but wasn't hungry. She'd not needed to relieve herself and not once had she felt thirsty. Brydie was sure that if they ever released her from this jewelled prison, she would emerge exactly the same as she had been the moment Jamaspa trapped her here. Not so much as a hair would be arranged differently.

If she was with child, it meant nothing. No foetus was going to grow into a baby in this static place.

Anwen's position as the future daughter-in-law of the queen meant she slept alone. At least that's what Brydie had always assumed was the reason she had her own room. Having seen and heard the court maiden and her queen in private, Brydie wasn't so sure about that anymore. She had the feeling it was because Anwen demanded it and Álmhath was afraid to refuse her.

Torcán often crept into her alcove at night. Although Brydie had never been close to the prince - she thought him a bore - one couldn't deny he was a handsome brute. He was aware of it, too, which was the main reason he was such a bore. Darragh had laughingly suggested the rest of it came from his unbearable sense of entitlement because his mother was queen.

Anwen, Brydie quickly concluded, was not in love with Torcán. But she seemed happy enough to use him for pleasure. The way they made love, Brydie couldn't think of any other way to describe it. The "do this to me, do that to me" way Anwen ordered Torcán about during coitus was all about Anwen having a good time. If Torcán happened to take some pleasure from it too, it was incidental to the business at hand.

Most times Anwen untied the necklace and placed it on the table by the bed, which meant Brydie didn't have to watch Torcán's grunting pleasure-taking, although there was no way to avoid hearing him. Once, the night Anwen had officially been gifted with her wedding present, she'd left it on while they made love, because Torcán wanted to look at her wearing it. Anwen seemed in the mood to indulge him and for once, she had let him enter her without demanding he work for the privilege by taking care of her needs first. That had been an unfortunate time for Brydie, being rocked back and forth while Torcán's face loomed above her - his expression more constipated than passionate - while he moaned and grunted and groaned and called out Anwen's name as if it was a plea for mercy as he reached his climax. It hadn't taken long, but she was feeling quite seasick by the time he'd collapsed on top of Anwen, smothering Brydie's view of him, thank *Danú*, leaving her with nothing to look at but his sweaty, hairy chest, magnified most unfortunately by the faceted walls of her jewelled prison.

What intrigued Brydie about that night, however, was that after she pushed him aside, promised she loved him and sent him on his way, Anwen had lifted her nightgown, reached down between her thighs, and taken care of her own pleasure once Torcán was gone. That made Brydie smile. Anwen might be marrying a handsome prince, but when it counted, he wasn't that much of a prize at all.

As *Lughnasadh* loomed Brydie worried Anwen would forget all about her being trapped in the jewel. The queen was no help, either. Álmhath seemed to be more and more distracted. Between plans for Torcán and Anwen's wedding, and everything that had to be organized for the ceremony transferring the power between the missing Undivided and their heirs, it seemed the inconvenience of one of her court maidens being entombed in an enchanted amethyst was the last thing the queen was inclined to worry about.

Brydie had never aspired to great office. The best she had ever really hoped for was a halfway decent marriage arranged by the queen, somewhere not too unpleasant, to a husband with enough wealth and good manners to make life tolerable. Although Anwen's attitude annoyed her, Brydie had never felt any jealousy toward her. The more closely she witnessed the life Anwen was about to embrace,

Brydie began to pity her. But maybe she didn't need to.

Politics was not Brydie's game, but it was Anwen's favourite pastime. The more time Brydie spent sitting at Anwen's throat, witnessing her day-to-day life, the more she came to understand why, of all the court maidens at her disposal, Álmhath had chosen this girl to marry her spoiled, easily manipulated son, but why she so often deferred to Anwen remained a mystery.

It was easy to lose track of the days. Brydie really couldn't say how long she'd been trapped now. *Lughnasadh* was getting closer, because of the feverish preparations. The wedding of Anwen and Torcán would take place at dawn, then the entire party was due to set out for the seventeen-mile journey to *Sí an Bhrú*. There, at sunset, the new Undivided heirs would be brought forth, and the queen of the Faerie would imprint the new twins with the magical tattoo on their palm, that would ensure the magic kept flowing to all the other Druids.

What was to become of Darragh and his missing brother after that was never discussed. Brydie had a feeling it wasn't going to be pleasant. The Undivided did not retire. There had never been a case where they simply stepped aside and allowed someone younger or more talented to take over.

One set of twins died and the new set took over. That was how it had always been.

There was some concern that Darragh was still missing. Álmhath had people scouring the countryside for him. Brydie could have told them they would never find him in this realm, because he'd gone rift running to another realm, but she had no way of sharing the information.

She learned something a couple of days before *Lughnasadh* that made her rethink everything she had believed about the relationship between the Celts and the Druids.

Colmán came to visit.

The Vate of all Eire was an irritating man, full of bad poetry and an implacable hatred for the *Tuatha Dé Danann* race, on whom his entire cult was reliant for their power. With his old-fashioned pointy forked beard, greased and threaded with gold beads, his humourless bearing and his complete devotion to preserving the oral history of the Undivided, he was the butt of more jokes than most Vates. Darragh had despaired of the man, and made fun of him every chance he got.

When he came to visit Álmhath, however, on the pretext of discussing the catering arrangements for the *Lughnasadh* feast, she was startled by the change in the man. He looked the same as he entered the hall, looked around, and began to intone something ridiculous and very badly rhymed, but as soon as he was alone with Álmhath and her future daughter-in-law, he dropped all pretence of bardic self-importance that he assumed in public, and began to speak like a conspirator.

"Have you any news of Darragh?" the queen asked, as soon the three of them were alone. Colmán glanced around the room as he spoke, perhaps looking for *Tuatha* spies disguised as creatures lurking in the corners, but there were none. Brydie thought his belief he could tell when he was being observed optimistic, given he had not discovered her trapped in Anwen's necklace, or realized there was a *Djinn* in *Sí an Bhrú*.

He seemed disinclined to answer with Anwen present.

"She can be trusted," the queen assured Colmán when she saw him looking at Anwen doubtfully. "I will vouch for her, myself."

"If you're sure, *an Bhantiarna*."

"I am," Álmhath said. "What news of the Undivided?"

"If you mean Darragh, then none at all," Colmán said. "And Ciarán is still missing, along with a few other Druids whose absence bothers me."

"What are the chances he'll be back in time for the ceremony?" Anwen asked.

Colmán shrugged. "I have no idea, and unless he arrives with Rónán at his side, I'm not sure it would make a difference."

"Is there no way we can delay the transfer?" Álmhath asked. The queen looked more worried than Brydie thought she ought to be, for someone who professed irritation at the control the Druids - and the Undivided who ruled them - had over her kingdom.

Colmán shook his head. "Not without revealing much more than we'd like about the *Matrarchaí* and the nature of the Undivided."

Brydie was surprised to hear Colmán talking about the *Matrarchaí* as if he was one of them. Surely the *Matrarchaí* was a society to which only women belonged? Until Brydie arrived in Temair and the queen had broached the subject, she'd assumed the *Matrarchaí* were simply glorified midwives. She'd learned on the way to *Sí an Bhrú* that they were much more than that, but she hadn't expected them to have members in the ranks of the Druids.

The queen began to pace, wringing her hands with annoyance. "I still can't believe we're even facing this nightmare," she said. "Those Undivided heirs should never have been discovered. We should have sent them out of this realm to be raised in secret." She stopped pacing and stared straight at Colmán. "Are we sure there are no more traitors in the Druid ranks?"

Colmán bristled at the accusation. "Why are you so certain the traitor who betrayed their existence - assuming there is one - comes from our ranks, and not yours? Plenty of your people know the truth, and far too many knew there were Undivided heirs to be had, any time we chose to reveal them."

"I have one word for you, Colmán," the queen retorted. "Amergin."

The old man tugged at his beard, something Brydie noticed he did when irritated. "Amergin was a gifted bard, but he was seduced by a *Leanan Sídhe* whore. And he was never one of the *Matrarchaí*. It was obvious, even when he was a younger man, that his fascination with the *Tuatha Dé Danann* made him an unlikely prospect."

"That insight was fortunate," Anwen remarked. Colmán turned to her, looking mightily displeased, Brydie thought, and because Brydie was hanging around Anwen's neck, it seemed as if he were looking straight at her. "You cannot deny it, Vate," Anwen added.

"He's not denying it, Anwen," Álmhath said with a short, bitter laugh. "He's annoyed because you're right. How far will this set us back, do you think?"

Anwen shrugged. "Hard to say. The circumstances that aligned themselves the night RónánDarragh were conceived were rare. We had the right bloodline in Sybille, and a member of the *Tuatha* royalty taken enough with her beauty to put his own prejudices against humans aside to lay with her during the *Lá an Dreoilín* festivities, and that from the coupling came a not just a child, but a set of psychically linked twins. When will this realm have that opportunity again? I hesitate to use the word never, but certainly not in our lifetime."

The queen muttered something under her breath but Brydie was too far away to hear. The conversation fascinated her. Who knew Darragh and his brother were conceived so callously? It sounded as though the *Matrarchaí* were breeding cattle, not princes.

And who was the member of the *Tuatha* royalty sufficiently besotted by Darragh and Rónán's mother, to lay with her during the winter solstice celebrations? They were drunken, wild affairs, admittedly, and plenty of the *Tuatha Dé Danann* came out to play, but it was almost unheard of for *sídhe* royalty to take part. Queen Orlagh - so Brydie had heard - frowned on her immediate family fraternising too closely with humans.

That's why she appointed Marcroy Tarth as her ambassador. She trusted him not to get too carried away at times like that. Brydie remembered seeing him from a distance at the Summer Solstice party earlier this year, moving among the revellers as if their antics amused him -the same way one might enjoy the frantic shenanigans of a disturbed nest of ants. But he hadn't lain with a human woman, as far as she knew. Apparently, he was above that sort of thing.

Which one of his brothers had braved Orlagh's wrath by laying with a Druid woman and impregnating her all that time ago? And what would Marcroy do to him, if he ever discovered the truth?

Brydie sat back on her heels and pondered the matter, while the conversation between Álmhath, Colmán and Anwen moved on to how many yearling calves were to be slaughtered to feed the ravening hordes of party-goers.

Darragh and his brother are more than just half-Faerie, she realized. They're *Tuatha* royalty.

What puzzled Brydie more than anything was why, if the Undivided could claim such a degree of Faerie heritage, the *Matrarchaí* were going to such pains to hide it.

And why had Álmhath thought it so important to mix the Undivided's mongrel-Faerie line, with the pure Celtic blood of Mogue Ni'Farrell's only daughter?

CHAPTER 31

Having sworn to kill herself if Ren tried to leave the Ikushima compound, Aoi seemed to think it gave her leave to become his constant companion. She rarely left his side after her brother, Namito, made his startling announcement about her promise. When he woke in the morning she was waiting outside his hut. She escorted him to meals, tried to engage him in conversation, offered him endless cups of foul-tasting tea to show off her tea-ceremony skills, and generally wouldn't leave him alone.

In another reality, he would have said she was stalking him.

He couldn't imagine why, but he missed having Trása around to complain about it to, more than he believed possible.

Ren's attitude toward his half-Faerie nemesis had softened considerably since acquiring his brother's memoires. Darragh and Trása were childhood friends. She had been banished from *Sí an Bhrú* around the age of fourteen, for some reason Ren couldn't quite access in Darragh's memories, but his feelings for her were warm and affectionate for the most part, spiced with a distrust and resentment that Ren thought may have been flavoured by his own feelings.

In the end, he supposed, it didn't really matter. The only person in this reality who didn't think he was Faerie and want something from him because of it, was Trása. That made her his best friend in the entire world. Literally.

Aoi was older than Ren by a couple of years, and a virgin, he guessed, by the way she blushed crimson at him, whenever she tried to flirt. And she *was* flirting with him. Big time. Strangely, her brother didn't seem to mind.

Things came to a head a few days after Trása flew off in search of a *Leipreachán*. As had become her habit, Aoi walked Ren back to his hut after dinner, making small talk - or trying to make it. They had nothing in common, so there wasn't much they could talk about once they'd exhausted the weather, the manufacture of traditional Japanese fireworks and his impending doom at the hands of either the Tanabe or the Empresses, as topics of conversation.

It was raining when they reached the hut. Ren turned to say goodnight, and to suggest that Aoi get back to the main house before it pelted down, when she suddenly rose up on her toes and kissed him. Her lips were sweet, and moist with raindrops, utterly enticing and the most dangerous thing he'd ever tasted.

Ren pushed her away in alarm. He was in enough trouble with the Ikushima already, without being accused of taking advantage of the eldest daughter of the House.

Aoi looked stunned that he didn't want her. "What is the matter, Renkavana? Do you not think I'm pretty?"

"I think you're gorgeous," he assured her. "But... well..." he was floundering, not sure what to say that wouldn't offend her. After all, Aoi had offered her life as security against his good behaviour. It was rude of him to just push her away.

On the other hand, laying a hand on this girl was - Ren was certain - a very short road to a whole world of trouble and pain.

Then something useful from his brother's memories popped unbidden into his mind - the first time he was grateful for the *Comhroinn* rather than confused by it. He might be all bumbling idiocy around strange girls, but his brother wasn't. "It's just... well, we hardly know each other, Aoi."

She smiled up at him and stepped a little closer. "It is my intention that we will get to know each other intimately, Renkavana."

Aoi meant it, too, Ren realized. On the verge of panic, suddenly Darragh's confidence around women didn't seem enough and Ren was out of his depth.

"That's really... flattering," he said, taking another step backward, until he was pushed up against the wall of the hut, "but what about your brother and your grandmother? What would they have to say about this?"

"My brother and my *Obaasan* would welcome a child of the *Youkai* into the Ikushima."

"Child?" Ren repeated, wide eyed with alarm. "Who said anything about a child?"

"I would bear your progeny with pride, Renkavana," she said. "For the honor of my House and my family."

"Okay, this is getting outta hand," he muttered in English, taking Aoi firmly by the shoulders to prevent her moving any closer. "Look," he told her in her own language, "I appreciate what you've done for me. It was very brave of you to take that oath to commit *jigai* to keep me here, but that doesn't make you my girlfriend. I like you, but you're too old for me. We can be friends, but there won't be any funny business. Is that clear?"

Aoi studied him for a moment and then she stepped back. She didn't look offended. She seemed... relieved.

My brother and my Obaasan *would welcome a child of the* Youkai *into the Ikushima*, she'd said.

Jesus Christ, did they put her up to this?

Ren wanted to ask, but he was afraid of the answer. Fortunately, now he had rejected her so forcefully, Aoi didn't seem to be interested in any further conversation. She merely bowed low to him, muttered a goodbye and turned and hurried through the rain to the main house, leaving Ren wondering if he wouldn't have been better off if he'd let Chishihero slit his throat the other night and be done with it.

Ren thought - or at least hoped - his rejection of Aoi would mean the end of her plans to seduce him, and for a day or so, he figured he'd taken care of the problem. Aoi avoided him all the next day, and when he saw Namito at breakfast the following morning, no mention was made of his sister's attempt to seduce their guest. Ren found himself missing Trása even more than he had before, figuring she might be able to give him some insight into this awkward situation. At the very least, she could tell these people he wasn't *Youkai* and put an end to this idea that he was able or willing to provide the Ikushima with any sort of child, let alone a half-*Youkai* one.

He was encouraged by her absence, though. If she'd been gone this long, perhaps she'd found a *Leipreachán* and was receiving instruction on how to open a rift in this realm, to get back to his own.

Time was ticking on. Ren figured he had less than a week until *Lughnasadh* and the power transfer. He tried very hard not to think about it - given he might well be dead in a few days - but it was always at the back of his mind.

Get a move on Trása, he urged her silently, wishing telepathy was one of his gifts. *We need to get out of here.*

But at dinner the following evening, the situation became infinitely worse. When he arrived for dinner, Aoi was there along with Namito and the old lady, and Kazusa, who was dressed up like a miniature geisha. Ren smiled at her, wondering at the outfit. "What's the occasion?" he asked. "Was I supposed to dress for dinner?"

Before she could answer, Masuyo smiled and indicated that Ren should take his seat. He sat down staring at them all, wondering where the food was.

"Do you find her pleasing, Renkavana?"

"Pleasing, how, exactly?" he asked, figuring the question was about as laden with danger as Kiva charging into to his room in a panic before a red carpet event - as she was wont to do - to demand "does this dress make me look fat?".

"Pleasing to the eye," Masuyo suggested. "Attractive. Desirable."

Oh... this is so not happening to me.

"Pleasing, yes," Ren agreed carefully. "And very attractive. But *desirable*?" He shook his head, wishing he were even half the diplomat his brother was, and not just pretending. "She's a bit young for that, don't you think? I mean... no offence, Kaz... but she's a little kid."

"She has already commenced her menses," Masuyo announced.

I really didn't need to know that.

"What is it you dislike, Renkavana? Her manner? Her appearance? Is she not young enough?"

"Oh... you are *sick*, lady," Ren muttered in English. In her own language he addressed her more carefully, hoping his talent for language was such that there was no way he would be misunderstood. "*Obaasan,* I don't find Kazusa desirable because she is a child, and where I come from, a person doesn't desire children unless they are sick in the head. I come from a reality where grandmothers protect their children, not whore them out to strangers." He hadn't meant the last bit to sound so harsh, but he couldn't help himself. What Masuyo was suggesting was monstrous.

Aoi muttered something under her breath that sounded suspiciously like "I told you so" to her grandmother. Namito's expression didn't change. Ren got the feeling he was a party to this under protest. If he wasn't, then to hell with Aoi's *jigai* oath. If this is what they did to children as a matter of course in this realm, he was out of here. They all deserved to die.

"You told Aoi she was too old for your taste," Namito said, breaking his silence. "Now you claim Kazusa is too young? Must we line up every nubile female in the compound for you to choose one the right age?"

Ren looked around the table at them in stunned disbelief. Kazusa was smiling at him, almost as if she was oblivious about what exactly it was her grandmother was planning for her. Aoi wouldn't meet his eye. Namito seemed frustrated and angry, but Ren wasn't sure if the *Daimyo* was angry at his guest or his grandmother. Masuyo looked determined. And annoyed.

"You people are crazy," he said, shaking his head. "Certifiable, card-carrying lunatics. The lot of you."

Aoi and Kazusa both gasped. Masuyo had turned purple and looked ready to burst something vital.

"You offend us at our own table?" Namito asked, bristling at the insult.

"You started it," Ren shot back, alarmed at how childish that sounded. And how inappropriate it probably was. This was a world where people committed suicide rather than face dishonor. Not a good idea to belittle their customs, he guessed. He rose to his feet, figuring he would be better served leaving now, before he did too much more damage. He'd lost his appetite and any desire to spend a moment longer in their company. Ren turned to Masuyo, the architect, he was sure, of this diabolical plan. "Thanks for the offer, *Obaasan*, but I decline. I decline your granddaughters. I decline every nubile

301

female in the compound. And I decline your hospitality." He glanced at Aoi, adding, "I'm sorry you took that oath, Aoi because you really shouldn't have. You don't know me. And if the choice I have is between you committing *Seppuku* and me sleeping with your little sister... well, bad luck for you, I'm afraid."

Without waiting for an answer, he turned and left the dining room, grabbing his *geta* on the way out and carrying them in his hand. He wasn't sure he had the guts to leave the compound itself, knowing Aoi would have to follow through on her oath if he did, but the least he could do was not share a meal with them.

It was fully dark when he emerged onto the veranda. He glanced up at the sky for a moment, hoping to catch sight of a white owl, but the sky was empty. *Where the hell are you, Trása? I've got to get outta here.*

He headed down the steps and along the raked path to his own hut. Someone had lit the torches lighting the path. Most people had eaten, he guessed, and were taking care of the last chores of the day before seeking their beds. That was another thing he'd learned about realms without electricity. They tended to go to bed much earlier than he was used to. He walked in stockinged feet across the compound, carrying his wooden sandals, back towards his own hut, the damp sand soaking his feet.

"Renkavana!"

Ren stopped, hung his head for a moment in resignation and then turned to find Namito coming up behind him, armed with a *katana* and carrying a spare.

"You have insulted my House, my family, my *Obaasan* and my sisters."

"What can I say, Namito? It's been a busy day."

"I demand you allow me the opportunity to restore my family's honor."

"Knock yourself out," he said, turning away.

He figured he was safe. Namito wanted to restore his honor. He wasn't going to stab Ren in the back. The *Daimyo* wanted a fight. Ren had no intention of giving him one.

"Stop!"

Ren took a deep breath. *This is going to get very ugly.*

He turned to face Namito again, under no illusions about how long he would survive a sword fight. His entire experience with bladed weapons involved a school term of weekly classes with Olympic foils, the odd bit of instruction with bored stuntmen while on set with Kiva, a few lessons with Ciarán that ended, every single time, with him getting his butt kicked, and the knowledge - but not the skill - acquired from his brother during the *Comhroinn*. He would last a minute or less, he figured, if he allowed this to escalate into an actual fight.

The problem was, in this world where people offered to kill themselves as a surety against a stranger's good behaviour, a mere sword fight to the death to restore a man's honor was probably a routine occurrence.

Everyone had stopped to watch. Aoi and Kazusa had come out onto the veranda with Masuyo. Fiery torches lined the path, making Namito look every bit the devastatingly well-trained samurai he was. Ren glanced around, his heart sinking.

The bigger the audience, Ren realized with despair, the less chance he had of talking his host out of this.

Namito tossed the blade to Ren, who took a step back so that it landed in the sand at his feet.

"You are a coward, Renkavana."

"Sticks and stones, dude," Ren muttered to himself. He looked at Namito, shaking his head. "I'm not going to fight you."

"Then I will kill you."

"Really?" Ren asked, wondering if it was bravery or complete idiocy to call his bluff. "Kill me? And then what?" *My brother and my* Obaasan *would welcome a child of the* Youkai *into the Ikushima*, Aoi had said. They'd thrown Kazusa at him, too. He was banking on Namito wanting him alive more than his honor restored.

"Wound him, Namito," Masuyo called out from the veranda. "He can still give us what we need without his limbs."

Charming, Ren thought, taking another step back as he watched Namito warily. Would he refuse to attack an unarmed man, or was offering Ren a weapon enough for the forms to be served?

It proved to be the latter.

With a roar, Namito raised his weapon and charged. Ren glanced at the blade on the ground, realized he had no chance of reaching it in time, even if he'd known what to do with it. The best he could do, in the split second between Namito's attack and losing an arm at the shoulder, was to turn away and try to protect his head.

Ren braced himself, waiting for the pain, wondering if he could manage to somehow zap himself away from here again, as he had when the Tanabe had tried to kill him...

But the pain never came. The air was suddenly filled with an angry screeching, a blur of feathers and cries of shock and alarm. Ren opened his eyes to discover Namito under attack from a huge eagle, furiously flapping its wings. He dropped his *katana* and fled the open courtyard for the shelter of the veranda attached to the main house as the eagle drove him back.

The bird didn't continue the attack once Namito was disarmed. Instead, it landed in front of Ren, stretched its wings in an awesome show of defiance, and then it morphed into a young woman, naked, magnificent and furious.

"How dare you!" she shouted, looking around at the terrified Ikushima. "In the name of the *Youkai* I demand you leave my mate alone!"

CHAPTER 32

Namito had found, or been handed, another *katana*. He raised it, prepared to continue his attack, now he realized he was facing a *Youkai* rather than a wild bird. He stepped down into the torch-lit yard, his sword at the ready and began to cautiously move forward. Ren was still breathing hard, his heart pounding at his narrow escape. He had not expected to avoid a fight with Namito by having Trása come to his rescue. He watched her facing down the *Daimyo* and smiled. In this mood, she truly was something to behold.

Trása laughed scornfully at the samurai as if he was a child waving around a bread and butter knife. "Are you so foolish, *Daimyo*, that you would attack a *Youkai* and her mate?"

"*Mate?*" Ren asked behind her in a low voice. It wasn't that he was ungrateful for her intervention, but he wasn't expecting her to claim him like some pre-historic cave girl in a really bad movie. "When did I become your *mate*?"

"Shut up, Rónán," she hissed, standing squarely between him and Namito. "And just play along." She glanced over her shoulder and added tartly, "Unless, of course, you'd *like* me to leave, so the nice little *samaurai* man can carry out his plan to cut you into sushi."

She had a point. Ren glanced at Namito and the sword he was waving about so angrily. "On second thoughts, why don't you just carry on saving me," he agreed and took a step backwards. This girl could morph into a tiger if she chose. Trása didn't need his help.

Namito was watching them through narrowed eyes, perhaps weighing up his chances of attacking Trása before she turned him into a toad, or whatever it was she was planning to do. It occurred to Ren at that moment, that other than morphing into a variety of avian wildlife, he really didn't know what Trása was capable of. He knew she was half-*Beansídhe*, but he'd spent most of his time with her in a reality without magic, and Darragh's memories of her were not in any way related to her magical ability.

"The Empresses have a bounty on your kind, *Youkai*. Those pointed ears of yours will make an ideal trophy to prove the loyalty of the Ikushima."

"I was thinking your balls would make an excellent necklace," she shot back. "But now I look at you, I think they would make better earrings."

Don't insult his manhood! Ren wanted to shout at her. *You'll just make things worse.*

Namito raised his sword even higher, her slurs bolstering his courage. "I will gut you like the vermin you are, *Youkai.*"

Trása glanced over her shoulder at Ren. "Time to wane out of here, I think."

"Wayne?" Ren asked in confusion. "Wayne who?"

Trása glared at him for a moment, as if he'd done something really stupid. "You don't know *how*?"

"How *what*, for chrissakes?"

"You don't know? Shit!" she said in English, and then she turned to Namito and held up her hand. "Stay your hand, *Daimyo* of the Ikushima. You have proved your courage. The *Youkai* honor you and your clan."

"*Hey*?" Ren asked, as Namito lowered his *katana*, looking just as confused as Ren felt. *What the fuck is she playing at?* One minute Trása was dicing with death, and the next, she was trying to play nice.

"You dare much, *Youkai*, coming into *Shin Bungo* and insulting the Ikushima." Namito didn't sound very certain, but at least he lowered his sword. Nobody watching the exchange from the verandas made a move to interfere.

"I dare much, because there is much I can offer you," Trása announced.

Ren was at a total loss as to what she might be talking about, or why she'd changed her tune so suddenly.

The next thing he knew, Trása was stepping up to Namito, so close she was almost nose-to-nose with him, and speaking in a strange, musical tone. "If I may beg your indulgence, *Daimyo*, I wish to speak to my mate in private. You will permit this."

Namito stared into Trása's eyes, as if he was bewitched, and nodded as he sheathed his *katana*. "You may discuss your private matter in Renkavana's quarters. I await the offer you speak of."

"Thank you." Trása bowed low to the *Daimyo* and then she turned, took Ren by the arm and all but dragged him across the raked sand to the hut, slamming the sliding door so hard once they were inside, she almost knocked it off its rails.

With a wave of her hand, Trása lit the candle on the table and the turned to Ren and punched him on the shoulder. "Why didn't you tell me?"

"Ow! Tell you *what*?"

"That the Undivided are *sídhe*. That you can wane like a *Leipreachán*?"

"I have no idea what you're talking about, Trása. Why did you tell them I was your mate?"

"Because *Youkai* mate for life. They'll stop asking you to mate with one of them if they think you're already spoken for." She studied him for a moment and then changed her tack. "Even if you didn't know, why didn't Darragh tell me about the Undivided being *sídhe*?"

"Probably because - like me - he didn't know anything about it," Ren said as he rubbed his arm, certain some memory of that startling news would be hiding somewhere in his brother's memories if he'd known about it. "What did you do to Namito?"

"What do you mean?"

"I mean that Jedi mind-trick you just pulled. That *these-aren't-the-droids-you're-looking-for* thing you just did to him."

"Oh that... I glamoured him, that's all."

"You can do that? Just make people do what you want?"

"Yes..."

He stared at her, not sure if what he was feeling was amazement or despair. "And you only thought to mention this rather useful trick now?"

"It's not as useful as you might imagine," she said, rolling her eyes as she put her hands on her hips which distracted Ren from the discussion, because she still wasn't wearing a stitch of clothing. "It only works if you can get close enough to someone so they're totally focussed on you. That's really the first time I've had a chance to do it."

Things had been hectic lately, he had to concede. Still...

"By the way, who the hell is Wayne?"

"Not who, *what*," she said, folding her arms crossly. "It's how you escaped the Tanabe, remember?"

"How did you know about that?"

"Why didn't you tell me you could wane?"

"Waning? Is *that* what you call it?" The word caused a whole world of interesting information to crowd the forefront of his mind as he realized what it meant. It made sense now. No wonder he hadn't been able to find any information in Darragh's memories. He'd been searching for *teleporting*, or *vanishing*, or *disappearing*. None of those words triggered a damn thing. *Waning* was the word he'd been looking for, and suddenly Ren discovered he knew exactly how to do it.

Not that the knowledge did him any good. If he waned out of here Aoi would have to commit *jigai*.

"Oh, so *now* you remember?" She shook her head as she noticed the dawning comprehension in his eyes. "It would have been a bit more useful if you could have had this epiphany out in the compound just now."

She had a point, but he didn't feel he deserved to be spoken to like that by someone wearing nothing but her birthday suit. "You do realize you're not wearing any clothes, don't you?"

Trása let out an exasperated sigh and snatched up the blanket from the futon. She wrapped it around herself impatiently and tied it off. "Better?

"Thank you," he said, and then shook his head. "And I didn't say anything out in the compound because I didn't know what it was called. Oh, and I can't go anywhere. Aoi took an oath. If I try to leave here she has to kill herself."

"Well, here's hoping she doesn't make too much mess when she falls on her sword," Trása said, with a complete lack of sympathy. "Let's go."

"No," he insisted, shaking his head. "I'm not going to be responsible for killing someone."

"You're *not* responsible," she said. "Did you make her take an oath?"

"Of course not."

"Then she's not your problem."

"Besides," another, rather cranky and impatient voice interjected behind him, "these be the Empresses' minions and they be the people that killed all of our people. Who cares if one dies?"

Ren spun around to find the strangest sight behind him. Standing there was a tiny, ginger-haired ninja, no taller than his knee, with a pointy ginger goatee and a belt full of tiny weapons made from ebony and *airgead sídhe*. Ren turned to Trása. "What is that?"

"A *Leipreachán*," she said. "What do you think it is?"

"It's like no *Leipreachán* I've seen before."

"And you've seen so many of them, haven't you? This is Toyoda Mulrayn. I think he's Plunkett's *eileféin*."

"Toyoda? Seriously?"

Trása ignored the question. "Toyoda, this is Rónán. In my reality, believe it or not, he's one of the Undivided."

"The Undivided be *Youkai* in your realm, too then?" he asked, stepping a little closer to examine Ren with a critical eye.

"I'm not *Youkai*," Ren said. He turned back to Trása, starting to get a little annoyed by this. "Why the sudden insistence that I'm one of you?"

"Because ye are," Toyoda said. "Can we go now?"

"I told you, I'm not leaving."

Trása threw her hands up. "Do you know *why* they want you here, Rónán?"

Ren felt himself blushing unexpectedly. "I was kinda getting an idea about that when you arrived. I knocked back Aoi, and "every nubile female in the compound" thank you very much. They even offered me a girl. A kid!"

The *Leipreachán* didn't seem surprised. "The Ikushima want children from ye because they have no family member in the *Konketsu*," Toyoda told him. "They be hoping ye will give them a magically gifted child, before they run ye through and offer ye head to the Empresses as proof they be loyal. 'Twould raise their family's social standing considerable."

But Trása smiled inexplicably. "You rejected Aoi?"

"Of course, I did. What do you take me for?"

"She's very pretty."

"She's a lunatic. Like everyone else around here. Have you found out how to open a rift yet?

"Ye need a folding spell." Toyoda answered for her.

"Great, where do we get one?"

"Ye don't just *get* one," the little ninja *Leipreachán said.* "Ye learn it. It takes years and years of study to master the folding magic. Only the most dedicated and highly trained *mahou tsukaino sensei* can open rifts."

"So we need one of these *mahou tsukaino sensei* who can fold the spell and we're good, yeah?"

"Tell him the rest of it, Toyoda," Trása said with a heavy sigh. She'd obviously been told the bad news already, by her expression.

"Even if ye know the spell, regular *washi* paper won't do," Toyoda explained. "It needs *gampi* paper for ye to fold the spell to open a rift between realms."

"Where do we get *gampi* paper from then?" Ren asked.

"That's the catch," Trása explained. "These Empresses everyone talks about? They are the daughters of the last Undivided. They took over this realm, banished or killed their father and uncle - there's something of a debate going on between the lesser*Youkai* about which it was. Then they killed all the pure *Youkai*, by driving them through rifts into magicless worlds, and kept the mixed-blood *Konketsu* to wield the limited amount of magic they allow them... and then... they destroyed all the *gampi* bushes except those in the Imperial Palace."

Why was everything to do with magic so damned complicated? "So, what you're saying is, we're screwed."

"Pretty much," Trása agreed with a shrug.

"*Lughnasadh* is only a few days away. They're going to transfer the power to the new twins and Darragh and I are going to die."

"Maybe you should have taken Namito up on his offer of all those nubile females, then," Toyoda suggested. "Be one way to pass the time until ye inevitable demise."

Ren glared at the *Leipreachán*. "You're a big help."

"I just be offering me wisdom on the matter. We *Leipreachán* not be as dumb as ye think we be..."

"Then how about using all that awesome *Leipreachán* intellect to come up with a real plan."

"Actually, Rónán," Trása said. "He already has. At least we have *kind* of a plan." She smiled at Ren, obviously pleased with herself. "We may just have figured out how to save you, if we can't get out of this realm in time for the equinox."

"Excellent. What about Darragh?"

Trása's smug look wavered a little. "What about him?"

"We're psychically linked, Trása. If one of us dies, the other will follow in a matter of days. You know that better than I do. I appreciate that you've come up with a plan to save me, but it's a waste of energy if you haven't thought up a way to save my brother at the same time."

CHAPTER 33

Once it was clear they weren't dealing with Chelan Aquarius Kavanaugh, but his previously unknown identical twin, Murray Symes no longer had a stake in the case. He tried to stick around, claiming some nonsense about knowing Ren and therefore being in a better position to judge his twin, Inspector Duggan thanked him for his help, dispensed with his services, and sent him on his way.

Then Pete had sat down with Darragh to interrogate him again and got nothing more than a repeat of this story about alternate realities, fairies, and Druids.

The following day, with nobody able to shake his story, Brendá Duggan ordered Pete to call in their own shrink, Annad Semaj, to assess Darragh, and decide if he was sane, if he knew where Hayley Boyle had been taken, or indeed, if he knew whether or not she was still alive.

Dr Semaj was the son of South African Indian parents who had come to the Republic of Ireland to study during the apartheid years. As "coloreds", they couldn't attend university in their own country and had chosen the University of Dublin for their medical studies. They'd never returned home. Annad, despite his name, had never stepped foot in the homeland of his ancestors and didn't speak a word of Hindi, or Zulu, either. He'd been raised in Dublin and spoke with an educated Irish accent that always unsettled the criminals he was assessing, because they'd judged him before he opened his mouth, and when he spoke, his soft Irish brogue was so unexpected, they were at a disadvantage right from the get-go.

Pete stayed in the observation room on the other side of the two-way mirror and watched him talking to Darragh. If anybody was going to get to the bottom of this kid's delusions and decide if they were real or not, Pete figured Annad would.

Darragh sat in the interview room, calm and composed. That bothered Pete. Most nut-jobs who claimed they were from other planet - or another reality as Darragh was insisting - tended to fidget. Most of them could barely sit still. This lad had a zen-like serenity about him that Pete found more unsettling than some of the violently agitated criminals he'd had to deal with.

Once they were past the pleasantries and formalities for the benefit of the recording equipment, Annad smiled, blew his nose and apologised for still having the flu. He studied Darragh for a long time in silence, taking note of his demeanour, Pete guessed.

What usually happened, Pete knew, was that the suspect would grow uncomfortable with the silence and start the conversation up themselves.

Darragh didn't. He waited Annad out.

"You have an interesting tale to tell, I hear," the doctor said eventually, which Pete found very interesting. Annad didn't often lose the "let's see who speaks first" game. "Tell me how you and your brother came to be separated as children."

Darragh nodded. "We were betrayed."

"I see," Annad said, in a non-committal tone, wiping his nose again. Pete was starting to feel guilty that he'd dragged Annad out of his sickbed. "Do you often feel as if people are plotting to betray you?"

"It is the nature of the beast, I fear," Darragh replied with a shrug. "The Partitionists actively call for our removal, but only because they don't understand the consequences." Darragh clasped his hands in front of him on the table. "Amergin's betrayal was particularly painful. He was like a father to us."

"To you and Ren?"

"My brother's name is Rónán."

"Ah, yes... Rónán. Does he remember this life you had in... what do you call it?" Annad consulted his notes for a moment. "The other realm?"

"He wasn't even four years old," Darragh said. "He remembers nothing."

"Does that bother you? That he won't believe your tale?"

Darragh cocked his head to one side. "He doesn't need to believe it, Doctor. He's been there."

"So... Ren... I mean, Rónán, can hear and see the same things you see and hear? The same voices? The same instructions?"

"Of course he can," Darragh said, and then he leaned back in his seat and nodded. "I'm not sure what you mean by instruct... oh, I see. You believe I am making this up."

"Are you?"

"If I were, would I admit it?"

"You might," Annad said, "if you were trying to fake insanity and discovered you can't keep it up. It's harder to pretend crazy than it looks."

"What reason would I have to pretend insanity?" Darragh asked. Pete thought he seemed genuinely puzzled by the notion.

"You're facing some serious charges, lad," the psychiatrist pointed out. "You might prefer a nice padded cell to a prison one."

Darragh shook his head. "Neither bothers me, Doctor Semaj, because sooner or later, they will come for me. Some discomfort in the meantime is tolerable. I won't be here long enough for it to be much more than an inconvenience." He smiled then, as if he'd just recalled something amusing. "It couldn't be any worse than sitting through a banquet in *Sí an Bhrú* with Torcán for company."

"Torcán?" Annad asked. "Is he one of your friends from the other reality?"

"A reluctant ally, perhaps. Hardly a friend."

"He's from the reality where you sent Hayley Boyle?"

"Naturally."

Annad stopped to blow his nose again, and to consult his notes. When he looked up, he changed the line of questioning. He was getting nowhere trying to trip Darragh up on the details of his imaginary world.

"What was Hayley's reaction to your intention to send her through to another reality?"

Darragh shrugged. "She was sceptical, I'm sure, but she trusts Rónán, or she would not have voluntarily gone with him. Truth is, I hardly spoke to her, so I couldn't say what her feelings were, one way or the other."

"How did she get away from St Christopher's?"

"Trása drove her back to the stone circle in Warren's car."

"Trása?" Annad consulted his notes again for a moment. "That's the girl claiming to be Jack O'Righin's granddaughter?"

"Trása lied about that to gain access to Rónán through his neighbour," Darragh said. "She has no family in this realm. She's half-*Beansídhe*. She is Amergin's daughter."

Pete heard the door open behind him, and saw Brendá Duggan's reflection coming toward him in the glass wall separating him from the interview.

"How's it going?" she asked softly, not that they could hear or see them in the other room.

"He's talkative enough," Pete said. "But he's really not telling us anything."

Brendá stared at Darragh and Dr Semaj for a moment before asking, "You've studied psychology. Do you think he's crazy?"

Pete shrugged. "There's a way to go yet. He fits some of the criteria for paranoid schizophrenia. He seems to believe things about reality and the world around him nobody else believes. He claims he has magical powers in the other reality, and that he's been betrayed by people plotting to remove him.

But he's lucid enough, and he doesn't seem to have any trouble making himself understood, nor does he seem particularly bothered if we don't believe him."

"What does Annad think?"

"Don't know yet. He's only just started." Pete turned back to the interview to watch, with the Inspector by his side.

"Do you sometimes feel others are controlling what you think, what you feel?" Annad was asking Darragh in the other room.

The young man smiled as the doctor pulled another tissue from the box to blow his nose again. "I may not control my destiny, Doctor, but my will is my own. That I am here talking to you is proof of that."

"How so?"

"If others were controlling me, I would never have left my own realm," he said. "The Undivided really aren't encouraged to go rift running."

"The Undivided?" Brendá Duggan asked beside Pete. "What's that?"

"It's the title he claims to share with his twin brother."

"He has a title?" she asked, raising her brow slightly. "Delusions of grandeur, too, eh? You'd better make certain he can't wiggle out of this by pleading insanity, Pete."

"That's what Annad's doing here," Pete reminded her. "Don't worry, if and when we charge him, we'll make it stick."

"Do you feel treated unfairly because others are jealous of your special abilities?" Annad was asking Darragh in the interview room. Pete hadn't heard the question before that because he was talking to

Brendá. He'd have to check the recording later, to see what he missed.

"See that you do," Brendá said, turning for the door. "Oh, before I forget, Logan just called me to ask if you could have the rest of the day off."

Pete turned to look at her. "Why?"

"Not sure. He wants you to meet him at your grandmother's place. I told him you would and that I wasn't your secretary."

He smiled briefly. "Thanks, boss."

Duggan didn't seem to want or need his thanks. "Just get this mess sorted before you go," she said with a scowl, pointing toward the interview room. "And as soon as he's finished, send Annad back home and tell him I said not to come back until he's well again. He's going to give everyone in the building that wretched lurgy, if he hangs about sneezing on everyone." With that unsympathetic decree she left the observation room, leaving Pete to continue watching Annad Semaj interviewing Darragh, curious about what his brother wanted, and why he hadn't simply contacted him directly.

God, he thought, with a sudden stab of despair. *He's not going to get engaged to that model is he?*

It was bad enough not being as visibly successful as his brother. He'd never hear the end of it if Logan got married first. Particularly if he married somebody their mother had set him up with.

Whatever Logan wanted, it could wait. Right now, he had other problems and they all began and ended with Darragh of the Undivided.

"Do you sometimes find it difficult to express yourself in words that others can understand?" Annad was asking the young man.

Darragh shook his head. "Quite the opposite. Like all Druids, I have a gift for languages. And language."

"So you're a Druid?"

"Of course."

"Do you ever worry you can't trust what you're thinking because you don't know if it's real or not?"

"No," Darragh replied. He seemed intrigued by the possibility. "Is that a problem in this realm?"

Pete smiled at that. *This kid is either a complete loon or a genius*, he thought.

Annad sniffed inelegantly before asking, "Ever talk to another person or hear other voices inside your head that nobody else can hear?"

"I would be quite mad if I did, wouldn't I?"

"Is that a yes or a no?"

"A most definite no," Darragh assured him. "Does that disappoint you, doctor? You seem to be fishing for an answer I am unable to provide."

"Does it bother you that I don't appear to believe you when you tell me about your alternate reality?"

Darragh shook his head. "How could you know about it?"

"You seem to know a lot about this reality for someone who claims he's only been here a few days."

"That is because I have shared the *Comhroinn* with my brother."

"What's that?"

"It is the mental sharing that allows us to know each other completely."

"I see," Annad said, leaning back in his chair. "Could you and I have this sharing? This *Comhroinn*?"

"No."

"Why not?"

"Because it wouldn't work."

"Why wouldn't it work? Because we are not brothers?"

"It wouldn't work because there is no magic in this reality," Darragh pointed out. "It is a magical sharing. No magic, no *Comhroinn*."

Pete shook his head, amazed at how consistent this kid was with his delusion. He could see even Annad had started to tap his pen on the table with frustration.

That made him smile. Pete hadn't been able to shake this kid's story for days now. It was something of a relief to discover he wasn't the only one who couldn't crack it.

The downside, of course, was that they were no closer to finding Darragh's accomplice, Sorcha, or discovering what had happened to Hayley Boyle.

CHAPTER 34

"Hate to be the bearer of bad news, mistress," Toyoda announced, peeking outside through a small crack in the door. "But it be debatable how much longer ye hosts be willing to let ye stay in here before they be storming the place. The glamouring be worn off and the *Daimyo* be pacing about out there like a caged cat. He seems mighty peeved 'bout something."

Trása threw her hands up and turned to Ren. The candlelight shadowed her face, but there was no need to guess what she was thinking. "We could be gone already if my *mate*, Rónán, here, would simply wane himself to safety."

"I told you, I can't leave," Ren reminded her, wishing he *could* do what she suggested. Now he knew what it was called, he knew exactly what to do and was rather looking forward to trying it again. Except for one small problem. "Aoi took an oath to guarantee I wouldn't try to escape. She'll have to kill herself if I leave."

"*So?*"

Ren stared at Trása, finding it hard to believe she meant to sound so callous. With the benefit of his brother's memories, he knew her much better now. Trása wasn't nearly as heartless and tough, he realized, as she liked to pretend.

He shook his head and folded his arms across his body. "I'm not going, Trása, so you might as well just get over it and move on to telling me your grand idea for saving me from certain death on *Lughnasadh.*"

"That *is* the plan," she told him in exasperation. "We get you out of here and take you to *Tír Na nÓg.* Or at least this reality's version of it. I've been there already. The place is so steeped in magic it all but drips from the trees. The magic there should protect you from the magic of the other realm."

"Should?"

"We'll know after *Lughnasadh,*" she said with a shrug. "The alternative is to wait here and find out the hard way that I'm wrong."

The idea of magic from one realm protecting him from the magic of another had some merit, Ren thought. But it still didn't solve the main problem. "What about Darragh?"

"He be trapped in a realm without magic, the *Beansídhe* tells me," Toyoda said, still looking out into the compound at Namito. Then he glanced over his shoulder at them. "Chances be good the transfer'll not reach him anyways."

He looked at Trása and her little ninja-*Leipreachán* companion. They seemed an unlikely pair to be taking advice from. "But you don't know that for certain?"

"Not for certain," Trása conceded.

"Then it's just what I said earlier. We're screwed."

"We don't know that," Trása said. "And if there is any chance taking you to *Tír Na nÓg* will mean you and Darragh will survive *Lughnasadh* then we need to try it. Unless you like the idea of being dead?"

"Not especially, but we're still back where we started and the problem with Aoi," he said, sinking down onto the futon with a sigh. "How did you even know I needed rescuing?"

"Toyoda told me about the *Konketsu* and how much the Ikushima wanted a magician of their own, and then I remembered the look on Aoi's face when I was here before." She smiled at him briefly. "It wasn't hard to figure out why they hadn't tried to kill you like the Tanabe did. That girl had designs on you then, Rónán. I was pretty sure you'd need some help fighting her off." She cocked her head sideways a little. "Of course, if you'd rather I *didn't* help..."

"No, it's fine. I'm glad you did. And you're right about them wanting a kid from the *Youkai*. Except I'm not *Youkai*, so why pick on me?"

Trása sat down on the futon beside him, shaking her head. "Trouble is, Rónán. You almost have to be one of us. There's no way you could wane if you weren't. Can Darragh do it too?"

He nodded. "Could and did," he told her. "That's how he was sneaking out of *Sí an Bhrú* to meet up with me." Ren closed his eyes for a moment to better access the memory. "Some chick called Brydie was covering for him."

Trása scowled at him. "Who is Brydie?"

"I don't know... his girlfriend?" Ren caught the look on Trása's face at that suggestion and quickly changed his tune. She was likely to lose it completely if she learned just how close Brydie and Darragh had been. "She's someone Álmhath introduced him to, maybe?" The memories were getting harder to separate from his own. It wasn't as clear-cut as just closing his eyes and letting the video replay in his head. There were emotions mixed up in there, and not just relating to the mysterious Brydie. Darragh's feelings for Brydie, Álmhath, Marcroy Tarth, and even Colmán, all clouded the memory, making it hard to be certain about anything.

Trása seemed set to interrogate Ren some more about Brydie and what she was up to with his brother, but Toyoda saved him from her questions. "Ye need to be swapping reminiscences some other time, mistress," he suggested. "It be time to leave."

Ren studied Trása for a moment and then rose to his feet. "Can you glamour Namito into releasing Aoi from her oath?"

"Sure."

"How long will it last?"

Trása shrugged. "I don't know... an hour if we're lucky."

"And then she'll have to kill herself?"

"I suppose. If she means it."

"She means it, to be sure," Toyoda assured them, straightening his weapons belt that never seemed to sit right for long. "These people not be fooling about when it comes to their honor."

"What if I convince them to let me go?"

"Sure," Trása said, looking at up at him. "But they're not going to. Don't you remember the old lady suggesting you can still give them what they need without your limbs?"

"That's my point," Ren said, a plan forming in his mind as he spoke. "You said you were going to make them an offer, so let's do that, yeah? I have something they need. That's the first law of negotiation, by the way. Go into the discussion armed with something your opponent wants, and know how badly they want it."

She frowned. "Is that something you picked up from Darragh's memories, too?"

Ren shook his head. "Actually, that one comes courtesy of one Jon van Heusen. He's my mother's manager. You remember him, don't you? Thanks to you, I got arrested for stealing his Ferrari."

"It was your idea to take the Ferrari," Trása reminded him. "I just said we'd get to the warehouse quicker if we took the shiny red car."

"Yeah, right," Ren said, and then he turned to the *Leipreachán*. "Open the door, Toyoda, and let's go make the Ikushima an offer they can't refuse."

With the glamour worn off, Namito seemed to be having a *what-was-I-thinking?* moment. He had started pacing across the raked path as Ren stepped onto the veranda. The night was much colder now, the temperature having dropped considerably while they were inside making their plans. Although he was sure he was imagining it, somewhere Ren thought he could hear the slow, rhythmic pounding of drums. Or rather he felt them, as if their pitch was so low he could only feel it through his bones.

Ren shook off the unsettling feeling and concentrated on the problem at hand. He wasn't sure if Trása was right about being safe from the power transfer happening on *Lughnasadh* in Darragh's reality if he was tucked away in this reality's version of *Tír Na nÓg*, but other than getting the hell out of this insane reality and trying to stop it happening at all, he didn't have any better ideas.

It was as good a Plan B as any other, but not if it was going to cost someone their life. Ren could deal with his own life being threatened, but he was not prepared to be responsible for Aoi dying, even if he thought she was crazy for taking such an oath, and her family equally crazy for holding her to it.

Aoi stood with her brother. Masuyo was still standing on the veranda of the main house, looking more angry than worried. The rest of the Ikushima workers had scattered or been sent away, leaving the *Daimyo* and his family alone in the compound. Ren was relieved that Kazusa was nowhere in sight. That she had been offered to him as a concubine was still enough to make Ren's stomach churn.

"Namito," he said, his breath frosting in the chilly air, as he walked from the hut with Trása.

"Renkavana."

He glanced at Trása for a moment before he spoke. "My *mate* ... is demanding that I leave with her and return to the homeland of the *Youkai*," he said. He didn't know the name of *Tír Na nÓg* in this reality. Homeland would have to do. "I have obligations there that I am honor-bound to fulfil."

"My sister is ready to commit *jigai* when you leave," Namito informed him stiffly. Aoi dropped her head beside her brother, refusing to meet Ren's eye. "It is for you to judge if your mate's wishes are worth an innocent life."

You people really are certifiably insane, he thought, resisting the impulse to run down the steps to Namito, grab him by the shoulders and shake some sense back into him. If Ren had learned nothing else travelling the world with Kiva, moving from one exotic movie location to another, he had learned that visitors never understood the locals as much as they liked to think. No matter how much one thought one's own customs better, people from other cultures usually didn't appreciate you breezing into town for a few days, weeks or months and trying to change theirs.

"I do not wish your sister harm, Namito," Ren said. "And I do not wish to belittle the value of your sister's oath, but if I stay here, *I* will die."

"Then you will die with honor," Namito assured him, solemnly.

Oh, well... in that case...

Masuyo had been listening to their exchange from her veranda, but when she heard Ren's life might be in danger, she clearly thought he was making it up to gain her grandson's sympathy. With a cry of disgust, she hurried down off the veranda and shuffled across the sand toward her grandson, her tiny steps limited by her wooden *geta* and the tightness of her kimono. She stopped beside Namito, who was standing between the torches lighting the path, puffing a little from the exertion. Masuyo glared up at Ren. By the light of the torches she looked haggard and furious. "Don't listen to him, Namito. He is lying to save his dishonorable, *Youkai* skin."

"Renkavana cannot give you what you want, if he is dead, *Daimyo.*"

Ren glanced at Trása, who had stepped up beside him, hands on her hips, looking faintly ridiculous wrapped in the blanket from his futon. "What are you talking about?"

"Doesn't take a genius to work out where you're going with this."

She stepped up beside him then and turned to address Namito, looking slightly ridiculous wrapped in the blanket, but no less fearsome than when she had been disguised an as eagle. "On *Higan No Chu-Nichi* ... the autumn equinox, a ceremony will take place in the realm from which we come that will destroy Renkavana, unless he is protected by the magic of his own kind."

"Let the *Youkai* die," Masuyo suggested to her grandson. She pointed at Trása. "Take the female. She looks healthy enough. You can impregnate her yourself."

"I'd like to see you try." Trása muttered in her own tongue so that only Ren could hear her.

He bit back a smile. Namito, to his credit, didn't seem too keen on his grandmother's suggestion. "*Obaasan* ... please..."

"You might be able to kill the *Youkai* in this realm," Trása continued, speaking to Namito, rather than his grandmother. He was, after all, the *Daimyo* here. He was the only one who could absolve Aoi from her oath. "But you can't keep us prisoner. The only reason you've kept Renkavana this long, is because he's too honorable to allow Lady Ouchie there..."

"Ow-ee," Ren corrected.

"... to run herself through if he leaves," Trása finished as if Ren hadn't spoken.

"What are you suggesting, Renkavana?" Namito asked, stepping forward a little, apparently to distance himself from his grandmother. Ren thought it interesting that he didn't want a *Youkai* child if he had to rape Trása to get one, but he seemed quite comfortable asking Ren to take his twelve-year-old sister to his bed to achieve the same aim.

Honor was something one could find ways around in this realm, it seemed. He stopped for a moment, still hearing the distant beat of drums, wondering if he was the only one who could hear them. Ren glanced around, but everyone seemed engrossed in the discussion and hadn't noticed them yet.

"Let Renkavana go," Trása said, "And I'll promise he'll return after *Higan No Chu-Nichi*."

"Assuming I'm still alive."

Namito seemed to be wavering. "What guarantee do I have that you will keep your word, *Youkai*?"

Ren took a step down from the veranda to the sand and stepped up to meet Namito, face to face. "Because I've proved I can be trusted." He stepped even closer and lowered his voice so that Masuyo couldn't hear what he was saying. "You told me Aoi had sworn to commit *jigai* and I stayed. I could have zapped myself out of here anytime I felt like it, and I didn't." That wasn't strictly true then, but it was true now, so technically, it wasn't a lie. "If that doesn't convince you my word is any good, I just refused to sleep with your little sister. The old lady might have thought that was a grand idea for the greater good of the clan, but you didn't like it any more than I did. That should tell you everything you need to know about me."

"If you do not come back," Namito said in an equally low voice, "Aoi will have to fulfil her oath."

"If I don't come back, it'll be because I'm dead," Ren assured him, "so you'll just have to take the chance both of us are going to see the sunrise after *Lughnasadh*, and let me go." He stopped and cocked his head. He hadn't imagined it - there were definitely drums. "Am I the only one who can hear that?"

Namito listened to the drums a moment, looking puzzled, and called to one of the guards patrolling the walls.

"What's the matter?" Masuyo asked. The drums were still pitched so low Ren could barely make them out. He guessed the old lady wouldn't be able to hear them at all. He glanced at Trása, but she seemed just as unsure. He thought she could hear the drums now. Aoi had turned toward the wall, awaiting some indication of direction.

"The Tanabe didn't have drums the last time they attacked," Ren said, wondering if that's what was happening.

Namito shook his head, bewildered. "That's not the Tanabe," he said, and then he turned to his grandmother. "Go inside. Take Aoi with you. And find Kazusa."

"You think we're under attack?"

"Just do as I command, *Obaasan*," Namito snapped, and then he turned for the wall.

Before Ren could follow, Trása was at his side. "Come on, now's our chance. Let's get out of here."

"Can you hear the drums?"

"Yes, I can hear them," she said. "And the tune they're playing is called *Trouble*. We have to go, Rónán."

"I can't. Namito hasn't released Aoi from her oath."

"Fine, we'll die here then," she said, throwing her hands up. "That's a much better idea."

"What happened to the *Leipreachán*?"

"He bolted the moment he heard those drums."

"Why did he zap out of here in such a hurry?"

"Because he's the only one of us with any common sense," she said. "And it's a sad day in any realm when the only creatures with any common sense are the *Leipreachán*."

The drums grew louder. There was a relentless stridency in the sound that set the hair on the back of Ren's neck standing on end. Slowly, as the sound became louder, others turned towards the walls, wondering what it was. People emerged from their huts. Even Masuyo seemed to have a change of heart and hurried Aoi away toward the main house. Ren looked around for Namito and saw him scaling the ladder to the walkway on top of the wall.

The drums were loud enough now that everyone could hear them.

For the first time, Ren got a glimpse of the Sight. He knew Darragh was gifted with prescience, but he'd never consciously experienced it himself before. He felt it now, however, and what he saw made his blood run cold.

"Trása?"

"What?"

"Get out of here."

"Excuse me?"

He turned to her, grabbed her by the arms to emphasise his point. "Go. Morph into the fastest thing you can and fly away from here. Now."

There must have been something in his demeanour that convinced her he wasn't fooling around. For once, she didn't argue.

"Come with me," she said.

"I can't," he said with utter certainty about where his destiny lay in these next few minutes. "I have to stay here."

She searched his face for a moment and then nodded in understanding. "You can See what's going to happen." It wasn't a question. "You have the Sight."

"Please, Trása. Go."

She nodded. "You've only got a few days until *Lughnasadh*, Rónán. You have to be in *Tír Na nÓg* by then, or-"

"I know."

The drums were now so loud there seemed to be no other sound in the compound. The walls were lined with people now, many of them in their nightclothes, staring down at whatever was approaching outside the walls. Ren let Trása go. "Fly away, Faerie. Stay free. For both our sakes."

She nodded, her eyes suddenly brimming with unshed tears, as if she too could see what was coming. Without warning, she threw her arms around Ren and kissed him on the mouth, but before he could grasp what she was doing and kiss her back, she turned into a striking white gull and slipped through his fingers.

With a squawk and a plaintive cry, Trása circled the compound once and flapped away towards the south.

Ren watched her leave, his fingers unconsciously touching his lips where she'd kissed him for a moment, and then he lowered his arm, squared his shoulders and turned toward the gate, as it slowly swung open.

The Empresses had arrived.

CHAPTER 35

The mystery of the relationship between Anwen and Queen Álmhath continued to intrigue Brydie. It deepened into something more sinister a few days after she learned the startling news that the Undivided were born of *Tuatha Dé Danann* royalty, in a complex and secret plan of the *Matrarchaí* for some nefarious purpose of their own.

As the betrothed of Álmhath's only son, Anwen wasn't bound by the same rules as the other court maidens. She had been in the sacred grove the morning Álmhath had selected Brydie as the one she would send to *Sí an Bhrú* to seduce Darragh. But Brydie wondered now, if Anwen had really been in the grove to oversee the selection, while appearing to be a part of it.

Anwen crept out of Temair in the middle of the night, waiting until Torcán was snoring softly in a stupor brought on by too much mead. She had made love to Torcán before he slept - or had let Torcán make love to her - and had forgotten to remove the necklace in her haste. Brydie had been treated to another one of those uncomfortably close encounters with Torcán, as he enthusiastically thrust himself into his betrothed, unconscious of her faked cries of pleasure.

Anwen checked that she could escape the fortress unseen and tied her cloak around her shoulders, hampering Brydie's view. She hurried barefoot through the halls, sneaking out into the chilly night, and went down to the sacred grove, out of sight of the main buildings. The guards ignored her, making Brydie wonder if there were magic involved. Álmhath's sentries were not so inept as to let a court maiden slip out in the dead of night, without someone asking what business she had, being abroad so late.

There was a woman waiting for Anwen in the grove. She was tall, slim and shrouded in a dark velvet cloak, her face concealed in the shadow of her cowl. Anwen dropped to her knees when she reached the grove, waiting until the woman gently touched her shoulder, before rising to her feet. She pushed back her cowl and Brydie saw an attractive, dark-haired woman of indeterminate age, with an air of elegance and command that she could feel, even through the faceted walls of her jewelled prison.

"*Bonsoir, cherie,*" the woman said, smiling as she signalled Anwen to rise. "You had no trouble getting away?"

Anwen shook her head, which always made Brydie a little seasick. "None, my lady."

"And how goes it, Anwen? Have you succeeded in the task we asked of you?"

Anwen hesitated before answering. *Task? What task?* was all Brydie could think to ask. Not that there was anybody about who could hear or answer the question.

This mysterious stranger might provide some answers, though.

"That depends on your definition of success, my lady," Anwen said, rising to her feet. "I have not been able to stop the *Tuatha* plan to transfer the power channel from RónánDarragh to the new heirs, BrocCairbre, on *Lughnasadh*. But I am about to be married to the queen's only son, which gives me more influence every day."

"Congratulations," the strange woman said, although she didn't sound especially enthusiastic.

"It will enable to me keep a steady hand on the helm here, but I fear not enough to wield true power. I have failed miserably in that regard, my lady."

"In the grand scheme, transferring power from one set of Undivided to another is not our problem. The death of RónánDarragh before we secure their bloodline is the *Matrarchaí*'s main concern."

"Ah... now there, I may have had more success," Anwen said, sounding a lot less contrite than she had a moment ago, Brydie thought. "I took your advice, my lady, and spoke to the queen about preserving their bloodline."

The older woman nodded. "I remember Álmhath. She was very keen to embrace the sisterhood when we first visited this realm."

Brydie could feel Anwen nodding in agreement. "She belongs to the *Matrarchaí* in this realm, although she doesn't appreciate the full depth and breadth of our reach. But she is no fool. She understands the power she would command, if she were to control the Undivided."

The woman frowned. "And how, exactly, does this unsophisticated Celtic queen imagine she can control the Undivided, when none of us have ever achieved the same feat?"

"By raising them to be loyal to her."

"I beg your pardon?"

Anwen sighed - impatiently, Brydie thought. "We need the bloodline preserved, my lady, you said so yourself. It wasn't hard to convince Álmhath to send a suitable vessel to Darragh's bed so his seed might be collected. Any children spawned from such a union, she plans to raise herself, ensuring their loyalty to her, rather than the Treaty of *Tír Na nÓg*."

Far from being pleased by this news, the woman seemed irritated. That made Brydie like her a great deal more than Anwen, who seemed to have little or no empathy for the task she had arranged for Brydie to undertake. "If only it were that simple."

"I didn't feel explaining the flaw in her thinking would achieve anything, my lady. Her ambition coincides enough with our needs to achieve the same outcome."

The visitor smiled sourly. "Well, you have to give her credit for trying, I suppose. It's a grand idea, but not one likely to succeed if the union results in offspring tied to the *Tuatha* by blood."

"I didn't have the heart to tell her how little chance her plan has of succeeding," Anwen said.

"It's not an impossible ambition though," the woman conceded. "There are realms where nobody has heard of the Undivided. Preserving the bloodlines in realms devoid of magic is much less problematic there. Believe me, I know. Who did you assign to the task?"

"Brydie Ni'Seanan," Anwen said. "Mogue Ni'Farrell's daughter."

Brydie pushed her face against the amethyst's surface wondering if her name, or her mother's name, would evoke any sort of reaction in the woman.

"Mogue had a daughter?"

"I thought you knew."

"She left the *Matrarchaí* in anger," the woman said. "We haven't spoken in twenty years. I lost track of her long ago." She pursed her lips thoughtfully. "Her daughter is not one of us, then."

"But she *is* pure human."

The woman wasn't pleased. Brydie was liking her more and more. "The *Matrarchaí* are not in the habit of whoring out young women, Anwen - even those not of the sisterhood - in order to secure our aims. Our issue is with those of *Tuatha Dé Danann*heritage. Not our own kind."

You tell her! Brydie silently cheered. And then she sank down to the floor of her prison, frowning. *But what does she mean about me being pure human? I thought I was special because I had some Faerie in me? I wish they'd make up their minds.*

"The girl in question was the right bloodline and had few prospects at court," Anwen replied in a dismissive tone that cut Brydie to the core. "She was destined to be someone's mistress, not a wife. The men who come to Álmhath's court looking for a woman to bear their children and a housekeeper to mind their estates, don't want a wife they have to fear every other man in their kingdom is lusting after. I did her a favour, my lady, not a disservice. Darragh of the Undivided was healthy, virile and not unattractive. One day, she'll thank me for the opportunity."

The Gaulish woman didn't seem mollified by Anwen's explanation. And Brydie found it vaguely unsettling that Anwen talked about Darragh as if he were already dead.

She was smarting a little over Anwen's opinion that she was too pretty to be marriage material, too.

"Perhaps," the woman agreed, with some reluctance. "Where is she now?"

Brydie saw Anwen's hands reaching up toward her, and she was thrown sideways as Anwen untied the necklace behind her neck and handed it to the Gaulish woman. "She's here."

The Gaul accepted the necklace on the palm of her hand and stared at it for a long moment, giving Brydie her first close look at her. It was impossible to tell the color of her eyes, between the darkness and the amethyst filter through which Brydie saw everything, but she was an attractive woman, and not as young as Brydie had first assumed. There was a maturity about her that marked her as a woman of some years.

"Did you... ? The woman began.

Anwen shook her head. "I've not the power to do anything of the kind, Lady Delphine. That's why I was chosen to come to this court. Had I any useful magical ability, the Druids or the Undivided, may have recognized the ability in me, and I would have been discovered as soon as I arrived."

"Then who did this?"

"I'm guessing it was one of the *Djinn*," Anwen said.

Delphine looked up, her concern obvious, even to Brydie. "What interest would they have in this girl? More to the point, what are the *Djinn* doing, sneaking around *Sí an Bhrú*?"

"I don't know, Lady Delphine. I just know that in this realm, the only species of *sídhe* who use inanimate objects to trap unwary humans, are the *Djinn*. She is trapped in the jewel."

Brydie stared up at the woman, pounding her fist uselessly on the walls. "So... get me out then!" she cried.

Lady Delphine, whoever she was, might know she was here, and what had trapped her, but she didn't seem to be in any great hurry to release her. Delphine studied the necklace with interest, but it was a detached, clinical sort of interest. She certainly wasn't whipping out her magic wand, or her stoking up her cauldron, or whatever it was she used to work her spells, so she could release Brydie on the spot. "Do they know you have her?" she asked Anwen, looking up from the jewel lying in her palm.

Brydie turned from watching Delphine, in time to see Anwen shrugging. "I don't know, my lady. I suspect not."

"Then for the time being, she is safe."

Safe! How can you call this safe! I'm a prisoner! You know I'm here! Get me out!

"It is almost impossible to release someone trapped by a *djinni* without the help of the *Djinn*," Delphine added. "If this girl succeeded and conceived, then we will have need of her. Until we can find a safe way to release her and the precious burden she may be carrying, she is safer where she is."

"And in the meantime?"

"In the meantime, the transfer will take place on *Lughnasadh* as scheduled, Darragh and Rónán will die, and we will be rid of one more threat to our plans." Delphine handed the necklace back to Anwen. "If Brydie conceived a child - or better yet, twins - then you did well to preserve the line. I wish we were having as much success in other realms."

Brydie was jostled again as Anwen tied the necklace around her neck. "There are problems, my lady?"

Delphine nodded as she raised her hood, pulling the cloak a little tighter against the chill. "The circle we use in the realm where I have been working was destroyed recently." She sighed, shaking her head. "Be grateful you've been sent to a realm where there is enough magic that you can leave anytime you need, *ma cherie*. Not all of us have been so lucky."

Sent? Brydie thought. *What does she mean by sent? Is Anwen not of this realm?*

What is she? A rift runner spy from another realm?

"The Matrarchaí *are the reason the line has never been broken,"* the queen had told Brydie in the wagon on the way to *Sí an Bhrú. "The reason why, after sixty-six generations, humans still occupy* Sí an Bhrú." She had also said, *"The* Matrarchaí *know the secret of producing the psychic twins needed to preserve the Treaty of* Tír Na nÓg."

But not the Matrarchaí *of this realm,* Brydie realized.

"It's going to take me days to get back," Delphine sighed, "and once I do, it's going to be difficult to leave again, until I can find another platform high enough off the ground to tap into the little magic that remains in the Enchanted Sphere."

The two of them began to walk toward the entrance to the grove. Presumably, Delphine was headed to the stone circle near Temair where she would open a rift and return to her own realm.

"It is easy to forget sometimes," Lady Delphine added, "just how the politics and religion of realms which don't even know of our existence, can impact upon our plans."

Where are you Darragh? Brydie wondered. *Do you know about these strangers lurking in your realm, plotting to bring you down?*

Does Álmhath know Anwen is a spy? She certainly knew something was afoot, but was she a party to it? Or was she being duped by these women of this alien *Matrarchaí?*

"You don't worry about being stranded in a reality without magic, my lady?" Anwen asked. She spoke to Lady Delphine with more deference and respect than she had ever shown Queen Álmhath.

"Constantly," Delphine replied. "And in the realm where I have been working these past thirty years, it is worse than most."

"Why take such a risk?"

"Because a realm with depleted magic is the one place we can be sure we are safe from *Tuatha Dé Danann* spies. It's frustrating to be working so hard toward securing magic for our own kind, from a world where our kind have all but destroyed it. Were it not for their engineering expertise I would never be able to open a rift in the realm."

"They have mechanical rifts?" Anwen asked, sounding surprised.

"They build ludicrously tall buildings," Delphine corrected. "So high they reach the Enchanted Sphere." The women reached the entrance to the grove. The moon remained hidden from view behind the clouds. Delphine stopped and turned to face Anwen, giving Brydie a much better view of her. It must have been cold, she thought, because Delphine's breath frosted faintly as she spoke. "The destruction of my circle has set my work back months. You are not my only charge, Anwen. There are other realms where Partition has already been achieved, and I am cut off from them temporarily. I'm not sure when I can get back here again. But you seem to have things in hand. There are other places where my intervention is needed."

"I can hold things together, my lady, until you return."

Delphine nodded and leaned forward to gently touch her fingertips to the amethyst around Anwen's neck. "Keep our little friend safe, then, Anwen," she ordered. "This realm will have need of her if we are to achieve Partition here in our lifetime.

She's a Partitionist, Brydie realized. She'd heard of them, of course. Her father bordered on being one. But his hope of one day escaping the bonds of the Treaty of *Tír Na nÓg* and what he called the oppressive rule of the *Tuatha Dé Danann* was something he merely ranted about around the hearth when he'd drunk too much mead with his friends in winter. She was sure he knew nothing of a group from another realm working to separate humans from *sídhe* magic.

"Can you find your way back to the circle from here, my lady?"

Delphine nodded. "I know the path very well, Anwen," she said. "I have visited many times before." She embraced the younger woman briefly. "You should return before you are missed." She took a step back, fixing her attention on Anwen's necklace. "Do you suppose your little friend in the jewel knows what's going on?"

"I doubt it, my lady."

Delphine leaned a little closer. Brydie could see her smiling. "Perhaps she is watching, listening, taking it all in." She straightened which enabled her to look Anwen in the eye. Her smile faded. "You may want to consider that."

Anwen nodded... or it felt as though she did - Brydie couldn't really see, but the jewel bobbed up and down for a moment. Delphine turned toward the trees and within moments she was lost in the darkness, leaving Anwen alone to sneak back into *Sí an Bhrú*.

Brydie sank to the floor with even more questions she couldn't answer, not the least of which was the most important...

Was there some way to tell whether she was now pregnant with Darragh's heir?

And if she was, what did the *Matrarchaí* want with her child?

CHAPTER 36

"What do you think?" Pete asked Annad Semaj when he emerged from the interview room.

Annad paused, sneezed and wiped his red, chafed nose before answering. "I think I could do a PhD on this kid."

"Is he schizophrenic?"

"Hard to say after only one interview. I'm guessing not. As a rule, schizophrenia is characterised by relatively stable, albeit paranoid, delusions, which our boy has in spades. But the delusions are usually accompanied by hallucinations, mostly auditory, and often perceptual disturbances as well. This lad displays none of that."

"He talks like he's hallucinating, but he doesn't act like it?" Pete asked.

"Exactly," Annad said. "He displays no disturbances of affect, volition or speech. On the other hand, he appears to have delusions of persecution, believes he's of exalted birth and that he has a special mission. He is Darragh of the Undivided, he says, and claims to rule this alternate reality he comes from." Annad walked over to the coffee vending machine and began to fish around in his pocket for coins. "Have you checked the local mental hospitals for missing patients? That could explain where he's been all this time."

"Not a bad idea. You think he's been institutionalised?"

"I have no idea, to be honest," Annad admitted. "I would have expected him to display more awareness of the process, if he had. Do you have any change on you?"

"I'm afraid not."

Annad shrugged. "Oh well... it's crap coffee in that machine anyway. Where was I?"

"You were telling me Darragh doesn't act like someone who's been institutionalised. Or he does. To be honest, I'm not sure."

"There's the rub," Annad said. "I don't know either. The paranoid schizophrenia may be episodic and we've got him on a good day. He might be in partial or complete remission. He might be chronic, although I doubt it. In chronic cases, florid symptoms tend to persist over a number of years. It's difficult to distinguish discrete episodes."

"We have to arraign him in the morning."

Annad pursed his lips thoughtfully for a moment and then nodded. "Well, if it's a preliminary assessment you want, then he's probably sane enough to appear in court. He knows right from wrong and he would be more than capable of assisting with his own defence. Today, at any rate."

"Did he give you any clue about where to find Hayley Boyle?"

Annad shook his head. "His story never wavered on that point. She has been sent to another reality to have her blindness healed, along with his twin brother and the girl, Trása. He insists *she's* half Faerie."

Pete sighed, shaking his head. "Christ, the tabloids are going to have a field day over this when he appears on tomorrow's docket."

"Only if they hear about it," Annad pointed out. "If there is anything positive to come out of that awful business in New York, it's that nobody is interested in anything else at the moment. Our boy may slip under the radar, if we're lucky. Does he have a solicitor yet?"

"He'll get a court-appointed one in the morning, I suppose. Kiva Kavanaugh has washed her hands of the whole affair, so at least we don't have the dreaded Eunice Ravenel to contend with any longer."

"Shame," Annad sighed. "I have this recurring fantasy about Eunice Ravenel cross-examining me."

Pete smiled briefly, but then his smile faded as he asked, "Between you and me, do you think he killed Hayley?"

"My gut feeling is 'no'."

"Then where is she?"

"In an alternate reality," Annad said with a grin. "Having her blindness cured by the *Tuatha Dé Danann*."

"You're a big help, Annad. I'll be sure to put that in my report."

"I'm here to help you, Pete," the psychiatrist reminded him, clasping his shoulder comfortingly. "You can be sure my remarkable contribution to your case will be reflected in my bill."

"You'll have something for me for court in the morning?"

Annad nodded. "I'll write something up about the delusions and how they're characteristic of schizophrenia, but that's about all I can give you at this stage."

"It'll have to do," Pete said. "In the meantime, I'll send him back to the cells. Maybe another night in remand will jog his memory." He glanced at his watch, and cursed when he remembered he was supposed to be meeting his brother at his grandmother's house.

"Is there a problem?"

"I have to be somewhere," he said. "Can you be in court tomorrow morning, in case his lawyer tries to pull a fast one and get him released because he's crazy?"

"I'll be there," Annad promised. "And not just for you. This young man intrigues me. I want to see how he acts in court when he's not so aware he's being watched."

"See you then," Pete said.

"You can count on it," Annad Semaj said.

There were almost as many people gathered at his grandmother's house, as there had been the night of her birthday party. Logan's Ferrari was parked in the drive. His cousin Kelly's Volvo was pulled in behind it, blocking him in. Pete took a deep breath - as he always did - before he knocked on the door. He needed to brace himself for whatever family celebration or catastrophe he was about to step into.

Logan opened the door. Pete stared at him, knowing instantly that he wasn't here to celebrate anything.

"Is Mamó okay?" he asked, thinking that the most likely explanation for this summons. She was an old woman, after all. It wasn't out of the realms of possibility that something had happened to her since Pete saw her last.

"She's fine," Logan told him.

"Then why the summons?" Pete asked as he stepped into the hall and Logan closed the door behind him.

"Come inside," Logan said. "I don't want to have to explain this over and over."

Pete thought his twin was being dramatic just for the sake of being dramatic, but he followed him into Mamó's stifling living room without telling him he thought that. Mamó was in her chair, as usual, Kelly was sitting on the sofa, her husband, Xavier, was standing by the window. Everyone was looking like someone had run over the family dog. In fact, the only one missing was his mother, who should be on her way back from her trip to America by now, probably with some young ingénue in tow, ready to unleash her on the European world of high fashion.

He crossed the room, kissed Mamó's papery, wrinkled cheek and then turned to his family. "What's wrong?"

"I got a text message from your mother on Tuesday," Kelly said, reaching for her husband's hand and squeezing it. She seemed in the verge of tears.

"Really?" he asked. "You made me take the afternoon off work in the middle of a really high profile kidnap case for that?"

Xavier leaned forward, offering Pete the phone. "Read it."

Pete flipped open the phone. The message was already on the screen.

Will call you Tuesday, cherie, the message read.

He read the message a couple of times, and then shrugged and handed the phone back to Kelly's husband. "What's the problem?"

"She never rang."

"After the World Trade Centre was hit, Kelly tried ringing her," his cousin-in-law explained. "When she couldn't contact her, she called me and I called her office here in Dublin. They told me she was due at the New York office that morning. Apparently it's not uncommon for her to disappear for days a time when she's travelling." He glanced around the room. "Did any of you know that?"

They all did, but it was such a part of their lives, none of them had given it much thought until now.

"I'm not sure you knew this, but New York office is located on the hundred and sixth floor of the World Trade Centre," Kelly announced.

"Do we know if she made it to her office in New York that morning?" Pete asked. He hadn't known about the office. The first tendrils of dread were starting to thread through his veins.

"Nobody has been able to contact her since Tuesday," Logan said in a toneless voice that was more disturbing than Kelly's overt grief.

Pete suddenly felt himself go cold all over.

"Jesus Christ," he said, giving voice to what everyone here seemed to know but was too afraid to say outright. "You think she was in the World Trade Centre when it was hit?"

"If she wasn't, why hasn't she rung us to let us know she's okay," Kelly asked, her eyes filling with tears. "She must know we'd be beside ourselves if we didn't hear from her."

Kelly had a point, but something bothered Pete more. He turned to his brother. "Did you know she had an office in the World Trade Centre?"

"Can't say I ever asked," Logan said. "Why?"

"Seems a bit over the top, doesn't it? I mean... a Dublin modelling agency with a penthouse office in what was probably the most expensive piece of real estate in the whole of New York?"

"For chrissakes, Peter," his grandmother growled. "Stop being a detective for five wee minutes and take a moment to grieve your poor dead mother."

"When did we decide she was dead?" he asked, alarmed at how quickly everyone had jumped to that conclusion. "You don't know that."

"They're saying nobody on the floors above where the planes hit made it out," Kelly said, sniffing back her tears.

"And you don't know she was anywhere near the place on Tuesday. Have you tried the Consulate in New York?" Pete loosened his tie. The room was stifling.

"First thing I did after Kelly called me," Xavier assured them, smiling down at his wife sympathetically.

"Which one?"

"The Irish Consulate, of course. Why?"

"Because she's French," Logan answered, slapping his forehead. "Of course! If she's laying wounded or unconscious in a hospital somewhere and she's been ID'd from her passport, they wouldn't even think to contact the Irish authorities."

Pete pulled out his cell phone and dialled his work number, without saying anything further to his siblings. They watched and waited as he got through to Brendá Duggan after a moment or two, explained the situation to his boss, and asked if she could pull any strings to cut through the red tape and find out if the French Consulate in New York had any news of their mother.

Pete could have rung the consulate himself, but he knew from experience that the higher one went up the chain of command, the more likely they knew someone who knew someone in the right place. The flow of information at Brendá's level would be more like water and less like treacle.

"I'll see what I can do, Pete," Brendá Duggan promised, when he'd finished telling her what he knew. "Do you need some time off until you find out what's happening?"

Pete shook his head, even though she couldn't see the gesture. "Thanks, boss. But right now, I think I'd rather be at work."

"I understand," she said. "But don't come back before you're ready. I'll make a few calls for you. I did a course on cross-border internet crime with Interpol last year in Paris. I have a some contacts over there who might be able to find out if there is any news of your mother. You'd better give me her full name and date of birth."

Pete covered the phone with his hand for a moment and looked at Kelly. "Do you know Mum's date of birth?"

"March eight, nineteen fifty one," she said, rolling her eyes. "Trust a boy not to know that."

Pete poked his tongue out at his cousin and repeated the date to Brendá Duggan.

"And what's her full name?" Brendá asked, after she'd obviously written it down.

"Adeline Monique Delphinia Sybilla Marguerite Bouvier Doherty," Pete said, amazed he could remember his mother's complicated full name but not something as simple as her birthday. "That's the official name on her passport, at least," he added. "But she rarely uses it. Mostly she goes by Delphine."

CHAPTER 37

The massive wooden gates of the Ikushima compound opened slowly to reveal the source of the drums. The Empresses' arrival was heralded by a platoon of drummers, dressed traditionally in *momohiki* pants, a wide red *haramaki* around the midsection, bare chests (despite the cold) and *hachimaki* headbands depicting a logo that was disturbingly similar to the traditional rising sun of Imperial Japan in Ren's realm.

Inside the compound, the place had erupted into chaos, and for a moment, Ren was forgotten. There were people running back and forth, children being dragged from their beds and hastily dressed as they rubbed the sleep from their eyes. Namito was shouting orders, Masuyo shouting other orders that directly contradicted her grandson. Aoi and Kazusa had both emerged from the main house. Kazusa was still dressed in all her finery, Aoi was smoothing down the wrinkles in a kimono Ren had not seen before. It was a shimmering green and red floral design edged with gold which reeked of an outfit saved for a special occasion.

If he'd been planning to escape, now would have been the perfect time. Amid this chaos, he could wane out of here without being noticed and never been seen again.

It was a tempting thought. Now he knew the name of what he could do, Ren was quite sure he could do it. But it meant Aoi would have to die.

He didn't want her blood on his hands.

And in truth, he was curious to meet the Empresses.

Daichi, Namito's commander who had joined them for dinner the first night Ren was a guest here, seemed to be trying to form his samurai into an honor guard along the wall, dragging those off-duty from their beds, haranguing them with shouts and insults about their poor family origins to get them moving.

Over by the main house, Namito was yelling at somebody else to bring fireworks. This was a fireworks factory, after all. What better way to greet the Empresses than with a fabulous display of Ikushima wares?

The theatricality of the Empresses' entourage made Ren wonder if the long line of drummers and the noise preceding their arrival was designed specifically to allow this sort of panicked preparation. He guessed they wanted their subjects to have advance warning of their imminent arrival. Ren had lived with a drama queen all his life, and knew a theatrical production when he saw one. It was hard to make an "entrance" after all, if nobody had been given time to roll out the red carpet. There really wasn't a need for any of this nonsense, that Ren could see, other than providing their hosts plenty of notice of their approach, so nobody could be accidentally dishonored - and perhaps required to commit *Seppuku* - by not having time to prepare.

The drummers - and there seemed to be scores of them marching through the gates, pounding away at their instruments - reminded Ren of the *taiko* performance he had to sit through when he visited Japan with Kiva. The performance was preceded by a tour of the troupe's community at *Kodo* and a lengthy discourse about the nature of *Taiko* and the wide range of percussion instruments common to classical Japanese and European musical traditions. Ren had zoned out a few minutes into the tour, paying little attention to the lecture, something he regretted later that day when they actually got to hear the musicians, because it turned out they were quite amazing, given they were making music with sticks.

The only thing Ren remembered clearly from that day, other than the drummers, was the story their guide told them about the origins of *taiko*. Ren remembered the goddess's name well, because Kiva had been so taken with the legend, she tried to buy the rights to it, with the intention of playing the sun goddess, Amaterasu, herself. Her manager, Jon, had eventually dissuaded her from attempting to hijack a story so steeped in a culture she didn't understand or have any claim on, pointing out that in a Japanese legend, it was unlikely audiences would accept a blue-eyed, blonde Caucasian playing the role of a Japanese sun goddess, even if she had an executive producer's credit.

That hadn't stopped Kiva insisting everybody refer to her as Amaterasu for a week or so, until she gave up on the idea. The thought made Ren wonder what Kiva was doing now. He hadn't had time to spare his mother - his adopted mother - a thought. Was she upset? Thriving on the drama? Genuinely concerned about what might have happened to her son, or trying to word a press release that put all the blame on him? Had Kiva done another feature in *OK Magazine*, to let the world know how devastated - and not responsible - she was for her errant son's criminal behaviour?

Thinking of Kiva sparked more than an uncomfortable wash of guilt. What about Kerry and Patrick Boyle, his pseudo-parents from his own reality? What had his impulsive but well-intentioned actions done to them? What about poor Neil? How did he respond to his sister's disappearance? Had he even noticed it? Were the Boyles worried that Hayley was missing, or did they trust Ren, confident he would never bring any harm to their daughter?

Ren realized he hadn't considered how Hayley's parents might react to her disappearance, something he was regretting, now he had time to think. Perhaps he should have left them a note. Should he have called them before stepping through the rift? He probably could have done something to reassure them Hayley was safe and would not come to any harm.

Don't worry Kerry and Patrick, he could have written in a note, *I've taken Hayley to another reality to have her sight healed by magic.*

Yeah, Ren thought. *That would have worked.*

It was a testament to the impressive length of the Empresses' entourage, that he had this much time to think before the drummers leading the parade had taken up position in the courtyard, followed by an escort of heavily armed samurai, surrounding four muscular Caucasian men, carrying a wide litter decorated in gilt and colored gemstones that reflected the torchfire across the courtyard in a spray of speckled rainbow light.

There was a loud bang on his right where the first of the mortar-fired shells were set off. A moment later the sky lit up with a glorious burst of red light as a starmine exploded overhead. Ren glanced up at the sky. The drums were reaching a crescendo. There was no sign of Trása. She might have been scared off by the fireworks in avian form or be watching from the trees.

Another brilliant starmine exploded overhead.

Ren was relieved beyond words that Trása - for once - had listened to him, when he warned her to get clear of the place. What he'd seen wasn't a clear vision of the future. That sort of vision was quite rare, according the knowledge his brother owned on the subject. And this vision wasn't exactly clear. He'd seen a glimpse of the Empresses' arriving in the compound and seen a glimpse of something else that might have been the future... or maybe the past.

Either way, it was disturbing.

It was the briefest of visions and it was of a herd of Faerie being pushed and prodded through a rift into a barren world beyond, while the Empresses looked on impassively, neither glorying in the *sídhe's* distress leaving this realm nor repulsed by it. They were just standing there, watching, as if the

Faeries suffocating on the other side was so everyday, so pedestrian, it hardly rated their concern.

Another array of red, silver and green star shells lit the sky as the litter-bearers lowered the curtained litter the ground. As it touched the raked sand, two identically dressed courtiers hurried from behind the litter, placing small, beautifully-carved wooden steps on either side. The courtiers bowed, and then, still bowing low, their eyes downcast, they pulled back the gold curtains to allow their mistresses to alight.

As another series of fireworks decorated the night sky, turning the compound to day for a few seconds, the Empresses climbed out in unison, in a move so well synchronised, Ren did not doubt they had practiced it until they got it right. One small wooden-sandalled foot followed another, then they emerged, dressed in identical kimonos woven from white silk and bearing the rising sun in a large pattern that reached from the hem to the wide red silk *obi* at their waists.

Around him, everybody in the compound fell to their knees. Except Ren.

He wanted to see them. He wanted to see if he'd been imagining things. He wanted to know if his vision had been true or just a wild fancy.

Ren watched the Empresses emerge from the litter and walk to the front where they smiled at each other and then turned to face him.

They were exactly as Ren had seen them in his vision. Blonde. Blue-eyed.

And barely ten-years-old.

CHAPTER 38

Darragh was not entirely unfamiliar with the judicial system. His brother had been arrested on more than one occasion in this realm - albeit for relatively minor infractions until Trása framed him for arson and murder. Since Darragh now shared his brother's memories, he knew roughly what was going on. Still, there seemed an inordinate number of people involved in the process of deciding a person's innocence or guilt in this realm. The process was complicated, confusing and, Darragh suspected, prone to substantial error.

It was much easier, he decided, when you had the magical ability to know if someone was telling the truth simply by looking into their mind. Justice was much more accurate in his reality and much swifter.

The court was full of people, surprisingly few of them reporters. Kiva Kavanaugh might not be directly involved in his case, now it had been established he was not the fugitive Chelan Aquarius Kavanaugh, but that he was the unexpected identical twin of her missing son, up on charges relating to the missing daughter of her chauffeur. There was a story for any journalist wishing to follow it through, but Darragh realized there were other things happening in the world. The antics of an actress's wayward offspring didn't rate a mention against the background of the attack on the World Trade Centre.

Even now, as Darragh was led into the dock by the prison officer assigned to guard him, the discussion in the public gallery wasn't about the next case, although a good many spectators, he gathered, were here for their own business and not to watch him being arraigned. The discussions were about whether or not there was a final death toll yet, what would happen next and if it was going to mean war, although exactly who was going to go to war with whom, was something Darragh still couldn't work out.

There were no familiar faces in the court besides the court-appointed solicitor he'd met earlier this morning in a small bare interview room set aside for prisoners to consult with their counsel. A frazzled, red-haired young man by the name of Mike O'Malley, he briefly explained the procedure to Darragh, asked how he wanted to plead and then hurried off to talk to his next client. His appearance would be necessarily brief, O'Malley assured Darragh. The charges would be read, bail would be set or refused, and then Darragh would be returned to the cells to either await his release once bail was posted or be remanded into custody. A trial would be arranged in the Criminal Courts at a later date.

Darragh listened politely to the explanation and told the young man he planned to plead "not guilty" to the charges when he heard what they were. It was certainly not what he was expecting. He thought they were holding him responsible for Hayley Boyle's absence, but the charges proved to be assaulting a police officer - which had been Sorcha's doing, not his - and stealing a police car. As the car they'd borrowed to help Rónán escape St Christopher's had been recovered by the Gardaí with no apparent harm, Darragh considered the latter charge simply a mischievous waste of time, and he certainly wasn't going to convict himself of it, voluntarily.

They were calling him Darragh Aquitania. This reality was so full of forms and procedures they even killed trees to write things down - which was foreign to the Druid reality Darragh came from where every event of import was committed to memory by a bard and nothing had to die to record it. A family name was everything in this realm and their computers wouldn't function without one. Pete Doherty had given him the name when he asked Darragh his full name in order to complete the form to qualify for legal assistance. At least, that's what Detective Pete had told him was the reason for the form. So he'd explained he was Darragh, son of Sybille, hoping that would help. He didn't mind the name Aquitania, but it was so new and unfamiliar that when they addressed him by it, he had to remind himself they were talking to him.

There was a note attached to his file, according to Mike O'Malley, saying he had been assessed by a psychiatrist and was deemed competent to stand trial.

"We've got your GSAS-1 form," he said, taking a seat opposite Darragh.

"I assume that's good news?" Darragh asked, having no idea what the form was, or its relevance to his current predicament.

"Well, it means you get legal aid," the solicitor said. "Did you confess to anything?"

"Only bewilderment at the legal process of this realm," Darragh replied.

O'Malley smiled briefly. "I hear you, brother. Why did they bring in a shrink to talk to you?" he added distractedly as he read through the file.

"I believe they were worried I might be suffering from some sort of mental disorder."

"Do you?"

"I don't believe so."

"Are you taking anything?"

"What do you mean?"

"Drugs," the lawyer asked. "Speed, smack, charlies, doves?"

Darragh looked at him blankly. "I have no idea what you are talking about, sir."

"Yeah... right..." O'Malley muttered, and then he glanced up at Darragh. "Did you assault a police officer?"

"Not at all," Darragh assured him, quite truthfully. "That was my companion, Sorcha."

"I see," O'Malley said, making notes on a large yellow pad. "So... where is this Sorcha now? If you can get her to turn herself in, maybe we can get those charges dropped."

"She has returned through the rift to the reality where she belongs." Darragh firmly believed that -

one way or another - his time in this realm was limited. And as these people had no reliable way to detect if he were lying, Darragh saw no need to betray Sorcha's continuing presence in this realm. He may yet need her help. He certainly wasn't going to aid her capture - or implicate Jack - by betraying her location, particularly as it seemed punching a Gardaí detective between the eyes in the process of helping a fugitive escape was a criminal offence worthy of incarceration.

O'Malley looked up. "*Excuse* me?"

"I am from another reality," Darragh explained patiently. "I am really only here until someone can open a rift from the other side so I can return home."

O'Malley was silent for a long moment. "I see. And you're saying you don't do drugs, eh? Well, that explains the shrink. Do you know anything about Hayley Boyle's disappearance that might help?"

"I have told them everything I know about it. Why?"

"It would aid your case considerably if the judge thought you were being more cooperative about finding her."

"I have been nothing *but* cooperative," Darragh pointed out, a little exasperated by the suggestion. "Almost everything I have told them is the truth."

"Almost?" O'Malley asked with a raised brow.

Darragh clasped his hands together on the table in from of him, the cuffs making a metallic sound against the cold metal table. "It is not my fault the people of this realm are not equipped with the knowledge to understand when I am telling the truth," he said. "You cannot know what I have seen or what I am capable of in my own realm, and I don't know how to explain it to you. I've been as truthful as I can."

The solicitor nodded and then pointed at Darragh's tattooed hand. "Is that a gang sign?"

"Excuse me?"

"The tat. Is it gang related?"

"No."

"Well, keep it out of sight, whatever it is," O'Malley warned. "You're up in front of Judge Riordan, and cracking down on gangs is his pet project. Let's not give him any reason to get upset."

"If you wish."

"You sure you can't give them something useful about the Boyle girl?"

"I have told them everything I know."

"I doubt we'll make bail unless you do."

Darragh shrugged. "It doesn't matter. I have no money to arrange bail, in any case," he said. "All my wealth, I fear, is in the other realm. Ironically, if I could get to it, I could return home, and these entire proceedings would be moot, wouldn't they?"

O'Malley sighed heavily. "Okay... I'll see if I can get you remanded into a psychiatric hospital for a full assessment," he said, closing the file as he rose to his feet. "And get you on some nice, helpful medication, maybe. At the very least, we should be able to get you remanded to St Patrick's. They specialise in kids your age. You really don't want to wind up in the general prison population."

Darragh nodded and smiled. O'Malley seemed competent and concerned for his welfare. His intention to have Darragh committed to a hospital rather than a prison was welcome. And it wouldn't be for long. Presumably Rónán or Ciarán were waiting for an opportunity to open the rift again so they could rescue him. The days were ticking by, after all. It wasn't long now until *Lughnasadh*. Darragh needed to be home with Rónán by then, or it really wouldn't matter what they did in this realm, because he would be dead.

It would be easier, Darragh knew, for Rónán to extract him from a poorly guarded hospital than a well-guarded gaol. It was the reason the Brogan and Niamh removed Rónán from the cells of the Gardaí station several weeks ago, rather than wait for him to be sent to prison, when they recovered Rónán from this realm the first time.

He refused to let their continued absence get him down. Darragh had spent his whole life looking for Rónán. Now that he'd found him and brought him home, he didn't doubt for a moment that his brother would do the same for him.

The remand hearing, when it happened, was over almost before Darragh realized it had started. He'd barely stated his name for the judge, before a quick exchange between the O'Malley and the prosecution took place and he was asked if he wanted to plead guilty or not guilty - to which he responded "not guilty" in a clear voice. A date later in the month was set and the judge was banging his gavel, ordering Darragh be remanded into custody. He didn't agree to the hospital suggestion O'Malley put forward, based on O'Malley's contention that claiming he came from another reality made him barking mad in this one, but the judge did order a full psychiatric assessment for his next court appearance. Before he knew it, Darragh was being hustled away and another prisoner brought into the dock.

O'Malley caught up with him and his prison officer escort in the hall. The solicitor was carrying a pile of other files, in addition to Darragh's slender volume.

"Someone from our office will be in touch," Mike promised, already pulling out the file for his next case. "Don't give them any grief, eh?"

"What do you mean?" Darragh asked.

"Just take your meds and answer their questions," the lawyer advised. "And keep your head down. Been inside before this?"

"I have been inside many times," Darragh told him, looking around the hall as people pushed passed them, heading for the courtrooms. "Are we not inside now?"

"Yeah... I get it," O'Malley said, rolling his eyes. "You're a tough guy. You can handle it." He thrust a small card at Darragh. "That's the office number if you need anything. Catch you later."

O'Malley turned and hurried back down the hall, leaving Darragh clutching his business card, without giving him an opportunity to speak.

"Come on," his escort said, taking Darragh by the arm. He was a large, taciturn, uniformed man with a bored expression that hadn't wavered the whole time Darragh had been in his custody.

"What happens now?" Darragh asked, still confused by the whole judicial process.

"You're going to gaol, my lad," the prison officer told him. "Weren't you listening in there?"

CHAPTER 39

Pete spent several days trying to track down his mother in New York, without success. Brendá had no luck with her contacts, and between them Logan and Pete had quite a few of their own. They called in every favour they were owed, every contact they knew and every slender lead they had. Pete refused to accept his mother was dead. Logan was a little more philosophical about it, but he was just as anxious to find her. So the brothers turned their considerable investigative talents and network of contacts to the task.

It was a waste of time. They found nothing and in the end, they needn't have done anything.

Delphine found them.

She rang Pete early in the morning, almost a week after the attack that all the TV news networks - who were still running images of the planes flying into the Twin Towers in an endless, maudlin loop -

were calling Nine-Eleven. He was asleep when the phone rang and it took him a moment to realize it was his mother calling when he answered it. Phone calls at that hour usually meant work. The bedside clock read 2:42 am.

Delphine sounded far away and tired. Pete had never heard anything so wonderful.

"I am so sorry, *cherie*," she said, her voice weary. "It is madness here. What you all must be thinking..."

"God, Mum! Where are you?" Pete asked, reaching forward to turn on the lamp. She'd called him on his landline. Pete grabbed his cell phone off the bedside table and started texting Logan, while they spoke.

"I don't want you to worry..."

"Where are you?"

"I'm in Chicago."

"What are you doing there? Your office told us you were in New York."

"Fortunately, we had some problems with a photoshoot, so I had to swing by Chicago, instead of staying in the New York office." She laughed softly. "Honestly, *cherie*, you're making things sound far more dramatic than they are."

He couldn't understand why she was laughing. "What about the other the people who worked there? Are they okay? Did they get out?"

"The office is closed on Tuesdays," Delphine said. "We lost some important equipment, but none of our staff. It's nice of you to worry about it, though, *cherie*."

Pete didn't think he was dramatising her disappearance at a time like this one little bit, but there was no point arguing about it. Nor did he think it strange that he worried over the fate of the people who worked for his mother. But there was no arguing with her at a time like this. He sighed with defeat. "Exactly where are you in Chicago, then?"

"The Rush Presbyterian Hospital."

"What are you doing in a Presbyterian Hospital?" Pete asked.

"A Presbyterian hospital is as good as a Catholic one, *cherie*," Delphine said.

Pete let out another exasperated sigh, certain she was deliberately misunderstanding him. "That's not what I mean, Mum, and you know it. We've been going crazy over here. You sent Kelly a text saying you'd call her, and then you disappear off the face of the Earth while the worst terrorist attack in the Western Hemisphere is happening in a building where you apparently have an office."

"I was having breakfast when the attack happened," she explained. "A friend of mine, Marguerite Villiers, is stationed in Chicago at the moment. Do you remember her? We went to the Sorbonne together. I'm sure I introduced you and Logan to her that time I took you to Paris... anyway... when I learned I'd be visiting Chicago unexpectedly, I rang Marguerite and we met for breakfast at the Sears Tower. I completely missed all the excitement."

Excitement wasn't quite how Pete would have described it, but he was relieved beyond words to learn she was alive and well enough to call. He could also tell there was something she wasn't telling him. No matter how innocent her side trip to Chicago, nobody had heard from her for days. "That doesn't explain what you're doing in hospital,

Mum. Or why we haven't heard from you for a week."

"I had... a little accident, *cherie*."

"What kind of *little* accident?" He knew what his mother was like. When his barely-remembered father was diagnosed with lung cancer more than twenty years ago, she'd smiled comfortingly and assured her anxious children he was suffering from nothing more than "a little chest problem". Six months later, he was dead.

"I discovered that when one takes on a taxi cab, one is going to lose."

"Jesus, Mum! You got hit by a taxi?"

"It's not so surprising, *cherie*," she said. "They're everywhere here. America is choked with them. You can't move without running into one of them. Quite literally."

"I'm coming over on the next flight," he announced, tossing his cell phone aside to fish his passport out if the drawer beside the bed.

"Don't be silly," she scolded. "Even if you could get the time off work and manage to get on a flight, this place is insane at the moment. I will be fine. Just ring the others and let them know I'm alive. I'd ring them myself, but Kelly panics when she's worried, and in her condition she shouldn't be stressing herself. As for Logan... well, you know your brother. He sensationalises everything. You, at least, I can trust to keep a level head."

"Are you hurt?" Pete realized it was a stupid question the moment he uttered it. Of course she was hurt. She was in hospital at a time when every hospital bed would be at a premium. If she was even remotely well enough to go home, she'd have been out the door the moment they judged her ambulatory.

"Just a little bit, *cherie*."

"How badly are you hurt?"

"They're not sure yet," she said, evading the question. "They have some more tests to run first. You must not worry, *cherie*. And you must tell your brother and sister not to worry, either. I have excellent insurance, many excellent doctors, and I will be home as soon as they let me out. Now promise me you will not overreact, or do anything silly, like flying over here."

"You're in hospital in a foreign country, Mum," he pointed out.

"I am in Chicago, Peter," she replied with a small, bittersweet laugh. "That is no more foreign to me than Dublin."

She had a point, but it didn't seem right to just leave her there without any family support. Especially at a time like this. "Even if I listen to you and I can convince Logan, Kelly's going to want to drop everything and come over." His cousin and his mother were more like mother and daughter than aunt and niece. Since she arrived to live with them when she was sixteen, Delphine had treated Kelly like she was a close member of the family.

"Then you must tell her not to. I don't think they would let her on a plane this close to her confinement, anyway. I am counting on you to contain her, Peter. And Logan, too. Promise me."

"I promise," he told her reluctantly.

"That's my boy. Now you give everyone my love, and stay safe until I get home, yes?"

"Okay."

She told Pete she loved him several more times before she hung up, leaving him wide awake and wondering if he should contact the others now, or let them sleep and break the happy news to them in the morning. Delphine was right about that much, Kelly did like to panic and Logan loved to sensationalise everything.

That decided him. He would tell them in the morning. Perhaps even lie a little and tell his brother and cousin he had applied his skills as a detective and located Delphine and not the other way around. Logan might not care so much, but Kelly would be devastated to learn his mother had chosen Pete to deliver the news she was alive, rather than ringing her in person.

The decision made, Pete was still wide awake and knew he wasn't likely to sleep again tonight. He glanced at the clock. It was almost three. The roads would be clear, and he could be at work in ten minutes, where the office would be quiet and probably empty. The time he'd spent searching for Delphine meant he'd missed Darragh's arraignment. He still had all Darragh's statements to go through, reports to be written, and leads to be tracked down. Despite his mother's disappearance, and the horror of the attack in New York, Hayley Boyle was still missing.

The transcript of Annad Semaj's interview with Darragh was on Pete's desk. Up on the noticeboard were the gruesome crime scene photos of another murder that must have been handed to the squad while he was trying to locate Delphine. He studied them for a moment, wondering what had happened. The victim was a middle-aged man who'd had his throat cut while putting out the garbage.

He sighed when he saw how thick the interview transcript was, glad he would have a chance to read through it while the office was deserted and the phones weren't ringing. He wasn't sure what he was looking for. He'd sat through most of the interview in the observation room. He'd missed a couple of questions when Inspector Duggan came in, and that was what he looked for now. It was unlikely, but Darragh may have said something useful while Pete was distracted.

Pete flicked through the document until he came to the part of the interview just before Brendá Duggan had walked in.

DARRAGH: I see. You believe I am making this up.

SEMAJ: Are you?

DARRAGH: If I was, would I confess to it?

SEMAJ: You might, if you were trying to fake insanity and discovered you can't keep it up. It's harder to do than it looks."

DARRAGH: What reason would I have to pretend insanity?

SEMAJ: You're facing some serious charges. You might prefer the thought of a nice padded cell to a prison one."

DARRAGH: Neither prospect bothers me, Doctor Semaj, because sooner or later, they will come for me. Some discomfort in the meantime is tolerable.

SEMAJ: Who is they? Do you mean your friends from the other reality?

DARRAGH: Of course.

SEMAJ: The reality where you sent Hayley Boyle?

DARRAGH: Yes.

SEMAJ: What was her reaction to your intention to send her through to another reality?

DARRAGH: She was sceptical, I'm sure, but she trusts Rónán, or she would not have voluntarily gone with him. Truth is, I hardly spoke to her, so I couldn't say what her feelings were, one way or the other.

SEMAJ: How did she get away?

DARRAGH: Trása drove her back to the stone circle in Warren's car.

SEMAJ: Trása? That's the girl claiming to be Jack O'Righin's granddaughter?

DARRAGH: She has no family in this realm. She's half-Beansídhe. She is Amergin's daughter...

Pete read it through twice, wondering what it was that bothered him about the conversation. It was something about how Hayley got away. Something that didn't sit right.

He read it through again.

SEMAJ: How did she get away from St Christopher's?

DARRAGH: Trása drove her back to the stone circle in Warren's car.

Pete finally worked out what was bothering him. It was the stolen car. *Trása drove her back to the stone circle in Warren's car.*

Why did he say that? Why not "the car" or "the Audi". Why *Warren's* car?

How did Darragh *know* it was Warren's car?

"Jesus Christ," Pete exclaimed aloud to the empty squad room. He scrambled through his file notes until he came to the sheet reporting the Audi stolen, filed by Warren's wife late Thursday afternoon. According to the statement, her husband, Warren Maher, walked home across the golf course on Wednesday night because he believed he was over the legal blood alcohol limit, and came back on Thursday to discover the car missing. She claimed he knew nothing about who had stolen it. She stated he hadn't even been aware the car wasn't sitting in the car park of the Castle Golf Club, waiting for him to collect it.

Trása drove her back to the stone circle in Warren's car.

Darragh knew the name of the man who owned the Audi. Which meant Darragh had probably met Warren, perhaps knew him well enough to address him by name.

Was Warren the missing piece of the puzzle? Could this innocent financial analyst shed some light on what had happened to Hayley Boyle? Or know where Darragh had appeared from?

Pete glanced up at the clock on the wall. It was just after forty-thirty in the morning. Too early to appear on Warren's doorstep to make a seemingly casual enquiry about his stolen car.

He stifled a yawn. He'd only had about three hours sleep. Time for a strong coffee and some checking into the not-so-innocent financier who claimed he knew nothing about what had become of his vehicle after he parked it at the golf club on Wednesday evening.

Grabbing his coffee mug from his desk, he looked inside and discovered a gelatinous goo at the bottom, the remains of the almost-finished coffee he'd left several days ago. It was going to take some scrubbing to get that out, and it was disgusting enough that even Pete wouldn't drink out of it until it had been washed.

He took the mug and headed for the kitchen, glancing at the bloody photos on the noticeboard as he passed them. The killing clearly wasn't an open and shut case. Most murders were committed by family members, friends or acquaintances. Despite what TV police shows liked to pretend, Pete was well aware that less than 20% of people murdered, were killed by strangers. This new case must fall into that minority. Someone - probably Frank Murphy who was fond of things like that - had drawn a rough layout of the crime scene on the whiteboard. There were other notes scribbled beside the photos. One of a bloody pile of clothes found next door. Another of the murder weapon discarded at the scene.

Pete wondered who'd been assigned to the case but didn't worry about it too much. He needed coffee and he had his own problems with the Hayley Boyle disappearance. It was going to take...

Pete stopped and turned to stare at the board again. The words *Castle Golf Club* caught his eye on the diagram. This new crime scene backed onto the course. And then he saw the victim's name scrawled beside a rough flowchart Frank had started, tracking the victim's last known movements.

"Oh, my God," Pete muttered in disbelief.

The victim's name was Warren Maher.

CHAPTER 40

The Empresses made no attempt to pretend they had arrived at the Ikushima estate for any other reason than to find Ren. They didn't spare Namito or his family a glance. They made a beeline for Ren, staring at him as if he were some rare and marvellous artefact they'd stumbled across.

The fireworks were dying down, the night growing colder as the little girls approached.

"Why did you come early?" the one on the left asked, not in Japanese, but in a language almost indistinguishable from the Gaelic spoken by the *Tuatha Dé Danann* of Trása's realm. "And here? To this place?"

The girls were identical, almost impossible to tell apart. Despite their traditional Japanese dress, Ren doubted they had a drop of Asian blood in them. They looked Scandinavian, not oriental.

"We've been expecting you," the one on the left announced, looking him up and down curiously.

"But we thought the *Matrarchaí* were going to send a woman," her sister agreed, looking a little puzzled. She walked around Ren, as if to study him from every angle.

"I am... what I am..." Ren said carefully, turning to follow the movements of the one who was checking him out so thoroughly. They had mistaken him for someone else, someone they seemed anxious to meet. Someone sent by the *Matrarchaí*, whoever or whatever the *Matrarchaí* were. He had a memory he thought must belong to Darragh about a organisation known as the *Matrarchaí*, but according to his brother's recollection, they were midwives, not inter-dimensional travellers.

"You didn't say why you came here?"

"To this realm?"

"To this godforsaken backwater colonial pocket of our empire," the twin on the left announced, looking around with disdain. "We had everything ready for you in our palace back in *Nara*. Well, nearly ready. We weren't expecting you for a while yet. Not until after *Higan No Chu-Nichi*."

Great... I'm probably destined to die on the Autumn Equinox in this realm, too.

"The *Matrarchaí* thought it better I keep a low profile," Ren told them, hoping it sounded plausible. He had no idea who they'd been expecting - other than probably a woman. He could only hope that for the time being, he would be able convince them he was the messenger sent by this mysterious *Matrarchaí*, and that whatever the messenger was coming here to do, he could persuade them to believe he was here to do the same. At least until he could get out of here, preferably without Aoi having to disembowel herself to preserve the precious honor of the Ikushima.

And before the real messenger turned up, would probably be advisable, too.

"That's not what Lady Delphine told us," the little girl on the left said, looking a trifle miffed. "She said there would be a great celebration come *On Higan No Chu-Nichi* ... the autumn equinox. You've spoiled all our plans by coming through the rift in this place. We were going to have such a grand party in your honor."

"Lady... um... Delphine thought it would be better to come through the rift here," Ren said, with no idea who Delphine was, other than the woman from the *Matrarchaí* who had arranged for somebody to visit the Empresses.

"She should warn us before she changes things like this," the right one said. "Do you have a name?"

"Ren Kavanaugh," he told them. He was about to ask the same question of the little girls but realized if he was sent here by the *Matrarchaí*, he should already know their names. "You're very hard to tell apart," he added, smiling. "Which one of you is which?"

"Guess!" the one on the left demanded.

OK... now I'm screwed...

The twin on the right nudged her sister. "Bet he can't tell."

Ren made a great show of studying each girl closely for a moment. It *was* possible to tell them apart. In the flickering light from the torches, it seemed the one on the left had slightly bluer eyes, and the one on the right had a smattering of fine freckles across her nose, barely noticeable in this poor light. After a moment, he threw his hands up. "I give up. Tell me, which one of you is which?"

The girl on the left responded. It was as if they were taking turns. She was grinning broadly at him. "I am Isleen and this is my sister Teagan."

Teagan and Isleen. He wondered, if they were the equivalent of this reality's Undivided, that made them TeaganIsleen or IsleenTeagan. Or maybe they didn't subscribe to the idiotic naming conventions of Darragh's realm in this one. That would be a relief.

"What happened to your pet?" Teagan asked, looking around. A small crowd of curious onlookers had gathered in the compound, watching the exchange with awe. Besides the numerous members of the Empresses' entourage, quite a few of the *Shin Bungo* residents, along with Namito, Masuyo, Aoi and Kazusa, were standing by the main house, their mouths agape. They hadn't known what to expect, he realized. The Empresses visiting their humble fireworks factory might set them up for generations, or destroy them utterly, depending on the whim of these two children.

"What pet?" he asked, dragging his attention away from their audience and back to these very dangerous little girls. Now was not the time to be distracted.

"The *Youkai* you had with you when you arrived," Isleen said. "The one who changed into an owl at the Tanabe compound and flew away?"

"Oh," Ren said. "*That* pet."

So the Empresses had been tipped off by the Tanabe. It was a wonder Chishihero Tanabe wasn't here with her troops, gloating over his demise. But perhaps the Tanabe had misread the situation. The Empresses were expecting someone from another realm, which meant they were presuming a magical guest. And that - if you believed Masuyo about magic-wielders all being of Faerie origin - meant the presence of a shape-shifting *Beansídhe* shouldn't surprise them.

Perhaps the Empresses weren't as hard on the *Youkai* as everyone seemed to think. His glimpse of the future said otherwise, but Ren wasn't sure enough of his ability to give his vision any weight.

"Delphine should have warned you to keep her under control," Teagan added, folding her arms across her chest with a frown. "We can't have them flitting about, stirring up the dregs of the lesser *Youkai* still left in this realm."

"She's harmless," Ren assured them, hoping Trása had the sense to stay away. "She was frightened, and changed shape without thinking what it meant. You know what the *Beansídhe* are like when they're startled... are there many lesser *Youkai*?" he added in what he hoped was a casual tone. Toyoda had been insisting they were on the brink of extinction.

Isleen nodded, her stance echoing her sister's. "More than we'd like," she said, and then she brightened. "But now you're here, we can take care of that, can't we?"

"Excuse me?"

"That's what you're here for, isn't it?" Teagan asked. She seemed confused. "That's why the *Matrarchaí* sent you? To help us? To unlock the knowledge she gave us? And to finish the eradication of the *Youkai* in this realm?"

Eradicate them? This was what these little girls were expecting from the *Matrarchaí*? An assassin? Ren stared at the two little girls in the firelight, trying to figure out how to answer to that.

"Did you bring her as a lure?" Isleen asked. "We thought of doing that, but we couldn't find a *Youkai* who would help us lure the others into our trap, and we didn't know the true names of any *Youkai* to force them to help. Do you know the *Beansídhe's* true name? Is that how you control her?"

Control Trása? That's a joke.

"I thought she might be useful," Ren said, hoping he sounded as if he had some knowledge on the subject. Somewhere among all the confused memories belonging to his brother, was something about every *sídhe* possessing a secret name, and that knowing that name gave the person with that knowledge complete power over the *sídhe*. It was how Trása had trapped Toyoda, although she hadn't mentioned such a trick would work on her.

Funny about that.

"You should tell us her true name," Teagan said. "That way we can control her if anything happens to you."

"Her true name?" he repeated, stalling.

"We're going to have to insist, Renkavana," Isleen said, putting her hands on her hips. "Lady Delphine said it would be a disaster to come this close to cleansing the realm, only to have some rogue *Youkai* we missed in the purges, rallying the troops."

"A complete disaster," Ren agreed, wondering if these girls had also shared something like the *Comhroinn* with an adult. They looked like children and seemed to have the emotional depth of children, but their words and ambitions were hardly that of children.

Ethnic cleansing, he was certain, was not a game played by little girls.

"It's Tinkerbell," he said, lowering his voice a little, so it seemed he was sharing a secret.

"*Tinkerbell*," the girls repeated in unison. "That's a strange name."

"Who can figure out the mind of a *Youkai*, eh?"

The name wasn't strange enough to worry the girls for long. Isleen brightened suddenly and turned to her sister. "Did you see the fireworks, Teagan? I wasn't expecting fireworks to greet us." She nudged her sister with a grin. "Can we make everyone do that?"

"The Ikushima manufacture them here," Ren explained. "They're very good at it, too. You saw them on the way in, didn't you?"

"Can we see some more?" Teagan asked, turning to look at him.

"I mean... we're here now," Isleen agreed. "We should probably stay the night at least, before we return home to *Nara*."

"We want to see more," Teagan demanded.

Ren nodded, beckoning Namito forward. "I am quite sure the *Daimyo* would be honored. In fact, I'm certain he'd like nothing more than to show you his wares."

A polite cough from one of the courtiers behind the girls interrupted them. It was a woman in her thirties, her streaked ash-blonde hair piled high in an elaborate arrangement that must have taken hours. She was dressed just as formally as the girls, but when she addressed them, it was with great deference. "Your Highnesses might like to consider returning to your palace in *Nara*," she suggested. "There are many petitioners awaiting your presence."

"Stop trying to act like a mother, Wakiko," Isleen informed the courtier with a dismissive wave. "We can spare time for a fireworks display. After all, we have a special guest to honor and tonight marks the beginning of the end for the last of the *Youkai* in our realm. We have much to celebrate. Why shouldn't there be fireworks?"

"Why indeed?" Ren agreed under his breath. The woman bowed and stepped back, as if she had somehow erred by pointing out the Empresses' responsibilities. Equally anxious to please, Namito hurried forward to greet his guests and arrange their fireworks display.

Ren stood by and watched, sick with the knowledge that the event these innocent little girls wanted to celebrate was only going to happen if he aided them in committing mass murder.

CHAPTER 41

"But they're only little girls!" Trása exclaimed as she morphed back into human form high in the branches of a huge mountain ash some distance from the Ikushima compound. Under normal circumstances, she wouldn't have risked changing back into her own form so high off the ground, but Toyoda had waved her down and indicated the branch was safe and strong enough to bear her weight.

At least, she assumed that's what was he was signalling. It was hard to tell in the dark. He could have been waving her off.

Fortunately, he wasn't. She caught the branches overhead to balance herself as she resumed her human shape, shivering as the cold air embraced her naked skin, but she ignored the chill. She was much more interested in what was going on down on the ground. She peered down through the almost barren branches into the Ikushima compound as Rónán faced a pair of creepily alike little girls, wishing she knew what they were discussing.

On the bright side, they hadn't killed Rónán on the spot, which was a good thing. But they had the ability to do it with a thought. Trása could feel the latent power in them from here.

"Those little girls look as if they escaped from *Village of the Damned.*"

"I not be familiar with that village, mistress."

"It's a special village. I saw it on TV in Rónán's realm," she explained.

The ninja *Leipreachán* looked at her sideways. "It be quite different to this realm then, where ye come from?"

"You have no idea, little man," Trása said, shifting around until she was sitting on the branch beside him. "What are they talking about, do you think?"

"Would ye like to know?"

"Do you have a way of finding out?"

Toyoda shrugged. "There be plenty of lesser *sídhe* still about in this realm, mistress, who might oblige if ye ask then. Mostly they be hiding out of fear, but there be wood sprites and dryads and plenty of the wee folk, who might be willing to aid ye in ye quest to put an end to these monsters."

Trása glanced at the *Leipreachán* a little alarmed. "Quest?"

"That be why ye came here, isn't it?"

He said it with such confidence. Trása didn't have the heart to correct him. Toyoda had been so pathetically relieved to be caught in her trap, it felt cruel to disillusion him by revealing she intended to be gone from this realm as soon as she found a way to open a rift.

"You're expecting *me* to save you all?" she asked, trying not to let her scepticism leak into her voice.

Toyoda nodded, smiling happily. "SvenHendrick said the gods would send help." He leaned across and patted her knee like a fond uncle. "It took a while, but I be so glad they sent someone so pretty."

For a moment, Trása was distracted by the compliment. She sat a little straighter and smiled, preening under his admiring gaze. "Really? You think I'm pretty?" Then she realized what she was doing, and shook her head to clear the thought. That was the sort of thing her mother would do. This world was so steeped in magic, the *Beansídhe* side of her was coming to the fore.

It felt very strange. Even when she'd lived in *Tír Na nÓg*, Trása had felt more human than *sídhe*. It was peculiar to be feeling the opposite.

"Tell me about SvenHendrick," she said, figuring that was a safer thing to ask than revealing her ignorance by blurting out "who are SvenHendrick?"

"They be the most powerful Undivided ever seen in this realm," Toyoda told her with a wistful sigh. "We be so happy when they be invested. It seemed like everything be exactly right with the world."

"If they were so powerful, how come the terrible twins down there are running the show?"

Toyoda shrugged. "I not be entirely sure. It started when Hendrick met Wakiko."

"Who is Wakiko?"

"She be mother of those abominations," Toyoda replied.

"Wakiko? Those girls don't look Japanese," Trása said with a frown. "They look like little Vikings."

"Wakiko be Norman," Toyoda said. "The Empire of the Rising Sun reaches far and wide, mistress." He pointed to the courtiers standing behind Rónán and the twins. "That be her there. In the blue kimono. She still be there for the girls, but they be the ones who rule the roost."

Down in the compound, Namito was hurrying forward, bowing obsequiously to the children. It seemed they were holding everyone in thrall with their mere presence.

"How is it in a realm ruled by the Japanese, you have Norman Undivided?" Trása asked.

"Isn't it the same in ye realm, my lady?" the *Leipreachán* asked, sounding surprised. "SvenHendrick's mother was a Gaul. The right twins not always be born in a place ye'd prefer. The *Matrarchaí* find the twins wherever they can find them."

"The *Matrarchaí*?" she asked, sounding just as surprised to hear of them in this realm, as Toyoda was to learn of the differences in hers.

"Have ye not heard of the *Matrarchaí*, mistress?"

"I've heard of them, Toyoda," she said. "I'm just surprised to learn that you've heard of them too."

"The *Matrarchaí* be at the root of all our troubles in this realm," he told her with a heavy sigh. "At least, that's what the elder *Youkai* believed, although being one of the lesser *Youkai*, they didn't confide in me 'bout it, as a rule."

Trása smiled, imagining her uncle treating a *Leipreachán* with anything other than disdainful contempt. "I'm sure they didn't."

"The *Matrarchaí* in this realm be the ones who oversaw the breeding of the psychic twins. They be the ones who brought Wakiko to court. They be the ones who started all the trouble between the Undivided."

Before she could ask exactly what trouble he was talking about, the sky overhead exploded in a brilliant burst of light. She blinked, the afterimage of the fireworks blinding her for a moment.

"They only be five or six when Lady Delphine came through the rift. She claimed to be of the *Matrarchaí* from a realm similar to ours where the Undivided had destroyed all the *Youkai* races. She said she came to warn us."

"She was lying, I suppose?"

"No. It be true enough about the dead *sídhe*. What she left out was that she hadn't come to be warning the *Youkai* about it, but to do the same here."

"Didn't somebody think to check what she was telling them?" Trása asked, as another brilliant shower of light burst overhead. "I mean... how hard is it to send a rift runner through to another realm to be certain?"

"It be very hard, mistress," he told her, flinching a little as it was followed by another starmine that blinded them with its brilliance.

Keeping up with this convoluted tale was making Trása's head spin. The distraction of the fireworks exploding overhead and the biting chill of the night air weren't helping much, either. "Hang on... let me get this straight. The *Matrarchaí* introduced the Undivided - or at least this realm's version of them - to some Swedish girl called Wakiko, who gave birth to those two down there and... what? They all lived happily ever after?"

"Not exactly."

By Danú, *this is like unraveling a felted fleece.* "What do you mean, *not exactly?*"

"Hendrick and Sven had a falling out, when Sven tried to kill Isleen and Teagan in the cradle."

Of course he tried to kill them. This realm is insane. She sighed, almost afraid to pose the obvious question. "All right. I'll bite. *Why* did he try to kill them?"

Toyoda shrugged. "There be various stories about. The *Djinn* claim Sven tried to kill them out of jealousy. The wood sprites say they heard it was because Sven be having a recurring nightmare about the twins. His visions showed the girls be the death of all the fey folk in this realm, and he had to kill them, because all the Undivided are part *Youkai*, so he was bound to defend the *Youkai* whatever way he could."

She shook her head. "That logic doesn't hold. If the Undivided are *Youkai* enough to want to kill their own babies to protect the *Youkai*, then Hendrick should have felt the same way."

The *Leipreachán* shrugged. "Maybe he didn't have the visions, so he didn't see the threat."

"It's possible, I suppose," she conceded. "But it's still insane." Trása watched the girls in question watching the fireworks below them, clapping delightedly with every new explosion. She figured Hendrick must have prevailed. "So Hendrick discovered Sven trying to murder his babies and stopped him. Then what?"

"They not be Hendrick's babies, mistress. They both be in love with her, but it be Sven who eventually married Wakiko and fathered the girls. The brothers never reconciled after Sven tried to kill them and it was left to Hendrick to raise them. The wee girls never forgave their father, neither, specially when the *Matrarchaí* told them their father tried to murder them in the cradle."

"But you said the Undivided went through the rift looking for help."

"That wasn't until Lady Delphine arrived and told them they must be rid of SvenHendrick and invest the girls as the Undivided in their place. And they found ye, mistress," Toyoda said, smiling up at her with adoring eyes. "I be surprised they didn't tell ye this before ye came through the rift."

"There wasn't a lot of time to discuss things," Trása told him, thinking it was the bald truth. She'd not even heard of SvenHendrick before today, let alone met them, so there never had been a chance to discuss any of this. "How did she convince them to rid themselves of two perfectly good Undivided and replace them with a couple of obnoxious little girls?" Trása well knew the consequences of such a plan in her realm. But the Undivided were not divided here. They were no separated youths, still testing the limits of their authority. They'd been grown men, healthy, hearty and more than capable of holding things together.

"Lady Delphine approached the *Konketsu* and warned them the argument between the Undivided was going to destroy the magic if it didn't end. When everybody agreed the brothers were never going to be reconciled, she suggested transferring the power to Teagan and Isleen, even though they only be little girls, back then."

"Not sure if you've noticed, Toyoda," Trása said, ducking instinctively as one of the starmines exploded almost directly overhead. "But they're still little girls."

"Only in body, mistress," Toyoda lamented. "Lady Delphine shared the *Comhroinn* with the new Undivided after the power transfer. They look like little girls, but they have the memories of a wicked, manipulative *Matrarchaí* bitch to call upon."

Trása looked at the little ninja askance. "Excuse me?"

"That be what Lord Hendrick called her, mistress. I just be echoing his words."

She smiled. "I see."

"After the transfer, things just went from bad to worse," Toyoda continued. "Turns out IsleenTeagan don't need the *Youkai* to channel the power to the *Konketsu*."

"But isn't that just because all the *Konketsu* are part sídhe?"

"Aye, they be that... but these girls can take the magic the *Youkai* loaned them, and channel the folding magic through their mongrel *Konketsu* without the help of our kind at all." For a moment Trása feared Toyoda was going to start crying again, but he seemed to get a grip of himself long enough to continue the story. "They not have any loyalty to our kind. SvenHendrick were compelled to protect the *Youkai*, but Wakiko is all human. Those girls don't have enough *Youkai* in them to be compelled to do anything for our kind. Once the *Konketsu* realized that, they started rounding up the *Youkai* and sending them to worlds without magic so we'd die. They told us they were better worlds they be sending us to. Worlds with *more* magic. Worlds where we'd be happy and not have to bother with humans at all." He sniffed back a tear, unable to continue.

Trása put her arm around Toyoda's shoulders awkwardly, thinking she'd never in her life imagined herself having to comfort a sobbing *Leipreachán*.

"Why didn't someone go for help?" she asked. There were plenty of realms out there, Trása thought, which must be similar enough to this one. Realms that would aid their brethren if they were under attack. And they must have had rift runners aplenty.

"They did," Toyoda told her. "But before they left, SvenHendrick destroyed the rift-making knowledge and killed all the *Konketsu* who could open rifts to keep the *Matrarchaí* out and to ensure nobody followed them." He sniffed and wiped his nose on his sleeve, leaving a silvery trail on the black fabric.

"When you say *destroyed*, Toyoda, do you mean gone forever?" Trása asked, more than a little worried to learn that small but significant fact. "Not just lost? Not just bundled up and put away somewhere for safekeeping?"

"They burned all the *ori mahou* texts that detail the folding for a rift and most of the gampi trees from which the folding paper be made. Those who can fold the *ori mahou* can still travel across this realm, mistress, but there be no gateways for us to escape to other realms any longer. That's why the *Konketsu* haven't been able to finish the job of eradicating the lesser *Youkai*. They no longer be able to send us through the rifts. We have to wait for *Youkai* like ye to come here, to save us."

Trása shivered, and she wasn't entirely sure it was because it was night, and she was sitting naked, high in a tree, watching a fireworks display while this strangely dressed *Leipreachán* shattered any hope she had of ever returning home.

He wiped his nose again. Down in the compound, the little girls responsible for driving all the Faerie in this realm to their deaths, jumped up and down, clapping with delight, their squeals of glee faintly reaching even Trása and Toyoda, high in the treetops.

"Is there no other way to open a rift?"

"Not that I be aware, mistress." He looked up at her curiously. "Doesn't ye have the knowledge from the realm ye come from?"

"Knowledge, yes," she told him. "Tools, no. We use jewels to open the rifts in my realm. And I don't have one with me. Why aren't they killing him?"

"Pardon?"

Trása pointed to the compound. Rónán was watching the fireworks display with the twin girls, cheering with them like he was their new best friend. "Why aren't they killing him? If these two little monsters down there are set on destroying all the *Youkai*, and Rónán is Faerie enough to be able to wane himself out of there, why is he staying and why are they treating him like an honored guest?"

"We be waiting for help and so be they," Toyoda explained. "Your friend be *Youkai* but he looks human. They might think Lady Delphine and the *Matrarchaí* sent him."

And Rónán is clearly playing along with that misconception, Trása thought, not entirely sure she blamed him for it. They needed to find a way out of this realm and they needed to do it soon, or Rónán and Darragh would...

"Hang on," she said, turning to Toyoda. "You said Sven and Hendrick went for help. How could they? I mean... the power was transferred while they still lived, wasn't it. In my realm, that means they should have died."

"The same holds true in this realm, mistress," Toyoda said. "Truth be, they were dying when they left. Sven looked as if he'd barely make it through the rift." He looked up at her with adoring eyes. "The gods must have been smiling on this realm if they were able to find help to send us before the magic withdrawal sickness took them."

His worshipful gaze made Trása very uncomfortable. She looked away, trying to pretend she didn't notice. "Apparently they were."

"Did it take long, mistress? For all that Sven fathered those abominations down there, I liked him and his brother. I'd not want to see either of them suffer before they died."

Trása momentary glimmer of hope died. "You're sure they're dead then?"

"Long dead I be supposing, mistress," the *Leipreachán* said heavily. "Nobody survives transferring the power from one Undivided to the next, in this world or any other. Why?"

"No reason, Toyoda... just wondering. Let's get out of here, hey? I'm freezing and there's nothing happening down there tonight." She glanced up at the sky. "It will be *Lughnasadh* soon. If I can't stop what's about to happen to Rónán, I'm not sure I want to be here to watch it."

"As ye wish, mistress," Toyoda said, climbing to his feet, which made the branch tremble alarmingly. "Where did ye want to go?"

"To *Tír Na nÓg*, Toyoda," she said, grabbing an overhanging branch for balance. "I want to go home."

CHAPTER 42

Old age was a terrible thing. It was bad enough, Sorcha mused, to suffer the steady decline of one's body over a period of decades - to feel the muscles withering, the ravages of time wrinkling one's flesh until one looked like nothing more than a caricature of the person they knew themselves to be - but to have it happen in a couple of weeks was beyond painful. It was soul-destroying.

And there was nothing she could do to stop it.

For much of her life Sorcha had been lithe and nimble, blessed with youth. That blessing was now revealing its dark side. Even returning to her own realm now would not undo the damage. Her aging had been delayed by her time in *Tír Na nÓg*. Returning through the veil to *Tír Na nÓg* would not restore her youth or reverse the damage wrought by this magic-less realm. Whatever happened, she was doomed. Her age had caught up with her.

It was not the first time she'd been touched by the cold hand of her apparently miraculous youth. She'd entered Tír Na nÓg with Marcroy Tarth when she was sixteen, naäÄ¢ve and full of hope, blinded by the promises of her Faerie prince. She thought she'd only been there five months or so. She emerged from the magical realm fifty years later. The pain of that agonising discovery she thought long forgotten. Sorcha had emerged to find her parents dead, her brothers old men, her great-grandnieces and nephews already starting families of their own. Her family had treated her like a pariah, fearful of the youthful stranger who claimed to be one of them.

She had tried to make a life with the remains of her family, but it proved too awkward for all of them. So after trying to fit in for a few uncomfortable and best-forgotten months, Sorcha had walked away. She sought a life using the warrior skills she had learned among the *Daoine sídhe*. If anybody asked - and few risked it - she would tell them she had emerged from *Tír Na nÓg* to find her entire family gone, everyone she knew and loved, long dead and buried.

It was easier for everyone that way. And it felt like the truth.

Jack's housekeeper, Carmel, didn't question Sorcha's rapid deterioration. A gossipy, generous woman who was rather fond of the sound of her own voice, and who had an opinion on pretty much *everything*, she took it upon herself to care for Jack's "cousin", even though Sorcha didn't want her help and tried - without success - to refuse it. As the days progressed, however, and her condition deteriorated, Sorcha reluctantly began to rely on the housekeeper's appearance each morning, not sure she was still capable of getting out of bed without assistance.

Sorcha had met plenty of old women in her time, some of whom reached their mid-eighties and were still collecting eggs and milking goats and generally looking after themselves as they had done for most of their lives, albeit a little slower than they once had. It didn't seem right that she was so fragile. Perhaps the speed with which her age had caught up with her was contributing to her weakness. Whatever the reason, there was no dash for a rift to her own realm in her future. No diving out of moving cars. No vigils in trees. Sorcha knew with a certainty bordering on prescience, that she would die in this realm.

All she could do was make sure she didn't endanger Darragh by betraying the truth about him.

That proved quite easy when it was just Sorcha in the house, with daily visits from Carmel, who made her a delicious, creamy pumpkin soup with soft white bread rolls and settled her in front of the TV, tut-tutting all the while about Jack's inconsiderate ways. "Fancy inviting his elderly cousin to stay and leaving her to fend for herself in this mausoleum," she would mutter as she fussed over her.

Sorcha entertained herself with the many ways she'd like to murder this well-intentioned but interfering old biddy, while being quietly grateful for her help. She could barely make it to the bathroom on her own these days and would have preferred to relieve herself in the garden among the bushes in the way she accustomed. Sorcha found the notion of flushing away one's bodily waste with perfectly good drinking water to be an indescribable folly.

Jack returned a few days before *Lughnasadh*, his book tour cut short by the attack on the World Trade Centre. Nobody wanted to read about terrorists any more. At least, not in a good way. Jack's story, the tale that had made him a wealthy man, now seemed self-serving and opportunistic. The Irish American ladies Jack was so scornful of - those society ladies who had so desperately wanted to pose with him for a photograph to show their friends how dangerously they lived, had cancelled their dinner places in droves. Feting a former member of the IRA - who'd been jailed for killing innocent bystanders by blowing up public buildings - seemed tacky and tasteless, in a place where the final death toll of another horrendous attack on a public building hadn't even been calculated but was likely in the thousands. He predicted the money would dry up for all organisations even remotely terror related in the aftermath of this attack. There would be no more Irish-American black-tie fundraisers held in New York to raise money for their poor put-upon cousins back in the Old Country. It wouldn't surprise him if the IRA decided to publicly disarm, Jack said, just to distance themselves from the scale and horror of the New York disaster.

Sorcha sat in the reclining armchair and listened to him going on and on about it, trying not to nod off in the afternoon sun. It was important to act as if she had some idea of what he was talking about because he was her host, and besides Carmel, the only person she knew in this reality. He was more than her only friend - if that was the word for their odd relationship - she figured if Darragh didn't miraculously escape custody and find a way back through the rift in the next day or so, he would probably be responsible for her body and laying her out. She owed it to Jack to pretend she cared.

To say he was surprised to find Sorcha still in his house when he returned from his travels was an understatement. Jack wasn't just surprised, either. He was livid. Sorcha wondered if his anger wasn't so much at her, but as a result of what he had witnessed while he was away. He didn't turn her out, though, despite his threats to do just that. Instead, he suffered her presence and watched her deteriorate a little more each day. Any lingering doubts he had about the existence of magic in the realm where his visitor belonged were fading with every wrinkle and liver spot that appeared on her ancient, wasted frame.

The morning of *Lughnasadh* dawned overcast and dull. Sorcha greeted the day with a certain amount of fatalistic acceptance. Tonight, back in the realm where she belonged, the queen of the *Tuatha Dé Danann* would make a rare appearance in the mundane world, to brand the new Undivided heirs with the magical tattoo that would allow the sharing of the magic between Faerie and human to continue. Heads of state from around the realm would emerge from the stone circle, bearing gifts for the Faerie Queen, to thank her for her generosity and to watch the ceremony unfold. It always struck Sorcha odd that they thanked her. There was really no need. Orlagh had given her word when the Treaty of *Tír Na nÓg* was first forged, nearly two thousand years ago. She couldn't break her word, even if she'd wanted to. Orlagh would continue to allow humans to share the *Tuatha Dé Danann* magic while ever humans were able to produce the special twins who were the vessel for the sharing.

The fate of the cast aside Undivided was well documented. Any chance Sorcha had of returning to her own realm, would die within a few days of the power transfer. As would Darragh. In all likelihood, he would not see out the night.

Wherever he was, if Rónán wasn't able to stop the ceremony, he would die too.

Sorcha was pondering this disturbing scenario when she heard the doorbell ring. She didn't try to answer it. Jack was in his glasshouse and wouldn't have heard it ring but Carmel was in the kitchen preparing lunch. Whoever it was and whatever they wanted, Carmel could answer the door and deal with it. Sorcha was quite certain the visitor wasn't here to see her. She lifted the remote and changed the channel. Sorcha liked watching the home shopping programs. They reminded her of the hawkers in the markets of her world, trying to entice passers-by who had no interest in, or need of, their wares.

"If you'll just wait in here," she heard Carmel saying, out in the hall. "I'll go and fetch him from the glasshouse."

"I can talk to him in the glasshouse," Sorcha heard a male voice offer.

"You'd best be waiting here for him, officer," she heard Carmel tell him. "He's not fond of visitors in his precious glasshouse. You wait in the living room. I'll be back in a tick."

Footsteps hurried away from the living room as the door opened and a young man appeared at the door. He was in his late twenties, Sorcha guessed. Certainly no older. He wore jeans and a suit jacket, with a blue checked shirt underneath, as if he couldn't make up his mind to dress up or dress down. He was a good-looking young man with more than a passing resemblance, she noted with curiosity - to Darragh.

He stared at her for a moment, frowning. "I'm sorry, I didn't realize there was anybody here." He stepped into the room, reached into his coat and produced a wallet, which he opened to display some sort of identification and a shiny badge. "Pete Doherty," he said. "And you are?"

"Tired and in no need of company," Sorcha informed him. She turned her attention back to the TV and the program she'd found. They were selling a rather clever blanket with sleeves, which she thought was quite a useful idea, but would have been better if it came with pockets to store one's weapons within easy reach on the outside.

"You're a friend of Jack's?" he asked.

Sorcha turned to look at him, this time more closely, and her heart skipped a beat. This was the man she had punched into unconsciousness in their stolen Gardaí car during Rónán and Darragh's escape from St Christopher's Visual Rehabilitation Centre.

She took a deep breath, and started eyeing off the nearest exit, until she realized Pete Doherty had no idea who she was. Even if did get a clear look at her in the car a couple of weeks ago, the girl who had knocked him out was nothing like this decrepit old woman sitting here watching the shopping channel.

"I'm a cousin."

"Do you have a name?"

"Of course."

The detective frowned, tilting his head to one side, as if he couldn't place where he'd seen her before. "Do I know you?"

"Not likely," Sorcha snapped, "if you don't even know my name."

"Now, now," Jack said, as he entered the room, wiping his dirty hand on a grubby scrap of towel. "You be polite to the nice policeman, girlie, or he'll take you away."

"Chance would be a fine thing," Sorcha muttered, and turned back to watching the presenter and his co-host gushing about the many uses of this amazing new concept of blankets with sleeves.

"How can I help you officer?" Jack asked, ignoring Sorcha's answer. He seemed cool and unbothered by the Gardaí detective's visit. Sorcha didn't know if that's because he really wasn't bothered, or because he had this sort of discussion down pat, given his long experience of being in trouble with the law. "You've come on your own, so I'm guessing you're not here to arrest me for anything."

"Patrick Boyle tells me he sent Ren Kavanaugh's twin brother and his accomplice to you, after he helped them escape the Castle Golf Club."

I knew that bastard would betray us, Sorcha thought, making a point of staring at the TV, for fear her anger at Amergin's *eiletéin* would betray them. But how did they know it was Darragh they had in custody? Had he told them who he was or did they have some arcane way of finding things like that out with their technology and sciences?

Jack didn't bother to deny it. "Aye. Little prick turned up here expecting a handout. I told him to piss off."

"Do you know where he went?"

"I'd be guessing, given the commotion going on at the Kavanaugh place a couple of days later with your lot invading the house like you had a hot tip on the location of Jack the Ripper, that he went next door," Jack said with a shrug, as if the ERU storming Kiva Kavanaugh's house was nothing particularly remarkable.

"What about the woman with him? Dark hair, about twenty-five. Maybe thirty. Maybe younger. Where did she go?"

Sorcha froze, expecting the detective would turn and look at her any moment and realize she was the one he was talking about. But he didn't and Jack didn't so much as spare Sorcha a glance to draw attention to her.

"Don't know who you're talking about," Jack said, without missing a beat. "The boy turned up on his own and I sent him on his way. I told the last cop who came to visit the same thing."

"I like to check these things myself."

"Check away, son," Jack said, placing his hands on his hips. "I've got too much invested in life outside of prison to get mixed up with that sort of trouble, these days. I pissed the lad off and got on a plane for New York. Wish I had stayed here."

Out of the corner of her eye, Sorcha could see the detective nodding, although she couldn't tell if he believed Jack or not. "Yeah... nasty business, that. Whose side are you on?"

"Excuse me?"

"That's your thing isn't? Blowing up buildings? Killing innocent civilians?"

"We never did anything like what they did in New York," Jack said, the contained anger in his voice obvious even to Sorcha. "And we phoned in a warning. Every time."

"Which makes it all right, I suppose." Doherty didn't wait for an answer. "Do you know a man called Warren Maher?"

Sorcha gripped the remote control so tightly the channel changed. Suddenly, she was watching a football match, but nobody seemed to be paying any attention to her.

Jack shook his head. "Should I? What's he do?"

"He's a financial analyst."

"Not my crowd, really," Jack said, feigning innocence. "Too busy planning terrorist attacks to talk to me broker. Should I know him?"

"Ren Kavanaugh and his brother, Darragh, stole his car last week."

At the mention on Darragh's name, Sorcha let out an involuntary squeak of alarm. *How does he know Darragh's name?*

Both men turned to look at her. Sorcha kept her eyes determinedly forward, fixed on the football match.

"Housekeeper's aunty," Jack explained. "Got dementia, poor old thing. Barking mad, she is."

"She seemed quite lucid a moment ago," Doherty said. She wasn't looking at him, but Sorcha could feel his eyes on her. And his suspicion. "Claimed to be your cousin."

"It comes and goes. What's the problem this broker fella? You think he was up to something with the lads?"

"I think he's dead," Doherty said, turning his gaze from Sorcha to watch Jack's reaction. "Someone slit his throat while he was taking out the garbage."

Jack barely hesitated. "Wish I could help you, detective, I really do. But explosives are my thing. I'm not a knifeman. If I'd done him, he'd be spread out all *over* the garbage, not bleeding on it."

"I never said you did it," Doherty pointed out. "Is that a guilty conscience talking?"

"Yeah, right," Jack snorted. "Is that all you wanted, detective? I have a *bromeliad* in dire need of a new home. I don't want to leave the roots exposed any longer than I have to."

"A *bromeliad*?"

"I'm halfway through re-potting a pineapple. Can you find your own way out, or do you need Carmel to show you the way?"

"I can find my own way out," the detective said. He turned to Sorcha, who was still glued to the TV, even though she couldn't have recalled a single thing that had happened on the screen these past few minutes if her life depended on it. "Ma'am."

She ignored him. *Barking mad,* Jack had described her. *Best this nosey young man keep thinking that.*

"Don't make plans for any more overseas trips in the next month or so, O'Righin," Doherty suggested and he opened the door. "I may want to talk to you again."

"Be my pleasure, detective. Now bugger off."

Jack waited in silence as the detective walked the long length of the hall. He didn't speak until he heard the sound on tyres on the gravel drive and then he turned to Sorcha.

"You killed him, didn't you?"

"It had to be done," she replied, seeing no point in denying it. "I had to protect Darragh and Rónán."

"One is missing, the other is in gaol," Jack pointed out. "You must be very pleased with your work."

She turned to glare at him. "You know nothing about me, old man. Or why I am here. It's of little consequence, at any rate."

"I'm not sure Warren's family would agree with that."

She turned back to stare sightlessly at the television screen. "It is September twenty second, Jack. It is *Lughnasadh*. By sunset, unless Rónán has found a way to stop the transfer, both he and Darragh will be dead in a matter of days, and me along with them, because with their death, I will lose any chance I have to return home. Warren's death was unfortunate, but necessary, a sentiment I am sure - given your background - you understand."

"I'd already silenced him."

"You silenced him until his conscience got the better of him," she pointed out, raising the remote control to change the channel again. "I took care of the problem permanently." The next station she flicked on to was a news program, once again showing the planes crashing into the World Trade Centre.

Jack stared at her for a long moment, and then shook his head. "Jaysus, it must be a cruel world you come from."

"No crueller than this one," she replied, pointing to the TV. "Because I can tell you this much, Jack O'Righin, nobody in my realm ever did anything like that."

CHAPTER 43

The investiture of a new Undivided was no small thing, and it brought representatives of the *sídhe* races from all over the realm. There were *Djinn* and *Tuatha Dé Danann, Youkai* and even a smattering of Egyptian deities, come to watch the festivities. There were probably not as many as once might have come. Nobody had seen hide nor hair of a Roman god in decades. The Indians believed each one of them was a manifestation of their own gods, so they didn't need them to appear at events like this and the African spirits - of which there was a numberless pantheon - considered the Treaty of *Tír Na nÓg* such a betrayal of their kind, that they generally refused to take part in the ceremony at all.

There were other guests, too, camped at *Sí an Bhrú*. The fields around the fortress were cluttered with colorful tents, the noise of a score of delegates and their entourages representing the rulers of lands as near as Albion and as far away as India and China. The delegation from Namibia had brought three caged lions - although the reason escaped Marcroy - probably to intimidate everyone else.

They had come through the stone circles with their Druids who opened the rifts and allowed them to travel the length and breadth of the world as easily as they traversed the distance between one town and the next in their own countries. Marcroy frowned as he looked down over the crowded fields, despairing of how many humans there were, not just in *Sí an Bhrú* but in general. There seemed to be more every year.

Why couldn't they be like the other animal species which shared this world, and die off when times were lean, to keep their numbers down? The curse of human intelligence, Marcroy often lamented, was their misguided compassion.

A herd of any other kind left the weak to die or for the predators to take, for the good of the herd. Humans spoke of kindness and caring, while they protected the weak and often allowed them to breed. In spite of that, they committed acts of appalling atrocity against each other in the name of war.

"You look pensive, brother."

Marcroy turned to face the queen of the *Tuatha Dé Danann*. Fair and flawless, her long hair flowing behind her in a cloud so fine it floated on the negligible breeze, she was dressed in a gown made of spider webs and light, her youthful face giving no hint of the thousands of years she had lived and ruled her people.

"I was just pondering the paradox of war, my lady," he told her, relieved beyond measure his older sister had arrived in time for the ceremony. She had promised she would be here to perform the power transfer from the absent Undivided to the new, less-talented and less-dangerous heirs, but Orlagh didn't keep time the way humans did. He would not have been surprised if she forgot... or missed it by a year or two.

"What is the paradox that vexes thee, Marcroy?" she asked glancing at her entourage. In her wake came a cascade of lesser *sídhe*, scores of them - small and flighty, sprites and spirits, and all hoping for a moment in her light, a glimmer of her favour. "Humans fight and sometimes they die. I have noticed they mostly prefer to maim each other with large sticks and pointed implements, and drink vast quantities of mead after the battle is done, convincing each other all the while, that they were not afraid of dying."

He smiled, reminded that Orlagh was much better informed about human nature than humans suspected. "They send the strong out to die, leaving the weak to carry on the tribe. I find that... inefficient."

Orlagh laughed - the sound a waterfall of delight that sent shivers down Marcroy's spine.

"You are the only one among us, Marcroy, who worries about efficiency. Are the rest of the Brethren here yet?"

He shook his head. "Not all of them. I have seen Jamaspa, but he seems preoccupied. He said he had lost something valuable and has gone to look for it." He swept his arm across the scene below. "We do have all the dregs of humanity, gathering like vultures circling a corpse."

Orlagh glanced at him curiously. "How can you loathe mortals so intensely, my dear, and yet spend so much time among them, scheming and plotting their demise? Do they never suspect your true feelings?"

"Some might," he conceded with a shrug. "But I have moved among humans long enough to have mastered their gift for duplicity. They have no notion of my motives. They think I aspire to be like them." He recalled the last human lover he had taken, although memory was vague, the woman's face lost in time. She was a Druid, he knew that much, but other than the wolf mask she wore, he remembered little about her or the winter equinox in question.

Orlagh frowned. "You promised me you wouldn't encourage that sort of thing. Or fraternise with them yourself. Not after the trouble with you caused with Sorcha."

Marcroy shook his head. Had he promised, being *sídhe*, he would have been incapable of breaking his word. "It served the required purpose at the time."

"You know what I think of *Tuatha Dé Danann* who fraternise with mortals," she said, frowning. "There are too many unwanted mongrels out there now. I would be appalled to find you adding to their number."

He gave her a reassuring smile. "Do not bother yourself, beloved. The last time I fraternised with any human was years ago."

"I trust you had a good reason."

He nodded. "The mortals were becoming suspicious of my motives, so I did what I must to assuage their concerns. I took part in one of their festivals, that's all. Nothing came of it."

She smiled at him, reaching up to touch his face. Her touch was electric, even to someone as used to it as Marcroy. This was what came of living entirely in the *sídhe* world, of never being tainted by mortals. For a moment, Marcroy wondered if he should simply do the same. Perhaps he should walk away from this life. Forget mortals and go back to where he belonged. What a delight it would be to stay in *Tír Na nÓg*.

What a thrill it would be to immerse himself in nothing more complicated than the wonder of being a prince of the *Tuatha Dé Danann* and put this mundane world of duplicity and strife behind him.

And then remembered *why* he was caught up in this mundane world of duplicity and strife. If he withdrew, the *Tuatha Dé Danann* would be destroyed.

Marcroy walked among humans so his beloved sister didn't need to.

Perhaps, after today he could arrange to spend more time at home. Once the threat of RónánDarragh was removed, his stewardship of the Druids needn't be quite so close. Of course, he would have to ensure another set of twins like RónánDarragh were never invested again, but surely he could do that without spending so much time in the mundane world?

"Beloved Marcroy," she said. "You have given up so much for your people."

"Not for my people, my lady. For you."

She laughed delightedly. "Now you are just trying to flatter me. Have you met the new Undivided?"

"I have. They seem personable enough. They are still children, of course, so it's hard to say what they will be like as adults." Truth be told, Marcroy didn't really care. Just so long as they weren't as powerful as RónánDarragh. That was all that truly mattered. "They have been waiting in *Tír Na nÓg* for this day to arrive."

"Was that wise?" Orlagh asked. "Won't they lose track of the time?"

"They are young enough not to notice," he assured her. "In their minds, they only arrived a day ago in the magical city of the *Tuatha Dé Danann*. Out here, weeks have passed, but at their age, time is fairly meaningless, whatever race one is."

"I suppose," she agreed, but already she was losing interest in the discussion. Across the valley, the sun was resting on the top of the hills. Soon it would be time for the ceremony to begin.

"I heard there was to be a wedding, too," Orlagh said, looking around for some sign of the wedding party."

"We've missed that, I fear," Marcroy told her, not bothering to explain that he had intercepted the queen's invitation and refused on her behalf. There were few things he cared less about than who Torcán of the Celts was marrying. The bride was one of Álmhath's court maidens - some orphaned and impoverished nobleman's daughter he supposed - who had caught the boy's eye. Why a woman in Álmhath's position wasn't using this marriage to fortify her throne made no sense to Marcroy, so he had no interest in the young lovers or their vows. If Álmhath wasn't smart enough to realize that her only child was too valuable a commodity to be wasted on a marriage based on anything other than protection of her borders or bolstering her wealth, he saw no reason why he should help celebrate her foolishness.

At his suggestion the marriage had taken place this morning, at dawn, presided over by Colmán. With the distraction of her son's marriage out of the way, he and Álmhath could move on to the important business, which was the investiture of the new Undivided. Marcroy needed that to happen - and not only to appease the Brethren. Although he couldn't prove it, Marcroy was certain Álmhath had known of these hidden Undivided heirs. He'd seen her fake her astonishment and delight when he'd told her of the find. Only a few weeks ago, he'd witnessed her momentary glimmer of surprise and alarm, when he had announced he had found them and planned to bring them to *Sí an Bhrú* to replace RónánDarragh. He had thought it would prove a much more difficult transition to make - and it might have been, had not Darragh played into his hands by behaving so foolishly over Brydie Ni'Seanan, the young woman Álmhath had thrown at him, no doubt in the hopes of getting a child from him before he perished in this evening's ceremony.

And he saw the speed with which she had tried to thrust a fertile young woman into Darragh's bed, as soon as she realized she couldn't stop the transfer of his power and that his bloodline, and that of his missing brother, might soon be lost.

Humans claimed there was no blood-link between the Undivided and insisted that the occurrence of these rare, psychically-linked twins was sheer happenstance. Marcroy had never been able to prove them wrong, but he had always had a feeling they were lying. Now he thought it even more likely because of the way in which Álmhath threw Brydie at Darragh.

"Ah well," Orlagh said, caring about Torcán's nuptials even less than Marcroy, "Do you suppose the Pristine Ones will come this time?"

"Hard to say," Marcroy told her with a shrug. "They weren't here for the last ceremony."

"They should get out more often," Orlagh said. "One needs to descend to the mundane world occasionally to be reminded why it is so much better at home."

Marcroy, for one, was hoping they didn't come. The Chinese deities were the oldest of the fey races and after the Africans, the ones most irked by the Treaty Orlagh had made binding the *sídhe* and humans so closely through the Druids. This day would be fraught enough without their stern disapproval. They might send Jamaspa to deliver their messages, but Marcroy had never been in any doubt as to whom the *djinni* was referring when he spoke of the Brethren, and who wanted RónánDarragh dealt with before they grew old enough to harm the Faerie races of this realm.

Almost as if thinking of him conjured his form, a wisp of blue smoke began to waver in front of Orlagh and Marcroy, taking shape before their eyes. A few moments later, Jamaspa appeared - from the waist up, at least - and bowed to the queen of the *Tuatha Dé Danann*.

"Ah, good lady, it is a pleasure to see you again," he announced with all the charm and elegance he reserved for those he considered his equal in stature.

"We are investing a new set of Undivided twins tonight, Jamaspa," she told him, smiling with delight. "Where else would I be?"

"Indeed, fair lady, where indeed?" Jamaspa agreed. "Shall I go down and announce you?"

Marcroy smiled as he looked down over the valley and the flurry of activity. The sun was almost sunk behind the hills now and in the east, the very first stars of the night were awakening against the velvet darkness. "I rather think they've noticed, don't you?"

Jamaspa glanced over the valley and the bobbed up and down in a nod. "I rather think they have. Will you walk on ahead with me, Marcroy, so that we may ensure the way is clear for your queen?"

Marcroy thought it an odd request. They could have all waned themselves down to the massive stone circle of *Sí an Bhrú* but Jamaspa must have something he wanted to tell him. Something that he did not want to share with Orlagh.

"Of course," he said, and then turned to his sister. "If that's all right with you, beloved?"

"Go, dear brother," Orlagh urged. "Play the diplomat for me. I will be down when the sun is fully set."

Marcroy bowed to his sister and turned to follow the *djinni*. Once they were down the slope a way, out of earshot of the queen, Jamaspa paused and glanced at Marcroy.

"Do you remember, cousin, the young woman the humans sent to *Sí an Bhrú* to collect the seed of Darragh of the Undivided before his demise?"

"Of course, I do," Marcroy said, hoping Orlagh had no notion of their discussion. He glanced up the slope at her, but she was paying no attention to them, engrossed in the horde of lesser *sídhe* that clustered around her, vying for her attention.

"Was this human girl important, do you think, in the grand scheme of things?"

"Only if she is with child and somewhere we can't do anything about it. Why?"

"Did you know she is missing?"

"The Druids pretend she never existed." He looked at Jamaspa with alarm. "You told me you'd taken care of her."

"Well..." the *djinni* said. "I did."

"And...? Marcroy asked impatiently. They were less than an hour from the power tranfer - less than an hour from RónánDarragh being removed from the equation - less than an hour from the threat they represented being eliminated forever. He didn't have time for this.

"I may have lost her... a little bit."

Marcroy felt himself go cold all over. "You *what*?"

Jamaspa's blue smoke thinned and faded with embarrassment. "It's not my fault. I thought I had her secured. I trapped her in the jewel we used to gain entrance to *Sí an Bhrú*."

"Then she is still trapped in the jewel, surely," Marcroy pointed out. "None but a *Djinn* has the power to release her. She is safely out of the way, imprisoned in the jewel. If you destroy the jewel then all will be well."

"And I would, cousin," Jamaspa muttered. "If I had it."

Marcroy stared at him in horror. "You *lost* the jewel?"

"I think it was stolen. You know what humans are like."

This can't be happening. Not now. Not tonight. "Then where is it? Where is the girl who might be carrying the get of RónánDarragh?"

"Not here to cause trouble," the *djinni* pointed out, a little defensively.

Marcroy shook his head, finding it hard to grasp how something like this could happen when they were so close to success. "We have to find her, Jamaspa. We have to find that jewel. Both of them - the girl and the jewel - need to be destroyed or everything we are doing here tonight will have been for nothing."

CHAPTER 44

Without intending to, Trása had become queen of the Faerie.

The role had fallen to her by default. In this reality where the *Tuatha Dé Danann* were a distant memory, where only the lesser *sídhe* and lesser *Youkai* remained, she was someone they could look to for guidance. Someone the lesser Faerie believed would protect them in a world where their eradication was all but assured if they didn't find a way to fight back.

The *sídhe* of this world were an odd mix of Faerie folk. Aelf and dryads, sprites and pixies, gnomes and nixes, many of them of no particular race or gender. These were the elemental creatures of the realm and had little interaction with the mundane species of their reality, which was the main reason they were still alive, Trása suspected. These were the creatures rarely seen by humans.

They had their own version of the Undivided here, although exactly how long ago they had shared their magic with humans was lost in the mists of time. Those who might remember... the *Tuatha Dé Danann,* the *Djinn,* even the greater *Youkai,* were all dead, driven through rifts where they perished from the lack of magic.

The lesser *Youkai* and *sídhe* that survived had coped as best they could. The *Leipreachán* had tried to embrace their new reality by emulating the warriors of this realm. Trása smiled every time she met another one, Rónán's description of them as *ninja faeries* still making her smile. They spoke the same language as the *Leipreachán* in her realm, but they had taken Japanese names - or mangled versions of them - and dressed like little ninjas. Their weapons were made of *airgead sídhe,* but they were the weapons of their conquerors, rather than the shillelaghs the *Leipreachán* of her realm carried. They carried *katanas* and *shuriken* and *nunchakus* - which Trása had a sneaking suspicion not a single one of them was capable of using without knocking themselves out.

Their relief at her arrival was pathetic. They were so hungry for guidance, for some sense that the greater *sídhe* of their realm were watching over the world, ensuring all was right with it. And they were universally convinced that SvenHendrick's dying act had been to find this brave and fearless half-*beansídhe,* half human saviour and send her to this realm to take care of the evil twins, Teagan and Isleen.

Trása wasn't really sure about their adoration. In her own world, she was an unwanted mongrel, belonging neither in the *sídhe* world or the human one. Here the wee folk just wanted to be near her, just wanted to bask in the glory of her presence, the way the lesser *sídhe* in her realm basked in Queen Orlagh's splendour.

There was no way of telling them the truth without breaking their hearts. There was no way of explaining that she had fallen through the rift into this realm by accident and she had no hope of opening another one on her own. There was no way to tell them she had never heard of Sven or Hendrick.

And it would be cruel to tell them that as soon as Rónán found a way out of this realm, she was gone from here and they would have to fend for themselves.

It was hard to say how long she'd been in this reality's version of *Tír Na nÓg*. Time moved differently here. When she arrived, she knew she only had a few days before *Lughnasadh*, but she wasn't sure exactly when it was. Trása wondered if she would feel anything - whether she should return to the fireworks factory and see if Rónán was still there or if he had already left with the Empresses for *Nara*.

She was still pondering that when she heard a sound behind her. Trása was standing on the edge of a wide bough, looking down over the glorious magical expanse of *Tír Na nÓg*, deep in thought. She turned in time to see a cluster of aelf blink out of existence with a giggle. They had left a basket behind, filled with apples, pears and persimmons. It was real fruit too, not the magical tastes-wonderful-but-doesn't-do-anything-to-quell-your-hunger sort of fruit that her mother was prone to serving. She smiled and called out a thank-you, guessing the laughter and rustling leaves above her head meant the pixies had retreated there, too shy to face her directly.

She reached down and picked up an apple, biting into it with a sigh, pushing aside the folds of the gossamer shift the water sprites had brought her as a gift, so she wouldn't tear the flimsy fabric. The apple was delicious. Even mundane food served in *Tír Na nÓg* tasted better than it did on the outside.

"Them pesky pixies not been bothering ye again, have they, mistress?"

She turned to discover Toyoda and two of his ninja *Leipreachán* companions standing on the branch behind her. Trása had to stop herself from laughing aloud at the sight of them.

"No, they're not causing trouble. They brought me food."

Toyoda frowned, not happy to hear that. Trása wondered whether he was jealous or just annoyed that he hadn't thought of it first. Not that he'd been here - Trása had sent him on a mission.

"Did you see him?" she asked, before Toyoda and his friends - who he'd introduced earlier as Isamu and Eita - had a chance to be distracted by a battle with the pixies over who was going to bring her the best gifts.

"He still be at the Ikushima compound, mistress," the one on the left informed her. Trása had no idea whether it was Isamu or Eita as they both had their faces wrapped in their ninja hoods, leaving only their eyes visible and some ginger whiskers poking out in odd places. "As be the Empresses."

"Really?" she said, thinking aloud as much as discussing the issue with three ridiculously dressed *Leipreachán*. "I thought they'd have taken him back to *Nara* long before now. How long have I been here?"

The three *Leipreachán* looked at each other for a moment and then shrugged. "Not sure, mistress. But it be *Higan No Chu-Nichi*, so that be telling ye something."

Trása frowned. She didn't know what Toyoda thought the date was telling her but she did know *Higan No Chu-Nichi* was what the Japanese colonists here called *Lughnasadh*. "It's tonight?"

Toyoda's eyes lit up. "Will ye be celebrating it with us, mistress?"

"Maybe," she said, not really listening. She was puzzled. Why hadn't the Empresses taken Rónán back to their capital in *Chucho?*

Or killed him outright when they realized he was Faerie?

"Are they holding Renkavana prisoner?" she asked, thinking perhaps the evil little Empresses had some nefarious plan in mind, perhaps a public execution. Perhaps they planned to make an example of Rónán and any *sídhe* foolish enough to step through a rift into this corner of their far-flung empire.

"He seemed fine to us, mistress," Eita said. Or maybe it was Isamu. She really couldn't tell. "Seems like he be in great favour with the Empresses, not their prisoner."

Why? she wondered. If the Empresses are determined to wipe out the *sídhe*, why are they feting Rónán like a long lost friend? Couldn't they tell what he was?

Or did being only mostly *sídhe* mean they thought he was from the equivalent of the *Konketsu* in another world.

"Do you suppose they'd welcome me with open arms if I went back there to fetch Rónán?" she asked. After all, she was only half-*sídhe*. Arguably, she had less Faerie blood in her than Rónán and would well qualify as *Konketsu*. Would she get the same reception? Or had Chishihero branded her irrevocably as a dreaded *Youkai* because she could shape-shift. Perhaps nothing she did would change the minds of those two little girls with too much power and a bloodlust for her kind that defied logic.

She glanced up at the sky but the position of the sun in *Tír Na nÓg* was never a reliable gauge of what was happening out in the mundane world.

If I leave here, will it even still be *Lughnasadh* by the time I get to Rónán?

And what could she do? The transfer would take place and Rónán would die. Perhaps not instantly, or even tonight, but at best he only had a few days. There was nothing she could do to save him. Perhaps her plan to bring Rónán here to *Tír Na nÓg* might work, but how would she get him here if he refused to wane out of *Shin Bungo*? For that matter, he had no idea where this place was, so he couldn't just will himself into the place.

Her heart sank. She realized that even if Rónán wanted to escape the Empresses, he had nowhere to go.

Was it fair that she hid here in *Tír Na nÓg* among her adoring new flock, while Rónán perished for want of the means to open a rift to his own realm?

Trása did not consider herself sentimental. She'd developed a hide thick enough to take the bruises life handed out to the half-human daughter of the most heinous traitor in living memory. She was surprised then, to find herself not only worried about Rónán, but almost overwhelmed with guilt at the thought that she had left him behind, even though he had sent her away and ordered her to stay away.

The *Leipreachán* must have mistaken her silence for concern - which was true enough, but she was not worried about what they assumed, or what they thought of her. "He seems fine, mistress," Toyoda assured her. "He not be in any immediate danger."

Not immediate, no, Trása silently agreed. *The danger to Rónán comes from another realm that we can't even reach.*

"I think I need to go back to *Shin Bungo*," Trása said, wondering how she could have contemplated leaving Rónán at a time like this. *What was I thinking? I can't sit here playing queen of the Faerie while Darragh's brother dies a horrible death from magical withdrawal, alone, in a strange realm, with nothing - not even a familiar face - to see him on his way.*

"But Renkavana told us to leave *Shin Bungo*, mistress," Toyoda reminded her. "To protect ye from the Empresses. He not be happy if ye endanger yeself - and the rest of us - by going back."

Trása smiled. Endangering "the rest of us" was the main concern of the *Leipreachán*, she figured. Her own safety probably came a poor second. "Renkavana's not going to be in a position to object," she predicted. "How long until sunset out there, do you think?"

"Not long, mistress," Toyoda said, looking worried. "Ye should stay here. It be *Higan No Chu-Nichi.* Stay and celebrate with us. Naught but trouble awaits ye in the mundane world."

"Naught but trouble awaits me wherever I go, Toyoda," she sighed, tossing away her half-eaten apple. "Why should this realm be any different?"

Toyoda glanced at his two companions before facing Trása. "Ye mean to go, then mistress?"

"Yes, Toyoda," I'm afraid I do."

"Then ye leave me no choice but to stop ye by force, mistress."

Trása laughed. "How are you going to stop me?"

"By ordering ye to stay... Tinkerbell."

She stared at the *Leipreachán* for a moment with a puzzled expression. "What?"

"I be ordering ye to stay... *Tinkerbell.*"

"Why are you calling me Tinkerbell?"

"We be sorry, mistress, but if ye insist on this folly, we be having no choice but to invoke ye true name," Eita - or was it the other one? - said.

"My true name? Who told you my true name was Tinkerbell?" Trása knew the origin of the name. She'd been in Rónán's reality for the better part of six months. She'd watched plenty of television, including the Disney channel.

"Renkavana betrayed ye, mistress," Toyoda told her heavily. "We didn't be wanting to tell ye, but he told the Empresses ye true name. One of the wood sprites overheard his treachery and brought us the news. And ye true name. We be so sorry, mistress, but we can't be letting you leave. We need you here."

So Rónán told the Empresses my true name is Tinkerbell. Trása appreciated the irony. And the dilemma she now faced. If she defied the *Leipreachán* and his friends, they would know Tinkerbell wasn't her true name. How soon would the information filter back to the Empresses? How soon before they learned Rónán had lied to them?

And what did it matter? It was almost sunset, the *Leipreachán* claimed. Rónán probably wasn't going to live long enough for it to be a problem.

"I'm sorry, Toyoda," she said. "But Tinkerbell isn't my true name. And Rónán needs me at the moment, a lot more than you and your friends do."

Before the *Leipreachán* could object, Trása resumed her hawk form and swooped toward the entrance to *Tír Na nÓg*, leaving her gossamer shift to float gently on the magical air and land with a whisper on the branch she had left behind.

CHAPTER 45

Anwen and Torcán were married in the sacred grove at dawn on *Lughnasadh*. It was a surprisingly simple ceremony, given the groom was the queen of the Celts' only son. Colmán presided over the ceremony, so of course, it rhymed, badly. Having seen Colmán when he wasn't trying to be Vate of all Eire, Brydie wondered, from her amethyst perch, if he deliberately mangled things to appear foolish, or if he really had no clue of how bad he was.

The vows, however, had been composed by Anwen, which served to highlight how painful Colmán's poetry was by comparison. Brydie watched Torcán and Colmán - the only members of the wedding party in her line of sight, as Colmán draped two strips of embroidered ribbon over Anwen and Torcán's joined hands, tied them together, and waited as they swore their troth.

"I belong to me and you cannot command me," Anwen announced, meaning every word, Brydie was quite certain. "But I will serve you, beloved, and bring you mead, while ever you treasure my heart. The bounty I bring you will taste sweeter, because it will be served by my hand, with my love and with my care, and my heart seasoning everything I prepare for you."

"I swear your name will be the first name to cross my lips each morn, and the last to cross my lips each night..."

Fat chance, Brydie thought, sceptical of this whole charade. Anwen might be good at composing vows, but Brydie doubted her sincerity.

"Each mouthful of food, I will save some for you. Each drink I take, I spare some for you. I will stand beside you in battle and know that your shield will protect us both. In the presence of *Danú*, and *Leucetios*, the *Bellona*, *Bel* and *Sionnan*, *Llyr*, *and Goidniu*, *Easal*, *Cebhfhionn*, *Finncaev*, *and Cliodna*. May these gods and goddesses bear witness to my pledge and hold me true to it, until death take me from you, or you from me."

Brydie was impressed, as much by Anwen's ability to name all those gods and goddesses without stumbling over a single name, as she was by the vows. Torcán repeated them, much less fluently than his bride, and then Colmán declared them wed and everyone cheered and retired to Temair for the wedding breakfast - a necessarily hurried affair given they were all due at *Sí an Bhrú* later that day for the ceremony investing the new Undivided.

The wedding breakfast was quite an affair, though. Álmhath had spared no expense, but the result was more than just a bountiful celebration of her son's nuptials. By mid-morning, almost everyone from Temair was well on their way to being drunk, which did not augur well, Brydie suspected, for the festivities this evening after the investiture of the new Undivided at *Sí an Bhrú*.

Brydie had a bird's eye view of the entire proceedings. Anwen didn't take the necklace off, even when she retired to her own chamber to change into something warmer for the journey to *Sí an Bhrú* later that morning.

Álmhath came into her chamber as Anwen was putting the finishing touches on her hair. It had been braided with rare golden samphire flowers for the ceremony. Now she was shaking her long hair free of the petals and brushing it out, before she braided it again for the journey. The daisy like flowers she had managed to retrieve intact sat on the table in front of the brass mirror. Brydie supposed Anwen was planning to press them as a keepsake of this auspicious occasion. At least, that's what she would have done with them. Who knew the workings of Anwen's mind?

"So," Álmhath said as she stepped up behind Anwen, watching her new daughter-in-law. "It is done."

"It was necessary, Álmhath," Anwen said.

"I do love my son, you know. I will be displeased if you hurt him."

Anwen turned from the polished brass mirror to face her mother-in-law. "I mean him no harm, Álmhath. But the greater good of the *Matrarchaí* is my overriding concern. You have no daughter to carry on your role as head of the *Matrarchaí* in this realm. That situation had to be addressed, and we don't have time for you to conceive a girl child of your own, or for your son and me to produce a granddaughter who can be trained in time."

"I knew it! I knew you were marrying Torcán for something other than love!" Brydie shouted triumphantly.

"I am sorry," Anwen continued, "but we all have to make sacrifices, and I would argue, my lady, that the greatest sacrifice here is mine, not yours. This business of separating the Undivided and Marcroy finding the replacement twins we were hiding has forced our hand. Sadly these new twins were never meant to inherit because they're barely gifted enough to empathise with each other."

The queen nodded, looking a little chastened. "I know. And I appreciate the reason you married Torcán, and your dedication to the *Matrarchaí* in doing so. I just wish I didn't have such a strong feeling we've failed miserably already."

Anwen must have smiled reassuringly, given her tone when she replied. Brydie could no longer see her reflection in the brass mirror, so she couldn't be sure. "We haven't failed, *an Bhantiarna*. Not yet. We have the seed of the Undivided." Anwen's hand briefly touched the jewel.

"Trapped in a *djinni's* spell," the queen reminded her.

"Which is better than nothing. I'm sure Lady Delphine will find a way to retrieve our prize."

"In the meantime, we must smile and nod while Marcroy thwarts our plans," Álmhath said, frowning.

"A temporary setback, sister," Anwen assured her. "Sooner or later, we would have removed RónánDarragh ourselves. You know that. In a few years it would have become very obvious they were not what they seemed."

She was talking about the Undivided being *sídhe*, Brydie realized. Why would *Matrarchaí* need to remove Rónán and Darragh?

"Because if they're mostly Faerie, they'd not age like ordinary men," Brydie said aloud, as the solution came to her.

Ye gods and goddesses, she thought. *This isn't the first set of Undivided twins to be removed prematurely, just the first time the Tuatha Dé Danann beat you to it.*

"How can we be sure they will be dead?"

"Nobody survives the power transfer. You know that."

Álmhath nodded. "And the *sídhe* know it too. And yet they allowed Marcroy to subvert Amergin and separate the twins. We don't know where Rónán and Darragh are, Anwen. So once the power transfer happens, we can't be sure they are dead."

"I see your point," Anwen said, jostling Brydie up and down with her nodding. She wished she knew what Álmhath was talking about. Brydie didn't get the point of this discussion at all. "You're afraid that if we don't confirm the death of RónánDarragh," Anwen continued, "we risk them appearing some day, returning from another realm, after our Undivided have achieved Partition. They could destroy everything."

Our Undivided? Brydie thought, rather confused by this discussion of which she was mostly ignorant. *Is she talking about the new heirs, BrocCairbre? RónánDarragh? Some other, as yet undiscovered, or unborn twins?*

Brydie glanced down and rubbed her belly. *Is she talking about me? About the twins I might be carrying?*

"We haven't failed, an Bhantiarna," Anwen had told the queen a few moments ago. *"Not yet. We have the seed of the Undivided."*

"Trapped in a djinni's spell."

"Which is better than nothing at all."

"The obvious solution," Anwen said, "is to keep our little friend trapped in the *djinni's* jewel, until we can confirm RónánDarragh are dead. Any twins gifted enough to achieve Partition can only be destroyed by their ancestors - and let's face it, it is almost unheard of for the retiring Undivided *not* to perish during the transfer of power from one generation to the next - then we do not allow those twins to be born until we know the danger is gone."

"That could take a very long time," Álmhath warned. "RónánDarragh are probably ninety per cent *sídhe*. If they survive the transfer, they could live forever."

Anwen shrugged, knocking Brydie off her feet. Again. "Your precious twins aren't going to survive you jumping about like that, Anwen," she called, annoyed but not harmed by the constant jostling. Anwen couldn't hear her, of course, but she felt better for yelling at her.

"RónánDarragh are long-lived, *an Bhantiarna*. Not immortal. We will ensure they are dead, one way or another. If not from the ceremony this evening, then the *Matrarchaí* will find them and kill them. Once we have confirmed their demise, we will release our vessel from her djinni spell and allow the next generation of Undivided to be born. These twins will be able to achieve Partition and rid us of the intolerable burden of sídhe interference in our use of magic. Once that is done," she added, turning back to the brass mirror to finish doing her hair, "we can start working towards what we have achieved in so many other realms - the annihilation of all Faerie races, because unlike the Christians are fond of saying, it is not the meek who shall inherit the Earth, Álmhath. It belongs to those prepared to eliminate any competition for it."

CHAPTER 46

The ceremony to transfer the power to the Undivided took place at sunset. Brydie was keen to watch, but more interested in seeing the queen of the *Tuatha Dé Danann*. Orlagh rarely left *Tír Na nÓg* and probably wouldn't do it again in Brydie's lifetime, so this was a rare chance to see a creature of legend, surrounded by scores of other celestial beings, all of whom had always been more myth than reality to a mere mortal like Brydie Ni'Seanan.

The exotic creature Brydie saw, however, was not Orlagh, queen of the Faerie.

It was Jamaspa the *djinni* responsible for her imprisonment and, if Anwen and Álmhath were to be believed, the only one who could free her.

So how she was supposed to attract his attention?

Brydie assumed Jamaspa would not recognize the stone itself, or surely Anwen would have gone to much greater pains to hide it. She certainly wouldn't be flaunting it for all to see, if she thought the *djinni* would know it instantly. He remembered a brooch - a gold filigree fancy worn to hold a cloak together. Now that the amethyst had been reset into a pretentious frippery amid scores of smaller, but similar stones, it was nothing like the item he remembered. And even if he looked at Anwen's necklace directly, could he tell there was someone trapped inside the centre stone? Would he even think to look?

The questions were far too many, the answers far too uncertain for Brydie to be hopeful this night would see her released from her jewelled prison. Anwen took her place beside Álmhath and Torcán, observers here, rather than participants.

This was a ceremony belonging to the Druids and the *Tuatha Dé Danann*.

The ceremony took place just as the sun rested on the crest of the hill in the west, illuminating the stones for the twenty minutes or so that the sun would bathe the circle and the Undivided heirs in her light, while Orlagh performed the ritual to share the magic, branding them to the bone, searing the magical symbol into the boys so deeply that even losing that limb would not interrupt the flow of power.

Usually that would be the end of it. The boys would be branded - often as babies - and they would remain in reserve until the Undivided died and they could assume their dying predecessor's powers.

Tonight was different. Tonight, the queen of the Faerie would brand the boys and then transfer the power conduit from the absent RónánDarragh to these shy, bemused seven-year-old boys, who stood naked in the centre of the circle, shivering as they were daubed in the blue woad with the triskalion symbol which would define them for the rest of their lives, once Orlagh had branded it into the palms of their hands.

Brydie felt sorry for the boys. They were pale, ginger-haired and thin, unprepared for what was to happen. As a rule, the Undivided heirs were identified much earlier and branded at an age where they would not remember life without the triskalion tattoo. Their lives from then on were full of privilege and preparation, waiting for the time they would take the reins of power.

These boys had received no such preparation. Brydie gathered, from what she'd heard between Anwen and Álmhath, that they had been identified years ago, but their presence had been kept secret. For some reason, the *Matrarchaí* had determined Rónán and Darragh were the preferred Undivided. They had not wanted to give anybody any excuse to threaten RónánDarragh's position until it suited them.

That plan had been thwarted, of course, by Amergin and Marcroy Tarth, when they separated the boys as toddlers, robbing the *Matrarchaí* of whatever it was they wanted of them.

She wondered if Amergin had understood that what the *Matrarchaí* wanted, more than anything, was the children of Rónán and Darragh. Brydie put her hand to her belly again, something she was prone to do of late. She still had no idea if she had conceived a child or whether all this plotting and scheming on the part of Anwen and Álmhath was for naught.

They would be more than a little disappointed, she realized, if her menses appeared a week after they released her from this jewelled trap. *That* would ruin all their plans.

The tall stones of cast their long shadows as the ceremony began. The boys were ready, a stag had been sacrificed to appease the gods, and the Druids had recited their part of the long, complicated ritual, and now the truly magical part of the ceremony could begin. Brydie watched Colmán and another, taller man wearing a stag mask. She guessed he was the Merlin from Albion, come to aid the Vate in this important task.

They spoke for a long time, so long that Brydie could feel Anwen starting to fidget.

And then they stepped up to the boys and turned to face each other.

"I invoke thee, first daughters of Ernmas, Ériu, Banba, and Fódla," Colmán called, "And their husbands, Mac Cuill, Mac Cécht, and Mac Gréine,"

"I invoke thee," the Merlin responded, "and beg thee *Tuatha Dé Danann* kings to bring this gift to bear."

"I invoke thee Ernmas's younger three - the *Badb*, the *Macha*, and the *Morrígan*," Colmán said raising his eyes to the setting sun.

"I invoke thee, *Anann's* sons, the brave *Glon*, *Gaim*, and *Coscar*," the Merlin added, opening his arms.

And so it went, back and forth between the Druids as the sun sank behind the hills of *Sí an Bhrú*. The boys, Broc and Cairbre, seemed confused rather than honored. Brydie felt sorry for them, standing there, so small, so insignificant, and yet so important to everyone here. She glanced across the circle to the *sídhe* who had gathered to watch, looking for Jamaspa, but she couldn't see his smoky blue form in the fading light. Marcroy Tarth was there, along with the achingly beautiful Orlagh and the contingent of lesser *sídhe* who hung about her like a cloud of insects in long summer grass.

Brydie turned her attention back to the ceremony, guessing her chance to catch Jamaspa's eye was fading fast. The *djinni* was unlikely to stay for the celebrations afterward. The feast. The free-flowing mead and the ensuing uninhibited revels that accompanied every solstice and equinox and resulted in most of the children born out of wedlock in Temair and *Sí an Bhrú* and probably every village in a ten mile radius of the celebration.

"I invoke thee, *Leucetios* god of thunder and storm," Colmán was saying, as Brydie turned her attention back to the Druids.

"I invoke thee. The Bellona, *Bel* and *Caireen*, mother Goddess. Defender of the young."

"I invoke thee *Caer Ibormeith*, goddess of sleep and dreams."

"I invoke thee *Sionnan*, goddess of the well spirits," the Merlin said, as Brydie started to wonder if this was ever going to end.

"I invoke thee *Scathach*, guard of the Underworld."

"I invoke thee *Cebhfhionn*," Colmán said, his voice starting to crack a little. "She who guards the Well of Knowledge to bring inspiration to these boys."

"I invoke thee *Finncaev*, that they may know of love and beauty."

"I invoke thee *Somhlth*, god of pure masculinity, divine energy, that ye bring these boys safely to manhood."

"I invoke thee *Uathach*, to teach these boys to be great warriors."

"We invoke thee *Cliodna*, goddess of the waves, who with every ninth wave that breaks on the shore, brings us closer to her bosom."

At last the Druids were done. As the last rays of the setting sun faded, Orlagh stepped forward to take each of the twins by the hand - Broc by the left and Cairbre by the right - to brand them magically with the symbol that would act as a conduit between the *Tuatha* and the Druids.

"I invoke thee goddess *Danú* ," she called, her voice sounding like the sweetest music imaginable, even to Brydie, trapped inside the jewel.

"And I invoke you, *Niamh*, goddess who helps heroes at death, to take the souls of RónánDarragh and lead them to the Underworld where they may find eternal peace."

And with that final word, the young boys standing before Orlagh cried out in pain as the triskalion made them its own and it was done.

The transfer was complete.

PART THREE

CHAPTER 47

Sorcha was dying. She knew it in her bones. Especially in her bones. She ached like an old woman.

In this reality, she was an old woman.

Her youth, which had been artificially preserved by her time in *Tír Na nÓg*, was a distant memory in this realm. It had only taken a couple of weeks for the magical effects of her time in the Faerie kingdom to shake themselves off like leaves falling from a tree with the approach of winter, leaving her bent, old and decrepit, barely able to care for herself, let alone perform her duties as guardian to the Undivided, a task at which she felt she had failed miserably.

Sorcha knew she would never see her home again. The implications were alarming. It wasn't that she had loved ones she would never see again. Any family Sorcha had in her own realm was long gone. Nor did she have any friend or acquaintance she would like to see again before she died. As *Lughnasadh* approached, and with Darragh still a captive and unlikely to be released soon, according to Jack, Sorcha fretted about dying because there was nobody left to perform the rituals required to see her into the otherworld, and that bothered her more than she could say.

Sorcha was left with no choice, she realized, but to take it upon herself to get things ready, confident she would know when it was time.

Her first task was to find some woad. She needed to paint her body with the right symbols, so the gods would recognize her when she stepped into their realm. She had thought it might be hard to find here, but it turned out Jack had some growing in a neglected corner of his garden. The old man was fond of his glasshouse, but he had reached an age, he claimed, where kneeling down to pull up weeds in dubious weather was no longer satisfying enough to justify the pain of kneeling. Carmel had one of her nephews lined up to come in and do the grounds, she claimed, when Jack remarked that he should hire a gardener, but there had been no sign of him yet. That meant - fortunately - the small patch of woad growing in Jack's garden remained undisturbed, and Sorcha had something to work with.

It was necessary to wait until Carmel left the house, however, before Sorcha could start her preparations. Sorcha knew the housekeeper wouldn't like the mess she was going to make, or approve of the plastic milk containers full of urine she had collected over the past few days. It was a pity it was already September, Sorcha mused, as she made her way out into the garden in a misty, chilly rain. The best time for harvesting was really July or August. She went to gather the patch of wild woad, hoping the sound she could hear in the distance was Carmel's car pulling out of the driveway, but she wasn't sure. Her hearing, along with all her other faculties, wasn't what it used to be.

With a great deal of effort, and a few embarrassing groans, Sorcha knelt down on the damp grass and grabbed a bunch of leaves from the woad nearest the edge of the garden bed. Woad dye was best made from plants in their first year. Once they blossomed and died in their second year of life, they weren't much good for anything but collecting seeds.

She cut the long dark leaves near to their base with secateurs borrowed from Jack's greenhouse, chopping away at the leaves of the younger plants until she'd filled a plastic supermarket carry bag. The plastic felt odd against her fingers, its texture unfamiliar and unnatural, but there was nothing more suitable in the kitchen.

Once she'd collected the leaves, she returned the secateurs to the glasshouse and headed back to the house, her pace frustratingly slow. She wasn't sure where Jack was. He tolerated her presence in his home - prompted, no doubt, by her galloping decrepitude - but was disinclined to engage with her, and acted as if he really wasn't sure what he was supposed to do about his unexpected and unwelcome guest from another reality.

With Carmel gone, Sorcha had the kitchen to herself. After she lined up the utensils and ingredients she would need, including her two bottles filled with urine, she washed the leaves well under the tap, marvelling still at the internal plumbing bringing clean water to so many rooms in the house. Once she'd rinsed them, she washed the leaves again, this time dipping them in a bucket full of warm water. Then she shook them out, a handful at a time, and cut off the stalks with one of Jack's awesomely sharp kitchen knives.

Sorcha tore up the leaves into smaller sections by hand when they were washed. Despite the keen edge on the blades of Jack's knives, it was much easier than chopping them. She threw the shreds into the largest pot she could find in Jack's cupboards. It was on the stove, two thirds full of water, slowly coming to the boil. Sorcha had left the pot out last night, under the eaves of the glasshouse, to collect rainwater. The sparkling water that gushed from Jack's taps had a strange smell about it that made her suspicious of its ability to react with the woad and make a decent dye. Unfortunately, Sorcha hadn't collected enough rainwater to fill the pot, so she'd had to top it up from the tap. Hopefully, she had enough pure water to make it viable.

Once the leaves had steeped in the almost boiling water for about ten minutes, she lifted the saucepan from the heat and lowered it into the sink, which she'd filled with icy water. This part was critical, Sorcha knew. The liquid must cool down quickly, or the woad would break down and the dye wouldn't work at all. Thanks to another invention of this realm that Sorcha considered a marvel - ice cubes - she was able to keep stirring the saucepan and adding ice to the sink, to cool the liquid down in as short a time as possible.

Once she was satisfied the woad tea was cooling, she put the lid on the pot and went about gathering the other items she needed for her journey into the otherworld.

In her own world, once she had passed on, Sorcha's body would be left exposed to the elements, away from the village and curious strangers, for at least nine days. Then her family would return and take whatever remains were left, dry them out and then bury them, either in the ground, or under water. In her realm, a body was supposed to decompose in a way that returned the person's essence to replenish the earth. That wouldn't happen here, of course. She had no family and she suspected the people of this over-governed realm would balk at a decomposing body laying about for any length of time.

The worst of it, Sorcha thought, as she opened the kitchen drawer to retrieve the largest carving knife - a poor substitute for the sword she would rather be buried with - *is that at my funeral, there will be nobody to perform the remembrances. There will be no drinking, no recounting of past deeds, no feasting... nothing.*

Just an anonymous old woman slipping away, without anybody in this realm aware of the great warrior she had been until recently, when duty and perhaps a cruel twist of fate had stranded her in this magic-less realm.

The thought made Sorcha pause. This world wasn't entirely without magic, she knew. The *Leipreachán*, Plunkett O'Bannon, had survived here quite well. The trouble with this realm was that any magic to speak of would be concentrated in the Enchanted Sphere. The more depleted the world, the higher the Enchanted Sphere, and more difficult to reach. On a world like this one would have to travel to the tallest mountain ranges. If one was lucky and had the talent and the resources to access them, perhaps tall buildings, like the one destroyed in New York, reached high enough to touch it. But down here on the ground, there was nothing useful.

Not that it mattered if there was. Sorcha lacked even the slightest hint of magical talent. This realm could have been dripping in magic, and she would not have felt a thing.

"What the feck is that smell?"

Sorcha slammed the drawer shut and turned to face Jack who was looking at the mess Sorcha had made of his kitchen, shaking his head.

"Smells like a cat pissed in here," he said. "A whole frigging herd of them."

"It's not cat piss," Sorcha informed him. "It's mine."

Jack stared at her. "Okay. I'll bite. Why?"

"I needed ammonia to extract the dye from the woad."

The old man walked across the kitchen, jerked open the cupboard under the sink, and reached inside. He pulled out a plastic bottle with a screw top lid and slammed it on the counter. "I suppose the bottle marked "ammonia" wasn't good enough for the job."

"I cannot read your language, old man. I'm am doing this the only way I know how."

"Why?"

"Because that is what I know."

"I don't mean why are you making woad the old-fashioned way," he said impatiently. "I want to know why you've trashed my kitchen and turned it into a public toilet to do it."

Sorcha turned to check the woad soaking in the pot, wondering if it had been there long enough yet. "I need to get ready."

"For what?"

"For *Lughnasadh*."

"What's going to happen on *Lughnasadh*?"

"Darragh will die, and with him any chance I have of finding my way home before I die of old age." She turned to face him. "Look at me, Jack. A week ago I was a young woman. Now it's all I can do to drag myself out of bed each morning and make it down the stairs. I am going to die, and I want my body to be treated according to the customs of my people."

"Don't be stupid," he said, looking at her in alarm. "You're not going to die."

"If it's possible," she told him, ignoring his denial. "I'd like you to leave my body outside for nine days, but I realize that might be difficult in this realm, so I need you to place my body in a large hole in the earth and then cover it. It would be good of you to cover it with layers of corn husks and maybe some small branches."

"Why small branches and corn husks?"

"Because over them, you'll need to put a layer of rocks. Once you've done that, you must fill the rest of the hole in and build a bonfire on top, which you must keep alight until the funeral is done. That should take no more than three days, or so."

"You're fecking serious," he responded, looking alarmed.

"Of course, I'm serious," she said. "So listen carefully. It's important to keep the fire going. It

452

will dry out my body so there is no smell and any risk of disease will be eliminated. After that, I'd like to be buried in the woods. Somewhere I'm not likely to be disturbed." She turned back to check the woad again. "I have a few things I'd like to have buried with me, too, which will make my journey into the otherworld easier."

Jack studied her for a moment, muttered something under his breath and left the room without answering her. Sorcha glanced up in time to see him leave and then turned back to her pot of woad. She had much to do before *Lughnasadh* if she were to die properly. She would have to trust that Jack, when the time came, would do as she asked and ensure her journey into the otherworld was as safe and comfortable as possible.

CHAPTER 48

Pete Doherty and his twin brother Logan had made a pact, when they were younger, to meet every Friday for a drink. They'd promised - somewhat optimistically - to never break this sacred pact sworn over a large jug of Guinness on their eighteenth birthday and promised each other that nothing would ever be allowed to interfere: not studying, not work, not girls. Nothing.

The pact had lasted less than a year. At first it was their different schedules and workload at university that got in the way. Then they both found part-time jobs - Logan working for a local paper covering community events like suburban cat shows and weddings on Saturdays, while Pete got a job pulling pints in a pub near the campus where they shared a student crib with three French girls their mother represented at her agency. They both had jobs that made it harder to get together these days. Even now, Pete always felt bad on a Friday when another slipped by and they didn't get a chance to catch up.

This week Logan made a special point of arranging a time to meet, even reminding Pete of their pact, although it was a Saturday and not a Friday, as their drunken oath stipulated. Pete assumed it was because of the news about their mother. Logan was concerned enough about her to forego a date with the lovely Tiffany, who was - in Pete's opinion - the reason they hadn't kept the Friday pact much in the past few weeks.

They met at the Foggy Dew next to the Central Bank on Dame Street. It was more Logan's taste than Pete's. The pub favoured live alternate music and was licensed to serve until two in the morning, so it was usually packed until the wee hours, especially on a weekend. Pete thought it a bit pricey and far too noisy, but he was willing to put up with it, for a chance to talk to Logan.

He arrived just after seven and found Logan tucked away in one of the odd assortment of nooks and crannies that characterised the cozy little pub. Over by the polished bar was a cluster of students from the nearby Trinity College, starting early with the birthday celebration of one of their number. Other than that, the pub was still reasonably quiet, the noisy Saturday crowd not yet arrived. The band was still setting up and most of the late night patrons were probably at home, getting ready for the evening.

There was a pint on the table waiting for him. Pete slid into the booth. "*Sláinte!*" he said, raising the glass to his brother.

"*Sláinte!*" Logan replied with a distinct lack of enthusiasm, his glass clinking against Pete's. Even without the morose expression, Pete would have known something was wrong.

He took a good swig of his beer and then stared at his brother, hoping he looked reassuring.

"Mum says she's okay, Logan," Pete told him, as he wiped the foam from his lips with the back of his hand. "She's getting the best care and she's not hurt."

"Gave us a scare, though," Logan said. "Why didn't she ring sooner?"

"Not sure. She says it's crazy over there at the moment."

"It's crazy everywhere these days," Logan said with a sigh. "How did Kelly take it when you told her?"

"She yelled at me a lot to start with, but Xavier calmed her down." Pete grinned. "He offered to take the kids to his mother's place up in Belfast, if she wanted to fly to the States to be with Mum."

Even Logan managed a smile at that. Kelly hated her mother-in-law and the feeling was mutual, as the family discovered during Kelly and Xavier's very tense and awkward wedding a few years ago. There was no way Kelly was going to let that Evil Bloodsucking Protestant Bitch - as she fondly referred to her husband's mother - a chance to corrupt her children, even for a few days.

"Did Mum sound okay?" Logan asked.

"She sounded fine. I told you that on the phone. What's really bothering you?"

"Nothing," Logan lied. "Had any luck with the Kavanaugh kid?"

"You mean *not* the Kavanaugh kid," Pete corrected. "He says his name is Darragh and he's sitting in remand awaiting a trial date, offering to tell us anything we want to know about the alternate reality he claims he comes from. Annad Semaj is having a ball talking to him. I think he wants to write a whole thesis on the kid. The guy whose Audi he stole has turned up dead in his back yard with his throat cut. There's no sign of the woman, Sorcha, who was with them. Jack O'Righin has an airtight alibi, even though I'm damn sure the old bastard knows something. Hayley Boyle is still missing, her father is still cursing himself six ways from Sunday for listening to a word Darragh said and not turning him over to us the moment he spotted him in that tree at the golf course. Nobody's seen hide nor hair of Ren Kavanagh since he disappeared in a flash of bright light and a hail of bullets a couple of weeks ago. How's your day been?"

Logan smiled. "Way to go, Detective. You've really got a handle on this one, haven't you?"

"Dublin's finest," Pete agreed. "That's me. What's up with you? And don't tell me you wanted to find out about Mum. You could have her phoned her yourself if you were really worried."

"I think I'm about to make all her dreams come true," Logan confessed, although he said it with such a glum expression, it hardly seemed something worth celebrating.

"Good for you," Pete said, puzzled by his glum demeanour. "How?"

"Tiffany's late."

Pete wasn't sure why that was relevant. "I didn't think she was joining us."

"Not that sort of late, idiot."

"Oh!" Pete said, as it occurred to him what Logan was saying. "Jesus. Are you sure?"

"I found three of those home pregnancy tests when I was taking out the trash last night. They all say yes."

Pete wasn't sure what to say. "Christ, what are you going to do?"

"That very much depends on what Tiffany wants to do."

He didn't like the sound of that. "You do know abortion is illegal in this country," Pete reminded him in a low voice, the cop in him never far from the surface. He wasn't trying to take the moral high ground, but the law was the law, even when it was inconvenient, and sometimes just plain unfair.

"No," Logan said with mock surprise. "Really? Thanks for that, officer."

Pete could feel Logan's despair, and was sorry he brought the subject up, but he knew his brother and he knew a lot of women travelled to Britain each year to have things like this taken care of. "What does Tiffany think?"

"I haven't told her I know." Logan swirled the beer around in his glass with a morose expression. "She'll probably curse me and accuse me of ruining her career."

Pete couldn't help but smile a little. "I gotta say, Logan, does she have much of a career to ruin? I saw her on TV in some ad for tampons or something the other night. She's drop-dead gorgeous, I'll grant you, but she's a shite actress."

Logan returned his smile briefly. "I wasn't dating her for acting skills."

"Still... you're a big boy. Haven't you heard of condoms?"

A flicker of remorse crossed Logan's face. "Haven't you heard of alcohol?"

Pete took another swig of his Guinness. "That'll be a grand thing to tell your firstborn when he asks you about how he came to be. Yes, son, I got pissed one night with this really hot bimbo, ignored common sense and then next thing I knew, I was a daddy."

"You know, you're really not being very helpful, Pete."

"I'm sorry," he said, and he meant it. He had no wish to add to his twin's despair. "What do you think she'll do?"

Logan shrugged. "I have no idea. I just have to hope Mum never finds out, unless Tiffany plans to keep it. Can you imagine our beloved mother's reaction if she ever discovered the mother of her precious grandchild hopped on a plane and disposed of it?"

"How will *you* feel if she hops on a plane to dispose of it?" he asked, watching Logan closely.

Logan shrugged, his conflict obvious. "I don't know. A part of me will be relieved, I think. Another part of me will probably spend the rest of my life wondering what he might have been like."

"It might be a girl," Pete said. "Hell, given the family history, Tiffany is having twins."

"Don't even go there," Logan groaned, downing the last of his pint.

"You gonna marry her if she decides to keep it... or them?" Pete asked, not sure what he'd do in the same situation.

Logan tilted his head sideways for a moment, staring at his brother. "I'm sorry, have you checked the date, recently? It's September twenty second, isn't it? *Two thousand* and one. Not *eighteen* oh-one."

Pete downed the last of his pint and grinned at Logan. "Maybe Tiffany's an old-fashioned kind of girl."

"She not, trust me," Logan assured him. "She's more the pre-nup and how-much-am-I-going-to-get-in-alimony sort. Christ, I only started dating her in the first place because Mum insisted we'd take a good photo at a red carpet event Tiff was invited to." He placed his glass on the counter. "The irony of this fateful event being the London premiere of *Rain Over Tuscany*, is not lost on me either," he added.

"Ah..." Pete sighed, a tiny part of him thinking Logan only had himself to blame for his predicament and when he got used to the idea, Pete was going to have a high old time giving his brother hell over this. "Is there anything more romantic than true love? You want another round?"

"Sure," Logan said, pushing his empty glass across the table.

Before Pete could stand, however, his beeper went off. Logan smiled, reaching for the empty glasses as Pete retrieved the beeper from his belt and checked the message.

"Damn. I have to go."

"You sure you just didn't time that thing to go off when it was your round?" Logan asked.

"It's nice you think I'm that clever, Logan. You gonna be okay?"

"I'll be fine," he said, forcing a smile. "There is a tiny bit of me that thinks I'd make a great dad, you know."

"It was the *tiny* bit of you that got you into this predicament," Pete chuckled, rising to his feet. "You need a lift somewhere?" He glanced around the pub. There were a lot more patrons crowding the bar and he could hear the band tuning up.

"I've got the Porsche," Logan said. "You'll call me if you hear from Mum again, yeah?"

"Of course," he promised. "You'll call me and tell me what's happening?"

"Don't worry," Logan promised. "You'll be the first to know."

When he called it in, the page turned out to be from Annad Semaj.

The message was to get to St Vincent's University Hospital on the double. Darragh had collapsed during an interview, the dispatcher informed him.

Pete arrived at the hospital sometime after eight o'clock. Annad met him at the entrance to the ICU looking very worried.

"What happened?" Pete asked, looking around, but he couldn't see Darragh anywhere. The dispatcher had only told him that Darragh had been admitted to St Vincent's, not the reason why. He'd been alarmed to realize the young man was here, and not sitting in a cubicle in the Emergency Department, complaining there was nothing wrong because he'd just fainted, that's all.

"I was just talking to him," Annad explained. The shrink had spent quite a bit of time talking with Darragh, fascinated by the elaborate fantasy world he'd built for himself, and hoping to document as much as possible of it, before Darragh officially went to trial. "He was telling me how it was *Lughnasadh,* and in his realm, the magic would be taken from him and given to another. One minute he was speaking, the next he dropped to the floor unconscious. To be honest, at first I thought he was faking."

"I'm guessing he wasn't, given he's in here," Pete said. "Where have they put him?"

"In the isolation ward," Annad told him. "They're worried it might be something infectious. I'm not allowed in there because of this wretched cold. They wanted to know where he'd been prior to his arrest. I thought maybe you could speak to the doctor. All I can tell them about is the alternate reality he thinks he comes from."

"I bet that was a big help."

Pete followed Annad through the ward to the isolation room, where a uniformed prison guard sat on a chair just outside, leafing though an old copy of a magazine with Kiva Kavanagh on the cover. Pete stopped at the observation window and looked in with concern. Darragh was lying on a bed, his arms by his side, palms up, wearing only a loose-fitting hospital gown. He was covered in electrodes monitoring his every breath and heartbeat. He appeared to be breathing through a ventilator. A drip was feeding him fluids in one arm, a motorised cuff on his right arm tracked his blood pressure and a clip on his right index finger was taking his pulse and his temperature. A doctor and a nurse were fussing over him, taking readings, checking his vitals. Pete watched them, growing more concerned by the minute.

"Is it possible he took something?" Pete asked, wondering if perhaps the boy had attempted suicide. He wouldn't be the first teenager to find himself unable to cope with being imprisoned.

"Unlikely," Annad said. "I was with him for nearly three hours before he collapsed. He was fine. Admittedly he was somewhat fatalistic and spoke a lot about his impending death, but he had no opportunity to take anything while he was with me, and he is not manifesting any of the symptoms of being poisoned by any chemical compound he could have gotten his hands on in the prison."

Pete looked at Annad with a frown. "It's Saturday, Annad. Don't you have a life?"

The shrink shrugged. "Doesn't look like it."

The ICU doctor must have noticed them waiting outside. She said something to the male nurse and headed for the door. When she emerged she lowered her mask, obviously expecting him. The doctor tuned out to be younger than Pete was expecting, but she was all business and had an air of competence about her that spoke much about her skill and the reason she worked in this particular unit of the hospital. "I'm Bernadette Regan, the ICU Registrar. You're the officer who arrested this boy, is that right?"

"Pete Doherty," he said. "Do you know what's wrong with him?"

"I can tell you what's wrong with him, Mr Doherty," she said. "He's in a coma. His breathing is erratic, his brain function readings are impossible, his heart is beating so fast I'm half expecting it to explode out of his chest, he has a fever that ought to have him in convulsions, his white blood count is through the roof... but they're just symptoms. What I don't know is *why* he has the symptoms."

"He dropped like a sack of potatoes," Annad said, shaking his head with a puzzled look.

Bernadette smiled briefly. "Is that your *medical* opinion, Doctor Semaj?"

He nodded, looking a little sheepish. "It's a clinical term in we use in psychology."

She smiled a little wider. "I picked the wrong speciality, I think." Then she turned to Pete, all business again. "What can you tell me about where he's travelled recently? Other than the fact that he is obviously dangerously ill, we can't find a reason for any of it. I'm inclined to rule out poison and he has no sign of drugs in his system."

"You think it's some kind of infection?"

"It may well be," she said, but she didn't look convinced.

"I've been in close proximity with the boy for days and I have the worst head cold," Annad told her. "Is it possible he's caught that?"

"I doubt it," she said, frowning. "His lungs are clear. To be honest, I can't tell what he's fighting. His blood work is bizarre."

"Bizarre how?" Pete asked, glancing through the glass at Darragh. He looked like death.

"His antibodies are all wrong. It's hard to explain. He has no immunity for things we vaccinate babies against, and antibodies for diseases nobody has seen in a first world country in decades." She sighed and shrugged helplessly, which was a very bad thing for an ICU doctor to do. "Right now we're leaning toward some exotic disease," she said. "But to narrow it down, we need to know where he's been."

Pete shrugged, wishing he knew more. "I really can't say, Doctor. He's been insisting he comes from another reality. And on the face of it, he might as well be telling the truth because we've had no luck tracking his movements in this one." He turned to study the lad, wondering what had brought down such a healthy young man so quickly.

And then he noticed something odd. He turned to Annad. "Hey, Annad. Look at Darragh and tell me what's different about him," he said.

Annad glanced at Pete oddly, but stepped up to the observation window and did as he asked. "Um... he seems paler than usual..."

"That's not what I meant."

"Am I looking for something specific?"

"Look at his hands."

Darragh was lying with his palms up, the right hand closest to the observation window. Annad studied the lad curiously for a moment, and then he turned to Pete, his eyes wide.

"Jesus Christ, Pete," he exclaimed. "The tattoo. On his right hand. It's gone."

CHAPTER 49

Trása flew back to *Shin Bungo* in hawk form, and then changed into a cat after she landed on an isolated section of the wall out of sight of the people of the Ikushima compound.

She was amazed at the difference a few days had made in the outside world. It was hard to keep track of the time in *Tír Na nÓg* but she hadn't realized so much time had passed and that *Lughnasadh* was already almost over.

The courtyard of the Ikushima compound was transformed. Gone was the pristine raked sand with its carefully laid-out pathways connecting the buildings, small and large, in an intricate, but functional design. Now there were huge rectangular *akunoya* tents covering the paths, housing the Empresses' entourage, maybe even the displaced Ikushima clan. Trying to explain what to expect now the Empresses were still at *Shin Bungo*, the lesser *Youkai* had warned Trása that the Empresses had probably taken over the family house, as was the custom among high-ranking officials. The common soldiery, the *taiko* drummers, the servants and the displaced family would be in these brightly colored temporary shelters, or just bedded down wherever they could find a dry spot inside the walls. Complete with tatami floors, the wooden-framed tents looked plentiful enough for a small army. This army was dedicated to the care and comfort, as far as Trása could tell, of two spoiled little girls.

There were six or seven of the *akunoya*, tall, decorative tents woven from brightly colored silk, dwarfing the main house with its pretty upturned eaves and deep shaded verandas.

Trása was both relieved and curious, not sure why the Empresses were still here in *Shin Bungo* when they were only a short trip through the rift to their capital, *Nara*, located faraway in *Chucho*, which was what the lesser *Youkai* - and presumably the humans of this realm - called this reality's version of Japan.

It made no sense, Trása thought, as she morphed into feline form, that they would still be here for *Higan No Chu-Nichi*. According to the lesser *Youkai*, everyone in this realm was preparing to visit their family tombs at this time of year. In this realm the autumn equinox was a time for honoring ancestors and that's where the Empresses should be - back home honoring their ancestors. Or maybe in Sweden or Gaul or somewhere, given their Nordic appearance. Celebrating the *Higan* and the end of the summer was a big event, the lesser *Youkai* claimed. It was something they would not want to miss.

Puzzled, Trása jumped down from the wall, wondering what the evil little girls were up to. It was almost sunset, she saw with concern - or at least as much concern as she was capable of as a cat. She began to walk towards the largest tent, thinking that would be where she was most likely to find Rónán, assuming the Empresses hadn't killed him already and were only still here because they hadn't finished celebrating his demise.

If he wasn't there, she would have to try the main house, but she wasn't sure what the reaction would be to a cat wandering inside. She might be able to roam about unobserved and unhindered, or someone might chase her away with a broom. Trása wasn't sure and decided if she couldn't find Rónán in the tents, she would stop and ponder the problem for a while, before doing anything rash. The smaller a creature one became, the harder and harder it got to retain the sense of one's self. A seagull was about as small as Trása was prepared to go without someone to watch over her. She had just found a way to break the curse that kept her trapped as an owl in her own reality. She didn't want to inadvertently trap herself in another animal form, just because there was nobody about to remind her of who she really was.

"*Atsusa samusa mo Higan made,*" the servants called to each other as they passed, rushing back and forth. *Heat and cold last until Higan.* She heard the phrase several times as she wove carefully between the tent pegs and the guy ropes securing the tents, and figured it was some sort of ritual greeting. Members of the Empresses' entourage hurried to and fro carrying bunches of wildflowers, ewers of incense and trays of sticky round *ohagi,* the treat made from *mochi* - a glutinous rice pounded into a paste and then rolled into balls and covered with soybean flour or *azuki* bean paste, known as *anko.* The lesser *Youkai* in *Tír Na nÓg* had been anxious to educate Trása about their realm. They had bombarded her with information like that. Some useful, some utterly absurd. The description of the *ohagi,* however, had been for a very practical reason. She might need to eat, Toyoda reminded her, while she was out in the mundane world. Real food. Like the food the humans lay out for their ancestor spirits, which the sprites and the pixies usually carried away in the dark of the night, to convince the poor souls their ancestors were actually paying attention to their pitiful mundane lives, and their ghosts had nothing better to do than hang about waiting for a snack every three months.

He had a point, although Trása was not yet hungry enough to steal food left out for the dead off their graves. It may have been her feline appetite at work, too. Cats were carnivores and had no interest in tasty balls of rice. They were much more interested in rats.

Trása reached the largest tent, a magnificent structure, striped with red, yellow, blue, white and black, adorned with gold trimmings and the Empresses' *kamon* painted onto the silk in gold paint. The pattern of the girls' family crest - their *kamon* - looked alarmingly like the triskalion branded onto the palm of both Rónán and Darragh, but she supposed it made a twisted sort of sense. Somewhere in history, the Undivided shared a common point of origin with these twins who wielded the power of the *Youkai* and yet were bent on destroying the true owners of that power. Every realm Trása had ever visited had something in common with another world. Even where the Undivided were unknown, there were still the same *sídhe* races. It was as if they populated the world and the humans came later, twisting their tradition, imposing their will on their more credulous magical neighbours, until eventually, whether out of ignorance, jealously or malice, they destroyed them. On closer inspection in the rapidly fading light, Trása realized even the guy ropes were made of a gold-painted rope and the pegs themselves seemed coated in the precious metal.

What a waste, she thought, wondering who was responsible for such frippery. Was it the girls who demanded such pretty shiny things or the adults charged with their care? Feline Trása realized she wasn't all that interested. She was more interested in the smells coming from this tent. Somewhere inside, she gathered, there was a meal going on, and they were eating fish. Raw fish. It smelled delicious.

Trása was able to slip into the *akunoya* on the heels of a servant rushing a platter heaped with the most delicious-smelling fish. She told herself that shadowing the food was probably the quickest way to find Rónán. That the food had the enticing aroma of raw fish was just a bonus for Trása's feline senses, and in no way influenced her decision to follow, she told herself.

Her instincts proved correct. The Empresses were hosting a banquet.

The Empresses, as well as each guest, were being plied with food and drink served on low individual tray-tables set up around the tent in a semi circle. The carved, ivory inlaid *honzen* tray-tables were quite small, so the number of dishes and the amount of food that could be served at one time were necessarily limited, hence the frantic if restrained efforts of the servants to ensure the royal guests remained sated. There were so many dishes, in fact, that beside each *honzen* was a second tray-table - the *ni-no-zen*. On the *honzen* - at a perfect height for a hungry cat - the servants had placed what Trása supposed were the principal dishes of rice, soup and *san-sai*, while the on the *ni-no-zen* she thought she could smell an additional soup and another couple of the *san-sai*side dishes.

Trása sat down to watch, hoping nobody was paying to attention to this uninvited black and white furry visitor. The smell of the food was driving Trása mad, her stomach rumbling louder than her purr. But none of the dinner guests noticed her, so she watched without them being aware of her.

The Empresses sat at the centre of the large canopy, naturally enough, Trása supposed, given that they were, well, Empresses. Rónán was seated directly in front of them, to make it easier to talk to him, she guessed. They were having quite a discussion, she could see, but she wasn't close enough to hear what they were saying.

On the left of the Empresses - she had no idea which girl was which - sat the woman Toyoda had identified as Wakiko, the long-suffering mother. She seemed disinterested in the discussion or anything else that was going on about her. On the right of the two little girls, trying to appear as if he was a part of the conversation between Rónán and the girls, was the Ikushima *Daimyo*, Namito. Arranged in the semicircle around them were the old lady, Masuyo, and the lovely Aoi and little Kuzusa, who spent most of the meal fixing her angry gaze on the Tanabe contingent opposite her. They must have been invited for the festival, and could not, Trása guessed, have refused the invitation without incurring the wrath of the Empresses.

Trása was puzzled by the seating arrangement, not familiar enough with the customs of this realm to know if Rónán's place was one of honor or something to be concerned about. The presence of Chishihero, the samurai Hyato - who'd tried to slit her throat - and several other Tanabe warriors was worrying, but not surprising, Trása supposed. Obviously, it was the Tanabe who had betrayed Rónán's presence in *Shin Bungo* - and this realm - to the Empresses.

It was hard to tell if Chishihero was pleased or angry with the seating arrangements. Unlike Kazusa, she was far better schooled at keeping her thoughts to herself.

Trása really wanted to know what Rónán and the Empresses were talking about. The conversation between him and the girls seemed to exclude everyone else. Rónán didn't look happy, either. Trása watched as the fading light was revealed every time the tent flap was opened by a servant hurrying in with a new tray of dishes. She wondered if Rónán realized how close they were to sunset. In their own realm, right now, Orlagh would already be halfway through invoking the aid of the gods...

You don't have time to sit here looking pretty, Trása told her feline self sternly, aware that with her long whiskers and her distinct markings, she was very regal, attractive and... *Oh stop that!* Trása moved off, hoping that once she had a purpose, she would find herself a little less susceptible to feline vanity.

Trying to act as if she belonged, she began to edge her way around the *akunoya*. For the most part, the dinner guests ignored her. One of the Tanabe even tossed her a scrap of raw fish, which tasted delicious, but she was sure it must be a dire breach of protocol. She didn't wait about to find out, working her way around until she was right beside Namito. Without being noticed, she sat down behind him. From this vantage, she could see Rónán's face, although only the back of the little girls.

"... release her from her oath," Rónán was saying, although it sounded more like he was asking a favour of the little girls. "I'm not leaving here until you do."

"If she was silly enough to swear such an oath," one of the girls responded, "why is it up to us to revoke it?"

"Because I won't leave this place unless you do," Rónán replied, in a tone that implied he'd made the statement many times before, to little or no effect. "She only swore the oath to keep me here until you arrived."

They're talking about Aoi, Trása realized, *and her insane oath to commit* jigai *if Rónán tries to leave* Shin Bungo.

Rónán was lying about why Aoi had sworn the oath, though. She'd done it because the Ikushima wanted this *Youkai* male to father a potential member of the *Konketsu* on one of their daughters to gain influence at court. They certainly hadn't been planning to hand him over to the Empresses, without gaining some advantage from the lucky accident that had placed him in their custody.

"Lady Delphine said she would send someone to aid us," one of the girls pointed out, sounding a little petulant. "Your oath to the *Matrarchaí* should mean more than some silly girl's oath to her social-climbing brother."

Trása smiled, and then remembered that these girls had shared a *Comhroinn* with the mysterious Lady Delphine. Perhaps that's why they weren't falling for Rónán's flimsy web of lies. They knew more than they appeared to know. Trása wished there was a way to warn Rónán of that. Or maybe he'd worked it out for himself. He wasn't stupid.

"And I will help you," Rónán promised. "I just need to go back to my own realm first, and get a few things I-"

"He wants us to open a rift," the twin on the left said to her sister. "If it's so important to go back and get something, why can't he open his own rift? Or bring it with him when he came here?"

Yeah, Rónán, Trása added silently. *Explain that one*. She could see what he was doing. The girls had been expecting someone from the *Matrarchaí* and he was playing along with the idea he was the one they were waiting for. He wasn't being very subtle about it though, and he was running out of time. The servants were already starting to place lighted candles on each diner's *honzen*, in preparation for the fast-approaching sunset.

"Lady Delphine promised us a guardian. How can you be our guardian if the first thing you do when you get here, is to leave again?"

Rónán opened his mouth to answer, but the words never came. Without warning, his eyes rolled back into his head and he stiffened, and then fell backwards, sending the *honzen*, the *ni-no-zen*, the rice, soup and *san-sai* flying.

The *akunoya* erupted in choas. The Empresses started screaming. Everyone jumped to their feet. There was food strewn everywhere, staining the tatami matting. Masuyo was yelling at Chishihero, as if she had done something to cause this. Someone was yelling something about poison. Aoi and Kazusa were trying to back away from what might well turn into a bloodbath. Hyato and Namito even drew their weapons, looking about for the invisible assailant that had taken down one of the dinner guests.

It was Wakiko, though, who reacted calmly to Rónán's apparent seizure. With the stoic calm that allowed her to care and nurture two monstrously powerful, spoiled brats, she pushed everyone out of the way, rolled Rónán onto his back and checked his pulse with her fingers, just under his ear.

Trása found herself unable to move. Through the forest of legs surrounding him, she could see Rónán was having trouble breathing. He was rigid and in obvious pain. She could only see the whites of his eyes.

It's happened, she thought, fighting the need to return to her true form so she could run to him. *Orlagh has transferred the power to the new Undivided.*

Somewhere out there, in a realm she couldn't reach, Darragh would be going through the same withdrawal, the same agony.

Trása wished cats could cry, because all she wanted to do was weep for Darragh. And for Rónán.

She forced herself to move, wending her way through the panicked legs of the dinner guests, until she reached Rónán's side. Wakiko shooed her away, but she refused to be deterred. Trása rubbed her face against Rónán's shoulder, as if she could will him to fight the effects of the devastating loss of magic that was going to kill him sure as darkness followed the sunset.

Wakiko pushed her away again, but she was determined. Ignoring the shouting and the accusations going on above her, as the Ikushima and the Tanabe tried to blame each other, she rubbed against his arm, pushing her face into his hand - as if that would revive him - as if he would realize that she wanted to be petted when he felt her soft fur against his fingers - as if that would be enough to counter the death sentence Orlagh had unwittingly carried out on this young man who had not, until a few weeks ago, even known what magic was.

It was a waste of time, of course. Rónán didn't respond. He was hardly breathing, although she could feel his racing pulse.

Trása pushed against his hand. *Don't die, Rónán,* she pleaded silently. *Don't die. Please* Danú, *don't let him die.*

It was a wasted prayer, she realized as his open palm fell lifelessly on the straw matting beside her. *Danú* had abandoned this young man.

The triskalion tattoo that marked him as *Danú* 's chosen was gone.

CHAPTER 50

It shouldn't be so easy to take a life.

The killer pondered that thought as he approached the cradle rocking gently in the centre of the warm, candle-lit chamber. Their mother would have set the cradle in motion, he supposed, to soothe the twins before she left the room, trusting their visitor so profoundly it would never occur to her the children might be in danger.

He reached the cradle and stopped to study it for a moment. The oak crib was carved with elaborate Celtic knot-work, inlaid with softly glowing mother-of-pearl. It looked antique, expensive. Probably a gift from their grandmother. Perhaps it had been in her family for generations.

Generations that would end now. Tonight. By his hand.

He glanced down at the blade he carried. The polished silver caught the candlelight in odd places, illuminating the engraving on the blade. He hefted the razor-sharp weapon in his hand. Faerie silver was useless in battle, he'd been told, but for this task, nothing else would suffice.

Warmed by the fire crackling in the fire pit in the centre of the large round chamber, the twins slept peacefully, blissfully ignorant of their approaching death. Even if they had been awake, it was unlikely they would recognize the danger that hovered over them. The man wielding the blade above their cradle - the man who had come to take their lives - was a dependable presence they trusted to keep them safe.

"You can't seriously mean to do this."

He glanced over his shoulder. His brother had appeared in the shadows by the door like a corporeal manifestation of his own conscience.

"It has to be done. You know what will happen, otherwise."

His brother shook his head and took a step further into the room. The assassin found himself staring at a mirror image of himself, except the face of his reflection was filled with doubt and anguish, while his own was calm and resigned to what must be done.

"They are innocent."

"They are death."

"If preventing our death requires the death of innocent children, then perhaps we deserve to die."

He didn't answer, turning back to stare down at the twin girls he had come to murder. It wasn't who they were, but what, that made their deaths so necessary.

Why am I the only one who sees that clearly?

His brother took another step closer. "I won't let you do it."

"How will you stop me?" he asked as he raised the blade, bracing himself for the fatal blow. One of girls was stirring. She opened her eyes to smile up at him, her face

framed by soft dark curls. Her sister remained asleep, still peacefully sucking her thumb.

"I'll kill you if I have to, to stop this."

The assassin smiled down at the twins, dismissing the empty threat. "Even if you could get across this room before the deed is done, turns out, you can't kill me without killing yourself, which would achieve precisely what I am here to prevent."

He moved the blade a little, repositioning his grip. The candlelight danced across its engraved surface, mesmerising the baby. He was happy to entertain her with the pretty lights for a few moments. His mission was to kill her and her sister, after all, not to make her suffer.

There was a drawn-out silence, as he played the light across the blade. Behind him, the presence that was both his conscience and his other half remained motionless. There was no point in his brother trying to attack him. They were two sides of the same coin. Since coming to this strange and terrible place, neither could so much as form the intent to attack without the other knowing about it.

The girls would be dead before his brother could reach the cradle to stop him.

"There must be another way to stop this." There was note of defeat in the statement, a glimmer of acceptance. And he wasn't talking about killing the girls. He was talking about mass murder. Genocide on a scale neither of them could have comprehended before stepping through the rift.

"I wouldn't be here if there was," the assassin replied, still staring down at the baby he had come to kill. "You know that," he added, glancing over his shoulder. "You've seen what I've seen."

His brother held out his hand, as if he expected the blade to be handed over, and for this night to be somehow forgotten. Put behind them like a foolish disagreement they'd been wise enough to settle like men. "They're just babies..."

"They are our death and the death of much more besides."

"But they're innocents..."

The assassin shook his head. "Only because they lack the capacity yet to act on what they were bred to manifest. It's nature over nurture, brother. Once they become adults..."

"Dammit... they're your own flesh and blood!"

He gripped the blade tighter and turned back to the cradle, steeling his resolve with a conscious act of will. It didn't matter who they were. It's what they were. That was the important thing.

It was the reason they had to die.

"They are abominations, bred to cause chaos and strife."

"What the Faerie showed us in other realities may not happen in this one."

"Of course it will," he said, growing impatient with an argument he considered long resolved. He reached into the cradle with his left hand to pull back the blankets covering the children. The twin who was awake grabbed his finger. Her blue eyes smiling, she squeezed it gently. Behind him, his other half watched, too appalled to allow this, too afraid to stop it.

"Help me, or leave," he said, feeling his brother's accusing eyes boring into his back. "Just don't stand there feigning disgust. It was your carelessness that brought us here."

His brother wasn't ready to give up just yet. "Perhaps what the djinni showed us won't happen in this reality..."

"I'm not prepared to take that risk."

"But you're prepared to have the blood of two innocent children on your hands?"

"Better the blood of two children, than the blood of the thousands who don't deserve to die."

He was still a little amazed he felt so calm. It was as if all the anguish, all the guilt, all the fear and remorse, all the normal human emotions a man should be battling at a time like this were a burden carried by someone else, leaving him free to act, unhindered by doubt.

If that wasn't a sign of the rightness of this deed, he couldn't think of anything else that might be.

He extracted his finger from the soft, determined grip of the baby girl, her skin so supple and warm, her gaze so trusting and serene, it was heart-breaking.

But not heart-breaking enough to stay his hand. He raised the blade, transfixed by the guileless blue eyes staring up at him. And then he brought it down sharply, slicing through the swaddling and her fragile ribs into her tiny heart without remorse or regret.

He was quick and, he hoped, merciful, but the link between the sisters was quicker.

Before he could extract the blade from one tiny heart and plunge it into another, her twin sister jerked with pain and began to scream...

Pete sat bolt upright in bed, bathed in a cold sweat, jerked awake by the horror of his nightmare. He was panting, trying to calm his racing heart. The clarity of his dream was terrifying, but not quite so terrifying as the underlying reason for it.

He glanced at the clock on the bedside table. It was just past three in the morning. Swinging his legs around so he was sitting on the edge of the bed, Pete put his head in his hands, trying to dispel the nightmare which was burned into his brain like a true memory, not the fading wisps of a soon-to-be-forgotten dream.

The nightmare shook Pete to his core, and not just because of the graphic nature of it, or even that he had it in him to imagine such a thing - he'd seen plenty of things in his job that would give a man nightmares. But Pete had studied dreams. He knew more than the average person about the pathology of what made them happen and the current thinking on what fuelled them and what they revealed about the dreamer. But if dreams were supposed to metaphorically act out one's unresolved expectations, what the hell did a nightmare where he murdered Logan's unborn babies mean?

Pete had never in his life, been jealous of his brother. He would admit to some irritation at the way Logan always seemed to land to the better job, the prettier girl, and now even be the first of them to father a child. To have such a nightmare, such a clear and unequivocal expression of such underlying - and until this moment unsuspected - rage toward his brother, so intense that he could imagine himself killing his brother's children made Pete question everything he knew about himself and his relationship with his twin.

Am I really that jealous of Logan? he asked himself, trying to find some trace of the emotion within himself, even a whisper of it - anything to explain the awful nightmare that kept replaying itself in his mind like a looped video tape. The nonsense about fairies and genies he dismissed as simply his mind populating his dream landscape with information it had on hand. He'd been reading the transcripts of Annad's interviews with Darragh, whose tortured mind was filled with mythical beasts that roamed his imaginary alternate reality at will, so it was easy enough to guess the source of that part of the dream. But the rest of it... where the hell did slitting babies' throats come from? In what dark part of his psyche was that lurking in, waiting to ambush him at the first sign of trouble? Was it jealousy of Logan? He'd never dreamed anything like this about his other nieces and nephews. Was it simply jealousy of his three-minute-older brother, or some deep-seated guilt about signing that pro-choice petition someone was handing around the pub a few months ago, manifesting itself into horror movie in his head, because they'd been talking about Tiffany getting on a plane to have the problem "dealt with"?

He'd certainly dealt with the problem in his nightmare. *What sort of sick, twisted monster does that make me?*

The phone rang before he could answer the question. He picked it up, knowing who it was without even glancing at the number. "Logan."

"The phone barely even rang," Logan remarked, not bothering with a hello. "It's after three in the morning. What? Were you sitting on it?"

"I'm not the one calling at three in the morning," Pete pointed out, sure his brother could sense the lingering guilt from his nightmare even across the phone. "What's up?"

"Nothing... I just had a feeling, that's all."

Another time, Pete may have laughed off Logan's fey feelings, but not tonight. "What sort of feeling?" *Like I might murder your kids some day?*

There was a long pause on the phone before Logan answered. "You remember the time you got stabbed chasing down that drug dealer in Killbarrick?"

Pete remembered it well. It wasn't much more than a flesh wound, really, but Logan had been on the phone to him within minutes of it happening. "Yeah, I remember."

"It was that sort of feeling."

"You're imagining things," Pete told him. "I'm at home. Safe and sound, tucked up in my bed."

"Answering the phone at three in the morning."

"Only because I have this idiot brother who insists on calling me at three in the morning."

There was another pause. Logan had something else he needed to get off his chest, Pete sensed. He waited, knowing there was no point in pushing his brother to speak faster than he wanted.

"Hey, Pete..."

Here it comes. "Yeah?"

"Do you think I'd make a good dad?"

Christ. He wants to talk about his kid. "Sure. Why wouldn't you be a good dad?"

"I dunno... I mean... you've studied that shit, haven't you? Cops deal with that sort of crap all the time. You don't think I'd ever hurt them, do you?"

Pete suddenly couldn't breathe. He couldn't speak. There was a long painful silence between the brothers, until Logan broke the silence with a sarcastic, "way to go there, little brother, with the quick but confident reassurance. Nice to know you think so highly of me."

Oh, for chissakes. "I... no... I mean... I didn't answer you, because I can't believe you'd even ask me something so insane. Christ, Logan, what sort of question is that? Why would even think that way?"

Logan was silent for a long moment, and then he forced a laugh. "No reason. Just a silly notion. You sure you're not lying in a gutter bleeding to death?"

"Positive. Go back to sleep, Logan. And stop worrying about stupid things."

"'Night Pete."

"'Night Logan."

The phone went dead. With a heavy sigh, he placed it on the side table and lay down again, but sleep eluded him.

Pete lay awake until dawn, certain that Logan had experienced the same nightmare he had, and that for some inexplicable reason, both of them were dreaming about killing Logan's unborn children.

CHAPTER 51

All hell broke loose with Rónán's collapse, a situation not helped at all by Trása morphing back into human form beside him, as Chishihero pushed her way forward to take charge.

"It's the *Youkai*!" the *Konketsu* magician screamed, as Trása fell to her knees beside Rónán.

Trása didn't know what to do. Rónán was so pale it was if all the blood had been drained from his body. His eyes were rolled up into his head and he was barely breathing.

Don't die, don't die, don't die, she repeated over and over to herself as she tried to cradle his head in her arms. *If Rónán dies,* she told herself, *then Darragh will die too.* She didn't want either of them dead.

"Kill the *Youkai*!" Chishihero was screaming behind her. "Kill her! Now!"

Trása ignored her. She let go of his head and grabbed him by the shoulders, shaking Rónán as if he was simply in a heavy sleep and that's all it would take to rouse him. That it was sunset here and in another realm the magic had been torn from him and his brother to be passed on to the new Undivided, mattered little to her. It couldn't happen like this. It couldn't end like this.

She would not allow it to end like this, stuck here in a realm where she was the only one of her kind left except for Rónán, although she still hadn't gotten her head around the idea that Rónán and Darragh were more *sídhe* than she was.

Rónán mustn't die, she caught herself thinking, a little surprised by the thought, because it was Darragh she loved. Darragh she yearned for. Darragh she wanted to be with.

"Wait!" someone called behind her. "You don't have to kill her. We know her true name."

Trása ignored them. She rolled Rónán onto his side so he wouldn't choke on his tongue - something she learned watching *Rescue 911* repeats in his reality - and tried to think what else she could do to keep him alive.

What's happening to Darragh? she wondered. *Is the same thing happening to him in Rónán's realm? Is someone with him? How will they know what's wrong with him?*

Trása had seen the medical wizardry of Rónán's realm first-hand. She'd considered it clumsy and inelegant and no substitute for magical healing at all. But she knew they had machines there, which could artificially sustain life. *When Darragh collapsed, has someone thought to intervene? Is he somewhere he can get help? Will they sustain his life with their incomprehensible machines and will that, because of the link between the twins, sustain Rónán in this realm, as well?*

The questions flashed through Trása's mind so quickly, she was unaware of the discussion going on above her, as Chishihero tried to have her killed and the Empresses tried to prevent it.

"We can control her, I tell you," one of the little girls said impatiently, and then Trása felt a hand on her shoulder. "Tinkerbell, take your hands of Renkavana this instant!"

Tinkerbell? Oh, for pity's sake, she's talking to me! Trása had only a split second to decide how to respond to the command. If she defied it, they would know Rónán had lied to them. If she obeyed it, on the other hand, the Empresses would think they had control of her and she might be allowed to stay with him. At the very least, Chishihero would not be allowed to have her summarily executed.

She snatched her hand back from Rónán and sat back on her heels, acutely aware that she was naked. Nudity didn't bother her normally, but here, amid so many unfriendly and accusing stares, she felt her vulnerability keenly.

"Yes mistress," she replied meekly, keeping her eyes downcast, and her tone resentful. She had seen Marcroy deal with enough *sídhe* whose names he commanded to know that invoking one's true name produced obedience, but a great deal of resentment, too. If she was to convince these humans they controlled her, she would have to behave like any other trapped and annoyed Faerie, forced to do someone else's bidding against her will.

"See!" the Empress who had commanded her announced. "I told you so."

"You cannot trust it, *Jotei*," Chishihero insisted. "Even if you know its real name."

"It seems to be working just fine," the other Empress said.

"Roll over, Tinkerbell," the first little girl said. "And shake your hands and feet in the air."

Sadistic little bitch, Trása said silently, as she did what the little girl commanded. She rolled on to her back and wiggled her arms and legs about - to the great amusement of everyone gathered in the *akunoya*, grateful she did not have to prove her obedience to anybody else. Teagan and Isleen were children, and what entertained them was far less onerous than any test someone like Chishihero could devise.

Isleen or Teagan - who could tell? - laughed delightedly and clapped her hands. "Oh, this is going to be so much fun."

"But what about Renkavana?" the other girl asked, looking down at Rónán's rigid body with concern. "What's wrong with him?"

Although they hadn't invoked her name, Trása used the question as an excuse to stop her ridiculous waving about. She quickly rolled back onto her knees and bowed low to the Empresses, glancing at Rónán with concern as she did. *Danú* , she asked the goddess silently, *is he even breathing?* "Something has happened in the realm from which Renkavana originates, *Jotei*," she told them.

"Is he going to die from it?"

Trása glanced at Rónán again and was inclined to tell the truth, but that might mean the end of both of them. She had to stall for time. Perhaps, against all the odds, Rónán and Darragh might live.

If not, she didn't want to hasten his demise. "I don't think so, *Jotei*," she said meekly.

"Can *you* heal him, Chishihero?" the twin on the left asked. Trása had decided that was Isleen. She seemed the more sensible of the two.

"I do not know what is wrong with him," the *Konketsu* woman replied. Trása couldn't see her face. Still kneeling, all she saw was a forest of stockinged feet, with an odd gap between the toes to fit the straps of the *geta* lined up outside the *akunoya*. "I cannot fold a healing spell unless I know what it is we are dealing with."

"We could try fixing him ourselves," Teagan suggested.

Trása wasn't sure that was a good idea, but she didn't know how to explain that. Telling these little monsters who had rid themselves of their own Undivided - their own father to boot - that Rónán was one half of the Undivided from another realm, might cause them to kill him, rather than save him. She wasn't sure magic was the answer here, either. Rónán had just had the magic ripped from him. The tattoo on his hand was gone. Trying to heal a magical wound so deep with more magic was, Trása suspected, akin to treating a serious burn with more fire. That Rónán was even still alive was a miracle. *What is happening to Darragh in the magic-less realm? Is Rónán still breathing because Darragh is too?*

Or maybe, it was just wishful thinking. Maybe Darragh was already dead and any minute now, Rónán will be, too.

"I don't know if it would help, *Jotei*," Trása said, trying to sound obsequious and angry at the same time. "What ails Renkavana comes from another realm. The magic you wield here may have no effect."

"The *Youkai* could be right," Chishihero conceded. "But I am happy to attempt a general healing fold, to see if that will help."

"It can't do any harm, I suppose," Isleen agreed. "I wish I could remember more of what Lady Delphine taught us about healing magic."

"It must be frustrating, *Jotei*," Chishihero said in a voice, that to Trása's ear, seemed laden with barely disguised contempt, "having all that amazing knowledge and not being able to use it."

"It is frustrating, Chishihero. So you'd better find a way to fix Lady Delphine's envoy," Teagan warned. "We can't do everything expected of us, if the person sent to unlock our power is dead, can we?"

Trása tried not to give the impression that she was listening intently, but the little girl's worlds intrigued her. Toyoda had warned Trása that Delphine had shared the *Comhroinn*, with these children, but he said nothing about blocking their power afterwards. *Did the mysterious Delphine understand how dangerous such power would be in the hands of spoiled children, or did she have her own nefarious reasons for her actions?*

"Should we contact her, Issy?" Teagan asked. "Maybe she knows the way to fix him?"

"I don't know," her sister replied. "What do you think Wakiko?"

Interesting that they don't call her 'mother', Trása thought, as she waited for the normally silent Wakiko to respond. *And that they still ask her for advice.*

"If this young man is important to the *Matrarchaí* and he is in danger, then I would be contacting Lady Delphine, *Jotei*. She should know there is a problem. And that it is not of our making."

"It's not of our making, is it?" Isleen asked worriedly. "I mean... you heard the *Youkai*. He has been felled by something that happened in another realm. She wouldn't blame us for it, would she?"

There was an awkward silence for a moment. Trása wondered what the rest of the guests were thinking about this odd conversation. It was sensitive information to be blabbing in front of relative strangers. Would the Empresses do something to the Ikushima to make them forget afterwards?

Or was their plan simply to eradicate them before they left *Shin Bungo*?

That would please Chishihero. Particularly if any plan to destroy the Ikushima involved the Empresses levelling the fireworks factory located squarely in the middle of her valuable forest.

She risked another glance at Rónán. He hadn't moved. He was still rigid, only the whites of his eyes showing, although he was visibly breathing now with an unnaturally even rhythm that made Trása wonder if back in the other realm Darragh was breathing with mechanical assistance.

"I think we'd better let her know," Teagan decided. "In the meantime, you can try whatever folding spells you think might help. As for you..." she added looking down at Trása.

"I would be happy to stay here and watch over Renkavana, *Jotei*," she offered. "You know my true name, so I cannot wane myself away from here without your permission. I could alert you to any change in his condition." Trása was lying about the waning, but then, she was lying about pretty much everything.

"We could have a futon brought in," Wakiko suggested softly. "It would make him more comfortable while you await instructions from Lady Delphine."

The twins shared a look that hinted at an unspoken communication between them, making Trása wonder if they were telepathic - at least with each other - and they nodded and ordered Wakiko to make it happen.

Trása kept her head lowered, and tried not to smile as she realized that Lady Delphine - whoever and wherever she was - might well pitch a fit when she got a message telling her the envoy she didn't send was injured.

And that meant she might have to come to this realm to fix the problem.

To do that, she had to open a rift.

If Rónán could just stay alive, if he would just beat the odds and achieve the impossible by not letting the power transfer kill him, they may have, quite inadvertently, found their way home.

CHAPTER 52

Ren opened his eyes, blinking in the bright, colored light. It took him a moment or two to figure out where he was, and then he recognized the striped silk *akunoya* belonging to the Empresses, and realized he must be inside one of them, and that it was daylight outside.

More importantly, it appeared he wasn't dead.

He had survived *Lughnasadh*.

Now what?

Stretching luxuriously, Ren was amazed to discover he felt quite well. He was lying on a futon covered by a warm comforter, and there was a large black and white cat curled up at his feet. The cat looked up in annoyance as he moved his feet and disturbed her. She glared at him for a moment and then she stood up...

... and morphed into Trása - stark naked and tearfully joyful to see him alive.

She threw herself at him, suffocating him with her hugs, her kisses and her tears, all the while repeating, "You're alive! You're alive! I can't believe you're still alive!"

Ren pushed her off him, smiling but bemused. "I won't be for much longer if you smother me."

She sat back on her heels, sitting astride him, grinning from ear to ear. "You're alive. You know what that means, don't you?"

"That... I'm alive?" he ventured, forcing himself to focus on her face. There really ought be some law against morphing from animal to human form without some sort of warning. Or clothing.

"It means Darragh is still alive, too."

"Are you sure?" Ren asked, not certain Trása was quite as keen on his survival as he'd first imagined, just that it portended well for his twin.

"If he died, you'd be dead," she told him confidently.

He was relieved beyond words. Ren was still growing accustomed to having a twin, and had still not quite come to grips with the understanding of how closely they were linked - so close in fact, that if one died, the other would die soon after. That he felt so healthy augured well for Darragh's fate, at least.

"How do you feel, now you've lost your magic?"

Ren hadn't really had time to take stock. "I feel fine."

"Do you feel any different?"

"No," he told her.

"Maybe the *Leipreachán* are right about you being *sídhe*. That would explain it."

Ren wasn't quite ready to accept that, so he decided to change the subject. "Where is everyone?"

"The Empresses have gone with Chishihero to inspect the plantation, so they won't be back for a while. Everyone from the Ikushima compound, from the *Daimyo* down, is making themselves scarce in case you die and they get blamed for it. They're in a lot of trouble, I think, for not reporting your arrival and Chishihero is doing her best to make trouble for them. Are you sure you're okay?"

"I'm fine. Would you get off me please? And put some clothes on?"

She smiled at his embarrassment, but did as he asked. "Oh, for *Danu's* sake, Rónán, you are such a prude."

"So how is it I'm still alive?" he asked, throwing covers back. He hastily replaced them when he realized he was naked. "Or did we get the date wrong?"

Trása smiled at his discomfit. She seemed to be in an extraordinarily good mood. "No, we got the date right. And it was touch and go there for a while. About dawn you seemed to fall into a deep sleep. Chishihero tried to take the credit for saving you, but I don't think she did, because her folding spells weren't working until the sun rose." Trása pointed to the scores of discarded origami shapes scattered on the floor around his bed. "Not that she didn't give it a good try once she realized the Empresses believed you were their much-anticipated envoy and not some *Tuatha Dé Danann* spy come to challenge her."

"Last few times I saw Chishihero, she tried to kill me," he pointed out with a frown, wondering what had caused her change of heart.

"Last few times she saw you, you weren't being feted as the envoy of the *Matrarchaí* sent to guard and guide the Empresses into adulthood," Trása told him, pulling on the *yukata* he'd been wearing last night, which someone - Chishihero perhaps - had removed while he was unconscious.

"What the hell have the *Matrarchaí* got to do with this reality?" he asked. Darragh's memories had knowledge of them, but it wasn't detailed and his brother certainly didn't consider them a threat. Or even associate them with rift running.

Trása sat herself down on the edge of the futon, and crossed her legs. Ren made no attempt to get out of bed, now she was wearing the only clothes available. He stayed safely under the covers.

"I don't know why they're here," she said. "In our realm they're an informal sort of sisterhood... just a loose collection of midwives, I thought. They're always around when there are babies being delivered. Marcroy thought they worked for the Druids, either indirectly or were allied with them, because it was the *Matrarchaí* who always seemed to be about when they found another set of the psychic twins needed to become the Undivided." She smiled. "He was pretty suspicious when he found Broc and Cairbre in that village and the queen acted as if she knew nothing about them. Marcroy didn't believe her. The queen of the Celts is the patron of the *Matrarchaí*. There's no chance those boys lived for seven years without her knowing something about it." She stared at him for a moment, as if she was expecting him to get out of bed, which was never going to happen while he was naked and she was standing there looking at him like that. "Are you ready to leave, your highness, or have you something else planned?

Some other event on your busy social calendar that means you have to stay here?"

"Can you open a rift to home yet?" he asked, thinking it didn't matter where he was in this reality. If there was no rift to cross nobody was going anywhere.

She shrugged. "I'm working on it."

"Yeah... well so am I," he said, thinking back to last night, just before he collapsed. From the moment he'd first met them and they'd mistaken him for their expected envoy from the *Matrarchaí*, the little Empresses often spoke of Lady Delphine and her many trips through the rift to this realm to instruct them on how they should rule their empire, now they had achieved Partition, whatever that was. Perhaps, Ren had been thinking, before he was rudely interrupted by his brush with death, if they couldn't find someone to open a rift for them here - or figure out how to do it for themselves - the trick was to wait until someone opened a rift from the other side. "And I've figured it out. We just need to do the *Comhroinn* with someone who knows how-"

"Not that easy, I'm afraid," she said, shaking her head. "It has to be voluntary and you have to be given the information. Even so, according to the *Leipreachán*, there is no equivalent to the *Comhroinn* in this realm. They learn things here, the hard way."

"That can't be right," Ren said, recalling several awkward conversations he'd had with Isleen and Teagan since they arrived in *Shin Bungo*. "The Empresses told me Lady Delphine had performed the *Comhroinn* on them, and they were expecting someone to come through the rift to help them sort out the information. That's who they think I am. She locked the information up so they can only access bits of it, apparently."

"Makes sense, I suppose," Trása said. "I'm mean, they're only children. Their brains would probably explode if you dumped all the knowledge of a master sorceress like Delphine into them."

"How do you know she's a master sorceress?"

"Well, she's certainly not your friendly neighbourhood Avon lady, is she?"

Ren smiled. "Do you even know what an Avon Lady is?"

Trása avoided answering the question. "It really doesn't matter. I have a feeling if we stay near the Empresses, sooner or later, the mysterious Lady Delphine is going to appear, and we'll have a chance to get out of here."

"That's a stupid plan."

"I don't see you coming up with a better one."

"We'd have no idea of the world we'd be stepping into," he told her, sounding like an exasperated mother explaining something to a small child. Ren might be inexperienced when it came to rift running, but he had Darragh's memories. Arguably, he knew as much about it as Trása did. "We jumped into this world without a clue about how to get out of it, and look how well that's turned out."

"But..."

"And you've no guarantee this Lady Delphine comes from any reality connected to ours. What if her world is like the one I come from, where the magic is all but depleted? Then we'd be stuck there."

"As opposed to *what*?" she asked pointedly, her good mood fading. "I've been sitting here all night, thinking about this."

"Then you know the only safe way out of here, Trása, is to figure a way to open our own rift, so we can control where it goes. Otherwise, we might as well stay put and let those little psychos murder us the way they have all the other Faerie in this realm. Which brings up an interesting point," he said, studying her closely. "What are you doing here, anyway? How come the Empresses didn't kill you on sight?"

"They know my real name," she said with a faint smile. "I have no choice but to obey them."

Ren couldn't hide his shock. "Bullshit! Your true name really is *Tinkerbell*?"

She rolled her eyes at him. "Of course it isn't, idiot. But they don't know that."

"Then how..."

"When you collapsed, I lost concentration and accidently morphed back into my true from."

"You were at the banquet?"

"I was a cat," she told him, a little impatiently.

"I didn't see you."

"That's because you weren't paying attention."

He shook his head in wonder. "I'm surprised the Empresses didn't disintegrate you on sight, if you suddenly appeared in front of them."

"One of them wanted to," she said. "And Chishihero was pretty keen on the idea, but then - thanks to your ridiculous claim to owning my true name - the other one reminded her sister that because they knew it, they could control me. I decided to play along."

"How long is that going to last?"

"Until they ask me to do something I'm not prepared to do," she said with a shrug.

That would work, he supposed, for a time. But he was still trying to get his head around that fact that he was alive. *Lughnasadh* had been looming as the date of his death for weeks now. Strangely, it was something of a let-down to find himself still alive.

"Do you suppose Darragh found his way back to our realm and stopped the transfer?"

Trása shook her head. "He may have found his way back home, Rónán, but he didn't stop anything. The magic is gone, I'm afraid."

"How can you tell?" he asked. "I don't feel any different. I can still sense the magic."

"You only think you can sense it," she said, with a sad little smile. "Look at your hands."

Ren did as she asked. When he saw the pale, clean skin where his triskalion tattoo had always been on the palm of his left hand, for a moment it didn't register what it might mean. His eyes suddenly welled with tears. He could not describe what he felt at the loss of the tattoo that had taunted and comforted him, all his life, not sure if he felt pain, or gratitude or longing or fear.

"Jesus Christ. It's gone."

"Why do you invoke the name of a Christian deity?" she asked. "Are you a follower of his?"

"It's just a saying in our world," Ren said absently, still staring at his hand.

"You should be careful invoking gods in realms with this much magic," she warned. "Sometimes they answer back."

"The tattoo is gone."

"Yes, I noticed that."

"But I don't feel any different. I can still feel the magic."

"Maybe you can feel it a little because you're part *sídhe*," Trása suggested. "But the Undivided magic is gone, Rónán."

He shook his head. "No... really, Trása. I can feel it." He looked up, suddenly filled with hope. "This realm is dripping in magic. We should be able to contact Darragh on the puddle phone, shouldn't we? Maybe even Hayley, to see if she's okay?"

"If Darragh made it home, we could," she agreed. "But if he got stuck in your old realm, there's no way of contacting him... although if he could find a talisman with sufficient magic, he could contact you. Or me. Any number of people for that matter. As for Hayley... it's hard to say. It would depend where she is, who she's with..."

Although he was anxious to ensure Hayley was alive and well, another thought occurred to Ren at that moment, which made him a little angry. "You mean, any old time in the last couple of weeks we could have called Ciarán or someone else in your realm for help, and got someone to open the rift for us from the other side?"

She refused to meet his eye. "Theoretically."

"But?" he prompted, guessing there was a reason he wouldn't like as to why she hadn't done just that and had Ciarán or Brogan come for them days ago.

"Marcroy wants you dead, Rónán. He separated you and Darragh when you were children. He arranged for the power transfer to take place, knowing it would kill you. What do you suppose he'd do if he learned you were still alive?"

"Gee... I don't know... open a rift maybe? Come get us?"

She shook her head. "He'd keep working on a way to kill you. And your brother. It's not safe to call our realm."

It sounded plausible, but there must be scores of other people, not related to the *Tuatha De Danann* that Trása could call for help. There had to be another reason.

"You don't want to go home," he said. "You don't want to be stuck here, but you're in no hurry to go anywhere else, are you?"

"I followed you through the rift without permission, Rónán. Marcroy is going to be very angry with me, too. He already cursed me once."

"So we're stuck here until your crazy uncle loses interest in us?"

"It's not the only reason, Rónán. As you so rightly pointed out, we don't know where we are. Yes, I could phone home, but what would be the point? If we tell someone to come get us, the next question will be "where are you?". There are an infinite number of realities out there. Do you know where we are?"

"But we can find our way home, can't we?"

She nodded. "You can always find your own home. It's when you start jumping about in realities you don't belong that rift runners run into trouble."

However reluctantly he wanted to admit it, she did have a point. "But we can contact other people," he said. "Even if they're not in a reality we can get to."

She nodded. "Scrying has more to do with the person than the realm they're in."

"So we can contact Darragh?"

This time she shook her head. "I doubt it. The realm were you grew up is very depleted. You saw the trouble we had when you and Darragh together tried to call Brogan in our realm."

"I have to get in touch with him, Trása. I need to let him know I'm alive."

"He knows you're alive, Rónán. He's alive too."

Ren wondered what the point of this whole psychic link business was. "It sucks, you know, that he can get punched in the face and I get a black eye across different realities, but we can't talk to one another."

"You don't get a black eye if he gets hit," she reminded him, a little impatiently. "You only manifest each other's wounds if they're inflicted with *airgead sídhe.*"

Ren knew about Faerie silver. At least he did now. He wished he'd known about it sooner because he'd suffered plenty of odd, inexplicable wounds during his lifetime. His sessions with the eminent Murray Symes, Psychiatrist to Troubled Children of the Stars, were a direct result of his link with his brother. His time in therapy had been a complete waste of time and served no purpose other than to make his mother feel better and Murray Symes a whole lot richer. Nobody had ever believed he wasn't cutting himself because of some deep-rooted psychosis that hundreds of hours of psychoanalysis had never been able to uncover.

And then another thought occurred to him. If he were cut in this realm with a blade forged from *airgead sídhe*, Darragh would suffer the same fate back in his reality.

Painful and bizarre as it would be, he might just have hit on a way to talk to Darragh. But it would be a one-way conversation. There was no *airgead sídhe* in his realm. Even if Ren carved an entire manifesto on his arm for his brother to read, there was no way for Darragh to write back.

"Did Darragh ever manifest a wound from me?" he asked. He tried to trawl through his brother's memories, but pain was something one tended to archive fairly quickly, so accessing Darragh's memories of every injury he'd ever acquired, and how he'd acquired it, was such a laborious process that it was much quicker to ask the girl who had grown up with his brother, if she remembered anything.

"Only once, that I can recall," Trása said, after a slight pause. "He was about nine or ten, I think. He woke up crying in the early in the morning. He was bleeding all over the bed."

Ren tried to imagine what had happened to him that would have that effect on Darragh, but he couldn't think of anything, offhand. "What sort of injuries did he have?"

She thought for a moment before answering. "Some deep scratches on his leg, as I recall. One of them so deep it was as if he had been stabbed with a very long, thin nail. I remember him refusing to heal it or have anybody else use magic to heal it, because it was the first hint he'd ever had that you were alive and out there somewhere and he might eventually bring you home."

Now she'd triggered the memory, Ren found himself filled with the same mixed emotions his brother experienced the only time he'd ever had one of his missing twin's wounds manifest itself on him. With the memory, came recall of the injury. "I remember now. I crashed my bike. It was really early in the morning. I was running away from home, I think." He smiled at the memory. "I only got as far the end of the street. It was winter and still dark and I slipped on a patch of ice and hit a tree. The bike was totalled. It was the spokes on the wheels that sliced me up, good and proper. My dramatic escape from my terrible life didn't seem nearly as heroic after I'd limped home, crying like a little girl."

She cocked her head to one side. "You had a bicycle made of Faerie silver?"

"Of course not." He stopped for a moment, trying to recall what the bicycle had been made of. Nothing else in his world seemed to have the same properties as *airgead sídhe*. He remembered the bike only vaguely. His memories of that incident were mostly about the pain he was in, as he hobbled home with his ruined bike, and the tantrum Kiva threw when she realized he'd been trying to run away. She had gone ballistic about the cost of the bike too, he recalled, and swore he'd never be allowed to own another. a threat she kept for all of two months before presenting him with a shiny new bicycle, in the hopes of easing the blow when she told him she was taking him out of school again to live in Prague for the better part of the year, while she made a movie there. Kiva's explosion about the cost of the bike was the key. "Now I think about it, I'm pretty sure it was titanium."

"Named for the Titans, do you think?"

He shrugged. "I guess. I wonder if Darragh could get his hands on something made of titanium, he could injure himself enough to affect me?"

"Probably," she agreed with a concerned frown. "But why would he want to?"

"Blood will have blood," he said darkly, thinking his plan both ingenious and horrific.

Trása looked at him blankly. "What?"

"It's a line from Macbeth," he told her. "It seems fitting."

"Who's Macbeth?" she asked.

"A Scotsman in my realm who exists solely to torture high school students," he told her, with a smile, figuring there was nothing to be gained by trying to explain Shakespeare to a Faerie. "Can you get your hands on an *airgead sídhe* weapon?"

"Are you kidding? Have you seen the *Leipreachán* in this realm? What are you going to do with a weapon?"

"Send my brother a message he can't ignore,"

"Wouldn't it be easier to scry him out?"

He shook his head. "Darragh was behind us, Trása, when the rift exploded and threw us into this realm. Don't you think, if my brother was anywhere he could contact us, he'd have called us on the puddle phone himself, by now?"

"I suppose," she conceded with a great deal of reluctance.

"So now we have a Plan B," he told her, with an encouraging smile. "How much longer have we got before the Empresses get back, do you think?"

She shrugged. "A while yet, I'm guessing."

"Then let's find you some clothes so I can have mine back, and then we can try calling my brother," he said.

"What are you going to tell him?"

"About the titanium, for one thing," Rónán said.

"Shouldn't you warn him about the *Matrarchaí*?"

"What would be the point? He's in a depleted realm," Ren pointed out. "What would the *Matrarchaí* be doing there?"

"I suppose."

He smiled at her encouragingly. "Cheer up, Trása. We're alive, and-" He stopped abruptly and the tent flap opened. A moment later a woman wearing a rich blue silk kimono slipped into the *akunoya*, looking furtively over her shoulder, before she dropped the flap and placed her finger on her lips, cautioning them to silence.

Outside, the rattle of metal against leather and footsteps marching in unison warned them a patrol was passing the tent, although Ren had no idea if it was an Ikushima patrol protecting the Empresses' camp from the Tanabe, or a Tanabe patrol protecting the camp from the Ikushima.

Ren stared at the woman in surprise. Their unexpected visitor was Wakiko, the mother of Isleen and Teagan. Her fair hair was piled up in the traditional Japanese manner and her lips were painted red, but her skin was so naturally pale, she needed no whitening powder to achieve the same look as the other courtiers in her daughters' court.

"You are alive," she said to Ren, nodding as if his continued existence confirmed something she already expected. "That is rare, and better than I hoped for."

"Can we do something for you?" Trása asked, climbing to her feet, a little like she was prepared to fight Wakiko to protect Ren, which he found rather touching.

Wakiko nodded and stepped further into the *akunoya*. "You can, little Faerie, and so can you," she added, looking directly at Ren.

He felt at a distinct disadvantage, naked and stuck under the blankets on a futon, but there was no chance he was going to climb out of bed with these two women watching. But he was curious about how Wakiko thought he could help her. Ren didn't feel able to help himself, let alone someone else. Maybe she wanted to intercede with the *Matrarchaí*. If she did, they were going to be in trouble when they discovered he had nothing to do with them.

"What do you want from me?" he asked.

"You are one of the Undivided in your realm, yes?"

Ren and Trása traded a glance, both of them instantly on guard.

"Why would you think that?" Trása asked.

"I saw the tattoo on Renkavana's hand before he collapsed. I have seen it before. I know what it means. And I know what its disappearance means."

Well you've got one up on me, right there, Ren was tempted to reply, but Trása answered for him. "What does it mean?"

"It means my prayers have been answered," Wakiko told them. "It means you can save my daughters."

"From what?" Ren asked.

"Themselves," Wakiko said.

CHAPTER 53

Darragh woke to find himself covered in electrodes with tubes poking out of every place they could find to put one. Choking on the tube they'd pushed down his windpipe, he instinctively grabbed at it and jerked it free, crying out as it scraped along his throat on the way out. Next came the drip in the back of his left hand, and worst of all, the catheter they'd inserted to collect his bodily waste. He pulled them all out, setting off a cacophony of beeps and whistles, and bringing the ICU nursing staff at a run.

He struggled to climb off the bed, pushing the staff away so violently he knocked one of the nurses to the floor. Everyone was shouting. Darragh was disoriented and afraid of what they might be doing to him with their machines. He didn't want to hurt anyone. But he was alive and couldn't figure out why. Or perhaps he wasn't alive. Perhaps this was some sort hellish afterlife, peopled by the cold, heartless, technology-driven gods of this realm.

There were figures all around him, trying to calm him down. He wasn't trying to make trouble. He called for Rónán, but his voice was dry and painful and he couldn't make himself understood. He didn't know what they were doing to him... or what they'd done to him.

Darragh tried to demand answers. He would have settled for a familiar face. But all around him were strangers, urging him to calm, while he thrashed about, trying to get free of them. A tall metal stand holding a bag of fluid crashed to the floor. Some inexplicable machine that screamed with a high-pitched squeal, rolled across the floor and slammed into the wall.

Darragh was panicked and lost and wanted, more than anything, to be gone from this strange place. The people around him could barely contain him. Then the door burst open and the guard posted outside his door charged in to help subdue him. On his heels was a woman with dark hair and a white coat... carrying a syringe.

Without having any idea what it was she carried, Darragh knew the syringe was meant for him and whatever it contained, he probably wouldn't like it. He redoubled his efforts to break free of the guard and others holding him down.

"Hold him still!" she ordered.

Darragh bucked and struggled, making it impossible for her to get a clear shot at him.

"I need to see Jack!" he demanded, as it dawned on him he wasn't it in the afterlife. There was no need for needles and syringes in the otherworld. He was still in Rónán's realm.

And he was alive.

"Jack O'Righin!" he tried to shout. "I need to see Jack O'Righin. I need to speak to Sor... ow!"

The woman in the white coat had managed to jam the needle into his thigh. Darragh redoubled his efforts to fight them off. But he couldn't fight them all. He struggled violently for a short time, and then, a few moments after the sudden sharp prick in his thigh, the room started to spin and this strange world of needles and machines and beeps and white lights brighter than the sun began to recede.

No matter how hard he tried to fight it, the drugs worked their magic on him and Darragh was soon drifting back down into the warm dark embrace of unconsciousness.

When he woke some time later, Darragh's eyes focussed more slowly than he would have liked. His throat was dry and raw and when he tried to move, he discovered he was strapped to the rails of the hospital bed with wide strips of Velcro.

But at least the tubes - especially the catheter - were gone.

He looked around, as much as he could with the restraints. He was in a hospital, he realized, calling on Rónán's memories of this reality, something he hadn't done the first time he woke up in this strange place - he had panicked because of all the tubes they'd thrust into him.

He was no longer in the ICU, he guessed. The machines were gone. The walls were a tacky shade of mustard, there was an inoffensive, matching geometric pattern on the curtains, a single hospital bed, a small basin with a mirror on the opposite wall. The detective who had caused his brother so much grief of late, Pete Doherty, was sitting beside his bed, flipping through a magazine.

"You're awake."

Darragh nodded, not certain there was an answer to such a blindingly obvious statement.

Pete put down the magazine, leaned forward in his seat and fixed his attention on Darragh. "What did you take?"

"What?" Darragh croaked. His throat was dry as driftwood. He looked at Pete imploringly. "Water?"

The detective stood up, poured some water into a plastic cup on the chest by the bed and then held the cup for Darragh while he drank. "Better?"

"Thank you," Darragh said dropping his head back on the pillow.

"All part of the service," Pete said insincerely. "You gave everyone quite a scare."

"I wasn't aware anyone in this realm knew me well enough to be concerned, Mr Doherty. I'm touched."

"What did you take?" he asked again. "All the tox screens have came back negative so far, but you went down too fast and bounced back too quickly, for your collapse to be just a bad dose of some nasty twenty-four hour bug."

Darragh frowned, not sure to what Pete was referring. He hadn't taken anything. He had - to his amazement - survived *Lughnasadh*. At least, he was alive for now. That didn't mean he would live for very much longer. Maybe this was a temporary reprieve. He might still be dead by the end of the week, although he felt well enough to believe that might not be the case. But he wasn't going to be falsely accused of trying to kill himself. "How could I take anything?" he asked. "I have been in prison."

"Sure... and nobody has *ever* smuggled anything narcotic into a prison."

"Then it could not have been something I took," Darragh agreed, pretending not to notice the detective's sarcasm. He glanced down at the straps holding him to the bed. "Are these really necessary?"

"You took some putting down the last time you woke up," Pete reminded him. "Hospital staff don't take kindly to that sort of behaviour."

"It was not my intention to hurt anyone," he said. "I was just surprised to discover I was still alive and in a strange place with tubes poking out of every orifice."

"That's what happens when you drop into a coma without warning."

"I warned Doctor Semaj something would happen to me."

"Yeah, he told me about that. *Lughnasadh* wasn't it?"

Darragh was pleased the detective seemed to have some grasp of the situation. "I am as surprised as you that I have lived through the night and I'm here talking about it, officer."

"*Let's* talk about it," Pete said, leaning back in the mustard-colored armchair that matched the disheartening décor of the rest of the room. He appeared quite relaxed, but Darragh had a feeling very little got past this man. He would know if Darragh was lying. That put the detective at a disadvantage, because Darragh hadn't lied about much at all.

It was not his fault what he was saying was completely unbelievable.

"What did you want to know?"

"I want to know about your relationship with Jack O'Righin," Pete said.

Darragh shrugged. "I barely know the man."

"And yet the first person you called for when you woke up out of a coma so deep you were damn near brain-dead, was the inimitable Jack O'Righin."

"From your tone, I gather you dislike him a great deal, detective."

"I dislike people who profit from other people's misfortune," Pete said. "O'Righin's a thug, profiting from the death of innocent people while masquerading as a political activist. It's people like him who give the other side all the ammunition they need to continue to suppress the very people he purports to help. *That's* what I don't like about him."

Pete's position made a great deal of sense, when he explained it like that, but Darragh, like his brother before him, still had trouble reconciling the old man who loved his glass house and his bromeliads, with the terrorist he had been as a younger man.

"I have no interest in Jack's politics, sir."

"So you're an opportunist."

"I don't mean to be," Darragh said, feeling as if he should be apologising for something. "Can you tell me what they did to my hand?"

Pete glanced at Darragh's right hand. "Your tattoo washed off."

"That's not possible."

"Clearly, it is possible. What did you do it with? Henna? A Sharpie?"

Darragh knew what henna was, but he had no idea about the other method Pete was talking about. "It must have been the ceremony at *Lughnasadh*.

516

When the power was transferred, the brand went with it."

Pete sighed. "I see. We're back to that again, are we?"

"I wish there were some way to prove I'm not lying," Darragh said.

"Let's start with why you were demanding to speak to O'Righin."

Darragh smiled. That was easily explained. "I want to talk to Jack, because he might know where Sorcha is."

"Ah... the mysterious Sorcha," Pete said, his tone giving away nothing. "I thought you said she went back through the rift to another reality with Hayley Boyle?"

"I thought you didn't believe me about the rift?"

"I don't," he detective said. "But the first rule of being a good liar is having a good memory, kid. Yours sucks, apparently."

"I lied about her still being in this realm because I didn't want Sorcha getting into trouble," he admitted.

"And all this time she's been at Jack's?"

"I assume so," he said, figuring the only way he was going to get a message to her, was to level with this man who had the power, he knew, to pass the message on. He vaguely remembered a guard in the room the last time he'd regained consciousness. Darragh realized being relocated to a hospital in no way altered the fact he was incarcerated, and that he was likely to remain that way until somebody from his own realm came for him, or the authorities in this reality accepted that he really hadn't done anything seriously criminal and let him go. But it was important to let Sorcha know he lived. She was too dangerous to leave in this realm without any sort of guidance or restraint, and who knew what she would do if she thought she was stuck here now, alone and friendless, in a realm she didn't know and didn't understand?

"Must be hard for her."

"More than I can say," Darragh agreed, genuinely concerned for the woman.

"What about Warren?" Pete asked.

Darragh's brow furrowed. "What about him?"

"Did Sorcha take care of him, too?"

"She was planning to take care of the matter the last time I saw her," Darragh told the detective, encouraged by how sympathetic the detective seemed to be to Sorcha's plight.

"Do you know what she was planning?"

Darragh nodded. "She felt it necessary to protect Rónán. I realize in this realm, such things are not nearly so cut and dried, but in our world - Sorcha's world - things are much more black and white."

Pete nodded, looking pensive. "Black and white, huh? Is that what you're calling it?"

There was a slight change in Pete's tone - an undertone of menace that made Darragh wonder if he might have inadvertently said something foolish. That memory of Rónán's rattled around inside his head again, along the lines of "never talk to the cops without a lawyer", but it was only now that the alarm bells rang in his mind.

"Rónán was quite insistent that we not kill him," Darragh assured the Gardaí officer.

"But you and Sorcha disagreed?"

Darragh nodded. "My brother has not seen what we have seen, sir. He did not really understand."

"But you and Jack understood he needed to be eliminated?"

Darragh nodded.

"Did Jack help?"

Darragh didn't worry for himself. He was confident someone would come for him, and he would not be held responsible for anything he had done in this realm. He knew Rónán would have preferred to keep Jack out of this, but Darragh wanted to protect his brother. To do that, he needed to make sure this detective understood Rónán had been innocent and any trouble they had caused was not Rónán's doing.

"He kept Warren silent until Sorcha could arrange a more permanent solution to the problem," he admitted.

"So Jack O'Righin, you and the lovely Sorcha conspired to murder Warren Maher?"

"Detective, you make it sound like-" Darragh cried out as a sharp pain attacked the lower half of his left arm. He struggled against the restraints as the pain grew worse, but there was nothing he could do, to relieve or stop the intense agony.

Pete jumped to his feet, to see what was wrong. He gasped when he spied blood welling on Darragh's forearm. "What the fuck is going on? What are you doing?"

Darragh cried out again and saw the wound taking shape. Then he knew. At least, he thought he did. He grinned delightedly through the pain. He recognized the timbre of the stinging agony, realized what it must mean. Although tears stung his eyes from the torment of an injury that was manifesting before his very eyes, he was filled with relief.

"I am not... doing... anything," he said, gritting his teeth, as he watched the blood bead amid the hairs on his forearm and then drip onto the pale blue cotton blanket.

Pete grabbed the emergency call button on the chest beside the bed. He pressed it a number of times and then ran to the door to call for help. Darragh bit back his pain and glanced down at his arm,

Slowly, painstakingly and with infinite care that only served to prolong the pain, a bloody word was slowly taking form on the flesh of his forearm, carved - he was quite certain - in another realm with *airgead sídhe* by his brother.

Darragh was elated. Rónán was alive and had found a way to contact him.

"Jesus, what is that?" Pete demanded, as he returned to pressing the emergency bell. The reaction time here in this ward was vastly different to the immediate response of the ICU staff. "What is that? Some sort of stigmata? How are you doing it?"

"I am not... doing anything," Darragh told him, gritting his teeth against the pain. "Rónán is."

"No fucking way," Pete insisted, refusing to believe what he was seeing.

Darragh leaned forward, trying to make out the words, but the angle his arm was tied to the railing with the Velcro and the blood dripping from the wounds made it hard to read. Then a nurse opened the door, stepped into the room, her put-upon expression changing to horror when she saw the blood. She shouted for help and shoved Pete out of the way.

A moment later there were more nurses filling the room, all of them shouting and ordering each other about and generally panicking about what was causing Darragh's sudden bleeding. With them blocking his view, Darragh could barely see the wound, although he could feel every agonising inch of the bloody characters as they were carved into his flesh. Unfortunately, the nurses were only interested in staunching the bleeding, not reading the message. Before long his arm was bound with a pressure bandage to stop the bleeding - obscuring Rónán's communication - and Pete was being shooed from the room.

They gave him something for the pain, and someone sent for a doctor, but Darragh wasn't paying attention to the medical staff. He dropped his head back on the pillow and closed his eyes, conscious of the words still cutting into his flesh, bringing him hope and maybe even a way home.

Darragh tried to recall the small part of the message he'd seen before it was obscured by blood, gauze and a clutch of very rattled nurses.

All he could remember seeing was one word, and it made no sense at all. Carved into his arm was the word "bike".

CHAPTER 54

It took several blows with a short police battering ram to break the lock in the solid oak front door of Jack O'Righin's house. Once they were inside, the armed ERU team spread out with practised efficiency, checking each room, and yelling "clear" as they verified there was nobody in the house brandishing a weapon, ready to die rather be taken alive.

Pete followed them in, carrying a handgun and wearing a bulletproof vest, but he let the team do its job, knowing he would only be in the way while they cleared the building. He listened to the radio in his ear as they moved, room by room through the house, expecting the call at any moment telling him they had found Jack or Sorcha. Part of him worried he wouldn't hear it over the comms, but rather shots ringing out somewhere in the depths of this large, echoing mansion.

Cold-blooded and merciless as she must be, Sorcha, he figured, wasn't going down without a fight. But with her arrest, finally, they might catch a break in the Hayley Boyle case. Darragh was delusional, but Sorcha, his accomplice, was much more focussed. So was Jack O'Righin. One way or another, Pete was determined, he was going to find Hayley Boyle and make someone pay for Warren Maher's murder.

It took the team less than ten minutes to get through the house.

It took them less than ten minutes to discover nobody was home. Not even the old lady who'd been here the last time Pete paid Jack O'Righin a visit.

Pete cursed as he entered the kitchen on the heels of the assault team, wondering who had tipped O'Righin off about the raid. It was the middle of the night, his car was parked in the drive, but there was nobody to be found inside. It didn't make sense that he wasn't here. The house had been under surveillance for hours. Other than the housekeeper leaving about four in the afternoon, there had been no other movement in or out of the house.

"Check again," he ordered into his radio, as he glanced around, wondering where the old man and the young woman were hiding. This was a big house, with lots of nooks and crannies. It was not inconceivable that they had gone to ground somewhere inside the house...

Another thought occurred to Pete. He reached for his radio but then decided to check out his hunch alone. Jack had a glasshouse out in the garden. Pete considered it a front to buy nitrates in case the old man decided to go back into the bomb-making business, but there was no evidence of that, just his own gut feeling, and the general dislike Pete had of anybody who cashed-in on killing people. He keyed the mike and then let it go again. It was only a glasshouse, which made it the worst place imaginable to hide. But Pete wanted to check it out. This was too important to leave any stone - or pot plant - unturned. Maybe he'd get lucky and discover Jack had been cultivating more than pineapples. A few drug charges might help if the accessory to murder charge didn't stick, after Darragh's confession yesterday.

He let himself out into the back garden. A gentle misty rain was falling, obscuring the glasshouse. He pulled out the uncomfortable radio earpiece and trotted across the lawn. As he neared the glasshouse, he realized there was a dim light coming from inside.

Pete should have called for back up, at that point, he knew, but something held him back. As he neared the glasshouse, its walls misted with rivulets of rainwater, the nature of the light became clearer. It was candlelight.

Inside the glasshouse, someone had lit scores of tea-light candles and placed them all over the stepped shelves inside.

Pete raised his weapon and opened the door carefully - although given it was glass, anybody inside with a gun could have killed him long before he got the door open. He stepped inside, the warm loamy smell of the vegetation, mixed with the smell of urea and blood and bone fertiliser, was almost overpowering.

Jack was standing opposite the door, but he wasn't paying any attention to Pete, who stopped at the entrance and took in the scene, not sure he believed his own eyes.

Laid out on the centre bench of the glasshouse was a dead body. Jack was standing there, looking down on it with tears silently rolling down his cheeks.

It was the old woman Pete had spoken to a few days ago, when he'd come here to ask about Warren.

She was not dressed like an old woman, though. She was naked, painted with blue woad, the symbols covering her limbs, her torso and her face, a mix of familiar Celtic designs and others he'd never seen before. Her arms were crossed over her chest. In one hand she held a carving knife, in the other, a small garden hatchet. Her thin, arthritic fingers clung to them like she was a knight laid out in state with his weapons.

The artwork on the old woman's body was amateurish but meticulous. Someone had spent a lot of time and expended a great deal of effort preparing this body.

Beside the old woman lay a variety of items. There were more kitchen knives, a block of cheese, several jars of what looked like homemade fruit preserves, and various other food items arranged around the body. On the centre of her forehead, Pete noticed, taking a step further into the glasshouse, someone had painted the same triskalion symbol that had - until so recently - graced the hands of Darragh and his twin brother, Ren.

Jack glanced up. It seemed he had only just noticed he had company.

"She must have known for days," Jack said, wiping his eyes, as if embarrassed to be caught with such an obvious display of emotion.

"Known what, you sick old bastard?" Pete asked, pointing his weapon directly at Jack's head. "That you were going to kill her?"

Jack smiled briefly. He didn't seem bothered by the gun. "I didn't kill her, lad. She died of old age."

Given the state of the old woman's body and the lack of any obvious wounds, Pete wasn't going to argue about that now. "Whatever she died of, O'Righin, the old woman didn't deserve to be defiled like this."

"Defiled?" Jack seemed surprised. "Jaysus, she did this herself, lad," he said. "She was going downhill fast. Had been for days. Once the equinox passed with no sign of help from her own people, she gave up, I think. But she wanted a warrior's burial. I tried to tell her they'd not let me leave her body lying about for days, or let me bake her in an underground oven in the back garden once she was ripe enough, but she was adamant." He gently moved a stray lock of grey hair from the old lady's face, adding. "I found her like this about an hour ago." Jack glanced up then at a shattering sound coming from the house, as if he'd only just realized his house was being torn apart by the ERU. "They'll be paying for anything they break in there."

Pete lowered his weapon. "Tell me where I can find Sorcha, and I'll stop them breaking things."

"You're looking at her."

Pete was tempted to raise his weapon again, pull the trigger and rid the world of this fool. "Really? *This* is Sorcha?"

"In the flesh."

"You know, I bet it seemed like a grand idea, when you and Darragh and Sorcha came up with that ludicrous story." He moved a little closer to the bench and examined the body more closely. The women seemed ancient. "But you're forgetting, Jack, I've met Sorcha. And this isn't her. You're out by about... eighty years, I'd say."

Jack nodded. "I met her the first time on September Eighth," he said. "She looked twenty-five... thirty at the best. I know you're not going to believe me, but I've seen her age, lad. Every single day since then."

"Sorcha helped kidnap an innocent girl and murdered a man for the crime of owning a car one of her accomplices stole, O'Righin. This woman wouldn't be able to get out of her walking frame long enough to get into a heated argument, let alone slash the throat of a grown man and then escape over the neighbour's fence."

"Nevertheless," Jack said with a shrug, "this is Sorcha. Aren't there tests you can do now, that will establish that?"

"Oh, don't worry, we'll be checking her DNA," he assured the old man. "And yours, too. If we find so much as a flake of dandruff belonging to you at Warren Maher's place, you'll going down for murder, not just being an accessory."

That got a rise out of the old man. "Me? An accessory to *what*, for feck's sake? Killing the broker? You can't pin that on me."

"Can and have," Pete told him. "Darragh's confessed to everything. He admitted to ordering the killing. He admitted sending Sorcha to do it. And he admitted to your involvement in keeping Warren Maher quiet until Sorcha could get to him."

Before Jack could answer, the glasshouse door shattered as the ERU burst in, weapons cocked, and trained them on Jack in a spray of red dots. The old man raised his hands in a gesture of surrender, however, his expression was anything but submissive. The captain of the ERU team quickly scanned the small building before he turned to Pete. "You were out of radio contact."

"Sorry," he said, lifting the earpiece off his vest where it had fallen when he pulled it out. "I must have dropped it."

The captain gave him a look that said volumes about what he thought of officers who lost radio contact for such a pathetic reason, and then he turned and ordered his men to take Jack into custody. He then fixed his attention on the old woman's body, intrigued, rather than disgusted by what he saw. "O'Righin did this?"

"He says not," Pete told him, as Jack was cuffed and marched out of the candlelit glasshouse. The old man muttered some comment as he stepped over the broken glass of the door, and then he was out of earshot. For a fleeting moment, Pete felt sorry for the old man.

He would probably never see his *bromeliads* again.

"There's no sign of the woman, Sorcha," the captain told him. "We've searched the house from top to bottom."

"According to Jack, that's Sorcha right there."

The man shook his head. "That's ridiculous."

"My sentiments exactly."

"Who is she, then?"

Pete shook his head. "I have no idea. Last time I met her, she was introduced as the housekeeper's demented aunt."

"She's laid out like a warrior," the captain said. He pointed to the weapons clutched in each hand. "See... the weapons, the food... that's meant for her journey into the otherworld."

Pete stared at man in surprise. "Are you telling me you think this woman thought she was some sort of pagan Celtic warrior?"

"The symbols on her body are crude, but they're unmistakable."

"I never realized you were such an aficionado of ancient Celtic mythology and symbolism, Mac," Pete said, rather impressed.

"We all need a hob- Hang on." He put his finger to his ear, to better hear the radio message coming through, and then he turned to Pete. "You're needed out front. Apparently the press has got wind of this."

"That's hardly surprising," Pete said. "The paparazzi have a permanent camp set up next door."

"This isn't the paparazzi," the captain said. "It's your brother. So go out there and talk to him. He needs to be gone before the crime scene people get here."

"I'll take care of it," Pete promised, and with one last glance at the curious old woman laid out like an ancient Celtic warrior, he turned and stepped out into the softly falling rain, wondering who she really was, why she would want to be laid out like that, and what the hell Logan wanted now.

CHAPTER 55

"My real name is Ingrid," Wakiko told Ren and Trása, as she ceremoniously poured their tea. She was kneeling in front of a low *honzen* table she had arranged for some of the Empresses' servants to bring in. The tea ceremony, she had assured them in a whisper when she sent for the paraphernalia to serve them, was a polite and thoughtful act for an honored guest. It provided her with a perfectly legitimate excuse to be here talking to them, should anybody - Ren assumed she was talking of the Tanabe - chose to question her about why she was fraternizing with the *Matrarchaí* envoy. "At least, that was my name once. I hardly remember that girl now. But like you, I am not from this realm,"

"You're from a magical realm though," Trása said. "Aren't you?"

Wakiko nodded, as she carefully laid out the charcoal fire she would use to heat the water for their tea. Ren had sat through a Japanese tea ceremony before, and knew it would take some time, and that it would be considered the height of bad manners to interrupt the ceremony. Wakiko, or Ingrid, or whatever her name might be, was a lot cannier than she appeared when she stood behind her daughters in public and appeared to grant their every whim.

"My realm is quite different to this. In my reality, there were no Undivided and the Faerie kept to themselves."

"So what are you doing here?" Ren asked, as Wakiko began to cleanse each of the tea bowls, her whisk, and the delicate ivory tea scoop in a precise order that only she knew, using prescribed motions that had probably been passed down from generation to generation for a thousand years or more. He wasn't a fan of Japanese tea, or the laborious and complex ceremony that went with serving it, but it was buying them time and gave Wakiko something to focus on, so she didn't have to look them in the eye.

"When I was sixteen, I was recruited by the *Matrarchaí*."

"Recruited for what?" Ren asked, as Wakiko began to spoon the powdered tea from the caddy into the tea bowl.

"To travel to exotic realms," she said, with a faintly reminiscent smile. She poured the water into the bowl and picked up the tea whisk. "The adventure of being a rift runner was irresistible to a sixteen-year-old farm girl from Normandy." She looked at Trása, adding, "As I am sure you will agree."

"In my realm, the *Matrarchaí* are midwives," Trása said, clearly suspicious of Wakiko and her tea ceremony. "Not rift runners."

"They are both, little Faerie," Wakiko told her. "In your realm and mine. Their influence is felt across countless realms, both magical and mundane. Trust me, if you know of the *Matrarchaí*, you are dealing with the same organisation that recruited me and brought me to this realm."

"To do what?" Ren asked again, accepting a bowl of thin tea with a bow. He took a sip and forced himself not to grimace. "Roam through as many realities as they can find, delivering babies?"

Wakiko smiled wanly and offered Trása a bowl, before carefully placing the lid on the tea caddy. "You would be horrified to learn how close to the truth that is, Renkavana."

"That's ridiculous," Trása said, glancing at Ren with a look that seemed to imply she thought Wakiko a complete loon. Ren wasn't sure he disagreed with that assessment.

"They are not just delivering babies," Wakiko said. "They are delivering very specific babies."

She paused, waiting for either Ren or Trása to get what she was telling them.

"The psychic twins who become Undivided," Ren said, after a moment, a little alarmed by the implications of that statement. "They know how to find them."

"They are not finding them, Renkavana. They are breeding their own."

Trása gasped.

"And therein lies the *Matrarchaí's* biggest problem," Wakiko continued. "Humans have no inherent capacity to wield magic. Not a drop of it.

533

To wield the magic of their hated enemy, to produce the twins they require, they must *become* the enemy."

"I still don't understand," Trása said, which saved Ren from having to admit the same thing. He put his tea bowl down and sat back on his heels, trying to decide if Wakiko was the answer to all their problems or the start of a whole new raft of them.

"If you are human and you can wield Faerie magic, then you have Faerie blood in you," Wakiko said flatly. "It is as simple as that."

"So Chishihero was right? My brother and I are part Faerie?" Ren asked, not sure how he felt about such a revelation.

She nodded, topping up Ren's cup of tea. "Almost pure *sídhe*, I'd say, to be as powerful as you are."

"I don't feel powerful."

"That's because you are ignorant of your full potential. Chishihero is not, which is why, when she first met you, she tried to kill you."

"Rónán can't be *sídhe*, or *Youkai* or any other Faerie race," Trása said. "Look at him! He looks so human it hurts. And he's been living in a realm without magic. If he was *sídhe* that fact alone would have killed him the same way the *Matrarchaí* killed the *Youkai* on this world."

"I said *almost* pure," Wakiko said. "That's the other thing the *Matrarchaí* breed for - *sídhe* who can operate in worlds without magic."

"What's the point of that?" Ren asked, thinking there wasn't much point in being able to wield magic if there was none to wield.

"They can tap into the Enchanted Sphere," Wakiko said.

"The what?" Ren and Trása asked in unison.

"The Enchanted Sphere," Wakiko explained impatiently. She was interested in what they could do for her and obviously resented the time taken from that to explain something she clearly thought they ought to know. "There is always some magic left, even on depleted worlds," she said. "It's pretty thin, but what is left tends to rise and concentrates in a band around the depleted world, that can be accessed if you can reach it."

"How high up are we talking?"

Wakiko shrugged. "I cannot say, Renkavana. I have only ever been to one world like that, on my way here. The stone circle was located at the top of a building - a building so tall I could never, in my whole life, have imagined mortal man could create such a thing."

"You could get higher climbing a mountain, I would have thought," Ren said, wondering why you would put such a thing as a stone circle in a building. "Wouldn't it be easier to tap into the magic from there?" He was already thinking ahead to when he found his way back to his old realm; to when he finally found Darragh and brought him home. If there was an Enchanted Sphere like that in his reality, then he might have stumbled on the way home for both of them.

"I made the same observation," Wakiko said. "Lady Delphine told me she needed the concentration of mundane life to allow her to tap into the Enchanted Sphere, which made buildings in cities better than isolated locations higher up, where there wasn't as much life."

"There's hardly any magical life-force in a mundane human," Trása scoffed. "You'd need... I don't know... millions of people for them to be of any use."

"In the realm I come from, you only build skyscrapers in cities with millions of people in them," Ren pointed out.

Wakiko smiled. "Skyscrapers? Is that what you call them?"

He nodded.

"It is a fitting a word."

"So Rónán is *sídhe* with enough human in him to survive outside the Enchanted Sphere," Trása said. "Like me."

"That is correct."

"And how did he get that way?"

Wakiko carefully placed the utensils from her tea ceremony on the *honzen* and sat back on her heels again. "If one is born of mixed blood, be it any race on Earth, in any reality, human or fey, one will manifest different characteristics of each race. If a dark-skinned man and a light-skinned woman have two children, one might be light-skinned and the other dark, but they would still be brothers."

"They breed for twins who don't look like Faerie," Ren said, perhaps grasping what she meant a little faster than Trása. He understood the principles of genetic engineering, even if it seemed ludicrous to be using the words "genetic engineering" and "Faerie" in the same sentence. "I take it the Faerie have no idea?"

"None at all," Wakiko said, shaking her head. "The *Matrarchaí* are relentless in their determination to keep the true nature of the psychic twins a secret."

Trása was listening to Wakiko thoughtfully, but at that, she shook her head. "It's not possible," she insisted. "Even if I believe what you say about breeding for human characteristics, rather than *sídhe* features, such a plan would never work. The *sídhe* are long-lived. You don't think somebody would notice when the Undivided don't grow old?"

"I do not know the history of your world, little Faerie, but I'd wager one of my limbs that all of your Undivided have died from accident or injury, rather than old age or illness."

"That's not..." Trása hesitated, and then frowned. "Actually, it is true. I can't remember the name of any Undivided who lived to a ripe old age."

"They have to kill them before they live long enough for people to notice they're not ageing," Ren said, a little stunned by what Wakiko was telling them.

She nodded. "Had you stayed in your world as the Undivided, you may have lived until your mid-thirties. Then you would have been killed in such a way that everyone would lament your passing and the tragic manner of your death, and the new Undivided would take over, gaining the *Matrarchaí* another ten or fifteen years without close scrutiny."

"How does that work?" Ren asked, intrigued, in spite of himself. "Neither of the previous Undivided was our father. How can they have been breeding toward a Faerie Undivided who doesn't look the part?"

"There is more than one bloodline, Renkavana, and they cross realities at times. The *Matrarchaí* have been at this for a long time."

"But why?" Trása asked. "It can't just be to have access to *sídhe* magic. They have that anyway, through the Treaty of *Tír Na nÓg.*

"In your world, they might," she replied. "But there are other worlds where the magic is not shared anywhere near so willingly. That is why they need to achieve Partition."

Trása let out an exasperated sigh. She wasn't buying a word of this, Ren thought.

"Seriously? The Partitionists? *That's* your reason for all this cross-reality breeding and subterfuge?" She turned to Ren. "Don't you listen to this, Rónán. She's talking nonsense."

Wakiko did not seem bothered by Trása's scepticism. "The Partition the *Matrarchaí* is working towards is not a political movement. It is, so I am led to believe by those with magical abilities, more a state of being."

"So the *Matrarchaí* are jumping across realities, breeding babies and murdering people like me for a bit of a buzz?"

Wakiko looked at Ren and sighed. "You poor boy, you have no idea how this affects you, do you?"

"I have a feeling you're going to tell me."

"You and your twin are *sídhe*, Renkavana, or Youkai or Faerie or whatever else you want to call it. You are bound to them. You may not realize it, but you will do whatever it takes to protect them."

"You don't know that."

"It's what you are," Wakiko said with a shrug. "If you don't believe me, try killing your *Beansidhe* companion and see how far you get."

"Be assured, my lady," Ren said with feeling, glancing at Trása who responded by pulling a face at him. "I've been tempted on more than one occasion."

"It doesn't matter," Wakiko said. "You cannot do it. And that is the flaw in the *Matrarchaí* plan to steal the magic on their worlds. The vessels they bred to take it for them, are by their very nature, compelled to protect their enemy, and not humanity."

"But if you achieve Partition, you can cut the ties?" Trása asked, looking thoughtful. She was starting to get it, Ren thought, and she didn't look happy about what this Norman geisha was telling her. "You'd have Faerie prepared to kill Faerie."

"That's where I come in," Wakiko said, nodding. "And others like me. I am human, you see. Not a drop of Faerie blood do I own, as far back as you care to go. I was recruited by the *Matrarchaí* to bear a set of Undivided twins."

"Because you're human?" Ren asked. "But if your logic is right, they'd need you to be *sídhe*."

Wakiko shrugged. "I do not know how it works, Renkavana, only that it does. If you breed the Undivided to the point where, like you, they look human but are almost pure Faerie, and then breed those twins again with a pure human, you get Empress, or Emperor, twins - twins powerful enough to channel the magic, but not compelled to protect the Faerie races."

"So then you're free to mass-murder my people," Trása said, her ire rising, "without the inconvenient need to protect your own kind getting in the way."

"That, I fear, is exactly right," Wakiko agreed.

"And that's what your daughters are?" Ren asked, putting a hand on Trása's thigh to calm her down. Somewhat to his surprise, she didn't bat it away, but placed her hand over his, as if seeking comfort from the contact.

Wakiko nodded. "Had I known what was in store for my children, I would never have agreed," she said. "But I was young and naïve and enchanted by the idea of magic and my mission to seduce myself a prince." She took a deep breath that seemed filled with regret. "I had visions of being a queen. Instead, I find myself the nursemaid to a couple of demons."

"They seem a bit spoiled," Ren said, thinking she was a little harsh. "My shrink would call it an over-developed sense of entitlement." He smiled at her, not sure what else he could do for her. "I'm sure they'll grow out of it."

Wakiko shook her head. "They have shared the *Comhroinn* but have not been allowed to fully access it yet. Once they are given access to that knowledge, they will not be my little girls any longer. They will be the heartless tools of the *Matrarchaí*."

It was all a bit much to take in, and Ren wasn't sure what Wakiko expected him and Trása to do about it. "Why are you telling us this?"

Wakiko glanced toward the entrance before she answered. "Because Chishihero has received word from *Nara* that the real envoy from the *Matrarchaí* is coming here," she said. Then she smiled. "Oh, don't try to look surprised. I knew the moment I met you that you had nothing to do with the *Matrarchaí*."

"Why didn't you betray us?" Ren asked.

"Because I need your help," she said. "When Lady Delphine gets here with the real messenger, she will unlock the *Comhroinn* and my daughters will transform from spoiled children into the monsters they are destined to become."

"I'm more worried why Chishihero has said nothing," Trása said, frowning, which made Wakiko scowl. She was a mother worried for her children and obviously considered it the only problem worth discussing. "She has no love for me, and I'm pretty sure she has even less time for you, Rónán. I would have thought she'd jump at the chance to expose you as a fraud."

"She will be planning to," Wakiko agreed, lowering her voice. "My feeling is Chishihero wants to wait until she has proof and someone powerful enough to take you down when she reveals you are not the real envoy."

"The proof being the real envoy," Trása said. She turned to Ren. "So what do we do?"

"Wait until the rift opens and get the hell outta Dodge."

Trása let out an exasperated sigh. "That means nothing to me."

"I mean we leave. As soon as the rift opens."

"You can't," Wakiko said. "Delphine will be there. She will not permit it."

"What do we do then?"

"It is simple, Renkavana," Wakiko said. "You must kill Delphine and anybody who comes through the rift with her."

Oh, Ren thought sourly. *Is that all?* "That will close the rift and we're stuck here." *Not to mention the whole killing someone in cold blood thing...*

Wakiko shook her head. "The last remaining book of *ori mahou*, is under lock and key in the Imperial Palace in *Nara*, along with the location of the few gampi trees left, from which the paper must

541

be made to open a rift between realms." She took a deep breath and looked both of them squarely in the eye. "If you save my daughters from Delphine, I will see you get access to everything you need in order to open a rift back to your own reality."

"But we have to kill someone," Ren said, to be certain he understood exactly what sort of deal she was putting on the table.

"You have to save my daughters, Renkavana." She shrugged and began to pack up her tea service. "It may involve killing Delphine and her envoy, or it may not. I have no feeling on the matter one way or another. I just need her to leave this realm and never come back. You are *Youkai*. You are one of the Undivided. You are far more powerful, magically, than she is, I suspect. If you do this thing, I will help you get home. I can offer you no fairer deal than that."

Ren glanced at Trása who nodded slowly. "I'm in if you are. And the lesser *Youkai* will follow if I ask them to."

He turned to Wakiko, for the first time in his life, feeling like Darragh must have when, as he'd ruled their realm. The unsettled boy who was Ren Kavanagh, indulged son of a rich and famous movie star, seemed to be fading into the distance. He was Rónán, one half of the Undivided, facing a life and death decision he was expected to resolve.

"How long have we got until they get here?" he asked. "We have some plans to make."

CHAPTER 56

Logan was standing in the rain outside Jack O'Righin's house, sheltering under a leafy oak whose leaves were already starting to turn. The Porsche was parked by the kerb with its engine burbling away, the wipers beating a slow tattoo across the glass. The streetlamps were set far apart in this area. Most of them were obscured by the evenly spaced trees lining the street, so it was impossible to make out anything other than Logan's silhouette waiting for him by the car. There was no sign of his cameraman or any other press. The paparazzi who normally camped at Kiva Kavanaugh's house next door were gone. It may have been the rain, the lateness of the hour, or perhaps there was some other function tonight with their presence required elsewhere.

Whatever the reason, Pete was grateful, although annoyed at his brother for trading on their relationship like this.

"Did you want me to spell 'no comment' for you," he asked his brother as he approached, "so you get it absolutely right when you're writing up your notes?"

Logan, who was always ready with a wise-ass comeback, didn't even crack a smile. As Pete neared him, he held something out to Pete. He took it from him and studied it curiously. "What's this?"

"Your passport."

"I can see that," Pete said, frowning. "What are you doing with it?"

"I called past your place but you weren't home. I thought I'd save you time by bringing it with me."

"Are we going somewhere?"

Logan nodded and pushed off the tree. "Paris tonight, then New York on Concorde in the morning. We're connecting with a flight to Chicago from JFK."

"Has something happened to Mum?" he asked, unable to imagine any other reason Logan would decide they needed to fly halfway around the world in the middle of the night. She was also the only person either of them had any interest in - as far as Pete was aware - currently in Chicago.

"Not yet."

"Not *yet*?" Pete glanced over his shoulder at Jack O'Righin's house and everything that it symbolised. Hayley Boyle, who was still missing, presumed dead at this stage. Darragh, the crazy young man who believed he came from an alternate reality. The dead financier, Warren Maher, whose only mistake was parking his car and having a few too many whiskies at the golf club while his wife was away visiting her mother. The old woman laid out in the glasshouse like an old Celtic warrior. The not-so-reformed terrorist, who would probably never know another day of freedom, once his parole was revoked.

And of course, Ren Kavanaugh, without whom none of this mess would have started in the first place.

"Logan, I just can't up and leave in the middle of a case to take a Concorde to New York... how in God's name did you swing that? Those tickets cost a fortune."

"Mum's agency has an account with British Airways."

"Good luck explaining that one to her, when you see her."

"She flies her models across the Atlantic on Concorde all the time. I happen to know that for a fact." Logan's tone was bitter and hard.

"You wanna tell me what this is about? I'm working, you know."

"I went to see Tiffany this evening. When I got to her place, she was gone. This is the note she left for me." He reached into his pocket and handed Pete a folded piece of lined paper torn from a spiral notepad.

Pete took the note, glancing over his shoulder to see if anyone had come to find out what had happened to him. Hopefully the ERU boys thought he was out here delivering a stern lecture to his reporter brother. He wasn't sure what they do if they realized he was taking time out to console his twin over a broken heart.

"What does it say?" he asked. He didn't want to read it.

"It says I'm not to worry, she'll be okay, she's flying to Chicago and that Mum is taking care of everything."

Pete's initial reaction was to say, *so what's the problem?* Then he realized what Logan was afraid of, when Tiffany wrote Delphine would be "taking care of everything". He shook his head. "No way. Mum's been harping on about being a grandma since we hit puberty. There is not a snowball's chance in hell that she'll arrange a termination for her own grandchild."

"Not if she knows it's mine," Logan agreed. "But what if Tiffany doesn't tell her? She's a model, Pete. Being pregnant isn't a great career move."

"But still..."

"If she lands in Chicago with runway shows already booked, and swears blind the kid isn't mine, Mum would help her to have the problem 'taken care of' in a heartbeat."

He was probably right. Delphine was a ruthless businesswoman when it suited her. "Then call Mum and tell her the kid is yours."

"I tried calling her," Logan said in exasperation. "Don't you think that's the first thing I thought of?"

"Sorry... of course you did. What happened?"

"She's not answering her cell phone. Her London office says she's in Chicago. The Chicago office claims she's away on a photoshoot with some of her girls and they can't contact her. I've left messages with everyone I can think of. Oh... and the hospital she rang you from? The one she claims she was in? I checked on that too. She spent one night there and then discharged herself. Days ago."

It all sounded very suspicious, but still not enough for Pete to walk away from his responsibilities here. Hayley Boyle was still missing. Jack O'Righin needed to be interrogated, and he was actually looking forward to that. "Look, Logan, I understand how you must feel, but-"

"I keep having this recurring dream, Pete," his brother cut in, in a low voice, as if he was afraid of being overheard. "We're both in it. And so are my kids. The kids that haven't been born yet. I keep dreaming I'm going to-"

"Kill them?" Pete finished for him, the hairs on the back of his neck suddenly standing on end. "That's why you rang me the other night."

Logan nodded, looking both relieved and puzzled. "How did you know?"

"Because I've been having the same dream."

Once, when they were about fourteen, Logan and Pete had been accused of cheating at school, because they'd written almost identical essays during an English examination. They swore they hadn't and Delphine had believed them. In high dudgeon - as only she could manage it - their mother had marched down to the principal's office and demanded the boys be allowed to sit another exam to prove their innocence. She made a big enough fuss that she got her way and when they compared the two papers after the second exam, once again, they were almost identical. That sort of thing happened less and less as they got older, but there was a feeling they had always shared when things like that happened, a oneness only identical twins understood. It was a state they could not begin to explain to anybody else. It was happening now, in that moment. Pete knew, without a shadow of a doubt, he needed to go with Logan. Nothing else happening in his world at the moment, was as important as the fact that right now, Logan needed him.

Logan would do the same for him. Pete didn't doubt it for a moment.

"I'll need to call Duggan and arrange some time off."

"You can do it in the car," Logan said. He didn't question Pete's change of heart or the reason for it. He knew.

"Give me a minute to get rid of this," Pete said, pointing to his rain-spattered bulletproof vest. "I'll tell Mac there's been a family emergency."

"True enough," Logan agreed. He didn't thank Pete or seem surprised.

"Can we call past my place to pick up some-"

"Clothes? No need. I packed a bag for you."

Pete searched Logan's face in the darkness. "You were pretty sure I would come, weren't you?"

"I was pretty sure of what you would do if I *didn't* ask you to come," Logan replied with the faintest hint of a smile.

Pete nodded. "Fair enough." Logan was right about that. There was a confrontation looming involving their mother, and in that, Logan was right. He would have been furious if it had happened without him.

He gripped his brother's arm. "We'll sort this out, Logan. I promise."

Logan smiled, but it never touched his eyes. "The world can't fight both of us."

"Not in this reality," Pete said. He turned and jogged back through the light rain toward the house. They were loading Jack into a patrol car in the driveway in front of the house. Although his face was lit only by the blue and red flashing lights parked around him, the old man looked defiant but resigned. Pete would miss not being the one to sit down and coax a confession from such an old legend.

Why did I say reality? Pete wondered, as he walked through the front door and began to rip the Velcro ties on his bulletproof vest open, while he looked for the captain of the ERU team. *I meant to say... hell... I don't know what I meant to say.*

Damn that kid.

It was bad enough to have it confirmed that he and Logan had been having the same dream. It was bad enough that he was walking away from all his responsibilities here, to follow Logan on what was probably a wild goose chase. He didn't need to start buying into Darragh's alternate reality crap.

Even if he'd seen, and still couldn't explain, how Darragh had made that bloody writing appear on his arm in the hospital.

Maybe it's a good thing I'm walking away from this case, he thought, as he spied Mac coming down the stairs into the hall and hailed him, *because apparently, it is driving me insane.*

CHAPTER 57

The gimmick of pretending the Empresses knew her real name was wearing a little thin for Trása, so she morphed back into a cat before they got back, and stayed out of their way for the next few days. Mostly she wandered around the compound, listening in to conversations she wasn't meant to hear - Chishihero plotting the downfall of the Ikushima, Masuyo plotting the downfall of Chishihero... It was all very fraught and in feline form, Trása was hard-pressed to care about the problems of these insignificant humans. She had whiskers to clean, furniture to mark and claws to sharpen on those delightful tatami mats they put down everywhere for her to walk on.

Rónán told the Empresses he'd sent her away, and Wakiko confirmed it, so the girls, although disappointed they didn't have their very own pet *Youkai* to boss around any longer, soon lost interest and turned their attention to other matters, such as preparing for the arrival of Lady Delphine and destroying the Ikushima.

Chishihero was using the arrival of the Empresses to advance the standing of the Tanabe, even a few old scores and remove the thorn in her side - the fireworks factory in the middle of her valuable tree plantation. She had recovered much of her family's honor by being the recipient of the message announcing the *Matrarchaí* were on their way. She would redress the last of her woes, when the rift opened and Lady Delphine - along with the legitimate envoy - stepped through from another reality and she exposed Rónán for a fraud.

They only had a few days, little to work with and Trása was not convinced Rónán had the balls to follow through on Wakiko's demand that he kill Lady Delphine and her envoy, even if it meant finding a way home.

The day before Delphine was due, she returned to *Tír Na nÓg* to check on the lesser *Youkai* who greeted her like a long-lost mother. Their pathetic need for guidance and comfort, for the security of knowing there was somebody in charge, left her wanting to weep for them. The *Leipreachán* were better at covering their distress, being cranky and curmudgeonly by nature, but the wood sprites, the undines, the kelpies and the like were more prone to showing their true feelings. Not a pool of water in *Tír Na nÓg* was calm, and when she walked past any water, no matter how small, it would roil in turmoil, as the dryads tried to reach for her, to beg her to make things back the way they had been before the *Matrarchaí* and the Empresses came to their world.

Rónán had come up with a plan, of sorts, but it required the cooperation of the Ikushima. Somewhat to Trása's surprise, he didn't balk at killing Delphine and her envoy as much as Trása thought he would. It was telling, she thought, that he seemed more and more like Darragh as the days went by.

His plan was pretty much to ambush the gate, using the Ikushima to distract the non-magical forces of the Tanabe while he took on Delphine. Chishihero was going to be Trása's task, one she accepted readily. She couldn't wait for a chance to confront that smug, murderous bitch of a magician. She would show her what a true *beansídhe* with a horde of lesser *Youkai* at her back, could do.

Trása thought Rónán would have trouble convincing Namito to help, and she was right. When he broached the subject, the *Daimyo* was adamant he would have nothing to do with such a treasonous plot. Unable to change the intransigent young man's mind, Rónán reported his failure to Wakiko, who promised to take care of it.

The following day, the Empresses held court in their *akunoya* and announced that the Tanabe were to be granted dominion over all the Ikushima lands, the factory was to be relocated to somewhere more isolated and for not notifying the Empresses immediately, of the arrival of the *Matrarchaí* envoy, Namito would be required to publically commit *Seppuku*.

The plan was, Trása supposed, to convince Namito, that he would better serve the survival of his family and the family estates, by defying the decree and teaming up with Rónán.

But Wakiko, despite all the time she had spent in this realm, and no matter how well she had mastered the art of the tea ceremony, did not understand the fundamental differences between the culture of her birth and this rigid, honor-bound realm. Here ritual suicide wasn't considered a disgrace, but a chance to restore the family's honor.

That it might cost him his life, apparently never occurred to Namito, which left Rónán seething. When Trása returned to *Shin Bungo* with only a day to go until the rift opened, Namito was preparing to die and Rónán still hadn't figured out a way to talk him out of it.

"Have you tried speaking with Masuyo?" she asked, when Rónán explained the problem on her return. She had flown into the camp disguised as a gull, slipping into the *akunoya* where Rónán was sleeping, before resuming her own shape.

He was expecting her. No sooner had she morphed back into her own form, Rónán thrust a thick cotton *yukata* at her. It was chilly in the tent and she was grateful he'd brought something for her wear, although she knew it had more to do with Rónán being embarrassed to see her naked than concern for her welfare.

"Masuyo believes Namito's death will restore the family's honor," he told her. "The fact they're going to lose everything, up to and including the roof over their heads, is apparently neither here nor there." Rónán was pacing, the same way Darragh used to pace when confronted with a dilemma he couldn't resolve. "Namito's already sharpening his *katana* and polishing his ceremonial armour."

"What's the point of that?" she asked, tying the belt around the *yukata*. "If you're going to do something as dramatic as kill yourself in public to restore the honor of the family, why would you wear something so bulky, so hard to stab through? You can't even show your face if you're wearing one of those *kabuto* helmets."

"Maybe he wants to cover his face," Rónán suggested as he paced. "I would. If I had to kill myself for such a stupid reason, I'd be crying like a little girl."

"It's not a stupid reason."

"Of course it is."

Trása shook her head and sat on the edge of Rónán's futon and looked up at him. "This world is bound by honor and the rules define the people who live here. It's the only thing they know, and it makes perfectly good sense to them. It's not what you or I would do, but it's the right thing for these people. That doesn't make it stupid. Just different."

He stopped pacing and turned to stare at her. "Wow... when did you turn into the voice of reason and tolerance?"

She smiled, inordinately pleased by the compliment. "I've been a rift runner for long enough to know when it doesn't pay to judge other people's values by comparing them to your own."

Rónán looked at her for a moment longer, as if seeing her in an entirely different light. Then he smiled. "Okay, Obi Wan, you're so wise... how do we convince Namito that killing himself to restore the honor of the Ikushima is a dumb thing to do. Not to mention hypocritical, I have to say."

"Why is it hypocritical?" she asked, intrigued to watch Rónán act more and more like Darragh with each passing day. She wasn't sure if it was the *Comhroinn*, or just Rónán's true nature coming to the fore, now his artificial world of movie premieres and private schools was taken from him. Whatever it was, she approved of the change. He still sounded like Rónán, but it was like having Darragh around without all the baggage that came with being one of the Undivided. The miracle of him being alive after*Lughnasadh* was something she chose not to question.

Rónán, and unquestionably, Darragh - wherever he was - had done the unthinkable. They had survived the power transfer and seemed none the worse for the experience. There would come a time when they would have to deal with the how and why of that, but they had to get out of here first, find Darragh and then find a way home.

"This is the bloke who offered me his little sister to get a child of the *Youkai*," Rónán reminded her, scowling at the memory. "I find it a bit rich now he's all about the honor of the family. Where was his honor a couple of weeks ago when he was pimping out Kazusa? When he let Aoi promise to kill herself if I tried to leave the compound? Instead of ritually disembowelling himself, Namito ought to hide his head in shame."

She smiled suddenly. "You know... I just had a thought."

"Lie down," Rónán suggested, sitting on the edge of the futon beside her. "It might go away."

Trása smiled even wider. "You're right about Namito hiding his head in shame. In fact, once he's wearing his full samurai get-up, it'd be hard to tell who was inside it."

"I have a bad feeling I know where you're going with this, Trása."

"Then you can see the logic in it."

"That's a bit of a stretch, but I'm listening."

She crossed her legs, sitting a little straighter on the bed. "The Empresses expect Namito to fall on his sword when Lady Delphine gets here. They want to show the *Matrarchaí* how clever they are - how they can make grown men kill themselves rather than displease them..."

"Tell me again," Rónán cut in, "why we think these girls are worth saving from the *Matrarchaí*?"

"Because they're little girls. And if you save them from the *Matrarchaí*, their mother will give us the tools to open a rift and be gone from here." If appealing to his nobility didn't work, she figured appealing to his self-interest would do just as well.

Rónán sighed with resignation. "How are you going to get Namito out of the way?" he asked. "I get putting on his armour and pretending that I'm him. I get that his troops will all be there and follow his lead, if they believe he's ordering them to attack the Tanabe and whoever else has come through the rift. And I agree that every single one of them would happily wage war on the Tanabe, and that we can probably rid ourselves of Lady Delphine and all the disasters that come with her. I think I may even have enough of Darragh's memories to fight off a magical attack by the *Matrarchaí*. Maybe even fight back. But how do we get Namito out of the way? *Without* killing him? I mean, that's the whole idea, isn't it? Saving him from himself?"

Trása smiled, feeling very smug. "You leave that to me and my lesser *Youkai* cousins in this realm."

Ren smiled at her. "You and a bunch of ninja *Leipreachán* are gonna take down a fully-trained samurai, huh?"

"Have you ever seen a piranha?"

"What?" he asked. "You mean, like the fish?"

Trása nodded. "Ever seen them feeding?"

"Sure... we have wild schools of piranhas all over inner-city Dublin."

She punched his arm. "You know what I mean."

He nodded and smiled at her. "Yeah... I get it. Small but lots of them. Are you sure the lesser *Youkai* of this reality will help, though? I mean, you're not one of them, strictly speaking."

"I am more welcome in this reality's version of *Tír Na nÓg*, Rónán, than I am in my own realm. Don't worry about me. When you need them, the *Youkai* will be there for you."

"At your command?" Rónán asked.

She nodded. "At my command."

CHAPTER 58

"I'm sorry, but Ms Doherty will be in meetings all afternoon," said the very pretty and unhelpful young receptionist at the offices of the ORM Agency. Her name was Summer, according to the engraved name tag she wore. She informed Pete and Logan, "If you leave your book and your contact details, she'll get back to you tomorrow." She smiled and added, "Identical twin models are rare. I'm sure she'll be interested."

The offices were sleek and stylish, the company logo engraved in a large mirrored sign behind the reception desk. Through the glass walls of the empty conference room behind the lobby, Pete could make out the spectacular Chicago skyline. From up here on the ninetieth floor of the Sears Tower, the view was unbelievable. Inside the office however, the lobby was identical to his mother's

Dublin office and the one in Paris, where an equally perky and persistent receptionist guarded the hallowed ground inside the ORM Agency from the unfashionable rabble trying to get in. Presumably, the recently-destroyed office in the World Trade Centre had been identical to this, too.

Pete smiled wanly at Summer's comment. Jetlagged and exhausted as he was from spending the last twenty-four hours in either airports or planes, he could still see the amusing side of this perky young woman having no idea who he and Logan were.

"If you tell her Pete and Logan are here, I'm sure she'll manage to drag herself away from her important business for a few precious moments."

"I really can't disturb her," Summer insisted.

"Is Tiffany Davis here?" Logan asked.

"I'm sorry, but I really can't tell you anything. If you-"

"Why don't you call your boss and tell Ms Doherty her sons are here," Pete suggested, putting his hand on Logan's shoulder to calm him down. He was fretting at the time they had taken to get to Chicago, particularly as they'd had no luck getting through to Delphine on the phone, despite the number of messages they'd both left her in the past day.

Summer's eyes widened. "Her sons? Oh... you're the ones who left all the messages!"

"That's right," Pete said. "So why don't you pick up the phone and tell Mum we're here. We'll wait in her office."

Pete didn't give Summer a chance to object. Working on the assumption that if everything in the lobby was identical, he knew where Delphine's office would be, Pete marched Logan past the desk, down the hall to the left and through the polished oak doors at the end of the corridor, before the receptionist could object or call security. He figured it was the fastest way to make sure he got Delphine on the phone.

Opening the door to Delphine's office, Pete was half expecting to find their mother sitting at her desk, leafing through some hopeful model's book, while her dreams of fame and fortune were crushed because she insisted on eating three times a day. But the office was empty, the desk bare, the modern, black steel and glass furniture giving the whole place a soulless atmosphere Pete had never liked - not in this office or any other.

"Do you suppose they're not in the building," Logan asked as he walked over to the window to take in the view, "because they're already at a doctor's office somewhere?" The sun was just starting to set in the distance. Pete couldn't help thinking the view would be amazing up here at night. Hopefully, they weren't going to be here that long.

"The receptionist said she was tied up in a meeting."

"So what?" Logan said, taking a seat on the windowsill. "She's paid to lie."

"Hey, I'm here for you, Logan. Don't take your anger out on me."

"I'm sorry," Logan said, turning to glance at the skyline again. Pete flopped into the leather armchair opposite the black, glass-topped desk and closed his eyes, wondering how long it would be before they could find a hotel to check into, and get some real sleep, not the fitful, broken sleep he'd be catching in snatches for the past day and night as they travelled halfway around the world.

"Why aren't we rich?"

Pete opened his eyes and stared at his twin. "*What*?"

"What aren't we rich?"

"Er... because we don't buy lottery tickets?"

"That's not what I mean," he said, frowning. "Look around you, Pete. This is our mother's office. Actually, it's only *one* of her many international offices. She has them all over the world. What must she be making with this damned modelling agency if she keeps offices like this? Can you imagine the rent on a suite here?"

"Can't say I've ever given it much thought, Logan."

Logan rose to his feet and looked around. "I mean... we never wanted for anything, but we didn't grow up with the sort of money this place reeks of. Suburban middle class, I always thought we were when we were kids."

"Nothing wrong with being suburban middle class," Pete felt compelled to point out, although Logan did have a point. "Maybe she doesn't make that much. Maybe it all gets sucked into overheads for hideously expensive office suites like this. What are you doing?"

Logan had started opening the drawers of Delphine's desk so he could go search through the contents. "Looking."

"Looking for what?"

"I don't know... something... anything."

"You can't just start rifling through Mum's office, Logan."

"Not a cop, little brother. Don't need a warrant."

"That's not what I meant and you know it."

Logan looked up and tossed something at Pete. "Here. Make yourself useful and find what these fit."

Pete caught the small key ring by reflex. He glanced at the keys and figured they belonged to a filing cabinet. There was only one in the office, a polished, low cabinet against the back wall. The sort of cabinet where the files were stored horizontally, rather than in drawers, like a traditional filing cabinet. With a muttered curse, he crossed the office and squatted down in front of the cabinet. He tried the key and it turned without resistance.

He stood up and turned to Logan. "There. Happy now?"

"Check the files."

"For *what*, for chrissakes? Jesus, Logan, get a grip. What in God's name do you think you're going to find in Mum's filing cabinets, other than the vital statistics of a whole lot of very tall, very skinny girls?" He grinned suddenly, and turned to the files. "And probably their phone numbers, too, now I come to think of it."

He grabbed a file at random and opened it, expecting to see a photo attached to the file of some willowy blonde or brunette, posing for the camera, looking fierce, and - more importantly - expensive, which he intended to wave at Logan to prove to his brother that he was losing the plot. But the file contained a baby photo, a chart that looked like a family tree, and a typed sheet detailing the child's name, address, date of birth and various other vital statistics.

He pulled out another file at random. It was almost identical - a baby photo, a family tree and a list of details about where the child was living. Pete pulled out two more files. They were the same, except one of them had a photo of identical twin girls.

"Logan, check this out."

His brother slammed the desk drawer through which he had been rifling shut, and crossed the office to Pete, who handed him the files. As Logan glanced through them, Pete pulled out even more files. All of them contained baby photos, a few had pictures of older children, and a number of them were twins. The files were color-coded with stickers along the bottom edge of the files, much the same way medical records were coded. The dates of birth belonging to the children varied greatly. Some were in the last year, others dated back to the 1940s.

"What the fuck is this stuff?" Logan asked, shaking his head. "Are they all like this?"

Pete nodded. Every single file in the cabinet was the same. "What's with all the family trees?"

"Maybe she likes genealogy."

"Maybe... but some of these kids must be old age pensioners by now."

It was intriguing, Pete thought, and decidedly odd, but there was nothing particularly sinister about it. It was just... bizarre. He turned and picked up another handful of files, and discovered more of the same. The last one on the pile, however, sent a shiver down his spine.

"Logan."

"What?"

"I think you need to see this one."

His brother looked up, looking over Pete's shoulder as he opened the file to reveal a photo of two chubby-cheeked, dark-haired boys, smiling at the camera. The photo was disturbingly familiar - it was the same photo their grandmother had of them, taken as babies, which sat proudly on her mantle. Pete scanned the vital statistics sheet, which told him nothing they didn't already know about themselves, and then flicked open the genealogy chart. Sure enough, their names, Logan and Peter, were given as the names of the two boys pictured, but they were spelled Logán and Peadar. Their family tree was nothing like they believed it to be, however. Their mother, according to this chart, was a woman named Lyonella, their father someone named Fionnbharr.

"What the fuck is this?" Logan asked, having no more luck than Pete at making sense of what he was reading.

"Something you were never meant to see, *ma cherie.*"

They both spun around to find Delphine standing at the door of her office. She took in the files scattered on the floor with a glance, and then focussed her attention back on her sons.

If we are *her sons.* The thought flashed unbidden through Pete's mind and Logan's too, he knew without a shadow of a doubt.

Delphine stepped into the room. She was wearing a fabulous blue and gold kimono, of all things, with a wide red sash. She walked toward them, her steps shortened by her outfit, her hands in her pockets, her expression reassuring.

"Is this us?" Logan demanded holding the file out to her, and then, as if he suddenly remembered why they were here, he added, "Where is Tiffany?"

"Upstairs," Delphine told him. "Safe and well."

"She's pregnant," Logan blurted out. "The kid is mine."

Delphine smiled at him. "I know."

"Did you help her get rid of it?"

"Did I...? Oh, for pity's sake, Logan. I would never do anything of the kind. I have been living for this moment. Tiffany has done us both proud."

"So we flew all this way for nothing?" Pete asked, glancing at Logan. "That's okay. It's not like I had anything fucking better to do."

"Tsk, tsk," Delphine scolded. "Language, Peter."

"It wasn't for nothing," Logan said, holding up the file with their photos in it. "Turns out it's been very informative."

"I was hoping you would never find out about that," she said with a regretful sigh.

"So... what?" Logan asked, obviously struggling to come to grips with what she was telling them. "We're *adopted*?"

She shrugged. "In a manner of speaking. Your birth mother... disappointed me. I was required to step in and take charge of your care." She smiled fondly at them and held her arms wide. "I did well, no? Look at you both. Clever. Successful... and now you have given me grandchildren. I could ask for nothing more."

"What happened to our real mother?" Pete asked, a little numb. This was all happening too fast, the ground shifting beneath his feet too quickly for him to know how to react.

"She... moved on."

Pete didn't like the way she was avoiding a straight answer. "What happened to her?"

Delphine stepped a little closer and put her hands in her pockets again. "She betrayed the cause."

"What the fuck does that mean?" he demanded angrily.

"That's no way to speak to your mother, *cherie*," Delphine said as she withdrew her hands from her pockets. With a short sharp breath, she blew a cloud of blue powder into their faces. The world went black so quickly, Pete didn't even realize he was unconscious until he came to, some time later, lying on the floor of a dark, cavernous chamber beside Logan, tied hand and foot, just in time to watch Delphine opening a rift into another reality.

CHAPTER 59

Chishihero waited alone at the stone circle for the rift to open as the sun sank below the trees and the gathering darkness brought the chill of the coming night with it. Trása thought it odd she hadn't brought reinforcements. Then again, maybe it wasn't so strange. She probably didn't want others seeing what was on the other side of the rift.

Or perhaps Kiba, the mastiff, was all the protection she thought she needed.

Trása sat down. Chishihero absently stroked the top her head. She still hadn't noticed her dog was now a bitch. That was the one drawback of shapeshifting. One could assume any form one was inclined to take, but one could not alter their gender. Kiba was an entire male. With the help of a few of the lesser *Youkai* and a healthy handful of *Brionglóid Gorm,* the mastiff was sleeping peacefully in his kennel back at the Tanabe compound. The almost identical mastiff sitting obediently at Chishihero's side now, was Trása in canine form.

She had not tried being a dog before. Marcroy favoured a wolf shape, and it had always felt slightly disrespectful to emulate the same species as her uncle. The mastiff form was different to anything Trása had tried before. It was powerful, strong. Trása like the feeling, although it was hard not to think about food. She found herself having difficulty concentrating at times because it seemed dogs considered everything around them potentially edible. She constantly had to fight the urge to sniff everything in the vicinity to see if that was the case.

Lightning crackled across the stones not long after Chishihero arrived, tying her horse and two spare saddled mounts to a tree far enough back from the circle so as not to spook them when the rift opened. She patted the top of Trása's head and muttered something soothing to her pet as the rift rent the air inside the stones, lighting the night with a radiance almost too bright to look upon. Trása had to resist the urge to flinch from her touch, as the opening rift left a jagged afterimage across her sight.

A few moment later, when Chishihero judged the rift stable, she stepped forward to greet the visitors from another reality. There were two women Trása could see, both of them dressed in kimonos, as if they knew they were coming to a world living under Japanese imperial rule, and wished to blend in.

Neither woman looked Japanese. The taller of the two was very pretty, with fair hair piled on her head and a slender frame that seemed too long and gangly for the traditional Japanese outfit she was wearing. This was, Trása guessed, the replacement for Wakiko, who was no longer toeing the party line, and about to lose her daughters because of it. The attractive woman beside her was older, shorter and obviously the one who had opened the rift, although what she had opened it with, Trása was too far back to see.

The women stepped through, but rather than close the rift behind her, Delphine - at least that's who Trása assumed the older woman was - beckoned Chishihero forward.

"You came alone as I requested?"

"Yes, my lady."

"Good, because I need your help, sister," the woman said.

Trása followed Chishihero to the edge of the stone circle as the Tanabe magician hurried forward, to see if she could recognize anything about the reality from which Delphine had emerged. But the world on the other side of the rift was, like this one, shrouded in darkness. It was impossible to make out anything other than a couple of prone shapes lying on the floor. The circle must be inside a building, she figured, because there was definitely a floor, rather than earth or stone beneath the bodies, and no hint of the world beyond the veil.

"I can't use magic to lift them until we get them onto your side of the rift," Delphine explained, "and my companion is with child. I don't want her straining herself."

Chishihero nodded and stepped through the rift to the other side. The blonde woman kept watch as

Delphine bent over one of the prone bodies and grabbed him by the shoulders. Chishihero took his legs and the two of them, with some difficulty, huffed and puffed and managed to lift the unconscious man from where he was lying in the other reality, to lay him on the ground just inside this one. Trása itched to get closer, but she remembered what happened the last time she crossed a rift in animal form.

There was very little magic in the other realm, Trása guessed, because Delphine didn't want to waste it lifting things. Once the first man was through, they went back to collect the other one, carrying it across the rift before dumping it, none too gently, beside the first.

A moment later, Delphine pulled a long thin rod that appeared to be made from crystal out of her sleeve and pointed it at the rift. Lightning sizzled for a moment and then the rift crackled shut, leaving the three women in darkness with two unconscious - maybe even dead - men, dressed in clothes that nearly shocked Trása back into her own form.

They were both wearing jeans. One of them was wearing running shoes with a Nike arrow on the side. Whoever they were, these men came from Rónán's reality, or one very much like it.

Trása's hackles suddenly stood on end. Had she and Rónán made a terrible mistake? Instead of helping Wakiko with her complicated plan to save her daughters in return for a way through the rift, should they have just waited here and simply jumped through this rift when it opened?

She'd suggested as much to Rónán not long after they first arrived. And she remembered him lecturing her about the dangers of jumping into an unknown realm. In fairness, he hadn't expected the rift to be opened with so little fanfare. But would Rónán have been so quick with his lecture, if he'd known one could buy Levis and Nikes in the world on the other side of the rift and that all they had to do to get to the rift, was run past three women, a dog and a couple of apparently dead bodies?

If Rónán was here now, could we have escaped?

And if these women came from a realm, depleted of magic, similar to the one Rónán had grown up in, how had Delphine managed to open a rift on a depleted world?

That question opened up new possibilities for Trása, but she couldn't act on them now. And certainly not while she was a dog.

One of the men was groaning softly as he regained consciousness. So they weren't dead, then. She padded over to them, sniffing them curiously. Who were they? And why had Delphine brought them here?

Chishihero must have been wondering the same thing. "You brought guests?" she asked Delphine.

Trása gently nudged at the man on the left with her muzzle, just as the one on the right began to groan, too. She turned to look at him and realized the men were twins. Identical twins.

"A last minute change of plans," Delphine said, sliding her crystal wand into her sleeve and straightening her kimono. "This is Trephina," she added, pointing to the blonde. "She will be taking over from Ingrid."

"Not a moment too soon," Chishihero said to Delphine. Then she turned to Trephina. "Welcome to my realm, my lady. I trust you will be happy here."

"Just don't point a camera at me," the young woman replied, although it was doubtful Chishihero knew what a camera was. She turned to Delphine and added, "If I never hear the words 'work it, baby' ever again, it will be far too soon."

Delphine smiled briefly at that but didn't comment. She turned and glanced at the men she had brought through the rift and realising they were starting to wake, she pulled out her crystal wand again and waved her it over them, binding the two men with magical ties that almost caught Trása as well.

"Who are they?" Chishihero asked, as Trása leaped back with a snarl of alarm at how close she had come to being trapped in the bonds that held the men rigid. It wouldn't matter if they woke now. They would not be able to move.

"A problem," Delphine said with a frown, putting her wand away. "They are the sons of another sister like Ingrid, who took it upon herself to alter the destiny of her children. I had to bring them to maturity myself."

"They are Undivided?" Chishihero gasped in astonishment.

Trása was equally astonished, but all she could do was wag her tail. It was disturbing how hard it was to control the betraying body language of a dog. She had renewed admiration for Marcroy, being able to control himself in wolf form. Trása looked down at the two men with renewed interest. They weren't just twins, she realized, if they were Undivided, that made them Rónán and Darragh's *eileféin*.

"Not officially, but they are the right bloodstock." Delphine smiled at her younger companion. "Trephina here carries our next set of Emperors or Empresses from their line, with luck."

"What are you going to do with them?" Chishihero asked, looking worried. "Kill them?"

Delphine paused but after a moment, she shook her head. "I'd prefer not to, until we know for certain we have a set of Emperor twins from them. But I can't risk leaving them here. They've been raised in a depleted realm, so they have no hint of what they might be capable of. There is far too much magic in this realm for me to leave an untrained pair of potential Undivideds here for very long, even if there are none left but the lesser *Youkai* to show them the way."

"Actually, my lady, there *are Youkai* here. They came through the rift several weeks ago."

Well, Trása thought, flopping down beside the captives. *That's blown it.*

"From where? Which realm?"

"I couldn't say," Chishihero said. "But they are the reason you were forced to come here and not through the *rifuto* stones in *Nara*. No sooner had I reported the arrival of the *Youkai* to the *Konketsu* in *Nara*, Wakiko was making plans to come here to visit them."

"No doubt she hopes to enlist their aid in defying me," Delphine said, looking mightily displeased. "And the *Youkai*? Have you taken care of them yet?"

Chishihero shook her head. "I've not had the opportunity, my lady, and the male, in particular, is far more powerful than I."

"Are you sure he is *Youkai*, and not just a magician from another realm?"

"I have seen him wane, my lady. And create fire with a thought. He needs no tools or folding spells like the *ori mahou* to ply his craft."

"Then you did the right thing waiting for me. Faerie like that need to be handled correctly." Delphine frowned and then turned her attention to Trása. "Is the dog trained to stand guard?"

"Of course, my lady."

The older woman nodded. "Then we will leave them here," she said. "We should be back by morning. I only plan to be in this reality for a few hours, even with these unexpected *Youkai* to deal with. If you trust the dog to guard them, they'll be safe enough here until I return at dawn. I assume everybody is waiting for us?"

Chishihero nodded. "They are," she said, and then she turned to her dog. "Kiba, stay!" she commanded. "Stand guard."

Trása had no idea how Kiba normally reacted to such a command, so she stood tall, pushed her ears forward and curled her lip in a silent growl. It seemed to be enough for the distracted *Konketsu* magician. Besides, Chishihero had no interest in these prisoners. She was more interested in her own problems, and they began and ended with the two *Youkai* who had the temerity to fall into her realm.

Her alert and attentive stance must have been enough like Kiba's behaviour not to arouse Chishihero's suspicions. Trása remained standing at guard as the women mounted their horses - no mean feat wearing a kimono - and turned their horses west for the Tanabe compound and the Empresses awaiting them there.

CHAPTER 60

Even though he knew he wasn't really going to kill himself, Ren still felt the weight of expectation as he walked up the long corridor of troops lining the path to the podium where the Empresses waited, along with the Lady Delphine, Chishihero and a tall, drop-dead gorgeous blonde who he supposed was the true envoy - the woman come to take the place of Wakiko, who no longer wanted anything to do with the *Matrarchaí* and the *Matrarchaí's* plans for her children. There was no sign of Wakiko, but Ren didn't worry about that. She had warned them Delphine would forbid her from attending the ceremony. She was around somewhere, no doubt, waiting in the wings to spirit her daughters out of the mÂ☐lée when the fun started.

Troops from both clans lined the path, Tanabe on one side, Ikushima on the other. Both were armed to the teeth, which Ren thought an insane idea, even if it did play into his plans for this evening. Each of the samurai held a flaming torch, lighting the path to his doom, filling the cold, still air with the acrid smell of burning oil.

The podium seemed a long way away.

Trása and the lesser *Youkai* had taken care of Namito earlier, before she left to accompany Chishihero to the rift disguised as the mastiff, Kiba, and the rest of the Ikushima left the compound in the Empresses' procession. Namito was magically bound and gagged, so he couldn't escape and raise the alarm. It remained to be seen what the *Daimyo* would do later, when he realized he'd been duped, but that was something else Ren couldn't afford to worry about now. He had a deal with Wakiko and a chance to learn how they opened rifts in this realm - not to mention a chance to thwart the plans of the *Matrarchaí* and what they would do to Teagan and Isleen, if Delphine unlocked the *Comhroinn* and gave the two little girls the benefit of her knowledge, memories and prejudices, particularly against the *Youkai*.

Once Namito was taken care of, Ren spent quite some time - with Kazusa's help - dressing in her brother's ceremonial armour. At sunset he had ridden out of *Shin Bungo* at the head of the Ikushima column, his head held high. He was, after all, posing as Namito who was off to restore the family's honor by disembowelling himself in a public spectacle that made Ren's blood run cold, just thinking about it.

Kazusa was the only member of the Ikushima clan who realized what was going on, and she had joined in the deception with enthusiasm. She was still young enough to question the mores of the adults around her, and willing to toss aside incomprehensible tradition when she could see the benefit. As Ren approached the podium, he caught sight of her out of the corner of his eye, standing with Aoi and Masuyo of the left of the dais, their faces stoic and implacable. They believed Namito's sacrifice would restore their family fortunes and would do nothing to interfere with that process.

Death before dishonor. Literally.

Ren thought they were all insane. Every last one of them.

Trása had come to check on him before she left, and to make sure he knew what he had to do. She was right to be worried. Delphine could not be defeated by mundane means. If it were that simple, Wakiko could have hired a ninja assassin to garrotte her as she stepped through the rift. Delphine needed to be defeated with magic, and only Ren - even Trása readily agreed - was strong enough to do it without the benefit of the folding magic the *Konketsu* used in this realm to wield their spells.

As they'd explained what he had to do, Ren had tried not let his doubts show. It was clear everyone was relying on him to save the day, so he wasn't sure how to tell them he didn't think he was the right person for the job - especially as he was the *only* person for the job. Wakiko kept insisting on that. It had to be Ren who faced down Delphine. She was too strong for anybody else in this realm. She had to be killed. Only someone like Ren, an Undivided who had survived the *Lughnasadh* power transfer, wielding a blade forged from *airgead sídhe*, was strong enough to take her down. Ren was surprised. Wakiko spoke as if it had happened before, but when he tried to question her, she changed the subject. She planned dealing with Chishihero and the replacement guardian for Isleen and Teagan that Delphine was bringing to this realm. The new envoy would not be a problem, Wakiko promised. She was human and if need be, she could be eliminated by other humans.

Trása had shooed Kazusa out and taken over tying the laces on Ren's new armour. It felt strange wearing something so intricate, that on closer inspection turned out to be made from bamboo. Ren had tried on a suit of medieval armour once, when he was on location with Kiva. The historical consultant on set didn't mind the questions of an inquisitive eleven-year-old boy. This Japanese armour was much lighter. It was easier to move in it too, which made sense given how fond the Japanese were of martial arts that required hand to hand fighting. Only the chest plate was made from a single, solid piece of metal embellished with the Ikushima family *kamon*, while the other vulnerable parts of the body, like the neck and the arms, were protected by scores of smaller pieces of metal tied together with blue and gold string, to match the Ikushima colors proudly hanging from the walls outside the compound.

Had he been serious about committing *Seppuku* in front of the Empresses, , the armour would come off, he would be allowed a last meal, and have one of his trusted samurai standing by to decapitate him, once he'd opened his belly. Of course, if everything went according to plan, things wouldn't go that far. Ren needed to get close to Delphine. Once she was dead, he fully expected all hell to break loose.

Trása stood back and admired her handiwork.

"How do I look?" Ren asked, picking up the *kabuto* and holding it by his side.

She eyed him up and down for a moment and then nodded. "You're taller than Namito, but you should pass muster if nobody looks too closely."

"I worry about plans that rely on nobody looking too closely."

Trása smiled and stepped closer to tie off one of the shoulder cords that had worked itself loose. "You'll be fine," she said.

"I'm not sure I can do this, Trása. I've never killed anybody before."

"Delphine is responsible for the murder of hundreds of thousands of *Youkai*," she reminded him. "In this realm and plenty of others, besides. If that doesn't help, think about this - if you *don't* kill her, she will unlock the *Comhroinn* and that will not only give Teagan and Isleen the power to kill us, it will make them *want* to do it, too. I'm guessing it'll be easier to kill one scary-evil old woman nobody in this realm really cares about, than two doe-eyed little girls everyone worships as their divine rulers."

She was standing awfully close, as she tied up the last of his armour. He was sure she was making perfectly good sense but it was hard to concentrate. Her hair smelled like summer - the same as it had that time in the old warehouse back in Dublin, when she'd been trying to set him up on a murder charge so he would be sent to gaol and kept out of harm's way. It was a monstrous plan, really, but he'd softened his animosity towards her the past few weeks. He understood Trása better now. He'd seen how she cared for the lesser *Youkai* of this realm who so needed a protector. Trása desperately wanted to belong somewhere. She didn't even seem to mind where. She was a mongrel caught between being *sídhe* and being human, and when the human world had rejected her, she turned to her Faerie family, and did whatever she must, to win the approval of Marcroy Tarth, and through him, the rest of the *Tuatha Dé Danann*. Ren wasn't sure, that in her place, he might not have done the exactly same thing. Maybe even worse.

Trása had smiled up at him and then, just as he was wondering if he could get away with kissing those tantalisingly close lips, she rose up on her toes and kissed him on the mouth.

Ren thought he might die. He slid his arms around her and pulled her closer. Just as he was thinking he might become lost in the taste of her, she yelped suddenly and pulled away from him.

She looked up at him, rubbing her back with a rueful smile. "Sorry. I didn't mean... Your armour scratched me."

"It's okay," he said, relieved she had a reason for jumping out of his embrace like she'd been burned. He'd been afraid she yelped like that when it occurred to her she was kissing Ren and not his brother.

Trása smiled at him again, a little shyly, which Ren found odd. After all, she'd just kissed him like a long-lost lover. "You can do this, Ren."

He nodded and lifted Namito's helmet onto his head. "Actually," he said, "I think I'd rather you kept calling me Rónán."

Eventually, sweating inside the armour despite the chilly evening air, his vision limited by the *kabuto* helmet, Rónán reached the podium, where he knelt and placed his forehead on the ground as Kazusa warned him he must. It was strange, but if he thought of himself as Rónán, he felt he had the courage to do this thing.

Ren wouldn't do it. Ren Kavanagh was the untested, cosseted and privileged son of a movie star - a private school boy with a credit card and a therapist. Rónán, on the other hand, was one half of the Undivided.

Rónán, not Ren, was the one compelled to protect the Faerie.

Rónán, not Ren, had the balls to kill someone when the occasion called for it.

"You may rise," the Empresses said in unison.

Rónán did as they commanded, keeping his head bowed. Although the *kabuto* covered most of his face, it wouldn't hide it enough to fool anybody if they got a good look at him.

He glanced up from the shadow of the helmet, fixing his eyes on Delphine. She looked vaguely familiar, but other than that - and her surprisingly modern blonde bob - she seemed unremarkable.

And she was holding a protective magical shield around herself.

It was strange that he could sense it. She wasn't trying to hide it. Was it for his benefit? Or for the benefit of the *Youkai* visitors to this realm that Chishihero had undoubtedly already warned her about?

It seemed she was expecting an attack.

"The Tanabe are to be granted dominion over all the Ikushima lands," Isleen announced to the gathering, her small voice ringing out on the still night air. "The factory that makes fireworks will be relocated to somewhere more isolated, for the safety of our magical forests. The lands currently held by the Ikushima are hereby granted to the Tanabe clan, as a reward for their faithful service."

"For not notifying us immediately," Teagan added, "of the arrival of the *Matrarchaí* envoy - for trying to hide their presence and gain personal advantage from an envoy to the Imperial court, Namito of the Ikushima is required to publically commit *Seppuku*, upon which time, and with his blood, he will wash away this dreadful stain on his family's honor. Do you willingly offer your life to us, *Daimyo* of the Ikushima clan?"

Before Rónán could say anything, Delphine leaned forward and asked Teagan something he couldn't hear. The little girl nodded and then glanced around. "Where is our honored envoy?"

The twins had obviously not been informed that Rónán and Trása were imposters.

Nobody answered the little Empress. She glanced at her sister and then at Delphine. "Perhaps Renkavana is waiting for you at the *rifuto* stones, my lady?"

Delphine's expression, when she heard Ren's name was quite unexpected. She looked genuinely surprised. "Ren Kavanaugh? Did you say the envoy's name was Ren Kavanaugh?"

"Surely you know that?" Isleen said, looking confused.

Delphine looked up, her eyes scanning the crowd. *She knows my name*, Rónán realized, wondering how that could be. *She's heard of Ren Kavanaugh.*

It was the last thing Rónán expected. Was it possible that Delphine came from, or had passed through, the reality he'd just left?

And if she knew the way back there, perhaps it wasn't such a bright idea to kill her.

No sooner than the thought occurred to Rónán, than the matter was taken out of his hands as a horse galloped down the corridor formed by the two lines of torch-bearing samurai. Rónán turned to find Namito bearing down on him, *katana* waving, shouting something about defiling the honor of the Ikushima.

Chaos erupted as the samurai lining the path realized their *Daimyo* was not standing before the Empresses on the podium, ready to restore their honor with his life, but galloping past them, dressed in his undergarments. The Tanabe samurai reacted predictably enough to the fury of the Ikushima troops, mistaking Namito's mad dash toward the podium as an attack on the Empresses. Realising that whatever the lesser *Youkai* had done to secure Namito, it hadn't been sufficient, Rónán turned back to face Delphine as the metallic ringing of scores of swords were unsheathed behind him. The *Matrarchaí* doyen took barely a fraction of a second to realize what was going on and turned her attention to Rónán.

Figuring his disguise was pointless now, he tore the heavy *kabuto* from his head and tossed in on the ground, just as Delphine hit him in the centre of his chest with an invisible sledgehammer blow. Rónán was thrown backwards and almost trampled under the hooves of Namito's mount who was dancing about, riderless now, trying to get free of the melee.

Rónán struggled to sit up as Delphine stepped down from the podium. Behind her, Wakiko was gathering up her daughters and hurrying them out of harm's way. The tall blonde woman accompanying Delphine moved to block her way.

Without so much as blinking, Wakiko pulled an ebony-hilted *kaiken* from her *obi*, and slashed it across the woman's throat in a spray of blood that spattered her daughters and set them to screaming as the woman collapsed at their feet. When Chishihero tried to stop her, she stabbed the *Konketsu* magician as well, just as efficiently and remorselessly. Rónán didn't see what happened to either Wakiko or the Empresses after that, because Delphine was blocking his view.

She raised her hand and slammed Rónán into the ground again, with another magical blow that drove the air from his lungs. "This is what I get for a moment of compassion," she said, staring down at him.

"*Wha...?*" Rónán gasped, wondering why he'd ever been stupid enough to think he could take this woman on. He tried to gather his strength, to marshal his power, but he couldn't breathe, let alone challenge this woman to a magical battle.

"I should have let you drown," she said, looking down at him with disgust. "And clearly, I should never have left you in the care of such an incompetent guardian."

Rónán had no idea what she was talking about. He assumed it was something to do with his arrival in the other realm when he was a toddler - the only time in his life he had come close to drowning. Did this woman have something to do with Kiva? Pushing himself up on his elbows, he wondered if he could even get to his feet, without her slamming him into the nearest wall.

"Who... the fuck... are you... lady?" he asked, as he managed to sit up. The air rang with the sound of blade on blade but Delphine filled his vision. And his thoughts. He knew the Ikushima and the Tanabe warriors were trying to kill each other all around them, but he had no chance to worry about it.

"Someone you are foolish beyond reasoning to think you could challenge," she informed him, apparently not threatened at all by the battle going on about them. "Even if you did survive *Lughnasadh*."

How does she know that?

"Wakiko is a fool," Delphine continued, sounding annoyed, rather than angry as she stepped even closer. "And you are a fool for listening to her."

Still trying to drag air into his lungs, Rónán scuttled along the ground backwards, hoping to escape her, certain beyond doubt that she was about to kill him and then turn her irritation upon everyone else in the compound.

"What did she tell you?" Delphine asked, her voice laden with scorn. "That I was evil incarnate? Did she mention the good the *Matrarchaí* have done? The worlds we have cleansed of the stinking *sídhe* so that humanity may have access to the magic the filthy Faerie hoard so selfishly to themselves?"

Delphine raised her hand again to deliver what Rónán was sure must be the killing blow. The movement gave him time, however, to grab the *kaiken* he carried at his waist. Smiling, Delphine looked down at the pitiful weapon he carried, stepping so close she was standing over him. "Is that the best you can do, little man?"

"Sometimes," Rónán said, as he stabbed the blade into her foot so hard it went right through and buried the tip in the wooden geta she was wearing, "less is more."

Delphine screamed, as the blade pierced her foot, but it wasn't the pain of a relatively minor stab wound that tore the agonising bellow from her. She went rigid, and so did Rónán, as the *airgead sídhe* blade with its wrought-silver hilt connected them as if the magical metal closed a circuit between them.

With a rush so intense, Rónán could barely contain his own agonising screams, the blade created an identical sensation to the *Comhroinn* he had shared with his brother. But this was no controlled sharing of memories and knowledge - this was darkness and horror. It was a sudden rush of memories and secrets of a woman whose life was being forcibly drained from her. Rónán clung to the blade with grim determination. Although it had only gone through her foot, the link between them was complete. He hadn't known it beforehand, but he realized now, that he must see this to the bitter end. He couldn't let go.

The magical link shredded his soul, buffeted his senses, tore at his very core, but he hung on until he felt Delphine's life force inexorably fading. He hung on until he felt the light in her flicker and die and she collapsed on the ground beside him, her open eyes staring into the distance, as if she was looking into the afterlife and didn't particularly like what she saw there.

Only then, with a head full of Delphine's knowledge and memories, did Rónán release his grip on the *airgead sídhe* blade, so he could let the darkness embrace him, and take away the pain.

CHAPTER 61

Trása waited until she could no longer hear the horses before she turned her attention back to the prisoners Kiba had been set to guard. They were beginning to regain consciousness and becoming aware, she guessed, of just exactly how unpleasant a *Brionglóid Gorm* headache could be. She studied them for a time, curious. Delphine had said they were Undivided raised unaware of their power. That made them just like Rónán.

What will happen, she wondered, *when they realize what they're capable of, here in this realm drenched in magic?*

"Logan..." the man wearing the jeans, leather jacket and the Nikes groaned, as his eyes - the only part of him besides his mouth that Delphine's magical bond had left him free to move - fixed on the dog standing guard over them. "You okay?"

"Some bastard's... buried an axe... in my skull," the one named Logan moaned. He was marginally better dressed than his brother, with a sports jacket over his jeans and expensive boots. "But I can't... move a muscle. How about you, Pete?"

The one named Pete didn't seem to be able to take his eyes off Kiba. "I can't move either," he said. "And ditto on the headache. You think that dog's going to kill us?"

"Only if we move."

"Well, that's not a problem then."

"Jesus... my head is splitting."

Trása wondered if she should do something about that. With a thought, she could resume her true form and cure their headaches. For that matter, she could release them, too. But she didn't know enough about these strange men to know if that was a smart move or the dumbest thing she might ever contemplate.

"Are we tripping on something?" Pete asked. "Last thing I remember, we were in Chicago, in Mum's office in the Sears Tower, going through her files."

"Turns out she's not our mother," Logan replied. "I remember that much."

Trása sat down, deciding to do nothing for the time being. While the brothers thought they were alone, they would talk freely. She figured she'd learn more about them this way, than releasing them and giving them the opportunity to lie about who they were and where they came from.

"We're tripping on something," Pete concluded. "This has to be a bad dream. All this bullshit about alternate realities and the Undivided... that's my subconscious playing tricks on me after reading too many transcripts of Darragh talking with Annad."

"Yeah?" his brother asked, unconvinced. "So how come I'm sharing the same trip?"

Pete was silent for a moment and then said, "I'm still working on that bit."

Trása dropped to her haunches, intrigued by these young men. They were in their late twenties, perhaps thirty at a pinch. If they were the *eileféin* of Rónán and Darragh, they shared little in the way of physical characteristics, other than the same dark hair and blue eyes. She didn't think she was looking at exact copies though, maybe a somewhat older version of the youths she knew. Given the infinite number of realities and the bloodlines the *Matrarchaí* had obviously been fostering, it was unlikely they shared similar blood.

But they *were* Undivided. They just didn't know it yet.

"You got any bright ideas about getting us out of this mess, little brother?" Logan asked, his eyes closing as he spoke, as if it hurt to even mouth the words. "I'd help with a plan, but I think my brains have leaked out of my skull - no functioning brain could possibly hurt this fucking much."

"I can't think either..." Pete agreed. "Christ. Whatever it was we been hit with, this is one seriously bad trip."

Trása was getting annoyed by Pete's insistence he was caught in a drug-induced nightmare. It was not an uncommon reaction among those inadvertently dragged across realities they previously didn't realize existed, but until the brothers overcame that pointless rationalisation, they couldn't begin to come to grips with the new reality in which they now found themselves.

"Maybe we're not tripping," Logan suggested. "Maybe this is real."

There you go, Trása said, although it came out as a short sharp bark. *That's the spirit!*

"That beast looks awfully hungry," Pete said, his eyes still fixed on Kiba. "Do you suppose they feed it on small children while they're training it?"

"That beast is the least of our problems," Logan groaned. "Do you think if we asked nicely, it'd kill me? At least then I'd be rid of this fucking headache."

It must have been Kiba's canine instincts overruling her compassion, but Trása felt herself drawn to Pete, rather than Logan. He seemed to be the stronger one. He was the one complaining the least, at any rate.

As the rising moon bathed the stone circle in moonlight, Trása turned to Pete, eyeing him closely for the first time. When she got a really good look at him for the first time, she realized, with a jolt so sharp she inadvertently resumed her true form, that she knew this man. She'd seen him before.

It was the cop who'd chased Rónán all over St Christopher's Visual Rehabilitation Centre.

Both Pete and Logan let out a yell of surprise as, without warning, the mastiff guarding them morphed into a naked girl. Trása didn't notice or particularly care. These men came from the realm they'd left Darragh in, which meant Delphine, when she returned through the rift, would be opening a doorway into the very realm they needed.

Without that knowledge, even with a jewel or an *ori mahou* spell, they might spend years trying to find the right reality again.

And right now, Delphine was riding into an ambush, from which Wakiko was determined she would not survive.

They had a way home. But only if Delphine lived and could be prevailed upon to return to it.

Trása glanced up at the sky. The moon was almost at its zenith. Back at the Tanabe compound, Delphine would be arriving with Chishihero and Trephina. Rónán, disguised in Namito's full samurai regalia was waiting, *katana* in hand, to give the signal which would set the Ikushima onto the Tanabe troops.

The plan was to kill Delphine, the unsuspecting Trephina and hopefully Chishihero in the ensuing meleé. With the *Matrarchaí* cut off from this realm, Wakiko would then be free to take her daughters in hand and steer them away from the moral precipice Delphine was driving them towards. There would be no unlocking of the *Comhroinn*. No more mass-murdering of the *Youkai* in this realm. With their mother guiding them, instead of the Empresses creating a magical world free of any Faerie, the girls could set things to rights. Even with most of the *Youkai* gone, there were still the lesser *Youkai* to protect. As one of the *Tuatha Dé Danann*, Trása was as compelled to protect them - even in another reality - as much as she would have been if they were lesser *sídhe* in her own reality.

It had seemed like such a good idea when Wakiko's plan was the only way out of here. Never, even for a fleeting moment, did it occur to Rónán or

Trása that Delphine would cross into this reality from the one they had just left.

Trása was torn, not knowing whether to morph into the fastest bird she could imagine so she could fly to the Tanabe compound to warn Rónán he must keep Delphine alive, because through her, they might have a way to rescue Darragh, or to do nothing and let the ambush play out as it was meant to, thereby saving the remaining *Youkai* of this realm.

"Trása!" Pete shouted, as she dragged her attention back to the immediate problem of what to do with Rónán and Darragh's *eiléféin*. "Oh my God! You're Trása, right? Jack O'Righin's granddaughter?"

She looked at him oddly for a moment, wondering why he would call her that, and then realized that in his world, her imaginary relationship to the old man who lived next door to Rónán was all he knew about her. She nodded and squatted down between the brothers.

"I can make your pain go away," she said. "And then, if you promise not to do anything stupid, rash or... violent, I will release you."

"Sweetheart, if you can make this headache go away," Logan groaned, "you can have my first born child."

Trása frowned. "Lucky I know you're joking," she said, placing a hand on his forehead. "I've met the firstborn of some Undivided and they're no fun, let me tell you."

Logan's face relaxed as his headache vanished. He sighed blissfully. "Whoever said there is no more euphoric feeling than the sudden cessation of great pain, knew what he was talking about."

She repeated the same gesture on Pete, drawing the pain of his *Brionglóid Gorm* headache away. He stared at her the whole time, his eyes full of suspicion. "How did you do that?"

"Magic, of course," she said. "How else?"

"That's bullshit."

"Suit yourself. It's not like Santa Claus. You don't have to believe in it, for it to work."

Pete scowled at her. He really was a suspicious, untrusting sort of fellow. "Can you really free us from this... this..."

"Go on," she prompted. "Say it."

"Magic spell holding us down," Logan said, not waiting for his brother. "Let us up. Please."

Trása smiled briefly at Logan and then rose to her feet. "Your brother has better manners than you do," she said to Pete, and then, taking a step back, she waved her arm, releasing the magical bonds that held to two men down.

Free of Delphine's magical bindings, they scrambled to their feet and looked about them, uncertain about what to do next.

"Where are we?" Pete asked, taking in the stone circle and the trees beyond with a disbelieving glare.

"Do you mean geographically, or in what reality?"

"There's a difference?" Logan asked, looking around. His gaze finally settled on Trása and he slipped off his jacket, holding it out to her. "Aren't you cold?"

Trása had been too busy to notice the crisp night air, but now Logan mentioned it, she was cold. She was also aware he was probably offering her the jacket because she was naked. The men from

Rónán's reality were oddly shy when unexpectedly confronted with a naked Faerie.

She smiled her thanks. "Of course there's a difference," she said, slipping the jacket on, grateful for its warmth, "but right now, I don't have time to explain it to you. I have to decide between saving the lesser *Youkai* of this realm, or Darragh in the realm you just came from." She glanced up at the moon. "I may already be too late."

"Darragh?" Pete asked. "There's nothing you can do for him now, Trása. He's going to be in prison for a very long time. Where is Ren?"

They'd only been gone from that reality a few weeks. She couldn't imagine what Darragh had done in that short time to get himself thrown in gaol. "Ren is busy. Why is Darragh going to prison? What did he do?"

"What *didn't* he do? Murder, kidnapping... where is Hayley Boyle, by the way? Is she here, too?"

Trása shook her head. "She made it home to my reality. I think. Who did Darragh murder?"

"Warren Maher. The bloke whose car you stole from the golf club."

"That would have been Sorcha, not Darragh," she said, shaking her head. Trása was sad Warren was dead, but she hadn't known him long enough for it to cause her lasting grief. She cocked her head sideways, as a thought occurred to her that changed everything. "Will Darragh be in prison long?"

"Twenty or more years at the very least," Pete told her. "It's a mandatory life sentence for murder."

The prospect didn't worry her nearly as much as Pete might imagine. A few weeks ago, that had been the plan she worked out with Plunkett to keep Rónán safe.

Maybe she didn't need to worry about Darragh, at all. If he was in prison for the next twenty-odd years, he was safe.

Understanding that lifted a huge weight from Trása's shoulders. If Darragh was safe, then her path was clear. She had to help the *Youkai* of this realm, which meant letting the ambush at the Tanabe compound go ahead as planned. Delphine must die.

The *Matrarchaí* sorceress had a crystal wand that allowed her to open a rift back to the world from where she had come. It might take some time to figure out how to use it, but oddly enough, time was the one thing Rónán and Darragh had, although they probably didn't appreciate that yet. Thanks to the interference of the *Matrarchaí*, Undivided twins were almost pure *sídhe*. They were long-lived. Now Darragh had survived the *Lughnasadh* power transfer, a few years in a Dublin gaol in Rónán's realm where there were rules about the humane treatment of prisoners was not so bad. If it took them the whole twenty years to find that reality again, in a lifespan liable to encompass centuries, it barely mattered at all. Better yet, they would know where to find Darragh when they got there. They wouldn't have to scour the world looking for him the way they did when they went looking for Rónán in the same reality.

Trása looked at Pete and Logan and realized the same applied to them. They were Undivided. They would live for centuries.

And they were part *sídhe*, which meant the magical time-dilating effects of *Tír Na nÓg* would not bother them.

Of course, they knew nothing about who they were or what they were. That was going to take some explaining, and Trása didn't really know where to begin.

Perhaps it would be easier to just show them. She could take them back to *Tír Na nÓg*, hide them there until Delphine was taken care of and let the lesser *Youkai* of this realm show these men what she didn't have the words to explain.

"That's all very nice," Logan said, looking about impatiently, "you two catching up and all, but are you going to tell us what is going on? What happened to our moth... to Delphine? And Tiffany? How come a few minutes ago, you were a dog? And how the fuck did we wind up here, anyway?"

Trása nodded. "I'll explain everything, all in good time," she said. "But right now, if you want to avoid Delphine taking you prisoner again, you need to come with me."

"To where?" Pete asked, full of suspicion and doubt.

"Home," Trása said in the language of the Faerie, figuring it was both the truth and the one thing that she didn't need to explain. "There is nothing to be afraid of LogánPeadar of the Undivided. I am taking you home."

CHAPTER 62

By Danu, the djinni was right. The Undivided are still alive.

Ciarán gasped when they brought Darragh in and sat him in the dock of the Dublin Criminal Court beside a uniformed prison officer who looked as if the task of guarding such a heinous prisoner was keeping him awake. He actually yawned as he took his seat, and then crossed his arms and lowered his head, probably so nobody would notice if he dozed off.

Until this moment, Ciarán had not believed that Darragh could have survived the *Lughnasadh* power transfer. To see him standing there now, alive and well - although in a great deal of serious trouble - left the Druid doubting everything he thought he knew about his own realm, and his loyalties.

Although he was shackled, someone had given Darragh a bright orange coverall and his hair had been trimmed. He looked like Rónán had looked, when they first brought him back through the rift to his own reality. The lad paid no attention to the public seating. Ciarán pulled the baseball cap he was wearing down a little, to avoid being recognized. He had not decided how he was going to extract Darragh from this reality yet. Until he did, it might be better if Darragh didn't start building up false hope of rescue.

Ciarán still wasn't sure he believed his eyes. Was Marcroy playing another trick on him? Did that wretched *djinni*, Jamaspa, have a hand in this?

It was only a few weeks ago that Ciarán had been lying in a crude hut in his own realm, battered, and broken following his torture for information about where Darragh and Rónán were hiding. Ciarán had sworn he would die before betraying the young men he was pledged to protect, an oath he had been very close to fulfilling. He had been resigned to his death - resigned to the knowledge he would never see either Rónán or Darragh again, and that in dying, he had saved them from the evil of the *Tuatha Dé Danann*.

Marcroy had released Brogan by then, to answer the scrying message from Darragh and arrange to open the rift. They'd left him lying there, alone and in agony, waiting for death or perhaps a wild pack of weremen, to find him.

Locked in magical bindings placed on him by Marcroy Tarth, unable to heal himself or escape from something so powerful, Ciarán was waiting to die when the *djinni* turned up and set him free.

"The Brethren have need," Jamaspa said, as Ciarán drank deeply from a pitcher of ale the djinni magicked up for him, "of a champion."

"Hope you find you one," Ciarán had told the *djinni*, wiping the foam from his lips. He put the pitcher down and glanced out of the door at the setting sun. Now he was healed and his thirst quenched, it was time he was gone from here. *Lughnasadh* wasn't far away and he needed to stop the transfer from happening, or the boys he was sworn to protect would die.

"I believe I *have* found him," Jamaspa said, looking at the warrior expectantly.

Ciarán shook his head. "I appreciate you letting me out of Marcroy's bindings," he'd said, "but that's all you're going to get from me, Jamaspa. My gratitude."

"My aid costs more than a mere thank you," Jamaspa said.

"Then tie me down again and leave me to die, *djinni*, because that's all I have for you. My allegiance is already sworn, and that's where I'm going. To save the Undivided."

"Then your purpose and the Brethren's coincide."

Ciarán turned for the door. "I find that unlikely."

"Perhaps you should hear me out, before you make such a hasty judgment." The *djinni* shimmered across the hut to block the door. "You owe me that much, at least."

Much as he disliked admitting it, Jamaspa had a point. "Talk fast then, *djinni*. I don't have much time, and what little I do have, I don't wish to waste listening to nonsense from you."

Jamaspa, oddly enough, didn't take offence to Ciarán's brusque manner. Instead, he shrank down to a smaller, better-formed blue cloud, with arms decorated with gold bangles and a discernible expression on his face. "You have travelled to many other realms in your time, have you not?" the *djinni* began.

Ciarán nodded, folding his arms across his chest. "So?"

"Then you have heard of Emperor twins?"

"Only rumours," Ciarán said, frowning. It was a long time since he'd gone rift running. The thrill tended to fade as one acquired years and common sense. What Jamaspa spoke of was something akin to legend, but a legend feared beyond reason by the *Tuatha Dé Danann*. The legend of Undivided twins inexplicably powerful and beholden to nothing and nobody.

"The rumours are more than rumours," Jamaspa told him. "There are realms - a growing number of them - where the Undivided have been created from Emperor twins and they have achieved Partition."

Ciarán knew the *djinni* wasn't referring to the vociferous but mostly harmless Partitionist movement who wanted humanity cut free of their bonds to the *Tuatha Dé Danann*, by destroying the Treaty of *Tír Na nÓg*, and returning to lives without magic or the need for it. Jamaspa spoke of true Partition, where the Undivided were powerful enough to take what magic they wanted without any help from the *sídhe* races. The Brethren's fear, Ciarán didn't doubt for a moment, was that in such a world, once humans had no need for the *sídhe*, they would decide to be rid of them, or enslave them or exploit them, which is what humans did to all the other creatures they came into contact with. They did it to their own kind too.

"And why do I care for these rumours?" he asked.

"Because there are other rumours that hint at a foe capable of defeating Emperor twins before they have a chance to mature."

"Then you don't need me," Ciarán said. "Your champions are already out there somewhere."

"In every realm where the Undivided have achieved Partition, they have turned on the *sídhe* and set out to destroy them, Ciarán," Jamaspa said. "We cannot ignore the chance to find a solution to that problem."

"I couldn't agree more," Ciarán said. "Good luck in your endeavours. Can I go now?"

Jamaspa swelled in size, blocking the entrance. "Rumour has it Emperor twins can be destroyed by the rare Undivided who *didn't* perish during the transfer of power from one generation of Undivided to the next."

That gave Ciarán pause. "Are you saying RónánDarragh might survive the transfer?"

"They are unusually strong," the *djinni* said.

"Legend says they have to be of royal blood."

Jamaspa nodded, which made him bob up and down in the air. "We believe they *are* of royal blood."

"That's ridiculous. Whose...?" Ciarán stopped, his jaw dropping as he realized what Jamaspa was implying. There was only one *Tuatha Dé Danann* of royal blood who spent any time among humans since Amergin brought his muse, Elimyer, to court. That had irked the Druids, but Amergin and his royal *Leanan Sídhe* had only ever produced one daughter. There were no psychically linked twins to worry about.

"By *Danú*... do you mean their father is-"

"Lucky the Brethren haven't extinguished him permanently," Jamaspa finished for him with a scowl. "Only the possibility that RónánDarragh might one day prove the salvation of our kind, maybe in this realm, but certainly in many others who need our help, has stayed the Brethren's hand."

"Does he know?" Ciarán asked, still a little gobsmacked by Jamaspa's revelation.

"He would never have helped Amergin throw Rónán through a rift to another world, if he had known," Jamaspa said. "We assume he doesn't."

This news changed everything. "Do you know for sure that the boys will survive the transfer?" Ciarán had asked, trying not to look too hopeful, too excited by what the *djinni* was telling him.

Jamaspa shook his head. "We won't know until the power transfer at *Lughnasadh* takes place. If Rónán and Darragh survive it, we have our answer. And maybe our weapon. If that happens, to protect this realm, we need to bring them home."

Ciarán nodded, beginning to understand the problem. "And you don't know where Rónán and Darragh are, or you would have arranged your own rift runners to bring them back."

"We know where they are. But they crossed into a realm without magic," Jamaspa reminded him. "We cannot follow them there. We need a part-human rift runner. Someone with experience dealing with this sort of thing."

"Why not send Brogan?" Ciarán asked, thinking of the young man who had been tricked by Marcroy into betraying the location of Rónán and Darragh, and exposing them to all sorts of charges by implying they were bringing *eileféin* through the rift. "He's clearly on the side of the *sídhe* these days."

"Brogan is Marcroy's creature now. For obvious reasons, we can't tell him anything about this."

"You'll get no argument from me on that," Ciarán agreed. "But even if what you say is true, give me one good reason why *I* should help you? There are no Emperor twins in this realm. How do I know you're not making all this about RónánDarragh up? Setting me up to betray the boys I'm sworn to protect, the same way Marcroy subverted Brogan?"

"We have no Emperor twins in this realm - *yet*," Jamaspa agreed, his size reducing to a more manageable shape. Ciarán had been grateful for that. It was hard to look a *djinni* in the eyes when you couldn't see both of them at the same time.

"*Yet*?"

"As soon as they got word we were planning to transfer the power from RónánDarragh to the new heirs, the *Matrarchaí* were throwing fertile young women at Darragh - the only twin they could get their hands on - in order to preserve his bloodline and perhaps get themselves a set of Emperor twins."

"The *Matrarchaí*?" Ciarán scoffed. "Seriously? *That's* the boogieman the Brethren fear? A bunch of gossipy old midwives?"

"What you think of our fears is irrelevant, Ciarán. What you seem to be missing here, is that Rónán and Darragh may be strong enough to survive the transfer. If that happens you must bring them home. Protect them. As you are sworn to do."

There had been no arguing with that.

Ciarán forced his attention back to the present, as the tipstaff ordered everyone to rise. A moment later, a dark-haired woman entered the court from the door behind the highest desk in the room. She was dressed in a long black robe with a stiff white tie at her neck and a ridiculous wig that fitted her very badly, as did the wigs sitting on the heads of the two men facing the judge.

As the judge took her seat, Ciarán glanced at the pamphlet he'd picked up outside the court, which offered a simple explanation of the proceedings, a description of the court and who did what. The tipstaff informed the people in the court they could sit. Ciarán glanced down at the brochure as he sat down, identifying the man who rose next and began to read the charges against Darragh as the Registrar. The list the man read was long.

Darragh had been busy the few short weeks he'd been residing in Rónán's reality.

They were charging him with conspiracy to commit murder, grand larceny, kidnapping, conspiracy to kidnap, assaulting an officer of the Gardaí, and a score of minor charges that hardly seemed worth the effort after the main charges were detailed. Darragh remained still and passive throughout the reading, as if he wasn't bothered in the slightest by the damning indictments.

All the while a young blonde woman sat beside the Registrar, tapping away on a machine Ciarán assumed was to keep a record of the proceedings. There were no bards in this world to remember the words spoken here, *verbatim*. They had to rely on mechanical means.

The jury box to Ciarán's right was empty. He didn't know if that was because they hadn't called the jury yet, or didn't intend to use one.

Eventually, the Registrar came to the end of the list and looked directly at Darragh, and asked "How do you plead?"

Darragh rose to his feet and looked at the judge. His gaze was serene and unflinching. "Guilty," he said in a clear voice that rang out across the courtroom.

Ciarán got the feeling he was the only one in the room who was surprised.

The judge nodded, as if she was expecting as much. "Do you understand what it means to plead guilty?" she asked.

Darragh nodded. "Yes, your honor."

The judge glanced down at her desk, and turned some papers over, read through them for a few moments and then looked up and spoke to Darragh again. "It is my understanding that despite being willing to plead guilty to these offences, young man, you are not willing to divulge the location of the kidnap victim or your accomplices to her abduction or any details regarding the murder of Mr Warren Maher. Is that correct?"

"I have given the authorities all the information I have, your honor," Darragh replied calmly. "They simply refuse to believe me."

The judge turned her attention to Darragh's barrister. Ciarán could not see his face, because he was facing the judge, but he was hard pressed to imagine Darragh was receiving adequate counsel from any man wearing such a ridiculous wig. "My client insists Hayley Boyle, the kidnap victim, and his accomplices, Chelan Kavanaugh, Trása Ni'Amergin and the woman known only as Sorcha, have gone through a rift to another reality, your honor," the barrister explained as he rose to his feet. "For this reason, we ask that her honor considers a sentence in an appropriate mental facility, where this young man's obvious psychiatric issues can be treated accordingly."

The judge pursed her lips, unconvinced. "Yes, I read your sentencing submission, Mr Gallagher," she said. "I also read the report from Doctor Semaj, who believes this young man is quite sane and trying to fake insanity for exactly that purpose."

"Our own psychologist disagrees with that assessment, your honor."

"Your psychologist is paid to disagree with it, Mr Gallagher," the judge pointed out, unsympathetically. "I am also bothered by your client's lack of remorse, and his unwillingness to take responsibility for his crimes."

"The Probation Report recommends the maximom sentence possible in this case, your honor," the prosecuting barrister pointed out, rising to his feet to stand beside Gallagher. "The offender doesn't believe he has committed any crime."

"Hence the reason we feel a secure mental institution would be the most appropriate place for him at this time," Gallagher responded, glancing at the prosecutor with a frown.

"I have no doubt your client has issues, Mr Gallagher," the judge said, closing the file on her desk. "But one sees offenders with *issues* every day of the week, and there are plenty of young men out there with *issues* who don't feel the need to deal with them by kidnapping and murder. My hands are tied in any case. You client is pleading guilty to conspiracy to murder. I am compelled to impose a mandatory life sentence..."

Ciarán closed his eyes, let the judge's voice fade into the background as she detailed the rest of his sentence, which didn't matter anyway, because

Darragh had just been sentenced to life imprisonment.

He opened his eyes and looked at Darragh. The young man was listening attentively to the judge, but didn't seem concerned. *He believes we'll come for him,* Ciarán realized.

And he knows if he is alive, Rónán is alive out there somewhere, too.

It would take some doing, to extract Darragh from this mess, Ciarán decided. They'd broken Rónán out of the Garda cells first time, but that wasn't as heavily guarded as a maximom-security prison. To make matters worse, this whole realm felt like it was under siege at the moment. Springing Darragh from his current predicament was going to take more knowledge of this realm than Ciarán owned.

He couldn't do it alone.

I need Rónán, Ciarán said to himself. *I need his knowledge of this world. I need to find him, bring him back to this realm, bust Darragh out of prison and then take both boys home together.*

Then they could deal with the *Matrarchaí,* Jamaspa, Marcroy Tarth, Colmán, Álmhath and the fallout from the superseded Undivided still being alive and well, when by all that was right and holy, they should be dead.

Ciarán looked at Darragh again, hoping... willing him this time... to turn around and look at him - to meet his eye, recognize his old mentor and friend and know that someone who cared knew where he was and would do whatever it took to get him home.

But Darragh stayed stoic and calm as the judge sealed his fate. And even when he was led from the court in shackles to begin his new life behind bars, Darragh held his head high and didn't look back.

EPILOGUE

Tír Na nÓg. Hayley said the words over and over to herself, as she waited for Elimyer to return with her food. She glanced at her wrist, wondering at the time, but in this world she had no wristwatch to mark the passing of the hours. She hadn't worn her watch since the accident. They'd been talking about giving her a Braille watch at St Christopher's, but she didn't need one now.

Hayley could see, better then ever.

What she was seeing was still hard to comprehend. This magical place didn't even exist in her reality. But here she was an honored guest of the Faerie, about to be served a meal by a real live Faerie princess.

Hayley glanced around to see who was watching and then pinched herself on the inside of her thigh to check she was awake. The pain made her grimace, but nothing else changed. *Tír Na nÓg* didn't vanish in a puff of smoke, to be replaced by her room at St Christopher's. The magical trees didn't recede to be replaced by the concrete rendered walls of the rehab facility with its brightly painted décor designed to cheer up the inmates, most of whom were blind, and therefore not able to appreciate the color scheme, anyway. Hayley thought it odd that she could tell the color of the walls now. She'd been blind the whole time she was at St Christopher's. How could she know what the place looked like?

Perhaps the doctors had been right. Perhaps her eyes had been able to see all this time, and it was her brain that let her down by not interpreting the messages correctly. She smiled, thinking of the shocked reaction she was going to get when she finally arrived home, completely cured and full of tales about being saved by Faeries.

They'll think I've gone mad.

"Here you are, my dear," Elimyer said, as she floated across the wide bough carrying a silver tray of fruit. "I hope you like it. These are my daughter's favourites."

Hayley still hadn't got her head around the idea that this girl was Trása's mother. It didn't seem possible. "Did Trása grow up here in *Tír Na nÓg*?"

Elimyer shook her head, and put the tray down beside Hayley. The fruit was a selection of apples, pomegranates, nectarines, peaches, apricots and strawberries. Each individual fruit was perfect, like the sort they showed in advertisements - flawless and nothing like the specimens available for sale in the shops. "No, we lived in *Sí an Bhrú* until she was almost a woman. I was her father's muse, for a time. And then they began to worry about her attachment to Darragh so it was decided it might be best to separate them."

"Why? What's wrong with Darragh?" Hayley had only had one brief encounter with Ren's twin, but he hadn't seemed so bad.

"Nothing is wrong with him, dear," Elimyer said, taking a seat on the bough beside her, "Are you a rift runner?"

"I don't think so. What's a rift runner?"

"Human and mongrel like my daughter," Elimyer said. "Funny... I thought that's how you came from another reality."

The idea that there were other versions of her having entirely different lives in an endless number of realities was almost too much for Hayley to comprehend. It was one thing to know about the theoretical possibility of alternate realities, quite another to confront the idea that somewhere out there in another universe, someone was leading her life and maybe even doing it better than she was.

It might be healthier, Hayley decided, not dwell on that idea for too long.

Hayley glanced down and realized the apple she'd selected was gone. She didn't even remember biting into it.

"Are you settling in?" Marcroy asked from behind.

She jumped a little at the unexpected voice and turned to find her Faerie prince standing on the bough behind her. She hadn't even heard him approach. Hayley smiled up at him, thinking it was criminal to be that handsome and have magical powers to boot.

"You're back!" Elimyer announced, quite unnecessarily.

"I have been at *Sí an Bhrú*," he told his sister. "The transfer is done."

"Is it past *Lughnasadh* already?"

Lughnasadh? Hayley thought. *How can that be?* "That's the autumn equinox isn't it? But that's weeks away." She was quite sure she had been here in *Tír Na nÓg* for little more than an hour or two.

Neither Elimyer nor Marcroy answered her question. But she wasn't bothered. She was well again, she was safe and the Faerie all seemed very friendly. They had healed her blindness, just like Ren said they would.

I'll just stay here a little longer, Hayley decided. *And then I'll get Marcroy to open the rift and he can send me home, and I can explain about the mix-up and they'll have to believe me, because I have proof. I can see.*

Ren and Darragh hadn't made it through the rift with her. They were back home, probably in a bit of trouble, given all the cops in Dublin were bearing down on them when she stepped through the rift. There were bullets flying around, too, although Marcroy now seemed fully recovered from his brush with a bullet from her realm.

Ren and Darragh will be fine. A night in gaol wouldn't hurt them. It certainly wasn't the first time Ren had spent a night behind bars. Kiva's lawyer, Eunice Ravenel, would have them out on bail before dawn, knowing how efficient she was.

I'll go home tomorrow, Hayley told herself, closing her eyes to appreciate the sublime flavour of the apricot she chose next. *And when I get back, I'll explain everything. After that, life can go back to normal. Like it was back before the accident. Back before Trása arrived in my world and everything went pear-shaped.*

It'll be just like none of this ever happened, she thought, smiling up at Marcroy.

Another day in *Tír Na nÓg* can't hurt.

SNEAK PEEK

BOOK 3 OF RIFT RUNNERS

REUNION

PROLOGUE

Pete wasn't expecting his home reality to be so ... white.

He'd imagined any number of scenes when they finally found this realm: the rolling green hills of Ireland were what he'd been expecting, but not necessarily the Ireland he knew. Perhaps a world where faerie roamed free and the air sang with magic, like it did in the reality they'd just come from - an odd reality where the rulers of Ireland were feudal Japanese lords answerable to a couple of precocious ten-year-old girls who seemed more Scandinavian than Oriental.

He wasn't expecting snow and ice, as far as the eye could see. "Where are we, exactly?"

Logan shrugged, looking about in bewilderment. Pete turned to the young man who'd brought them here. He was dressed in a loose cotton yabagin, the marrow-freezing cold not touching him through the magical shield of warmth he had, in fact, woven around the three of them.

Ren's expression was grim as he studied the barren snowscape. "I think it's Hawaii."

"That's a glacier over there."

"Clearly they're not having problems with global warming, then," Logan quipped, flashing his brother a quick grin. "There's magic here, though. I can feel it."

"It's fading," Ren said.

"What do you mean?"

"Magic needs living things to sustain it. This world is dead."

"We don't know that for certain."

"This is the fourth stone circle we've tried, Logan. They've all been the same. No sun, no life, just snow and ice."

"Maybe there are other, warmer places ..."

"We're virtually standing on the Equator. Where do you suppose it's going to be any warmer?"

"What did this?" Pete asked. He directed the question at Ren and it wasn't rhetorical. This was the world from which Delphine had stolen Pete and his twin brother as babies. She had planned to use them as breeding stock for the Matrarchaí, while ensuring they were ignorant of their heritage. She thought they would never learn that they were powerful sorcerers in their own right, because they were Undivided. They only lacked the magical tattoo on their palms which would make them capable of sharing their magic with other human sorcerers, as well as wielding it themselves.

Then Ren and Darragh had happened along, and nobody's life had been the same since. Especially now that Ren had all of Delphine's memories, so he had the answers the others wanted. Ren had shared some of her surface memories through the *Comhroinn*, but the really meaty stuff that Pete and Logan were interested in was hoarded almost jealously by Ren. He claimed Delphine's memories were too hard to sort out, therefore too hard to isolate and reveal in the Comhroinn, the Druid magic mind sharing that was more art than magic.

Pete knew that some things Ren learned from his Comhroinn with Delphine were near the surface and so could be easily accessed and shared. Other things were hidden, requiring Ren to delve far deeper. His reluctance to do so annoyed Pete, who believed the answers to all their questions were hidden in Ren's mind. It was selfish of Ren to deny them answers, just because the memories were unwanted and he was afraid of a little bit of a headache.

"Hey, did you hear me?"

Ren was staring off into space. There was a blank look on his face suggesting he was either bored, or lost in the memories he'd accessed to bring them to this place.

"Kavanaugh?" Logan looked at Ren with concern. When Ren didn't answer he turned to Pete. "Is he usually this annoying?"

"Yes," Pete said. He stepped up to Ren and snapped his fingers in front of the young man's face. "Hey! Wizard boy! Snap out of it!"

Ren blinked and fixed his gaze on Pete. "You should be dead."

"Yeah, pity about that. Now why don't you -"

"You should both be dead," Ren said, casting his eyes over Logan as if Pete hadn't spoken. "I cannot permit you to live, knowing what you are. You were never meant to gain this self-knowledge."

"Ren?" Pete said.

"I don't think that's Ren any longer," Logan said, as the air about them suddenly chilled. Ren - or whoever it was - had dropped the warming shield.

"Delphine?" Pete's breath frosted as he asked the question, afraid he already knew the answer. This was what Ren had feared. He wasn't skilled enough to hold back the memories he carried. Pete shivered, and not entirely because of the cold.

"I was prepared to let you live ordinary lives," Ren said, although it was clear the words were not his. This was Delphine, just before she died. Before Ren killed her. The Delphine who was able to justify the murder of two men she had raised as her own sons. "But you just couldn't help poking your nose in where it wasn't needed, could you? I told you I was safe. You should have left it at that."

With the preternatural instincts of identical twins, Pete knew that if he could distract Ren long enough, Logan would be able to get around behind him. Pete didn't know what it would take to shake Delphine loose from Ren's mind, but he was pretty sure that neither he nor Logan understood their newfound magical abilities enough to counter someone as powerful as Ren - souped up as he was with Delphine's centuries of knowledge about how to use that power.

"Who'd have thought some mundane little terrorist attack that had nothing to do with the Matrarchaí would interfere with your plans to rule the world?"

Ren raised his hand and Pete started to choke, as if his windpipe was being crushed by an invisible hand. "How dare you mock me? After all I've done for you. And for your information, the *Matrarchaí* has much bigger plans than just ruling one world."

Pete couldn't breathe. He collapsed to his knees, wondering where Logan was. He didn't have much time, he knew, before the memories of Delphine that were possessing Ren crushed the very life out of him.

"Ren ..." he gasped with his last breath, appealing to the young man who owned this power crushing the life from him. Surely Ren could fight back? He wouldn't have surrendered willingly ...

And Logan ... where was Logan?

In answer to his question, he saw his brother fly past him and land heavily against the bole of a dead, snow-covered palm tree. Pete couldn't tell if he was unconscious or dead. He just knew there'd be no help coming from that direction.

If he was going to survive this, he needed to get Ren back. But he was already starting to black out. Desperately, he groped around on the snow-covered ground until his hands closed over the closest thing he had to a weapon. The rock he found was rough and cold. Pete scooped it up and smashed it down onto Ren's foot, the only part of him he could still focus on.

Ren cried out in pain and the pressure eased on Pete's throat. He staggered to his feet and lurched at Ren, driving his fist into his solar plexus with the full weight of his body behind him. They crashed to the ground. Pete landed on top on Ren and raised the rock, ready to crush Ren's skull if that's what it was going to take to shake Delphine loose from his mind.

"No! Pete! It's me!"

Pete hesitated, the rock still raised above his head. He sat astride Ren, who was staring up at him with genuine fear. The arrogance of Delphine was gone.

"How do I know it's you?"

"Delphine wouldn't be talking to you. She'd go back to killing you."

Cautiously, Pete lowered the rock. "Are you sure she's gone?"

Ren nodded.

"What happened?"

"I did what you asked, Pete. I tried to access her memories. Next thing I know, I was Delphine. Are you going to let me up?"

"Maybe." Pete glanced across the snow-covered stone circle to where Logan lay, relieved see him groaning as he pushed himself up onto his hands and knees. He turned back to Ren. "Can you stop her doing that again?"

Ren shrugged. "I think so. Darragh knew how to do it. I'd have to lock down her memories, though, and everything she knows will get locked down with it."

"Small price to pay if it means you're not going to go postal on us without warning."

Logan staggered over to them, studying his brother - sitting astride Ren and still clutching the rock - with a puzzled expression. "Is that Ren?"

"For the moment," Pete assured his brother and then turned back to Ren. "Do it."

"Now?"

"You ever want to leave this realm?"

Ren nodded and closed his eyes. Pete could feel him drawing from the faded magic of this world and then, after a few moments, he opened his eyes. "It's done."

"How can we be sure?" Logan asked.

"Because as soon as we get back to the ninja reality, we're going to hand him over to Trása and she can make sure it's done."

"Do you trust Trása to do that?"

"I trust her to want her boyfriend to stay alive," Pete said, climbing to his feet, "because if he goes Delphine on us again, we're going to have to kill him." He reached down and offered Ren his hand. "You okay with that?"

Ren nodded as Pete pulled him to his feet. "You're not staying here, then? This realm is your home."

"What's to stay for?" Logan asked, looking around.

"Besides," Pete said, "Delphine said the *Matrarchaí* has much bigger plans than ruling the world. I think we need to find out what she meant by that."

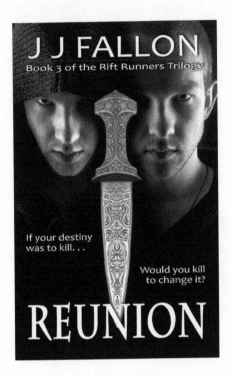

THE WORLD OF THE UNDIVIDED AND THE FAERIE

Proper names are in bold type

A Mháistir (a MAW ster) Master.

A Mháistreás (a MAW stress) Mistress.

A Stóirín (ah stor-een) Term of endearment. Roughly translates as "My love".

Aintín (ann-teen) Faerie word for Aunt.

Airgead sídhe (AR-gat Shee) Faerie silver.

Airurundo (air-RU-run-doe) Japanese name for Ireland in the *ori mahou* reality.

Amergin (aw-VEER-een) Vate of All Ireland until his death. Trása's father.

An Bhantiarna (on can-teer-na) Lady.

Aoi (ow-ee) Eldest daughter of the Ikushima clan.

Arigatou gozaimasu (ah-ree-gah-tou Go-zai-mah-su) Thank you very much.

Banphrionsa (ban frinsah) Princess.

Bealtaine (byawltuhnuh) Summer equinox.

Beansídhe (ban-shee) Faerie with long hair and red eyes due to continuous weeping. Their wailing is a warning of a death in the vicinity.

Brendá (BREN daw) Queen of the Celts. Mother of Torcán.

Bríghid (breed) Celtish princess. Niece of Brendá. Cousin of Torcán.

Brionglóid Gorm (bring-load gurm) Roughly translates as "Blue Dreams". Magic powder used by the Druids to induce instant unconsciousness.

Brithem (bree-them) A Druid judge or an arbitrator. They specialise in lexichemy - magic using the spoken word.

Broc (brok) Undivided heir.

Brógán (BRO gawn) Druid healer.

Brydie Ni'Seanan (BRY dee nee SHAR nan) Celtic princess; niece of Álmhath; cousin of Torcán.

Cainte (KIN-cha) Master of magical chants and incantations.

Cairbre (CAR bry eh) Undivided heir.

Chishihero (chee-she-here-oh) Japanese sorceress in charge of the *kozo* plantation in Dublin. Head magician of the Tanabe Clan.

Ch□ch□ (choo-cho) Middle Kingdom. Alternate name in the *ori mahou* reality for Japan.

Ciarán (KEER awn) Ciarán mac Connacht, Warrior Druid.

Cillian (KIL ee an) Half-Faerie/half-human *sídhe*.

Colmán (KUL mawn) Vate of All Eire. Amergin's successor.

Comhroinn (KOH-rinn) Name of the sharing ceremony that transfers knowledge between Druids.

Daiko (dy-ko) Japanese drums.

Daimyo (die-mee-oh) Head of the clan.

Danú (DA nu) The Goddess worshipped by both Faerie and Druid alike.

Daoine sídhe (deena shee) "People of the Mounds". Refers to the Faerie race as a whole. Also known as the Tuatha Dé Danann.

Darragh Aquitanina (DA-ra) Druid prince. One half of the Undivided.

Éamonn (AY mun) Elimyer's latest lover.

Eblana (e-BLAN-uh) Druid name for Dublin.

Eburana (eb-oo-rah-nah) Japanese name for Dublin/Eblana in the *ori mahou* reality.

Eiléféin (ella-phane) The alternate reality version of oneself.

Elimyer (ellie-MY-ah) Trása's mother. *Leanan sídhe* who becomes Amergin's muse.

Farawyl (farra-will) Druidess and High Priestess of the Barrows.

Futagono Kizuna (foo-tah-goe-noe-kee-noo-zah) The Undivided.

Gochisosama (go-chee-sosah-mah) Thank you for the meal.

Hai (HI) Yes.

Haramaki (ha-ra-ma-kee) Belly protectors, containing chain mail or articulated plates of iron, made of silk and lined with various materials.

Hayato (hi-AH-toe) Head of the samurai charged with protecting the Tanabe Clan's *kozo* plantation.

Hayley Boyle (Hay-lee Boil) Daughter of Patrick Boyle and his first wife, Charlotte. Stepdaughter of Kerry Boyle.

Higan No Chu-Nichi, (hee-garn-no-choo-nee-chee) Autumn equinox in the *ori mahou* reality.

Iie (i-ee) No.

Ikushima (ick-ISH-oo-mah) One of the clans of *Airurundo*.

Imbolc (im-bolk) Spring equinox.

Isleen (izs-lean) Empress of the *ori mahou* realm.

Itadakimasu (ee-tah-dark-eemar-soo) I gratefully receive.

Jamaspa (j'MAS puh) Djinni. One of the lords of the Djinn.

Jotei (joe-tay) Title used when addressing the Empresses.

Kabuto (kah-boo-toe) Samurai helmet.

Katsugi (ka-tsu-gi) Lightweight drum played while carried by a strap.

Kazusa (kah-zoo-sah) Youngest daughter of the Ikushima clan.

Konketsu (kon-ke-tsu) Humans with Faerie blood able to practise folding magic.

Lá an Dreoilín (lah-ahn-droh-il-een) Also known as Wren Day. The winter solstice. Celebrated on December 26.

Leanan sídhe (lan-awn shee) A Faerie muse of exquisite beauty who offers inspiration, fame and glory to an artist in exchange for his life force.

Leathtiarna (lah teerna) Half-Lord.

Leipreachán (LEP-ra-cawn) One of the lesser fairies.

Liaig (lee-aj) Druid Healer.

Lughnasadh (loon-a-sah) Autumn equinox.

Mahou tsukaino sensei (mah-hoo-tsooo-ky-no-sen-say) Magic master.

Mara-warra (MA ra WOR ra) Sea-people also known as the Walrus People.

Marcroy (MARK-roy) Lord of the Tarth Mound. Elimyer's brother.

Máthair (mahar) Mother.

Merlin (MER-lin) Head Druid in Britain. Second only in power among the Druids to the Vate of All Eire.

Namito (na-mee-toe) Head of the Ikushima clan.

Niamh (neev) Druidess.

Oceanus Britannicus (o-she-AR-nus-bree-TAN-ee-eoos) Roman name of the English Channel.

Ori mahou (oree-mah-hoe) Folding magic.

Orlagh (*OR-la*) Queen of the Faerie.

Ossian (Ocean)

Prionsa (frin-sah) Prince.

Ráth (rar) Ring fort consisting of a circular area enclosed by a timber or stone wall with a ditch on the outside called a cashel.

Ren/Rónán Druid prince. One half of the Undivided.

Rifuto (ree-foo-toe) Rift.

Samhain (sow-en) Winter equinox.

Shàngqıng (shang-ching) The Supreme Pure One - One of the three Chinese Faerie Elders who make up the Brethren.

Shillelagh (shil-LAY-lee) Short, gnarled club usually fashioned from a tree root. Commonly made with a knobbed head, they often serve a secondary purpose as a walking stick.

Shime Daiko (shee-meh dy-ko) Small Japanese drum. Has a short, wide body with thick rawhide on both sides and is tuned by either rope or a bolt system.

Sí an Bhrú (shee-ahn-vroo) Traditional home of the Druids.

Sídhe (shee) Common name for the Faerie race in general.

Si☐illinn a (shool-leen ah) "Walk with us..." Druid ceremonial chant invoking their gods and goddesses.

Sorcha (shore-shah) Druid warrior.

Stiofán (stee-farn) *Tuatha Dé Danann* refugee living in *Tír Na nÓg* in the *ori mahou* realm.

Tàiqıng (tie-ching) The Grand Pure One - One of the three Chinese Faerie Elders who make up the Brethren.

Tanabe (tan-ah-bee) One of the clans of *Airurundo*.

Teagan (tee-g'n) Empress of the *ori mahou* realm.

Tír Na nÓg (tear-na-knowg (with a hard g)) Land of Perpetual Youth. The traditional home of the *Tuatha Dé Danann*.

Torcán (TURK awn) Prince of the Celts. Son of Brendá.

Trása (TRAY-sah) Trása Ni'Amergin. Half-Faerie/half-Druid offspring of Amergin and Elimyer.

Tuatha Dé Danann (tua day dhanna) Commonly known as the Fae.

Faerie or Fairy. Also known as: Children of the Goddess Danú, the True Race, or the *Daoine sidhe*.

Uncail (UN cayl) Faerie word for Uncle.

Vate (VART eh) Druid. Second only in power to the Undivided. Acts as regent when the Undivided are not yet come of age at their ascension to power.

Wagakimi (wa-goh-kee-me) My lord.

Yabangin (ya-bahn-gin) Savage, feral.

Youkai (yo-kigh) Faerie Yukata (yoo-kah-tah) Informal, unlined cotton kimono tied with a narrow sash (obi).

Yùqɪng (yoo-ching) The Jade Purity - One of the three Chinese Faerie Elders who make up the Brethren.

ALSO BY JENNIFER FALLON
(JJ FALLON)

Hythrun Chronicles
Wolfblade
Warrior
Warlord
Medalon
Treason Keep
Harshini

Second Sons
Lion of Senet
Eye of the Labyrinth
Lord of the Shadows

Tide Lords
The Immortal Prince
The Gods of Amyrantha
The Palace of Impossible Dreams
The Chaos Crystal

Rift Runners
The Undivided
The Dark Divide
Reunion

ABOUT THE AUTHOR

JJ Fallon has Masters Degree in Research and is a trainer and business consultant with over 20 years experience in designing and delivering courses ranging from basic computer training to advanced project management.

Fallon currently works in IT and spends several weeks each year at Scott Base in Antarctica.

Made in the USA
Lexington, KY
30 July 2014